Praise for Theresa Howes

'I absolutely loved this . . . Vivid and heartbreaking.' Lana Kortchik, *USA Today* bestselling author of *Sisters of War*

'War, passion and tragedy unite in this atmospheric and moving tale.' S D Sykes, author of the Oswald de Lacy Medieval Murders series

'A wonderfully immersive, emotional read.' Annabelle Thorpe, author of *The Enemy of Love*

'A truly gripping read, both tragic and romantic, and I loved it.' Jill Mansell, *Sunday Times* bestselling author of *Maybe This Time*

THERESA HOWES lives in London, and has a background as an actor. Her work has been long-listed for the Mslexia Novel Award, the Bath Novel Award, the Caledonia Novel Award, the Lucy Cavendish College Prize and the BBC National Short Story Award.

Also by Theresa Howes

The Secrets We Keep

The French Affair

THERESA HOWES

HQ

ONE PLACE. MANY STORIES

This novel is entirely a work of fiction. The names, characters and incidents portrayed in it are the work of the author's imagination. Any resemblance to actual persons, living or dead, events or localities is entirely coincidental.

HQ
An imprint of HarperCollins*Publishers* Ltd
1 London Bridge Street
London SE1 9GF

www.harpercollins.co.uk

HarperCollins*Publishers*
Macken House, 39/40 Mayor Street Upper,
Dublin 1 D01 C9W8

This paperback edition 2023

1
First published in Great Britain by
HQ, an imprint of HarperCollins*Publishers* Ltd 2023

Theresa Howes asserts the moral right to be identified as the author of this work.
A catalogue record for this book is available from the British Library.

ISBN: 9780008547912

FSC www.fsc.org MIX Paper | Supporting responsible forestry FSC™ C007454

This book is produced from independently certified FSC™ paper to ensure responsible forest management.

For more information visit: www.harpercollins.co.uk/green

Printed and bound in the UK using
100% Renewable Electricity by CPI Group (UK) Ltd

To Bill
For putting up with it all

Prologue

London, Summer 1943

If the war had taught Iris anything, it was that it was easier to lie during the blackout than in the cold light of day, and so it was with good reason that she always insisted on meeting Guy Mason after dark. And it was for this same reason that she also insisted on making love with the lights out. Not that it was about making love as far as she was concerned but about *lying back and thinking of England* – and of victory. The first time she gave herself up to him, it struck her that *lying in bed* had more than one connotation, and as the realisation dawned, it was as much as she could do to hide her smile.

Already, only a few weeks after their first meeting, Mason's luxurious mansion flat, with its thick carpets and antique furniture, situated just off Mayfair, held no secrets for her. Every time his back was turned, she took the opportunity to acquaint herself with every nook and cranny, every hiding place. Guy Mason might have considered himself the smartest and most well-connected civil servant in the British government, but he was too vain, too eager to impress her to have the sense to guard his secrets closely.

Iris had learned enough about life to know that men like Mason were quick to underestimate intelligent women. Subterfuge was easily found in a tube of scarlet lipstick, while a certain type of male brain was easily fogged by a cloud of Shalimar. Mascara, pancake and rouge were just as much battledress as any khaki uniform.

While Mason stamped his feet in the shower, Iris wrapped the top sheet tightly around her body and slipped out of his bed, shuddering in the dark, shaking off the memory of his rough hands against her skin, hands that knew how to feel, but not how to touch, not in the way of a true lover. With one eye on the bathroom door, she crouched beside the bed and slid her fingers beneath the mattress, moving them slowly until she found the object of her search.

Forming her hand into a claw, she dragged the papers from their hiding place, triumph rising in her chest like a budding rose. Leaning back on her heels, she flicked on the bedside lamp, the words *Top Secret* in bold letters striding across the top of the page, warning her against transgression. With practised hands, she reached into her bag and retrieved the small camera, hidden in an interior zipped pocket, and photographed the papers before slipping them back beneath the mattress.

Already the water had stopped. Mason was out of the shower, the low murmur of his distracted humming a warning that he was towelling himself down and slipping into fresh pyjamas, the leather and tobacco top notes of his cologne already drifting through the gap under the bathroom door. Time was almost up.

She was stashing the camera in her bag when a loud rapping on the front door broke the late-night silence. Mason stepped out of the bathroom, made irritable by the disturbance.

'What the devil . . .?'

His demand to know what was going on was interrupted by a rush of voices from the street below, which Iris suspected had been timed to coincide with the continued knocking on the door.

A cold dread crept over Iris's body. Something wasn't right. She raised her hand to silence Mason and stumbled to her feet, struggling to keep herself covered by the bedsheet. A cornered animal, her attention shifted to the bedroom window as a small stone hit the glass.

'I'll take a look.'

She turned off the lamp, throwing them into darkness before she pulled aside the blackout curtain, blinking at the sudden flash of a bulb from the camera that must have been trained on the window, waiting for someone to reveal themselves.

Startled by the light, Iris stepped back into the room and closed the curtain, reeling as if she'd been shot. But it was too late. She'd been seen, her image captured, naked, but for the flimsy cover of a bedsheet.

She'd been caught.

Panic ran through her like a hot wire as she thought of her beloved Jack, somewhere far away, risking his life to report on the war. His heart would never recover if he found out what she was up to.

Already there were shouts from the men waiting on the pavement below, strangers calling Mason's name, cracking the silence of the early hours, denting the leaden atmosphere of the blackout.

While she rushed to get dressed, Mason remained in the bathroom doorway, tugging irritably at the collar of his silk paisley dressing gown. The knocking on the front door was louder now, more insistent. Whoever it was, they weren't going away and they didn't sound in the mood to take no for an answer to their demands.

'What's going on, Mason?'

He muttered at the sound of the front door being forced open. 'I'm sorry, so sorry.'

Pinheads of sweat from the hot shower erupted on his forehead as heavy feet approached along the hallway. It was too late. There was nothing he could do to stop the men bursting into the bedroom, guns pointing.

Chapter 1

One week later

Iris pressed her back against the wall, every muscle in her body tense as she forced herself to remain still. One twitch, the slightest flinch would give the game away. The smell of rot drifted from somewhere under the floor, the intermittent sound of a rodent's squeak reminding her the basement was far enough underground to put them on a par with the sewers.

Her eyes blinked in time to the splash as Yvette's head was forced under the water for the third time, her heart beating to the rhythm of the thrum as the young girl's body was thrust against the side of the bath.

Twenty-five, twenty-six.

She counted the seconds in her mind. How long could Yvette hold out? She studied the tension in her body as she clung to the air in her lungs, the skin taut on her knuckles where her fists strained against the rope that had been lashed around her wrists. How old was she? No more than sixteen: fit, strong and determined. She'd lied about her age at first, but Iris soon got the truth out of her. It was almost as if she had a sixth sense when it came to knowing when people were lying. It was what made her so good at her job.

She glanced at her watch. 2.03. Was it morning or afternoon? Time lost its essence in this room where there were no windows and only one bare bulb of artificial light. They'd been locked in here together for two days and nights now, or was it three? She lit a cigarette and held it between her fingers, its burning tip a single point of heat in the airless room.

Forty, forty-one.

'That's enough.'

Iris only had to murmur the order. The officer who'd been holding Yvette's head under the water let go and stepped away from the bath. Yvette raised her head and threw it back, sending a spray of water around the room as she gasped, lungs and shoulders heaving, the blue tinge of her skin rapidly returning to pink.

At Iris's nod, the officer untied her wrists and ankles. Once she was free, Iris passed her the cigarette.

'Are you all right?'

Yvette took a long pull on what was left of the stub and nodded, the smoke mixing with the newly found air in her lungs prompting a fit of coughing. Iris handed her a towel, giving her a minute to compose herself and ordered the officer who'd held her underwater to leave the room.

'Well done. You held out better than most.'

Yvette remained on her knees, the towel covering her head. 'I need to build up my lung capacity so I can stay under for longer.' She slipped the towel around her neck and looked up at Iris, her eyes still wild from her panic to hold on to life. 'I'll have to do better, won't I?'

'You can never be too prepared. Once you're dropped into Occupied France, the most important thing is to always be quick and clever. Keep at least one step ahead of the enemy or of anyone who might have a reason to betray you. Assume the worst of every person you meet. It's the best way to avoid being captured and interrogated. Just because you're French and working for the Allies, you can't assume everyone will be on your side.' She helped Yvette to her feet, brushing aside a curl of wet hair that clung to her face. 'Get yourself a hot shower and something to eat. We'll pick up again tomorrow after you've had some sleep.'

Iris was locking the door of the training room when she spotted Ambrose coming towards her along the narrow corridor, his head ducking to miss the bulb that hung from the ceiling by a single cord.

'Ah, Iris, there you are. How did Yvette hold up during the mock interrogation?'

It took less than a second for the switch in Iris's head to flick from speaking and thinking in her native French to English.

'What day is it?'

With the interrogation over, she was suddenly exhausted, disorientated from spending so many unbroken hours in this dingy underground place.

Ambrose frowned, visibly irritated by her failure to answer his question. 'It's Wednesday. Why do you ask?'

It couldn't be Wednesday already. She'd spent longer with Yvette than she'd realised. It was credit to the girl that she'd stood up to such sustained questioning. 'Day or night?'

Ambrose tugged at his sleeve, making a great show of checking his wristwatch. 'It's 2.17 p.m. Now, tell me about Yvette. Will she do?'

'She shows great promise.'

Iris didn't elaborate. She wanted the conversation over with, so she could go home and get some sleep. She stepped around Ambrose's great bulk, her shoulders brushing the wall in the narrow corridor. If Ambrose sensed her desperation to leave, he didn't react to it.

'That's what I like to hear.'

The most striking thing about Ambrose was his ordinariness. His nondescript hair and unassuming face made him instantly forgettable to anyone who happened to pass him in the street.

Even his grey jacket and tie, his white shirt with its crumpled collar seemed designed to make him invisible. Being easy to overlook was what made him so good at his job.

He fell into step behind her as she continued along the corridor. 'We're looking at dropping her into France by the next moon. The resistance network in Lyon has lost its wireless operator. They need a replacement *toot sweet*.'

It was only three weeks since Natasha had been sent in to do the job. Iris had spent an intense couple of months helping her to prepare for it. She'd even accompanied her to the aeroplane to see her off, consoling her with a few last words of reassurance. Iris had warned Ambrose that Natasha was too nervous to send, but he had insisted on her going, because they were desperate for anyone skilled in Morse code who could operate a wireless. For Iris, there was no satisfaction in knowing she'd been right.

'What happened to Natasha?'

Ambrose's face clouded over. For all his gusto, he took it personally when one of his agents was lost.

'Shot in the back as she tried to flee a German patrol. It seems she took the wrong turning down a side street and ran right into them.' He held up his hands as if he too were about to be shot. 'You told me not to send her in. I should've listened to you.'

There was no point in Ambrose employing her if he wasn't willing to take her advice. How many times did she have to be proven right before he realised this?

He clicked his fingers and clapped his hands as if such a gesture could draw a line under the tragedy and make it disappear. 'Better luck next time, eh?'

She wanted to scream at him, but it wouldn't do any good, and after everything she'd put Yvette through during the last three days, she didn't have the energy. When it came to it, nobody knew anything about how best to prepare agents for the field. They were all amateurs in this new kind of warfare.

'It's important to learn from these mistakes. Let's not rush into dropping Yvette into France until we're sure she can cope.'

Ambrose rolled his eyes, resistant to taking advice from a woman. 'We're desperate, Iris. You've said yourself she's the best we've got.'

'She's no more than a child. Let's not forget that.'

When he didn't answer, she turned to face him, blocking his way along the corridor. 'You offered me this job because of my ability to dissect what people are thinking, to separate their lies from the truth. Why did you bother, if you're not prepared to listen to what I tell you?'

Iris had been a journalist for fifteen years when war broke out. At first she'd resented that as a man, her husband, Jack, had been allowed to follow the fighting to report on it, while the authorities had refused female journalists permission to travel to the front line.

During the London Blitz, she'd put herself in the thick of it, capturing the devastation of the bombing and the aftermath. Anyone could take pictures of burning buildings, but she'd focused on the reactions of the victims, often following up on their stories for weeks and months afterwards.

It was this work, which demonstrated her acute observation and her ability to see through the surface image to the truth of what people were thinking, that had attracted the attention of Ambrose. At their first meeting, he'd realised that as a French woman, she had a unique capacity to assess French agents for their ability and loyalty. More than that, they'd trust her in a way they'd never trust a British Intelligence officer.

'We'll discuss Yvette later. There's something more important I need to talk to you about first. Come to my office as soon as you've had something to eat.'

'I need to catch up on some sleep first.'

He tapped his watch as if it were a ticking bomb. 'There's no time. There's a war on, in case you hadn't noticed.'

Chapter 2

Iris returned to her office to collect her coat, her mind drifting to the Women's Voluntary Service canteen parked near the embankment, where she planned to pick up a cup of tea, a sandwich and if she was lucky, a currant bun. Ambrose couldn't deny her a few minutes of fresh air after she'd been locked in the basement for so many days and nights with Yvette.

Pushing her hand into her coat pocket, her fingers brushed the crumpled envelope from Jack. His letter had arrived just as she was leaving the house three days ago. She'd buried it into her pocket while she ran for the bus, putting off reading it until she had a moment alone. Now, after all this time, it still remained unopened.

She sank into the chair behind her desk, all thoughts of food and sleep forgotten. It had been months since she'd had a proper letter from him, and even longer since she'd seen him. At the beginning of the war, he'd been given permission to accompany the British Army and report on the action in Western Europe and the Mediterranean. More recently, he'd attached himself to the RAF bomber crews in the north of England as they'd carried out air raids on Germany. It wasn't only the miles that had kept them apart, but the fighting he'd witnessed that had put a distance between them.

Over time, she'd come to rely on his dispatches in *The Daily News* to know he was safe. She could tell they'd been heavily censored. She knew his style well enough to spot the work of another hand disrupting the rhythm of his finely tuned prose. His voice was different. If she hadn't known better, she'd have thought they'd been written by a stranger.

She forced herself to open the letter, dreading what it might contain. She'd written to him the morning after Guy Mason's arrest, asking him not to jump to the most obvious conclusions over the pictures they'd printed of her in the newspapers, looking out of his bedroom window wearing nothing but a bedsheet. She couldn't put off reading his reply any longer. Sooner or later, she had to face up to what he thought about it.

Iris

They say absence makes the heart grow fonder, but it isn't true. Absence has made strangers of us. I saw your photograph on the front pages of all the newspapers. I told myself it couldn't possibly be you, but there you were, wearing nothing but a bedsheet, shamelessly staring out of Guy Mason's bedroom window.

I received your letter the following day, begging me not to believe what I'd seen in the papers, asking me to trust your word, rather than my own eyes. You said it wasn't what it seemed, but you couldn't tell me what it was exactly. I can only assume that was because you couldn't come up with a convincing enough lie.

You can't imagine the humiliation I feel, knowing my wife has betrayed me with a traitor. War has changed us all, but I don't know who you are anymore and I can no longer find it in my heart to call you my wife.

Jack.

The relentless clack of a solitary typewriter echoed along the corridor, as if to remind Iris that the world hadn't suddenly ended. She turned the letter over, hoping Jack had continued on the other side, that he'd had a change of heart after signing it, and added a *PS*, remembering that he loved her, because losing him was unthinkable.

Their marriage couldn't end like this, not because of what had happened with Mason. It was only by becoming his lover that she was able to get close enough to him to find the evidence that proved he was a traitor. Jack couldn't tear up the life they'd built, simply because she'd been driven to do what was necessary by the demands of war. Their commitment to one another was stronger than that. It had to be. And if it wasn't, then what were they fighting for?

And yet, there was no point denying what he'd accused her of. She'd been a fool to think he wouldn't find out what she'd been up to, that she could manage the situation with Mason and not hurt him.

She folded the letter and pushed it back into her coat pocket. There was only one person who could help her mend things with Jack, and that was Ambrose.

Iris walked into Ambrose's office without bothering to knock. She had too much on her mind to worry about pleasantries.

Ambrose looked up from the documents on his desk, seemingly unruffled by the intrusion. 'Ah, there you are. There's something I want you to do.'

'Before we get on to that, I need your permission to tell Jack about the work I've been doing.'

Ambrose had a way of shaking his head that reminded her of a dog. 'Absolutely not.'

'He saw the photos of me looking out of Mason's bedroom window the night he was arrested. He thinks I've been unfaithful. It's ruined our marriage.'

'You tell him nothing, Iris. You're sworn to secrecy.'

'Can't we make an exception? We can trust Jack not to tell

anyone.'

'You're talking about the same Jack Foley who tried to defy the official censors over the bombing of Hamburg last month?'

Iris sat in the chair opposite Ambrose's desk. If she waited for him to offer her a seat, she'd wait all day. 'Jack's a journalist. It's his job to report the facts as he uncovers them. The air attacks were excessive and inhumane. The public have a right to know.'

'Rumour has it, he's a Communist.'

'That's rubbish, and you know it. He's a man of honour. It's a rare trait these days.'

'There's no place for honour in war. You have to win by whatever means you can.'

'So what are we fighting for, if not for truth and justice?'

Ambrose sighed, tapping his fountain pen against the back of his hand. 'You did an excellent job for us with Mason. If it hadn't been for the evidence you gathered against him, who knows what strategic military secrets would have ended up in enemy hands. Think of the countless lives you've saved. You have to consider your marriage as one of the sacrifices of war. People have suffered far worse.'

The comment was designed to make the ruin of her marriage sound like a noble act. She understood how Ambrose was so good at his job, how he had the ability to always get his way.

'You're an attractive woman, Iris. You'll soon find yourself another man.'

'I don't want another man. I want Jack.'

'You didn't have to take the assignment when we offered it to you. You knew the risks.'

Originally, this was only a backroom job, helping to prepare French agents for their work in Occupied France. It was only recently, when she was asked to cultivate a relationship with Mason, that the job had taken a different direction.

How could she have said no to an active role in the war when both her parents had been shot in Paris in 1941 for producing leaflets promoting the Allied cause? Active service, however covert, however little difference she was able to make, went some way to avenging their deaths. Her sacrifice might have been nothing compared to what others had suffered, she accepted that, but it was enough to destroy her and Jack's lives and their future together.

'You promised Jack would never find out. How did you expect to honour that promise when the photograph of me wearing nothing but a bedsheet appeared on the front pages of all of the newspapers? Jack's a journalist. How did you think he wouldn't see it?'

'It's the nature of the game, Iris. You knew the rules when you signed up for it.'

'In that case, I'd like to be released from further duties. I've worked closely with all the agents you've sent into the field during the last couple of years. On top of that, I helped you to trap Guy Mason. Surely, I've done my bit.'

'Publishing that picture of you looking out of Mason's bedroom window was the only way to ensure he didn't suspect you were the one who betrayed him.'

'That wasn't the agreement.'

'We had a change of plan. There was no time to discuss it with you. We had to act quickly to keep you safe.'

'You promised he'd be sent to prison for life. Isn't that supposed to keep me safe?'

Ambrose paused, his eyes furtive as they scanned her face. 'We kept your name out of it, didn't we?'

Iris was growing annoyed with Ambrose's games. Everything had gone further than she'd expected and she'd been left feeling out of her depth. She'd agreed to befriend Guy Mason after one of his colleagues in Whitehall noticed him handling top secret documents that shouldn't have been in his possession. She was only meant to have drinks with him once or twice, perhaps go out to dinner with him to assess his character, but once she'd raised her suspicions that he might be passing military secrets to the enemy, Ambrose had instructed her to become more intimate with him as a way of finding evidence that would incriminate him as an enemy spy.

'You kept my name out of it, but not my face.'

For once, Ambrose had the decency to look abashed. 'We'd originally planned to pull you out of the operation much sooner, but you were doing such a good job.'

'It's time I went back to being a journalist. I need to convince Jack I'm the same woman he fell in love with all those years ago. I can't do that while I'm bound by so much secrecy.'

'We're grateful for the work you've done.'

'Then show your gratitude by releasing me from further service.'

'If I release you now, you'll have to remain in isolation at a remote location of our choosing until everything you know about our operations is no longer pertinent.'

Iris frowned, fury rising in her veins. 'What does that mean?'

'You'll essentially be under house arrest in a secure establishment.'

'For how long?'

'It's impossible to say, but at least until the end of the war.' He gave her a serpent's smile. 'I can't let you go. You know too much about the work we do here, and you're too bloody brilliant at it.'

This man had her bound up, whichever way she turned. When she didn't answer, he leaned forward, spinning his pen with his fingers as if it were a game of chance.

'Anyway, back to the new plan.'

'Hold on a minute . . .'

'Originally, we were going to put Mason on trial, make a big splash in the newspapers that we'd caught a traitor to boost public moral, then lock him up and throw away the key.'

'You said this was the only way to keep me safe if he worked out I was the one who gathered the evidence against him.'

Ambrose nodded, overemphatic. 'Absolutely. But the *powers*

that be have decided not to put him on trial. It would prove too much of an embarrassment for the government to admit we had an enemy spy in Whitehall. You don't have to look far into Mason's history to find his German associations. He should never have been given the position in the first place, despite his English public school education and his connections to the political establishment. His mother is part of the German aristocracy, for God's sake, and everyone knows how closely tied up they are with Hitler.'

'So what happens now? Are they setting him free?' Iris's stomach tightened as she thought of Mason's strength, of the violence in him. 'What if he works out I was the one who trapped him?'

'I'm told you still have a family member living in France. Eva Fournier, the famous cookery writer.'

'She's my aunt.'

The word *aunt* did her a disservice. Eva was like a second mother, and the only blood relative Iris had left. From the age of seven, she'd spent every summer in her beautiful house in Dijon. Iris hadn't been able to contact her since the Germans invaded, and never stopped worrying about her being alone in Occupied France.

'Do you want me to go and stay with her until all this blows over?'

'Yes and no. Just because Mason has been let off a show trial and a prison sentence, it doesn't mean he's to go unpunished.'

'What will happen to him?'

'Right now, he's still in custody. We're going to offer him his freedom on the condition that he leaves Britain and never comes back. This is where you come in.'

'What is it you want me to do?'

'Thanks to your photo being printed in the papers, he doesn't suspect you of being involved in his capture. Write to him in prison. Let him know you've given up on England and are returning to France to live with your aunt. Tempt him to follow you.'

'And then what?'

'Kill him.'

The idea was so absurd, she almost laughed. 'Why not just do it here and now?'

'It'll raise too many suspicions. The government intends to put out the message that he's innocent and make a big show of releasing him. If he's suddenly found dead in England so soon after being released, it'll raise too many questions. If it happens in occupied territory, the British public won't find out.'

'Why do I have to be the one to kill him? You have plenty of agents far more skilled in such matters than I am.'

'Because you're closer to him than anyone, and he trusts you. You've trapped him once, you can do it again.'

'I don't know. It seems . . .'

'You want to punish him for destroying your marriage, don't you? For breaking Jack's heart?'

'Yes, of course, but . . .'

'Wouldn't you like to go back to France? You're always complaining you've abandoned your country in its hour of need. This is your opportunity to change that.'

'And if I kill Mason, what then?'

'Dijon is a place of strategic importance, thanks to its road and rail network. Once you've dispensed with Mason, it wouldn't do any harm to have you working as another pair of eyes and ears on the ground. As long as no one suspects you're connected to us, of course.'

Iris thought of Natasha, so scared and inexperienced and sent out into the field too soon, shot trying to evade a German patrol, because she'd taken the wrong turning down the wrong street. If Iris had been there, she might have been able to prevent it.

'I know the area well. I could support your agents with local knowledge.'

'First, you have to assassinate Mason.'

Ambrose had done it. He'd reeled her in, convincing her to stay in his service. 'What about Jack? What do I tell him?'

'Let's concentrate on winning the war, shall we? You can worry about Jack later.'

Without Jack, there was nothing to keep Iris in England. She could be of more use in France.

'I'll go and pack a bag.'

'You've got twenty-four hours. I've already organised the appropriate papers and the money you'll need. Have a safe trip.'

Iris's marriage was in ruins, but Mason would be punished for betraying Britain, and at least Iris would have the satisfaction of being the one to do it.

Chapter 3

It was mid-afternoon when Iris stepped off the train in Dijon. Ambrose had organised a small boat to secrete her across the channel into northern France in the dead of night. From there, she'd caught a train to Paris and another to Dijon.

Before leaving, she'd replied to Jack's letter, informing him she was going to stay with her aunt Eva for a while, in case he had a change of heart and tried to find her in London. In the closing paragraph, she professed her love and her faithfulness, her determination to rebuild their marriage.

For now, she had to allow Mason back into her life, but she made a vow never to let him back into her bed. It was the one promise she could make to Jack, even if she couldn't tell him directly without betraying her mission.

She left a second letter for Jack with Ambrose, asking him to pass it on, should she not survive the mission. This one was more explicit, explaining that everything she'd done had been carried out in the name of duty, for his country, and for hers. She didn't expect it would be delivered to him until after the war, but at least one day he'd know the truth, even if it would be too late to mend his broken heart.

The sun was still high when she arrived in Dijon, the air

heavy with the continental heat she'd missed so much during the cold wartime years in London, the branches of the plane trees casting long shadows across the narrow medieval streets and cobbled lanes.

She closed her eyes and took a deep breath, filling herself up with the scent of the limestone buildings baking in the sun, and the memories of happier times: the summers spent with Eva as a child, and later as a young woman, finding her feet, growing away from everything she knew and loved, until it pulled her back. For all London had been her home for twenty years, France was the place that claimed her soul. Now, without Jack's love to anchor her, she wasn't so much free of England, as set adrift.

On the surface, the town seemed unchanged, apart from the German street signs and the swastikas flying from the public buildings. Yet, it was the smaller things that pointed to the insidiousness of the Occupation: the way the women and the old men looked away as they passed her on the street, the sense of mistrust that made her suspect murder was possible in what had once been a quiet town. It was the shock of the German soldiers, strutting like pigeons in their grey-green uniforms, instilling fear with a single glance that was the most unsettling. Just the sight of them left Iris feeling exposed, as if they could read her every thought and motivation.

Her decision to take a shortcut down a narrow side street proved to be her first mistake. Knowing it had always been a quiet road, she expected to avoid the German patrols. By the time she heard the thud of boots and fists landing on soft flesh, it was too late to turn back.

Three German soldiers had a young boy cornered. Already she could hear them laughing and jeering as he sank to his knees. She could smell his blood in the air, taste it on her tongue as he cried out. Her instinct was to intervene. But what could she do against three armed soldiers? For the sake of her mission, she knew to disappear before she was spotted, but the words were out before she could stop them.

'Leave the boy alone.'

Her safest bet would be to retreat to the main street, but it was too late. They'd seen her. Instead of running, she held her ground as they trained their eyes on her. Of all the things they might have been thinking, she knew to assume the worst.

'You'll turn around and walk away if you know what's good for you, madame.'

The soldier, who was barely old enough to shave, gave the order in stumbling French. His only authority lay in his fists and his heavy boots, the brutal uniform he hid behind.

'Let the boy go before you cause him serious harm.'

The young boy, no more than fourteen, struggled to his feet, using the distraction she'd provided as an opportunity to escape, coughing out words of thanks and gesturing to her to leave. 'Do as they say, madame. Run. Run for your life.'

Already, he'd fled, disappearing around the corner onto a busier street, where with luck and speed, he'd quickly become impossible to trace.

The second soldier advanced towards her, tugging his gun from his belt. 'Go, before I shoot you. Don't tell anyone what you just saw.'

Iris backed away. She couldn't risk being arrested or killed before she'd even begun her mission. She should have learned from Natasha's mistake. The danger on the streets was far worse than she'd anticipated. She must be more careful, avoid being stopped and searched, make sure any Englishness that had rubbed off on her wouldn't be detected. If anyone asked, she'd been living in Paris since before the war, not London.

Picking up her pace, she turned the corner onto the busy street, where life continued as it had before, as if the horrors that were taking place just out of sight all over the town were not occurring. This wasn't the welcome she'd hoped for. It wasn't home she'd returned to but a war zone.

* * *

It hadn't been possible to let Eva know in advance that she was coming, and so for the first time in all her years of visiting, her aunt hadn't been waiting at the station. Usually, she'd be running along the platform to greet her as the train came to a halt, the impossibly wide brim of her straw hat flapping in the breeze, the pale blue ribbon tied under her chin to keep it in place, tugging to be set free. At least by surprising her at home, Iris had spared her witnessing the incident with the soldiers.

Eva had always been ageless, a goddess of love and wisdom. Now, as Iris reeled from the incident with the soldiers, she wondered how the years of living under enemy occupation had changed her.

Eva's home was an old three-storey townhouse, set in the corner of one of the busy local squares, with shuttered windows, a green front door and a large back garden, surrounded by a high brick wall. Eva loved every stone and lintel, every roof tile and chimney, and was proud to tell everyone that it had been bought *with the efforts of my pen, my spade and my wooden spoon.*

Despite the time of day, the window shutters were closed and there was no answer when Iris knocked. Reluctant to be seen loitering outside, she retrieved the spare key from beneath the pot of lavender by the front door and let herself in, calling as she entered the house.

When there was no reply, she moved from room to room, hope fading with every unanswered call. Despite the emptiness, everything was just as it had always been. Dried rose petals scented the air, and the solid country furniture still filled up the space and made it a home. The polished oak floors were still scattered with the antique rugs Eva had picked up on her travels between the wars. Her portrait, painted by a lover who might have been Pierre Bonnard, still sat above the fireplace. Every sight and smell offered Iris the promise of comfort and familiarity, apart from Eva's absence.

Usually, she'd have a beef daube slow-cooking on the stove,

or if the weather was hot, there'd be a salad chilling in the cold store, laden with capers and goat's cheese, the olive oil caressing every blushing curve of the tomatoes. Today, there were only leftovers in the pantry, the stale reminders of the food shortages everyone was forced to endure under the German occupation.

Iris was opening the window shutters in the kitchen when she sensed someone standing behind her.

'Aunt Eva, is that you?'

Her voice faltered at the sight of the familiar figure in the doorway. Not Eva, but a neighbour.

'Clemence. I didn't hear you come in.'

'Forgive me. I didn't know it was you. I heard someone opening the shutters and wanted to check there wasn't an intruder.'

The slanting shadows of Clemence's face told Iris something was wrong. 'Where's Eva?'

'I'm sorry, my love. She's not here anymore. Eva died.'

Eva was a force of nature, a force for good: brave, accomplished and resourceful. It was impossible to believe she'd gone.

'It happened suddenly last Tuesday. It was a great shock to everyone who knew and loved her.'

'How could she have gone without saying goodbye?'

The war had forced them to spend the last few years apart, and now they'd missed each other by a matter of days. The timing of it was too cruel.

'I'm sorry you had to find out like this, my love, but I had no way of contacting you to let you know.'

If only Jack were here. He'd know what to say, even if he couldn't put it right. Remembering his last letter, loss snatched at her heart. She swallowed back the lump in her throat. Grief, layered on top of grief, was making it hard to breathe. She'd lost the only two people in the world who loved her. She forced back her tears. Eva wouldn't have wanted her to give in to them, not while Clemence was watching. Eva was stronger than that, and so was Iris.

'I've been letting myself into the house to keep an eye on it, but you can have the key back now you're here.'

The gesture made Iris feel even more alone. 'Please keep it. While this is Eva's house you'll always be welcome. Don't wait to be invited.'

Clemence had been Eva's close neighbour and friend for thirty years. There was never a time when Iris visited that Clemence hadn't been a constant presence. She'd lost her husband in the Great War, and with Eva having never married, they'd taken care of each other when they were sick, or needing company. Her stout figure was slighter now than before the war and she'd aged ten years since the fall of France, but then so had many people. Yet, whatever it was she'd suffered, it hadn't sapped her energy or her dignity. Her long grey hair was pinned in a chignon at the base of her neck, her face was freshly powdered and her daisy print dress was spotless.

'Is Jack not with you?'

Iris shook her head, trying not to show how much his absence mattered. 'He wasn't able to come.'

'The war has a lot to answer for.'

Clemence made them a chamomile tisane, using fresh tufts of the fragrant herb which she picked from the garden while she waited for the kettle to boil. Her brief absence from the kitchen allowed Iris the privacy she needed to gather herself together. She was too laced up to betray any emotion, even in front of the most sympathetic heart.

The tisane was one of Eva's recipes, and designed to soothe. Together they sat at the kitchen table, avoiding the chair where Eva used to sit. Clemence wrinkled her nose at the drink, which wasn't as good as when Eva used to make it.

'I told the bees about Eva, so they wouldn't fret. They'll be pleased to know you're here.'

Iris hadn't considered the bees and wasn't ready to venture into the garden, a place that had meant so much to Eva.

'I'll speak to them at dusk.'

It had been a fraught summer the year Eva taught Iris how to manage the bees. At first, she'd been terrified of being stung, until Eva had shown her how to relax around them, how to charm them while she removed the best of the honey.

Without Eva, every task suddenly seemed overwhelming. 'How am I supposed to carry on without her?'

'You have everything she taught you. It might not seem like it now, but it will be enough. And you don't have to worry about the funeral. Everything's taken care of. There'll be a big turnout. Eva was admired by everyone in the town.' She retrieved a newspaper cutting from the dresser and handed it to Iris. 'I kept this for you. I knew you'd be back one day and want to see it.'

Cookery writer, Eva Fournier, age 67, who was famous all over the world for her works on French cookery, died at her home in Dijon yesterday morning. Mme Fournier, who had never married, was about to wed her lifetime friend, Albert Lavigne. Her publisher has said she was also working on a new recipe book.

'She'd finally agreed to marry Albert?' After so many years of Eva turning down his proposals, Iris would never have believed it.

Clemence nodded. 'It's a tragedy that we'll be saying goodbye to her when we should have been celebrating her wedding.'

It explained the piece of lace, neatly folded on top of the dresser, the sewing box open beside it. Iris ran her fingers through the delicate fabric, avoiding the fine needle glistening at the edge where Eva had left it, mid-stitch. It was a reminder that she'd seen her beloved Eva for the last time, that there'd be no new memories. From now on, her birthday would be a day of remembrance rather than a celebration. Eva was in the past. She'd gone and was never coming back, and she'd taken all her love with her.

Clemence gathered up the wedding lace and bundled it into

a drawer. 'I should have put this out of sight. It doesn't do any good seeing it. It's too cruel, that's what it is.'

'How is Albert?'

'Heartbroken. You know how much he loved her. He waited a lifetime to marry her, and just when he thought she was finally going to be his wife, he loses her for good.'

'Was it you who found her?'

'I did, my love. She was still warm to the touch when I arrived.'

Iris's eyes searched the room. Was there a spot on the rug she'd always need to step over, a chair she'd need to avoid?

'Where did it happen?'

'In the garden. Beneath the almond tree. At least she was in her favourite place. And she was finally able to call her home her own again, since that filthy German had gone.'

'She wasn't living alone here?'

'A German officer had been billeted with her for over a year. His name was Max Schiller. He went not long before she died.'

Iris shuddered at the thought of the enemy living in the house. 'Will he be coming back?'

'I don't think he'd dare to show his face around here again. He wasn't a nice man. He gave Eva a terrible time while he lived here, in that quiet, bullying way some men have. Eva was more than a match for him. She never showed the effect he had on her, but endured it with dignity. Still, he was a brute.'

'Was he sent somewhere else?'

Clemence shrugged. 'Who knows? He was here one day and gone the next. No one was sorry when he went.'

'There's still a large German presence on the streets. He must have been the only one to have left.'

'There's a lot of resistance fighters hiding in the hills and disrupting the transport network. Schiller was put in the town to stamp it out. His reputation for brutality was well known and they thought he'd be a deterrent.'

'And was he?'

'He's the one that's gone. The Resistance is still here.'

'Couldn't Eva refuse to have him here?'

'Schiller insisted on being billeted with her because of her reputation as a cookery writer. He knew she'd feed him well. With so many local producers, food isn't as scarce here as in many parts of France. It's one thing we're thankful for. He also had access to all kinds of food, which he gave to her, expecting her to cook it for him. He pretended to admire her work, but it soon turned to contempt.'

It was unimaginable what life must have been like for Eva with a German officer living in her home. Yet, however terrible it had been, she'd found a way to cope with it. It was even more of a tragedy that she'd died just as she was free of him, while in the middle of hemming her wedding lace and working on a new recipe book.

'What did she die of, Clemence? You said it was sudden. Does anyone know what caused it?'

'You mustn't worry yourself about that, my love. Eva wouldn't want you to dwell on it. It won't do any good and it won't bring her back.'

'Had she been ill?'

Clemence turned away, fussing with Eva's sewing box, rattling the cotton reels as she struggled to close the lid with trembling fingers. 'You mustn't ask so many questions. What's done is done.'

What's done is done. The phrase had a deadly ring to it. Iris was experienced enough in interrogation to know Clemence was hiding something important.

'What happened, Clemence?'

'It's not worth fretting over.' Clemence refused to look up, continuing to fumble with the sewing box.

'If you don't tell me, someone else will, and I'd rather hear it from you.'

'She was shot.' Clemence sobbed as she forced out the words.

'Shot?'

'It was a single gunshot, straight to the heart. She wouldn't have known anything about it.'

'Who did it, Clemence? Have they been arrested?'

'A filthy German soldier did it. He left the gun beside her body, just to make sure everybody knew what our enemy occupiers are capable of.'

'Why did he kill her?'

'Who knows? But if they were prepared to kill her, they'll kill anybody.'

'It doesn't make sense.'

'They're ruling by fear. It's the only way they can keep control.'

If this were true, then Eva's death had been for nothing. People wouldn't be cowed. They'd stand up to their aggressors.

'Is there any way of finding out who killed her?'

'It could have been any one of the nasty creatures you see roaming the streets. Like predators they are, in their vile uniforms. It doesn't do to ask any questions unless you want to be next. Summary beatings and executions aren't uncommon. They'll attack anyone without a second thought. No one holds them to account, not even their own high command. They might give the impression of being courteous, offering smiles and sweets to children, but it's a different matter when they think no one's looking.'

'Whoever killed her must be held to account.'

'Don't start asking questions, Iris. It's too dangerous.'

Iris had already witnessed enough on the streets to understand the dangers she was facing. And even if she hunted down Eva's killer, it wouldn't bring her aunt back. The only way to avenge her death was to make sure the regime responsible for it was driven out of France. Their ultimate defeat would be the only way justice would be served for Eva's murder and for the deaths of countless others. If she was to play her part in their downfall, she had to focus on her mission for British Intelligence.

Without Eva, Iris was navigating a new and frightening world. If Mason took the bait and followed her to Dijon, she'd be completely alone in her mission to kill him. There'd be no one to help her, or soothe her if things went wrong. Without her beloved aunt, Iris's life was suddenly much lonelier.

Chapter 4

Iris moved from room to room, trying not to disturb anything. It seemed wrong to be in Eva's house without her, when everywhere she looked, there was evidence of her living presence. Clemence might have folded her wedding lace and put it in a drawer out of sight, but Eva's reading glasses were still on the kitchen dresser where she'd placed them, her pink flannel still draped over the bath where she'd left it to dry the day she died.

Everything was the same as it had always been, but soon it would all be different. Each small change Iris made as she moved around the house erased a little more of Eva. It was as inevitable as the dust settling, as the rising and the setting of the sun. Life was forcing her to go on, even as she resisted it.

She left exploring the garden until last, conscious that it was the place where Eva had been killed, knowing the bees would be wondering where she was, and how badly they'd have been affected by Eva's death.

If anywhere reflected Eva's soul more than the house, it was the garden. It was here, among the flowers, the fruit trees and the vegetable beds, that Eva's work as a cookery writer began. The produce she grew in this speck of land, bound by the old stone wall, was the inspiration for every recipe. Eva didn't only write about the food she cooked, but about where it came from, how she'd grown and nurtured it. Her books were as much about gardening as about eating, each one written with the spirit and the sensitivity of a poet. She revealed her soul in every word, and it was this that connected her with every cook and gardener who picked up one of her books, and why she was loved in so many countries and not just in her native France.

The leaves on the trees were restless in the warm breeze. It wouldn't be long until the storms came, breaking the humidity with the force of the thunder and the driving rain. Change was in the air, even as it had already happened. Now Eva was gone, nothing would stay the same.

The beehives were farthest from the house, the area around them planted with lavender and heather. Eva had believed in laying on a feast, so the bees didn't have to work too hard to find the ingredients to make the best honey. *Love nature and it will love you back*, she used to say. *It will give you everything you need to survive.* Iris wasn't immune to the cruel irony of this, knowing she'd died in her beloved garden.

She was sitting on a bench, pulling on Eva's rubber boots, when she heard a noise. She peered around the neat rows of vegetable beds and the tall canes holding up the last of the peas, straining to see what it was: a bird scratching among the dropped leaves, or the fall of an overripe quince from the branch of a nearby tree, but it was none of these things. Someone was in the garden.

Tracking the sound, she followed the beat of footsteps on the brick path, jumping at the sudden bang and the resulting shudder of the wooden gate as it slammed hard against its frame.

Could it have been Mason? Following Ambrose's instruction, she'd written to him before leaving England, while he was still in custody, giving him Eva's address, so he'd know where to find her once he was released. But if it was him, surely he'd have marched up to the front door, such was the sense of his entitlement, rather than slipping in through the garden like an intruder?

By the time she reached the gate, whoever was there had retreated down the alleyway and disappeared. It could have been anyone from the town, but what if it was a German soldier? They had the right to go anywhere these days, to take whatever they pleased and destroy anything that offended them.

Her thoughts turned to fear as she remembered seeing the young boy savagely beaten in a quiet side street. Then there was Eva's murder, which had taken place close to where she was now standing. Eva had always considered the house and the garden to be secure, but she'd been naive. Iris pushed the gate, testing its strength, and rattled the latch, which had worn loose over so many years of use. There'd never been a bolt on it because there'd never been a need for one, although it would have been sensible to secure it once the Germans moved in.

Whoever was in the garden must have been up to no good. Why else would they disappear unless they were worried about being caught? She scanned the flower and vegetable beds, the espaliered fruit trees, looking for clues. Half a dozen bees buzzed lazily above the lavender, unconcerned by the disturbance. Was the intruder someone they were accustomed to? Nothing in the garden seemed out of place, or at least she didn't think so. But whoever had been there had visited for a reason.

The shed door banged, the sound echoing through the silence and disrupting Iris's thoughts. She slipped behind the yew hedge and crept towards it, conscious that someone might be inside. And there it went again, the crash of the door, sounding as if someone had slammed it.

But it was only the wind that had taken it. Just like the back gate, it had only a rattling old latch to secure it. In Eva's philosophy, what else would it need when this was her private world and there was no one to bother her in it?

Inside the shed, everything was the same, the smell of warm compost and leaf mould as reassuring as it had always been. Iris only had to close her eyes to remember Eva sitting on the three-legged stool in the corner, cleaning her pruning shears with a soft rag, her elbows leaning on the long handles as she rested them across her lap. It was too perfect a memory to linger over without getting upset, and she forced herself to turn away, quietly closing the door as she left.

Behind the shed, there was a patch of ground, part of which had been given over to the compost heap. The rest of the space had become overgrown with rhubarb and oleander, and a hydrangea which was now in need of dead-heading. The larkspur and foxgloves, long past their seasonal peak, had grown leggy, and were overreaching themselves from neglect, or perhaps Eva had simply forgotten them, tucked out of sight of the house and the rest of the garden. The hemlock and the corncockle, creeping around the feet of the taller plants, showed she'd failed to keep on top of the weeding, their seeds, dropped seasons ago from the beaks of passing birds or carried on the wind.

On her way back from the shed, Iris spotted the upturned basket of almonds Eva must have been harvesting when she died. She stood in the shadow of the tree, rigid with grief, imagining the moment of Eva's murder as she confronted the spot where it happened, picturing the horror when Clemence found her.

The air temperature was much cooler in the shade. Iris shuddered as she gathered the scattered almonds and tipped them into the abandoned basket, topping it up with the remaining nuts on the tree, hulling them as she went, before carrying it down to the cellar where Eva always left them to dry. It was a job that needed doing and Iris did it without thinking, just as Eva had taught her.

The cooking was done in the kitchen, but much of Eva's experimental work happened right here in the cellar, out of sight, where no one would disturb her. Iris's eyes scanned the secret space, wishing Eva back. Nothing had changed since the last time she'd visited. The rush matting on the stone floor still crunched underfoot, and the shelves were still lined with glass jars filled with dried herbs, fruits and flowers, edible seeds and nuts.

The copper still, used for distilling essential oils, remained on the wooden table in the centre of the room, the conkers to keep away the spiders, tucked in every dark corner. Jars of last season's honey and preserves filled every available space. Most surprising of all were the bags of sugar, which these days, was more precious than gold. Remembering what Clemence had said about Schiller giving Eva extra supplies, she imagined he must have provided it to satisfy his sweet tooth, or else she'd stockpiled it at the first hint of war. Eva hadn't changed. She'd been productive right up to the moment of her death, storing and preserving food for the months ahead.

Eva's last notes, outlining the ideas for her next cookery book, were on the desk in the corner. Beside them was a recent letter from her publisher, discussing the recipes they should focus on after the war.

There was a chestnut cake beside the letter, wrapped in paper and string, which Eva must have baked just before she died. Its proximity to the letters suggested it had been intended as a gift for her publisher. Now a relic, it seemed too precious to eat, but it wouldn't keep forever. Knowing Eva wouldn't have wanted it to go to waste, Iris took it to share with Clemence.

Clemence was feeding her hens in the garden, humming a gentle song as she scattered chopped carrots and grain across the lawn, encouraging the birds to forage and scratch for their dinner. Her face clouded with emotion at the sight of the cake, which appeared as an unexpected gift from the recently dead.

She ushered Iris into the house and cut her a tiny slice, watching her bite into it as if it were a sacred act. 'We should make the most of it. No one else could bake quite like Eva.'

The sensation of the cake in her mouth took Iris back to the moment she'd first tasted it. She was seven years old, and her mother had left her with Eva for the first time, promising to come back for her at the end of the summer. At that point, Eva had been a stranger, and to a child, the months spread out before her, an eternity of empty days and loneliness, but the syrup, oozing through the soft crumb of the cake, had put an end to her tears. Suddenly, she'd felt cherished in this unaccustomed place and it had no longer felt strange, but full of the possibility of happiness.

Iris rubbed the crumbs from her fingers as she told Clemence about the intruder in the garden. 'Who do you think it was?'

'There's been a lot of strange behaviour since the Occupation. France is full of displaced people trying to make their way to freedom, all of them on foot and with nothing but what they stand up in. It could have been an escaped prisoner of war, trying to get back to his family, or someone avoiding being sent to a forced labour camp. They might not even have been from this town.'

'Do you feel safe here, Clemence? Are you closely watched?'

'Look what happened to Eva. Of course it isn't safe, of course we're watched.'

'You said Schiller was billeted here for a while. Are there other German soldiers living close by?'

If Iris tempted Mason into Eva's home as means of trapping him, she had to understand the risk. He could appear at any moment and she needed to be prepared for all eventualities.

'If you want to survive here, Iris, you must keep yourself to yourself, have one eye over your shoulder and don't ask too many questions. If you can't do that, you're better off going back to Paris.'

'It's occupied there too. Do you think I don't know the risks?'

'Dijon is much smaller than Paris. Word travels fast if anyone starts asking questions about safety and risk, and there are fewer places to hide. There's death on the streets whichever way you turn.'

Iris cut Clemence a slice of cake, trying to take the tension out of the air. Dijon had become a different place since the Occupation. If she was to lead Mason into a deadly trap and avoid being implicated in his eventual murder, she had to ensure she was above suspicion. There was no room for mistakes.

Chapter 5

Iris pulled the black leather gloves onto her hands, smoothing the bends and the dips across the fingers where they'd moulded to the contours of Eva's knuckles. She wouldn't have minded her borrowing them on this of all days, and it was a comfort to know she'd be carrying something of Eva with her as she said her final goodbye.

There was a man waiting on the doorstep when she left the house. She hadn't heard him knock and didn't know how long he'd been standing there. He smiled too brightly, given the nature of the day, and offered her a bottle of wine as she opened the door.

'Iris, at last. It's good to see you.'

Iris stared, leaving him holding the bottle in the air between them. Paul. She wouldn't have recognised him if it hadn't been for his voice.

'A gift from my vineyard. The Germans don't get their hands on all the barrels.' He waved the bottle at her until she took it. 'It's good to see you.' He ran his fingers across the top of his head and gave a nervous laugh. 'Did I say that already?'

Since she'd last seen him, Paul had become the image of his father. He was only two years older than her and yet he looked like an old man. She tried not to stare at his receding hairline, his gaunt features. He could only have been half his previous body weight, his legs almost too brittle to hold him up. He'd always been strong-limbed and muscular from working on the family vineyard. Now, there was nothing left of him. She could hardly relate the man standing before her to the tearaway who'd been her childhood friend.

'I can't invite you in. I'm on my way to Eva's funeral.'

He nodded a little too fervently. She'd never known him to be nervous before. 'I've come to escort you.' He tilted his head to one side. 'Let's go.'

It was only after they'd set off that she noticed he was wearing a black suit and tie rather than his usual flannel shirt and trousers. He must have bought the outfit especially for the occasion, or seeing how ill-fitting it was, he'd probably borrowed it.

'How's Nathalie? Is she still living in Dijon?'

Paul looked away, mouthing the words as if he were spitting them on the ground. 'My sister moved to Paris a few years ago to teach in a new school. When the Germans took the city in 1940, she joined the convoys of people trying to leave. We received a letter from her the day before her departure, telling us she was coming home, but she never arrived. The German planes shot countless people from the air as they tried to flee. She must have been one of them. We'll never know what happened to her.'

'I'm so sorry, Paul. I had no idea.'

'If you hadn't stayed away for so long, you'd have known.'

The sharpness of his tone was understandable, but still it came as a shock. His experiences of war had hardened him, and Iris no longer knew what to say to him.

His eyes darted here and there, scanning the roofs of buildings and every street corner, as if he expected to spot a sniper at each turning, expecting the worst, just as the worst had happened to Nathalie.

'I don't suppose Jack could risk coming. The Germans would shoot him as soon as he opened his mouth.'

He said it as if Jack's absence was some kind of victory. 'Who told you I was back?'

'Everyone's talking about it. You wouldn't miss Eva's funeral.'

It was a reminder that everyone had an interest in everyone else's business. Since she'd returned, the glances were more furtive than ever. There'd never been any malice in it before, only curiosity and often a willingness to help. Now, there was real fear in the air. With enemy soldiers patrolling the streets, looking for an excuse to pounce, any unwanted attention could be a threat to life.

As they crossed the square, Paul pulled a crumpled sheet of paper from his pocket. 'Christophe couldn't come today. He asked me to give you this poem. He wanted you to know he was sorry about Eva.'

Christophe had been a quiet young man, always with his head in a book when he wasn't helping his parents to run the local hardware shop. She couldn't imagine his gentle soul coping with the war. She pushed the poem into her bag to look at later. 'How is he?'

'His father died a couple of weeks ago, days after being beaten by German soldiers in a street brawl. How do you think he is?'

The words sounded more like an accusation than the breaking of terrible news. 'Poor Monsieur Janot. I'm so sorry to hear it.' How many unnecessary deaths had there been since the Occupation, and how many more were still to follow?

'Was Christophe called up to fight before the fall of France?'

'Yes, but it didn't last long. He was shot and captured by the Germans who made him a prisoner of war. After the armistice, he was sent back home. He wasn't fit enough for hard labour, so they had no use for him.'

'His injury must have healed by now. I'm surprised he hasn't been reinterred.'

'The bullet damaged the muscle at the top of his right arm, rendering it almost useless. It's a sorry state for a young man to be in and he feels it deeply.'

'How about you, Paul? Are you still running the vineyard?'

What she really wanted to ask was, what happened? What did they do to break you into so many small pieces and leave you like this?

'After France fell, I was sent to a forced labour camp in Germany. Instead of avenging Nathalie's murder, I was made to work for the regime responsible for killing her, until they broke me too. It's me you've got to thank for all those enemy tanks rolling across Europe, destroying everything in their path.'

Iris recoiled at the bitterness that had crept into his voice. 'You're home now, that's all that matters.'

'When I became too ill to work in their factories, they sent me back here to run the vineyard, just as I've always done, only now the Germans take most of the wine as soon as it's in the barrels.' He lowered his voice. 'I make sure they only receive the poorest quality of what we produce.'

They were almost at the church when they found themselves in the path of a group of French prisoners, their emaciated faces and shabby clothes indicating they were long-term captives being moved to another labour camp, although how they could be expected to work when they hardly had the strength to walk was anyone's guess.

Iris looked the other way as they marched towards her, refusing to catch the eye of the German guard who was leading them, trusting he'd consider her gesture one of disinterest rather than a refusal to engage with him. She thought she'd got away with it, until his sudden cry of *halt* told her she'd misjudged her tactic. The prisoners sagged, feeble as kittens, as they were forced to stop.

'Madame.'

The officer angled his head, searching out her gaze until she had no choice but to look at him. He was too tall and too broad, his innate clumsiness undermining his assumed sense of superiority. His voice, a pitch too high, made him ridiculous. He could have been any one of a number of soldiers occupying their homes and their streets, tormenting the life out of them. It was as if a whole generation of German men had been bred specifically to fulfil this duty. Iris set her expression to neutral, sensing each set of hungry prisoners' eyes on her face, willing her to get the better of their captor as she met his stare.

'Monsieur.'

'Are you well, madame? You look pale.'

It wasn't concern in the German's voice, but the thrill that he might be terrifying the life out of her. She felt the tension in Paul's body as he stood beside her, his hand gripping her arm. Silently, she urged him not to react, to leave the soldier to her.

'Thank you for your concern, monsieur. I'm on my way to my aunt's funeral. It's an emotional day. She was very dear to me.'

The officer stepped back as if her grief were contagious. 'Please accept my condolences for your loss.'

His expression failed to match the sentiment of his words. He was enjoying himself, revelling in her sorrow. He might as well have been the monster who stole into Eva's garden and shot her in cold blood.

The eyes of the prisoners were still on her, each man relying on her to show the soldier up for the aggressor he was by remaining dignified in his presence, her defiance taking the edge off their humiliation at being herded through the town like cattle as if France no longer belonged to them. She'd only been here a few days and already she hated the way the Germans behaved, pretending to be the victors, when in truth they were already losing the war.

She pulled out her powder compact and checked her face in the mirror, distracting herself until the guard and the prisoners had passed by, not wanting to catch anyone's eye. It was too dangerous to risk being considered as anything other than what she was supposed to be.

Paul loosened his grip after the last of the prisoners had filed past, the shuffle of their broken-down shoes fading in the distance.

'Are you all right?'

She snapped the compact shut, showing him her brave face. 'I'm fine. Let's go. We don't want to be late for the funeral.'

At least he'd had the sense not to intervene when the guard approached her. She hadn't trusted him not to say the wrong thing. Now, as he held on to her once again, guiding her to the church as if she didn't know the way, it was like walking with a stranger.

It was hard to believe he was once the boy who'd taught her to swim and to climb a tree, to milk a goat and to predict a change in the weather on the coming breeze, filling her childhood summers with happy memories, inspiring physical courage in her like no one else could. It was because of him that she knew the words to all the rude French songs they never teach you at school, and how to judge a good wine from a bad. He was the first boy she'd held hands with, the first boy she'd ever kissed, and she'd grown to love him as the brother she'd never had. Now, she wouldn't have recognised him if he'd passed her in the street.

Clemence had said everyone in the town would turn out for the funeral and it was a shock to find the church almost empty. Iris consoled herself with the thought that Eva would have been amused by the rows of empty chairs, the hollow sound of so few voices making an attempt at the hymns, and would have claimed it to be *just punishment for all the glum funerals I refused to attend.* Eva had believed in celebrating life, not death, and she wouldn't have expected anyone else to do anything different.

Iris reminded Clemence of this later, back at the house, where the few mourners had gathered to drink to Eva's memory.

Clemence offered her an olive, determined to make sure none of the food she'd put out was wasted. 'People are tired of funerals. It's only a couple of weeks since we buried Monsieur Janot. Before that, it was Monsieur Legrand. The town can only stomach so much sorrow.'

This was the first Iris had heard about Monsieur Legrand's death. 'The Mayor died?'

'He didn't die, he was killed. The Germans dragged him out

of his office without warning and shot him in the town square.'

Summary executions were becoming a familiar story. 'Why would they do that?'

'Because the only way they can rule is through fear.'

'The same reason they killed Monsieur Janot.'

'He made the mistake of saying the wrong thing to a German soldier. It's all it takes these days.'

Paul appeared from the kitchen and handed Iris a glass of wine 'Will you be staying in Dijon or will you be leaving us again?'

Iris's stay depended on so many things. On Mason taking up her invitation to join her, and on her being able to assassinate him without it looking like murder. The situation here was more perilous than she'd first imagined. It was unlikely she'd be able to stay on as Ambrose's eyes and ears on the ground if there was any suspicion around her after she'd completed her mission. She'd underestimated the dangers of living under enemy occupation.

And then there was Jack. There was no hope of mending their marriage while they were living in different countries. All of this was too complicated, too secret to confide to Paul. 'Honestly, I don't know.'

Monsieur Vallery must have been waiting to catch Iris alone. As soon as she moved away from Paul, he stepped forward.

'May I have a quiet word please, madame?'

Iris followed him into the garden where there was no one to overhear them.

'Forgive me for taking you away from your guests, but I wish to speak to you privately, not only to express my deep regret at your loss, but in the capacity of Eva's solicitor.'

The old man's faded blue eyes were full of concern, his delicate features set in sympathy as he tried to hide his pain at losing his dear friend so as not to burden her with it. She knew him too well for him to get away with such a disguise. She wondered if he'd have the courage to mention the nature of Eva's death when no one else had.

'As you know, Eva had no immediate family. You were the closest thing she had to a daughter and so it might not surprise you to learn that she has left everything to you, including this house. Please come to my office tomorrow morning to sign the papers.' He forced a smile, his formality straining at the seams. 'Congratulations, madame. Eva has left you well-provided for.'

This was more than Iris had expected or even considered. Eva's death was nothing but a loss and she hadn't thought to gain anything from it.

'Are you sure? She never mentioned anything about it.'

'We'll discuss it further tomorrow when you've had time to take it all in.'

Back inside the house, Albert was sitting in the corner, gripping a glass of pastis that had barely touched his lips. He was wearing his best suit, his white hair and beard neatly trimmed for the occasion. Iris kissed his forehead and sat beside him.

'Look at you, Iris. You're as lovely as ever. How Eva missed you these past years.'

Iris had promised herself she wouldn't cry in front of anyone and was determined not to let herself down. 'I wish I could have come sooner, if only . . .'

'There's no *if only*. There's nothing you could have done.'

Once again, the nature of her death was to remain unspoken between them, a secret born out of fear that mustn't be shared.

She rested her hand on his sleeve. His jacket was too warm for the time of year and the fabric was rough beneath her fingertips. 'Was she happy, Albert?'

'She was happier than she'd been for years.' Albert looked at her, his eyes hollow with grief. 'She was finally going to be my wife. I'd loved her since I was sixteen years old. I only married Bernice because Eva wouldn't have me. Once I was widowed, I started courting her again. Do you know how many years it took her to say yes?'

'I'm so sorry, Albert.'

'Every year of waiting would have been worth it to have one day of being able to call her my wife.'

'She loved you very much.'

'I know, but she was independent and always put her work before anything else, and I even loved her for that. I wouldn't have wanted to burden her with children when we were younger, knowing there were books she wanted to write, places she wanted to visit to discover their food. It wouldn't have been true love if I'd have stood in the way of her dreams.'

Albert had loved Eva enough to respect her need for freedom. And yet, during all those years apart, he never gave up on her. Iris thought of Jack, eating his heart out over a glass of whisky in a bar somewhere in England. The situation wasn't the same, but when it came to it, he hadn't had enough faith in their marriage to trust her. She couldn't blame him. He didn't deserve the humiliation of seeing his wife's infidelity displayed on the front page of every newspaper in Britain. She'd made a fool of him on a very public stage.

It wasn't long before the guests began to leave. Iris was washing up the used glasses when Albert's son, Fabrice, came into the kitchen to say goodbye.

'I'm sorry about Eva. My father is heartbroken over her death. It was foolish of him to ask her to marry him at their age. I don't know what he thought he'd gain from it.'

Love, thought Iris, *companionship, and the joy of having someone who cares for you forever at your side. And if forever isn't possible, there's still the joy of today and tomorrow and the day after that.* Instead of saying it, she handed him a bowl of salad to take home, and accompanied him to the door to say goodbye.

Paul was outside having a cigarette. She tensed when she realised he was watching her. 'I thought you'd gone home.'

He put the cigarette out and dropped the remains of the stub in his pocket. 'You look like you've had enough for one day. I have a bottle of our finest 1928 Côtes du Rhône in my bag. Come and sit on our bench in the square and we'll drink it.'

The other guests had already left, and despite her unease at Paul's lingering presence, she couldn't face being alone in the empty house. 'I'll fetch a couple of glasses.'

By the time she came back, Paul had already settled on the bench. The first mouthful of wine slipped down her throat like silk. Before she knew it, she was on her second glass. She rested her head on Paul's arm, relaxing for the first time that day. Sitting together like this had taken them both back years, and despite the changes in him, Paul was beginning to seem more like his old self.

'Did I ever tell you what an excellent winemaker you are?'

'We have to give my father the credit for this vintage. He was still running the vineyard in 1928 when it was produced. I was just his lowly assistant.'

'Did your mother keep the vineyard going while you were in the labour camp?'

'Yes, but she couldn't have done it without the help of the women in the town. The Germans took most of what was produced, but she survived on the little that was left.'

Iris clapped her hands a little too loudly. She'd hardly eaten all day and the wine had gone to her head. 'Bravo to every wartime wine-producing woman in the town.'

'These days, I make sure the Germans taste only the very worst of our wine so they won't come back for more.'

As they sat side by side, looking up at the sky, it was easy to pretend the years had fallen away. Iris could imagine herself at fifteen again, stealing out of the house to meet Paul after Eva had forbidden her from seeing him. *He's too wild*, she used to say. *He'll lead you astray*. How many nights had she crept home, having drunk too much wine? For all Eva had disapproved, they still remained some of Iris's fondest memories.

Of course he'd been wild, but he was also gentle and sweet. She'd always felt protected whenever he was around. Now instead of strength, all she sensed was anger.

Already the bottle was empty and Iris's head was swimming. 'I should go home. It's been a long day.'

Paul dropped his arm around her shoulder and pulled her closer. 'I missed you so much during these past years. The thought of sitting on this bench with you again and getting drunk is what helped me to survive the labour camp. Now you're back, you'd better stay for good.'

She felt his arm tense around her as she tried to move. 'You've forgotten I'm married to Jack.'

'And yet, here you are, sitting on a bench with me. You were mine first. I won't let you forget that.'

Iris slid to the end of the bench, untangling herself from his embrace. 'Why haven't you ever married? Lots of women in the town would be glad to have you.'

He shrugged, folding his arms against the sudden cool breeze. 'There was never anyone I liked as much as you.'

She remembered their first kiss. It had been a drunken, stumbling affair, embarked upon out of curiosity rather than anything else on Iris's part. After all, she'd only been fifteen and couldn't be blamed for experimenting. At the time, she hadn't realised how much it had meant to Paul. Not wanting to upset him, she'd allowed him to keep on kissing her and holding her hand for the rest of the summer until she returned to her parents in Paris. By the time she came back the following year, she'd put it behind her, but Paul had never forgotten it.

'That summer . . . we were hardly more than children.'

'If it hadn't been for Eva, we'd have been married years ago.'

She leaned away from him as he spat the words. The rise of his temper made her nervous. She'd never known such rage in him. 'You can't say that, Paul. It's not true.'

What they'd had was no more than a youthful flirtation, as fleeting as the summer that it lasted. It had never been mentioned since, at least not until now.

'Eva turned you against me. She did it so cleverly, that even now you can't see it.'

'If you feel that way, you shouldn't have come to her funeral.'

'I came for you, Iris. Everything I've ever done has always been for you.'

The mood had darkened and the cool breeze was getting stronger. The sound of soldiers' boots, echoing along the cobbled streets, was getting closer. She had to get home before the curfew. She got up from the bench, unsteady from the effects of the wine, gently pushing Paul away as he tried to kiss her.

'Goodnight, Paul. Don't stay out too late.'

Chapter 6

Iris lay awake for most of the night, trying to comprehend the changes in Paul. His physical degeneration was understandable but the contortion of his heart was another matter. This wasn't the same person who'd taught her to ride a bicycle when she was ten years old, steadying her as she wobbled, pedalling around the square, squealing at him never to let go of her. In those days, she'd been glad to feel the security of his hands gently circling her waist. Now, she wondered if he'd taken her instruction too literally when she'd begged him not to let go.

Had he hung on to her all these years, keeping his heartbreak to himself as he watched her fall in love and marry Jack? Or had his time in the prison camp generated a part of him that had never been there before, a part that had caused him to rewrite the past, challenging their joint memories and punishing her for roads not taken?

She would never regret leaving France to live with Jack in London when he asked her to marry him at the age of nineteen. Nor would she wish to take back the twenty years she'd already given him. Paul's display of jealousy, his quickness to anger, wouldn't make her regret any of it.

Perhaps it was Natalie's death that was to blame. The two of them had been so close as children. Paul must have felt as if a part of him had been ripped away as he tried to come to terms with the slow realisation that she was never coming home. And with the vineyard now under German control, what else was there left? No wonder he harked back to their idyllic summers of the past, when so much of what he had back then had since been snatched away.

Iris was still thinking about Paul the next morning when a messenger appeared with a note.

Arriving on the 5 o'clock train from Paris. Meet me at the station.
Mason.

Mason had taken the bait. He must have been released from prison, and had agreed to the condition that he leave Britain. She hadn't believed Ambrose's plan would work, and there'd been a chance it wouldn't, but Mason was on his way. Her mission to assassinate him would begin today. But first, she had an appointment to keep.

Monsieur Vallery's office was in a quiet back street, away from the bustle of the market. Only the occasional grumbling of the patients visiting the dentist next door interrupted the silence of his working day. He welcomed Iris inside and invited her to take a seat, apologising for the absence of his assistant, who'd slipped out to run an errand.

The dark panelling that covered all four walls and the ornate walnut desk spoke of a bygone age, the half-closed blinds creating a drowsy atmosphere. The Oriental rug, long admired by Eva, had been trodden away with wear, giving the room a sense of shabbiness that he'd probably failed to notice, as year after year, he went about his daily business. Quietly spoken and introverted, he'd barely looked up from his desk in almost half a century, and seemed largely oblivious to the changes that were going on around him. She wondered if he even realised there was a war on.

He pushed his spectacles onto his nose and turned to the mahogany filing cabinet, tugging at the top drawer where the runners had warped, until it lunged open. After considerable rummaging, he retrieved a brown folder, bursting with papers.

'It's simply a matter of signing a few forms, madame. Eva made sure everything was in order, so the handover of her property to you would be straightforward. She didn't want you troubled with the paperwork.'

Eva must have thought everything through carefully before she died. The only thing she'd neglected to do was to tell Iris about it.

'When did she arrange this?'

Monsieur Vallery squinted at the date on one of the papers. 'Eighteen years ago. As soon as you reached twenty-one.' He gave a sad smile. 'I remember her sitting in the chair where you are now and saying it was to be your belated coming-of-age birthday present.'

So Eva had put everything in place nearly two decades ago and had never told her. Iris's hand shook as she signed the papers, reading through each one carefully before committing her name to it. Not only had Eva left her the house and everything in it, along with the considerable contents of her bank accounts, she'd also put her in sole charge of her literary estate.

'She has left you well-off, madame, but with that comes the responsibility of taking care of her legacy.' Monsieur Vallery's face softened. 'She had great faith in you and wasn't prepared to entrust it to anyone else.'

It was too much to take in. Iris hadn't expected anything from Eva and now she'd been given everything. She asked Monsieur Vallery for a glass of water, giving herself time to gather her thoughts while he went to fetch it.

He placed it on the desk in front of her, his face full of sympathy. 'There's much to be thankful for as well as to mourn. Eva wouldn't have wanted you to be sad. She always believed in celebrating life.'

'Clemence told me she ran to you for help after she found Eva in the garden. Do you think she suffered?'

Monsieur Vallery rubbed his thumb across the smooth half-moons of his fingernails as he considered his reply. 'There's no point in dwelling on what happened, madame. The past is the past and cannot be changed.'

It was a way of shutting down her questions with tact and sensitivity, reminding Iris that he was mourning Eva as a long-standing friend, that his grief was probably still too raw for him to discuss it.

'We will win the war, madame. There will be an end to this.'

He had to be right. The loss and suffering couldn't all be for nothing.

He shuffled in his seat, suddenly eager to be rid of her. 'Is there anything else, madame?'

'No. You've made everything perfectly clear.' Refusing to discuss the nature of Eva's death proved the Occupation had made cowards of them all.

Monsieur Vallery straightened the papers on his desk and slid them back into the folder. The issue was closed and he wouldn't be returning to it. 'Then you won't mind seeing yourself out.'

Chapter 7

The news of Iris's inheritance was still sinking in after she left Monsieur Vallery's office and made her way through the busy market. It was impossible to consider the beautiful house and garden as belonging to anyone other than Eva. It had been a second home to Iris for most of her life, yet she couldn't think of herself as having sole possession of it, and couldn't believe herself worthy of it.

Her thoughts were interrupted by the sound of a man clearing his throat. She looked up, suddenly aware that a German officer had fallen into step beside her.

'Madame, I don't believe I've seen you before.'

He was tall and thick-limbed, and spoke in clumsy French. He reminded her of the officer who'd stopped her on the way to Eva's funeral, but it was just that they all had the same look about them, the same false pleasantness that was as unpalatable as their bad breath.

She gave him a passing nod, so as not to seem rude, refusing to fill the silence when he didn't respond. She was more skilled in interrogation techniques than he could ever imagine, and she could sense a trap at twenty paces.

Assuming he had nothing else to say, she carried on. She'd only taken a dozen steps when he called after her, ordering her to stop. Iris obeyed, waiting while he took his time to catch up with her.

'Show me your papers.'

She slipped them out of her bag and handed them over in one smooth action. Her slow, deliberate breaths steadied her shaking hands as he studied them, comparing the photograph on her identity card to her face a little more carefully than was necessary, to make the point that he had the power to do so.

'Why haven't I seen you before? I know the face of every woman who walks up and down this street.'

'I've recently arrived from Paris.'

'Why did you leave Paris?'

'My aunt died. She lived in the house in the corner of that square over there.' She shouldn't have given him so much information. It was nerves that had made her do it.

His eyes drilled into her as she spoke. Not blue, like a perfect Aryan specimen, but a mottled grey.

'The famous cookery writer?'

She didn't like the way he asked the question, but she stood her ground. 'Yes. She was very well known.'

He thrust her papers at her, his eyes still fixed on her face. 'It's not always good to stand out from the crowd. You'll do well to remember it.'

The words could have been a threat or a warning. His tone gave nothing away other than malice. She stood patiently, waiting for his permission to leave. He wasn't confident in his superiority. She could tell by the way he held himself, but if anything, this made him more unpredictable.

'When will you be returning to Paris?'

'I don't know. I have to work out what to do with the house and with my aunt's things. It might take some time.'

He clicked his heels, folding his hands behind his back. 'Then I'll keep my eye on you.'

If it was fear he hoped to see on her face, she made sure he was disappointed. 'It's a small town. I'm sure our paths will cross again.'

He held her gaze, his mouth a thin line of contempt. 'I promise you they will. Don't forget, I know where you live.'

Iris's heart was thumping like a bass drum. She checked her pace, making sure she didn't appear hurried or troubled after the solider finally allowed her to go. Everyone knew Eva, even the occupying enemy. They also knew the true nature of her death, even if no one dared to mention it. Now she was known to be associated with her, it was going to be difficult to keep a low profile.

Passing the church on the way home, she spotted Christophe sitting beside the gate, kicking his heels against the crumbling stone wall, his right arm strapped to his body. His attention was focused on a small leather notebook, no bigger than a pocket Bible, which he held close to his face with his good hand.

Iris was shocked by the physical changes in him, just as she'd been shocked by the changes in Paul. These days, no one appeared to be the person they used to be, and it made her uncertain of everyone she met.

Christophe looked up when she shouted hello, dragging himself back from whatever world had captured him in the pages of the book. It was the first time she'd seen him in spectacles, and his eyes narrowed as he looked at her, as if the lenses weren't strong enough to help him to see into the distance. His hair, cropped close to his head, and his moustache reminded her that he'd been made to live a soldier's life and a prisoner's life. It was more than any young man should have been forced to endure, especially one as sensitive as Christophe.

He clambered down from the wall, slipping the book into his pocket as she approached him. There'd still been so much of the boy about him when she last saw him that it came as a shock to see him transformed into a young man. She was tempted to comment on how he'd changed, but given the circumstances that had forced it, he probably wouldn't want reminding of it.

'Thank you for the poem. It meant so much to receive it on the day of Eva's funeral.'

'I couldn't face coming. Not so soon after burying Papa.'

His voice had grown deeper. Each word he pronounced sounded as if it were stirring up gravel at the back of his throat. She imagined he'd become popular with the young women in the town.

'I was sorry to hear about his death.'

'Everyone's sorry, but it won't bring him back.'

Monsieur Janot had been such a vital man before the war, with boundless energy and a willingness to do anything for anyone. It was hard to believe he was no longer a part of the community.

'What happened?'

'Papa had a disagreement with a group of German soldiers. He only appeared to have a few cuts and bruises, but he died two days afterwards.'

If only Monsieur Janot had kept his head down, or turned the other cheek, he'd still be alive. Aggravation was part of the enemy tactics, but insisting on having the last word wasn't worth dying for.

The Mayor, dragged out of his office and shot in the main square, must have been killed under similar circumstances, just as Eva was. It was a pattern that had to end. France had to become smarter if it was to win the war. But there was no use saying this to Christophe, who'd already lost so much, and none of it was his fault.

'How's your mother?'

What Iris really wanted to ask was, how was she surviving the war since her only son had been called to fight and returned to her in this state? Since her husband had been killed? Was she the same person she used to be or had it changed her too, just as it had changed everyone else?

'She complains there's too much work to do, running the hardware shop without Papa to help her.'

'She must be glad to have you at her side.'

'I'm no use to her like this and I'm no substitute for Papa.'

He nodded to the bicycle propped against the wall, an oversized wicker basket strapped to its handlebars. 'These days, I'm nothing but her delivery boy and not a very good one. It's impossible to cycle in a straight line with only one decent arm. She's had to employ Solange to help in the shop because I can't do anything that needs two hands.'

Solange had been in the same year at school as Christophe. The last time Iris saw her, she was teaching herself to be a seamstress and dreaming of working for one of the couture houses in Paris. No doubt the war had put a stop to her ambition.

'If your mother has employed Solange, business must be good.'

'She's busier than ever now we have the enemy living among us. No one is safe in their beds anymore. Everyone wants bars on their windows, bolts and locks on their doors.'

Iris had seen little evidence of destruction in the streets, but with German officers billeted in the town, the damage probably took place behind closed doors. The Occupation had taken the war from a military conflict and made it into a domestic one.

He looked at her over the top of his spectacles. 'What did you think of my poem? Is it any good?'

From what Iris could remember, it had been a jumble of phrases that hadn't said much at all.

'I didn't know you wrote poetry.'

'After I was released from prison, I met a man on the train who said he was a doctor. He asked me where I'd been sent to fight, but I couldn't tell him because the words got stuck in my throat. The carriage was crowded and there was nowhere to sit and hardly any room to stand. It smelled like a goat shed, only worse. A goat shed only smells of shit and animal. The train smelled of other things too: blood and fear, anger and despair.

'We stood pushed up against each other for hours and hours because we couldn't help it. There was no room to breathe and I didn't want to anyway. Not with the smell. He said he was tired. He'd also recently been released from prison and couldn't wait to get home. He wanted to crawl into bed beside his wife and sleep for a month, to be oblivious and wake up with his mind clean and refreshed so he could pretend the things he'd seen and done had never happened. I told him I couldn't do that. I had to stay awake because of the images that had stuck to the back of my eyelids.

'He said I should write it all down. Eventually it would drive the images out and I'd be able to sleep again. So now I write every day, forcing out the unspeakable thoughts by expelling them onto the page.'

'Is it working?'

He pushed his good hand into his trouser pocket as if to retrieve something he'd hidden there. 'Do you think I'm good enough to be published?'

'I'm no judge of these things. If you're serious, you should send your work to the poetry magazines. They'll tell you if they think you're any good.'

This wasn't the answer he'd hoped for, she could tell by the way he pressed his lips together, but she didn't want to give him false hope. Life had let him down badly enough as it was. She said goodbye, her mood bleaker than before, now she'd witnessed the state of him. Christophe had always been brittle; now he was completely broken.

Chapter 8

Iris was approaching Eva's house when she remembered the spare key under the pot of lavender. It had been careless of her to leave it there, when anyone could find it and let themselves in. She'd been so shaken by Eva's death that she wasn't thinking clearly. She crouched down and lifted the pot, her fingers searching blindly beneath it for the key, but it had gone. She took a steadying breath. No one else knew it was kept there. It had always been her and Eva's secret. Now someone else must have discovered it.

She slipped inside the house and closed the door quietly behind her. Something in the atmosphere warned her to be on her guard. It wasn't her imagination. She could definitely sense a change.

'Hello.'

No one answered. She hadn't forgotten the intruder in the garden. Now, that same intruder could be lurking in the house. Moving from room to room, she looked for clues: the rearrangement of dust, a disturbed fringe at the edge of a rug, but there was nothing. She sniffed the air and listened. Was that a foot scraping across the floor, the sound of a throat clearing, or was it her imagination? She took a closer look around, searching every corner and crevice until she spotted it; a long brown hair, thin as gossamer on the corner of the rug that lined the narrow passage to the cellar. It was only a single strand, but it was enough to give away the intruder's presence.

Iris crept down the steps to the cellar. Whoever was there remained silent. Between the two of them, not a breath stirred. Turning the handle, she pushed open the door. The trespasser knew they were about to be disturbed and was waiting in the dark. Iris flicked on the light, hoping the sudden brightness would startle them long enough for her to gain the upper hand.

'Iris, thank God it's you.'

Before Iris could place the voice, Yvette crawled out from her hiding place beneath the table. She was wearing a checked skirt and a dark blue blazer, woollen tights and low-heeled Oxford shoes. Her brown hair was braided in two long plaits that bounced off her shoulders every time she moved her head. No one passing her in the street would have thought her anything other than a schoolgirl.

Iris stepped into the cellar and closed the door, shutting them both in, relieved to be facing a friend rather than an enemy. 'What are you doing here?'

'I overheard Ambrose telling someone you'd returned to your family in Dijon. I knew your aunt was Eva Fournier, the famous French cookery writer, so I guessed you might be with her. It wasn't hard to find the house. She mentioned it so often in her books.'

Despite the danger, Iris couldn't help being proud of Yvette's ingenuity in tracking her down. She'd taken her instruction well. 'It's not safe for you to stay here.'

'Just one night, please. I beg you. I've been on the move for days. I need somewhere I can sleep for a few hours, where I don't have to keep looking over my shoulder. Nobody need ever know.'

The desperation in Yvette's voice was palpable. She couldn't have been in France for more than a week, but already she appeared like a hunted animal. She was still only a child, and in need of someone to run to.

'I won't stay long. I have to keep on the move so the enemy doesn't track the signal when I transmit messages.' She nodded to the brown leather suitcase in the corner which was used to transport the wireless.

If the wireless was discovered, they were both as good as dead. 'You can stay for one night, but no more. It'll put us both in too much danger.'

With Mason due to arrive in Dijon that afternoon, it was more than Iris should have offered, but she didn't have the heart to turn Yvette away. One false move on the streets and the young girl would betray herself. Her desperation would be an obvious target for any German patrol.

'How did you get into the house?'

'I found the key under the pot of lavender by the front door. I wouldn't leave it there again, if I were you. It's too easy for someone to find.'

'You'd better keep it. But don't come here again unless you're absolutely desperate. If I'm not here, move the pot of lavender to the other side of the path as a signal, in case there's someone with me when I return.'

Yvette nodded, visibly relieved to have found a safe place. The bloom in her cheeks reminded Iris she was only sixteen and too young to be facing such danger. When she'd questioned Ambrose's judgement on selecting her for training, he'd insisted the fact that she could pass as a child would give her a stronger cover. In a country where women were overlooked and underestimated, a smart young girl such as Yvette could get away with almost anything. With luck on her side, he might be right. Luck, however, was something they couldn't rely on.

'I've been on the move for three days and nights. Is it all right if I have a bath?'

Iris checked her watch. She still had three hours before Mason arrived. It was time enough to settle Yvette and make sure she was well hidden. 'Of course.'

While Yvette had a bath, Iris made soup, using a butternut squash kept from last year's harvest and freshly picked sorrel from the garden. They ate in the cellar, wrapped in Eva's blankets to keep off the chill from the stone floor, and spoke in whispers, even though there was no one to hear them. Iris didn't ask Yvette for any news and Yvette knew better than to question why Iris was there.

After they'd eaten, Yvette explained how Ambrose had arranged for her to be parachuted into France the day after Iris left.

'I didn't get to improve the length of time I can hold my breath underwater. I was determined to achieve a full minute.'

Iris pulled her blanket more tightly around her shoulders, suddenly cold at the thought of Yvette being interrogated. 'Let's hope you won't need it.'

Yvette tore off a corner of the bread and stuffed it into her mouth, displaying all the ravenousness of youth. 'I'll keep at least one step ahead of the enemy, just as you taught me. If I get out alive, it'll be all thanks to you.'

And if you don't, thought Iris, *it will be all my fault.*

Chapter 9

Time was ticking on. Mason was due to arrive within the hour. How was Iris supposed to murder him without being found out? Distracted by Yvette's arrival, she had yet to come up with a plan beyond meeting him off the train. She couldn't have him staying in Eva's house, not while Yvette was there, and she was determined to keep the vow she'd made never to go to bed with him again.

It was probably too late to salvage her marriage to Jack, and he'd never know of her pledge, but it was the one thing she could do to prove to herself that she was worthy of winning him back. To honour this, she had to dispatch Mason quickly, before he could suspect she'd been the one to trap him. The most important thing was to keep his trust while she worked out how to kill him without any suspicion landing on her.

On the way to the station, she stopped off at a hotel and booked Mason the best available room. She had to take control of the situation from the start, and not give him a choice as to where he would sleep that night. Until she'd formed a plan, she'd take one step at a time and worry about tomorrow when it arrived.

She was waiting on the station platform when his train pulled in, bracing herself to look pleased to see him as he stepped down from the carriage and moved towards her. Suddenly, the reality of her task struck home. Even if she managed to murder this great brute of a man, how was she supposed to dispose of his body?

'Iris, there you are.' He dropped his suitcase and held out his arms, expecting her to run into them.

'Mason, welcome to Dijon.'

She pecked his cheek with the lightest kiss and stood back to look at him. His woollen overcoat and brown leather brogues marked him out as an Englishman, as surely as his loud voice and bumbling tones. With any luck, it would be enough to get him arrested.

'I heard about your aunt's death. It must have come as a shock.'

She passed off his comment with a nod, refusing to sully her grief by discussing it with him. He had a way of demeaning everything and she wouldn't allow him to do that to Eva's memory.

'Did you have a good journey?'

'There was nothing that half a bottle of decent brandy won't fix.'

From a man who found fault with everything, this was better than she'd anticipated. She gestured to him to pick up his suitcase, urging him to hurry. It was important they weren't seen together too much in public.

He gathered his pace as she marched out of the station, a stranger in town, not wanting to be left behind. She didn't imagine his French went beyond schoolboy level and he'd struggle to communicate with the local people. Now he was here, she had no idea what he intended to do, but dressed like an Englishman and with limited French, he'd find it difficult not to stand out.

'I've booked you into the best hotel in town. If they can't supply you with a good brandy, nobody can.'

'A hotel? Why aren't I staying with you?'

'This isn't London. Everyone knows me here. Gossip travels fast. I'm a married woman. Having you stay in my home would damage my reputation.'

'Why do you care what people think?'

'I won't insult the memory of my aunt by betraying the moral standards she brought me up to respect.'

'But you're with me now. No one would dare to say anything against you.'

He had a very high opinion of himself, considering he was in a foreign land where he could barely speak the language.

'Do you have the right papers? You'll need to show them at the hotel before they'll give you the room.' She wondered how he'd manage this. If his Englishness was discovered, he'd be arrested. He didn't have the social status here that had served as a cover for his spying in London.

Mason tapped his top pocket. 'No need to worry. I'm travelling on my German passport.'

Of course he was. She should have guessed. He'd told her about his German heritage when they first met. It came as a shock now to think of it, but it was also a reminder that he was the enemy.

She stood apart from him in the hotel reception as he checked in and collected his key. The young woman on the desk shied away when he showed her his passport, the warm smile of greeting on her face rapidly freezing as he switched from speaking faulty French to fluent German when she struggled to understand him. She didn't understand his German any more than his terrible French, but it reinforced that he was the enemy and she'd better not cross him.

Iris made a point of not catching her eye. With any luck, she wouldn't remember she'd been here, or that she had any association with Mason. But Mason had other ideas. He turned to her, waving his key.

'Are you coming up?'

He meant it more as an order than a question. She paused while she pretended to consider it, making her refusal sound more like a sacrifice. 'I'll let you settle in first. You must be tired after your long journey.'

The porter was standing by, waiting to show him to his room. Iris gambled on Mason being too proud to press the point in front of the hotel staff, but the look on his face told her he was furious. 'Very well. I have some business to attend to in any case. I'll see you soon.'

Once again, the tone wasn't one of a casual goodbye, but an order. Iris had bought herself some time, but probably not long. Her distant behaviour had angered him, but she wouldn't go back on her vow to keep him out of her bed. Now he was here it was proving harder to keep up the pretence of being pleased to see him than she'd anticipated. The most important thing was not to panic. If she was to kill him swiftly and efficiently without arousing suspicion, a cool head was needed. She couldn't risk making mistakes.

Chapter 10

Yvette left after the end of curfew the following morning, hauling her heavy suitcase through the streets while they were still quiet enough for her not to be noticed. Iris didn't know where she was going or when she'd see her again and that was as it should be.

As soon as she'd gone, Iris went to the bakery to buy bread. Now her mission to kill Mason had begun, it was important to keep to a regular routine, so nobody suspected her of anything other than going about her everyday life. Too much had happened since the Occupation to make her certain of anyone. People no longer appeared as they once were. The change in Paul had proven this. She wouldn't have believed he was capable of such anger, while Christophe appeared a shadow of his former self, his gentle soul beaten and broken. Given the suspicious mood of the town, and the threat of the occupying enemy, it was vital she didn't do anything to draw too much attention.

The café in the square was busy when Iris returned from the bakery. Before the war, she'd visited at least a couple of times a week, and so now she must do the same. It was already mid-morning and the tables had been set outside, the green earthenware jugs filled with white chrysanthemums, anchoring the red checked tablecloths against the late summer breeze.

She chose to sit in full sun, determined to make the most of the weather. The air was rarely this warm in England and she'd missed its comforting heat. She waited while Adele took an order from a woman in a German uniform sitting at a nearby table. Adele held her notebook at arm's length, struggling to contain the baby strapped to her chest as he waved his tiny limbs and grizzled.

The German woman's eyes darted from face to face, examining everyone in the café, alert to every cough and sigh. These young German women, brought over to work as auxiliary staff for the officers of the Third Reich, were known as Grey Mice. Judging by her watchfulness, Iris understood why.

Once Adele had written down the Grey Mouse's order, she turned to Iris. 'I heard you were in town.'

'I came back for Eva's funeral.'

The baby's face was puce with suppressed fury at his containment. Adele adjusted his position against her chest, his hands following the movement of her pencil like airborne starfish. 'Yes, of course.'

Like Christophe, Adele had still been a child when Iris last visited. Now she was all grown up with a baby of her own. 'Is this your little boy?'

Adele nodded, the corners of her mouth turned down as if he wasn't her proudest moment. 'His name is Georges.'

The Grey Mouse's eyes shifted from Adele to Iris as she followed their conversation. Adele must have taken it as a hint to get a move on with the order because she began to untie the shawl that held Georges against her chest.

'I can't do this with him throwing his arms about. Will you hold him while I fetch the coffee?'

Before Iris could say yes, the baby had landed on her lap. Free of her burden, Adele dashed into the café to get the drinks.

Iris shifted in her seat, trying to find the best position to settle him, worried he might slip from her grasp as he wriggled in her arms. The Grey Mouse studied her for a full minute before she finally spoke.

'I couldn't help overhearing your conversation. You were a friend of Eva's?'

Her French was flawless. She was also too curious for comfort. Georges threw his head back with a sudden burst of rage. Iris leaned to one side, dodging the impact of his skull against her nose, and forced herself to relax. She mustn't behave in a way that might make the Grey Mouse suspicious.

'She was my aunt.'

There was a slam of the café door as Adele appeared with the drinks. Iris hadn't said what she wanted and Adele had brought her the same order as the Grey Mouse's. She took Georges in exchange for the drink and threw herself into the chair next to Iris.

'Thank you for holding him. Sometimes it's impossible to cope with him and serve everyone in the café as quickly as they demand.'

'What does Georges's father think about it?' Adele wasn't wearing a wedding ring, which made Iris cautious of using the word *husband*.

The colour rose in Adele's face. 'How would I know? I have no idea where he is.'

A woman with a child and no husband would have caused a scandal in the town. Iris was too tactful to ask any further questions. The gossip would reach her sooner or later, informing her who the father was, and explaining in unnecessary detail why Adele remained unmarried.

Adele pushed the coffee cup across the table, away from Georges's tiny reach. 'I'm sorry I didn't come to Eva's funeral.'

Before the war, Adele had been a great favourite of Eva's, teaching her how to cook and sew when her mother had shown no interest in doing so. Considering their closeness, Iris had been surprised that she hadn't been there to say a final goodbye.

'I couldn't leave the café. This place doesn't run itself.'

Iris took a sip of the coffee, which wasn't coffee, but an infusion of chicory in lukewarm water. The Germans kept the real coffee for themselves.

'Did you see much of Eva before she died?'

'Not as much as before.'

Was she lonely or frightened? Iris wanted to ask. *Did she know her murder was coming?* But it was too much to put onto Adele, who already had enough of her own concerns.

Clemence said it was because they'd recently buried Monsieur Legrand and Monsieur Janot that so few people attended Eva's funeral, but it didn't seem a good enough reason when Eva had been so well loved. It must have been the nature of her death that kept people away, fear that if they rubbed up against cold-blooded murder, they might become a victim of it too.

'It's Eva's fault I'm stuck with Georges. He's ruined my life.'

Anger had hardened Adele's voice. She might be a mother, but she was still the same petulant child she'd always been.

'I was supposed to be in Paris, studying to be a teacher, but now I have to stay and look after him. Instead of an apartment overlooking the Seine, I'm living in two rooms above the café and at the beck and call of customers for ten hours a day. It's not fair.'

The Grey Mouse spoke up. 'Your little boy is beautiful. You're lucky to have him.'

Adele snatched the Grey Mouse's cup. 'We were having a private conversation.' She turned to Iris, suddenly contrite. 'Ignore what I just said. I shouldn't have let my tongue run away with me. I'm tired. It makes me bad-tempered. There's no charge for the drink. Thank you for looking after Georges.'

Before Iris could insist on paying, Adele had disappeared inside the café with Georges and slammed the door behind her.

The Grey Mouse placed her money on the table and stood up to leave. 'My name is Frieda. I work as a translator for the senior officers of the Third Reich. I couldn't help overhearing what the waitress said about Eva. I was sorry to hear about her death.'

Such sympathy was impossible to stomach, coming from a member of the regime responsible for killing her. It was the height of hypocrisy and an insult to Eva's memory. Iris tried not to betray her fury.

'You mustn't take any notice of Adele's anger. She seems to be under a lot of strain.'

'I spent some time with Eva in the weeks before she died. I had admired her work for many years and felt honoured to get to know her. Her books are very popular in Germany. She let me into her home and showed me around her famous garden. I hope it can be preserved in some way. It would be terrible to think it will be lost now she's no longer with us.'

The words were almost enough to dissolve Iris, even as they dropped from the mouth of the enemy. 'She always loved to meet her readers.'

'It was an honour to have known her.'

Eva had been the same warm-hearted person she'd always been, right up to her murder, so why had Adele taken against her?

The mood in the town had changed and Iris suddenly felt among strangers. It was heartbreaking to think Eva might have felt the same way at the end of her life. Living under enemy occupation had hardened people more than Iris could ever have imagined. She no longer felt part of the community and she no longer knew who she could trust.

Chapter 11

As Iris approached the house, she heard a loud clatter coming from the kitchen, as if one of Eva's cast-iron saucepans had been dropped on the stone floor. Surely Yvette hadn't been reckless enough to come back so soon? Iris already suspected the Gestapo were watching her. She'd been stopped and questioned too many times for it not to be the case. Now Mason had arrived, she had to be more careful than ever. She let herself in and moved quietly along the hallway.

'Hello, is anyone . . .?'

The rest of the sentence lodged in her throat at the sight of the unexpected visitor. It wasn't Yvette as she'd anticipated, but an enemy soldier, standing with his back to her as he peered inside the cupboard where Eva kept her best china.

He turned around at the sound of her voice. It wasn't a member of the Third Reich, but Mason wearing the uniform of a German officer. His expression barely changed at the sight of her.

'There you are, Iris. I wondered where you'd got to.'

She did her best to hide her shock at seeing him dressed as one of the enemy. At least he was finally showing himself for what he actually was.

'Mason. I hardly recognised you in that uniform.'

'Where do you keep the coffee? I can't find it anywhere.'

She'd forgotten his propensity to loom over her whenever they were in a confined space. Whatever company he kept, Mason was always the tallest man in the room. His receding hairline was the only part of him that knocked his sense of superiority. Even his rugged complexion, a testament to his years of outdoor activities and drinking too much brandy, he considered a badge of honour.

'Why are you in uniform? Have you joined the military?'

He grinned, taking her as a gullible fool. 'You might have seen me play the part of an English gentleman in London, but my mother is from a noble German family. I told you this when we first met. What I didn't tell you, is that my cousin is very close to Hitler. The Third Reich has awarded me an honorary rank for the information I passed on while I was working in Whitehall.'

His use of the word *noble* seemed rather questionable, given his activities. He was proud of working as a spy, of exploiting his English connections, his public school education and his privileged upbringing, to pass secrets on to the enemy.

Iris didn't react. For her own safety, she had to make sure he didn't suspect she was working for British Intelligence and that she'd been doing so long before she met him.

'That explains why you were arrested that night in London, why the photographers were outside your flat, waiting to take your picture.'

He puffed out his cheeks. 'British Intelligence couldn't prove their allegations, of course, which is why they released me.'

She knew this was untrue, because she'd been the one to provide the evidence against him, but now wasn't the time for all that. 'How did you get into Eva's house?'

'I jemmied the lock on the sitting-room window. Don't let anyone tell you an English public school education is a waste of money. I learned my most useful life skills from the second-generation criminals I shared a dorm with.'

His English tones rang through the house, subtle as church

bells, and at odds with his German uniform.

'What will you do now? Will you settle in Dijon or return to Germany?' Was he planning to stay for good, or was he only passing through? How much time did she have to carry out her mission?

'First, I'm going to find out who betrayed me. I still have friends in Whitehall. They're having a sniff around. When I find out who it was, I'll destroy them.'

'It was probably nobody. You know how things are during wartime. People will do anything for money.'

'Then I'll make them pay.' He moved closer, his broad body casting shadows in the sunlight as he tugged at the buttons on her blouse. 'I didn't come all this way to talk about that. Why don't you show me how pleased you are to see me?'

She used the excuse of looking in a cupboard to slip away from him, making a play of seeing what there was to eat. 'You should have let me know you were coming. I'd have had lunch ready.'

He frowned at her dishevelled hair, her lack of lipstick. 'I thought I'd surprise you. I assumed you'd be pleased to see me, but obviously I was mistaken.'

'I wasn't expecting you, that's all.'

He must have forced his way in while she was queuing at the bakery or sitting outside the café, chatting to Adele and the Grey Mouse. If anyone had seen him entering the house in his uniform, they'd think her a collaborator. Word would spread around the town in no time.

He threw himself into Eva's chair. 'Now I come to think of it, I'm starving. Bed can wait till later. What have you got to eat?'

'I'll freshen up and then I'll make you something.'

'Be quick about it.'

She dashed upstairs to wash her face and run a brush through her hair, giving herself a few minutes to settle her nerves. She had to stay calm. It wouldn't do for Mason to see she was scared, but it was too much of a stretch to pretend she was pleased to see him.

When she returned to the kitchen, he was sitting at the table with a couple of eggs from Clemence's hens and the day's bread ration in front of him.

'This was all I could find worth eating. What have you been living on?'

He'd ransacked Eva's pantry while she'd been upstairs. 'There's not much to be had. The Germans take the lion's share of everything.'

He rolled his eyes. 'I suppose it'll have to be tea, if there's no coffee.'

'Mint or lemon balm?' If he was hoping for Ceylon, he was going to be disappointed.

'You are joking?'

'I don't shop on the black market. That's the only place you can get such things.'

She lit the stove, fumbling with the matches as she ignited the gas and then reached for the eggs, trying to appear casual as she cracked them into a pan.

He retrieved a pouch of tobacco from his pocket and began filling his pipe, tamping down the tobacco with his finger.

'I was surprised to receive your letter while I was in custody. It was a pleasant surprise, though, very pleasant indeed.'

'It was only right to let you know I was leaving London after we'd been getting on so well. I didn't want you to think I was the kind of woman to abandon a man when he's in trouble.'

'I was flattered by your invitation.'

Suddenly, he was out of the chair and sliding his hands around her waist, his lips sticky against her flesh as they brushed the back of her neck. Panic ran through her at the force of his physical presence. If she was going to kill him, she had to act quickly, and there was no time like the present.

The eggs started to burn. In her efforts to hide her fluster, she'd forgotten to add any fat. She grabbed a knife to scrape them off the bottom of the pan, but instead of using it on the eggs, she faked a spell of dizziness, aiming the knife at the back of Mason's hand as it gripped her waist. If she could cause him enough pain to disable him, it would be easier to inflict a second, more deadly knife wound.

Mason shouted out, grabbing her wrist to steady her as the knife lunged towards him.

'Steady on, you nearly did me an injury.'

Iris dropped the knife and placed her palm against her forehead, faking more dizziness. 'Sorry, I thought I was going to faint.'

He led her to a chair and pushed her into it, his manner lacking any trace of sympathy. 'Take deep breaths. You'll feel better in a minute.'

Iris nodded. She didn't need to act as if she was shaken. It had been an ill-thought-out and ruthless attempt to kill him. What had she been thinking? Certainly not of the consequences. If the attack had succeeded, how would she have disposed of his body?

He turned off the heat under the eggs. 'This place is no good for your health. Don't you think it was a bit reckless, returning to an occupied war zone?'

'France is my homeland. Why wouldn't I want to come back?'

His answer was stalled by a knock on the door. Iris went to answer it before Mason could intervene. Whoever it was, she had to get rid of them before they realised Mason was there.

Paul was standing on the doorstep clutching a dead rabbit, its scrawny neck making its premature death all the more heartbreaking as he gripped it in his hand.

'A woman was selling these in the market. I thought you'd like one.'

Hearing his voice, Mason appeared at her side and draped his arm around her shoulder. 'Who's this?'

The triumphant look dropped from Paul's face. 'Don't choke on it.' He pushed the rabbit into Iris's hands and let out a noise like the sound of a small child crying as he began to walk away.

'Paul, wait.'

She shook herself from Mason's grip and ran after him, calling his name as he crossed the square. She had to find a way to explain Mason's presence. What had Mason been thinking, showing himself like that, making his assumed possession of her so obvious?

Mason ran to catch up with her. 'Get back inside and be quiet. You're making a show of yourself.' His voice was sharp and insistent as he gripped the top of her arm and dragged her back to the house.

Tomorrow there'd be deep bruises where his fingers had dug into her flesh, but she couldn't think about that now. She resisted pushing him away as he shoved her into the kitchen. She couldn't risk angering him or give him anything to question her loyalty. It was vital he didn't guess she'd been responsible for his arrest in London, if he hadn't already worked it out. Nor could she let him see how much he disgusted her.

'Who was that at the door?'

He must have known his name. He'd heard her call it across the square. He just wanted her to say it. She threw the ruined eggs in the bin, grieving at the waste, before wrapping the rabbit in newspaper and putting it in the pantry. The thought that Paul had bought it for her when he probably could have done with it himself made her wretched.

'Who was it, Iris?'

'That was Paul. He's an old friend.'

Mason lowered his fist quietly onto the table. 'I see. Well, that makes things rather awkward.'

He glanced around the kitchen, looking for evidence of Paul's presence and picked up a piece of bread, ripping into as if he'd never been fed. He'd gained weight since she'd last seen him, so he hadn't had too terrible a time of it while he'd been in custody. Yet, the experience had taken its toll. He was less self-assured than when she'd first met him. The charm he'd employed to get his own way had lost its polish, revealing the rough coat of the bully underneath.

'So, will you settle in Dijon or return to Germany?' He still hadn't answered the question. She needed to know how much time she had to complete her mission. She couldn't risk any more botched attempts at killing him.

He looked at her, his mouth full of bread. 'That depends on you.'

This was where she was supposed to make a commitment to him. She stared at the heel of bread in his fist, refusing to meet his eye. 'Is your hotel comfortable?'

'It has better hospitality than I'm being offered here.' He sneered at the bread. 'You'll have to do better than this if you want to please me.'

'If I'd known you were coming, I'd have bought extra food.'

'I expected to pick up where we left off in London, but I now realise it's not as straightforward as that.'

'Life's more complicated here than it was in London. There's the Occupation for a start.'

'The war was never an obstacle to us before. I came here at your invitation, and now you treat me like a stranger. It's time to decide what you want.'

He stuffed the last of the bread into his mouth before getting up to leave, the anger coming off him in waves.

She tried to keep her hands steady as she opened the door to see him out, putting enough distance between them, so he wouldn't lean over to kiss her, knowing if he did, it would be an act of violence rather than affection. She remembered the bruises he'd inflicted on her in London, how he'd laughed when she'd shown them to him the following day, blaming them on his uncontrollable desire, when it had been something else altogether. She'd had to learn to brace herself against him, training herself not to flinch every time he came near her.

Now, once again, his capacity for violence was palpable. She could see it in the whites of his knuckles as he clenched his fists, in the way he'd eaten every scrap of her bread ration out of spite.

She didn't flatter herself that she meant all that much to him. She was just someone to run to after he was forced to flee England. His ego had been damaged and he was here to reassert himself. Her first attempt to kill him had been clumsy and driven by panic. She could only hope he didn't inflict too much harm on her before she managed to carry out her orders more efficiently.

Chapter 12

Madame Janot was sorting nails in the hardware shop when Iris entered. She greeted her without looking up, scribbling a number on a scrap of paper, so as not to lose count.

'Sorry I wasn't able to come to Eva's funeral. It was Solange's day off and I couldn't leave the shop unattended.'

'There's no need to explain.'

Madame Janot's hair was neatly curled around her square face, the chestnut brown dye she'd used to colour it, rich and glossy. Beneath her apron, she was wearing a smart skirt and blouse, the trim on the sleeves an exact match to her lipstick. Iris imagined that Solange, with all her dressmaking skills, must have been responsible for the improvement in her appearance.

'I'm rushed off my feet most of the time. Christophe is no help with that useless arm of his. Since he came back from the prison camp, he's got it into his head that he wants to be a poet.'

'He gave me one of his poems on the day of Eva's funeral.'

'Was it any good?'

There it was again, the awkward question. 'I suggested he send it to a poetry magazine, to see what they think of it.'

'He doesn't need any encouragement. I need him here, making an effort to be useful. His father never used to let him get away with such laziness.'

'I was so sorry to hear about Monsieur Janot's death.'

'It came as such a shock. It's as much as I can do to keep the shop running, but moping won't put food on the table.' She smoothed her apron, ready to return to business. 'What was it you wanted?'

'I'm looking for window locks and bolts for Eva's house.'

Madame Janot considered the shelves behind the counter, her eyes narrowing on the rows of empty boxes. 'Solange, I need your help. I can't find a damn thing.'

Solange appeared the moment she was summoned, greeting Iris with a manner perfectly poised between courtesy and friendliness.

'The locks are in the storeroom, madame. There's just a few left.'

'Yes, of course.' Madame Janot tapped her forehead, displaying her frustration at her lapse of memory, and patted her pockets in search of the key.

'I'm surprised Eva didn't secure the house when the enemy first invaded. I've never known such a rush on locks as we had then. Still, I suppose living with a German officer was all the protection she needed. Things are different now, of course. It must be strange for you, living there alone.'

'There was an intruder in the garden. I need to make the property secure.'

She didn't mention that she had to stop Mason breaking in whenever he felt like it. She couldn't leave herself vulnerable. If he'd discovered Yvette with her wireless, it would have been the end of everything.

Solange retrieved the storeroom key from the till and handed it to Madame Janot, who jabbed the air with it to strengthen her point.

'You probably imagined it. It's understandable, after what happened to Eva, and the Mayor, of course. What a shock that was to everyone. How many window locks do you want?'

'I'll start with twelve. Also a bolt for the garden gate. The biggest you have.'

'I'll see what's left in the storeroom. Supplies have dried up since the Occupation. The Germans have seen to that.'

Solange took Madame Janot's place behind the counter, ready to serve any new customer who might appear. She'd grown taller in the years since Iris had last seen her, and fine limbed. Her dark hair was now neatly pinned to the back of her head, where once it had hung in schoolgirl braids. She was wearing a blue-and-white checked button-through dress, neatly belted, with short sleeves and a pointed collar.

'That's a pretty dress.'

Solange beamed. 'Thank you. I made it myself. I copied it from a picture in *Vogue* from before the war.'

'Do you still want to work for one of the couture houses in Paris?'

'Oh, yes, but not while they're forced to dress the wives of German officers. Until then, I shall stay here and continue to improve my dressmaking skills.'

As she spoke, Christophe appeared outside the shop on his bicycle. Solange watched him through the window, her eyes alert to his every move as he dismounted. 'It's the duty of every woman to make the best of herself during these difficult times, don't you agree?'

'I do, but it's important to do it for yourself, not just for others.'

'Yes, and that's why . . .'

Solange fell silent as Madame Janot returned with a box of assorted locks and bolts. 'Have you got someone to fit these for you?'

Iris examined the locks, wondering what size would be right for which window, which bolt would be best for the gate. 'I'll do it myself.'

'Quite right. There's no point in relying on a man for anything. They all abandon you sooner or later, and what are you left with?

Nothing but disappointment and a broken heart.'

'Monsieur Janot's death must be very hard on you and Christophe.'

'He didn't consider us when he got into a brawl with a group of German soldiers. What a miserable life he's left me with.' She relaxed her frown as Iris handed over the money. 'Don't take any notice of me. I'm not usually this gloomy. You've caught me on a bad day. If the locks aren't right, bring them back and I'll change them.'

Christophe was sitting on the wall outside the hardware shop when Iris left, his bicycle abandoned on the ground beside him. He looked up from his notebook as she closed the door behind her, the bell above it giving a solitary ring.

'What were you talking to Maman about? You didn't mention my poems, did you?'

'Your mother was the one who brought them up.'

Iris understood why Christophe didn't want his poems mentioned. It wasn't about the poetry, but the fact that his mother seemed to criticise everything he did, no matter what it was.

He slipped his notebook into his pocket, dropping his pencil in the process, his fingers clumsy as he struggled to contain both objects in one hand.

Iris picked it up as it rolled towards her feet and handed it back to him. 'You're still writing poems?'

'The doctor I met on the train said it would be my salvation.'

The poetry was making him too introspective, closing him down from the rest of the world, when what he really needed was to start living again. The best way for him to find salvation was to fall in love. She thought of the way Solange's eyes had lit up when she noticed him outside the shop and wondered if she was the reason he'd stayed outside.

'It's not good to spend all your time alone. Do you see your friends these days?'

'Did Solange tell you to say that?'

'No. Why do you ask?'

'No reason.'

'Is she one of your friends? I remember you were at school together.'

'Everything's different since the war. Friends aren't the same.' He slipped the pencil into his pocket, changing the subject as he made it disappear. 'What are those locks for?'

'Eva's house. I want to make sure it's secure.'

'Are you frightened someone will harm you?'

They were living under enemy occupation. Surely, he could understand her need for more security?

'The old locks are rattling. I want to replace them.'

'It's not good for you to be living alone. You should have a man to protect you. No one's safe these days.'

She smiled at his old-fashioned gallantry. 'You don't have to worry about me. I can look after myself.'

He retrieved his notebook from his pocket, as if to indicate their conversation was over, that he was putting his concern for her safety to the back of his mind. Her reassuring words must have done the trick. Lies came so easily to her these days that she could almost fool herself into believing them.

Chapter 13

Iris had always slept in the same room in Eva's house. From the first summer she spent there, it became her room. Eva had even let her choose the pale-yellow wallpaper, splashed with pink roses. When Iris was twelve, Clemence had stitched her a quilt made of patches from the clothes she'd outgrown, each one a memory of summers past, of the rites of passage that had made her the person she'd become. Even now, half a lifetime on, it remained on the bed as a reminder of happier days, its endurance a promise that a more certain future lay ahead.

Now, the familiar feather bed no longer felt like a place of comfort and safety. It had become somewhere to stare at the ceiling in the darkness as she tried to work out how to kill Mason. Her attempt with the knife had been clumsy. She couldn't risk failing again. It wasn't the only thing that kept her awake. Since discovering the intruder in the garden, she was constantly listening for the sound of illicit feet on creaking floorboards, imagining the splinter of wood as someone tried to force open the windows or the doors.

Listening so hard for so many hours fed the darkest parts of Iris's imagination, until the scattering hoot of every owl seemed to carry evil intent, the leaping shadows of the bats, an intricately choreographed dance of death. But that night, the disturbance wasn't all in her mind. The faltering shuffle of feet was real. Someone was loitering in front of the house.

She crept out of bed and opened the window shutters, squinting at the slanting blue light of the moon. Whoever it was shouldn't be there and they knew it. Four years of war had taught her that guilt could be heard in the hesitancy of a footstep, and whoever was out there had *trespass* written all over them.

'Iris, it's me.' A man stepped out of the shadows. 'I didn't mean to alarm you.'

It was Jack. Jack was here. It was impossible, but it wasn't a dream. He was really here. She ran downstairs and let him in before he was spotted, her heart settling to a steady beat, knowing it was him, knowing she didn't have to worry that it might be somebody else.

The night was cold and they were both shivering, the blackout reducing them to shadows as they stood face-to-face in the hallway, not knowing how to be with one another. Her desire to touch him, to feel his arms around her, was almost overwhelming, but she couldn't forget the tone of his last letter. She'd do anything to make him love her again. To take away the pain she'd caused.

'What are you doing here?'

She waited for him to explain his presence, wishing them in an alternative world where the war wasn't happening, where they'd been allowed to live happily ever after, as they deserved.

He ran his fingers through his hair and looked up at her from beneath his fringe. His hair had grown out of the close crop he'd adopted when he'd lived alongside the troops on the front line, and it was the first time she'd seen him this unshaven.

'I was in the area. You mentioned in your last letter that you were returning to Eva's house.'

'What do you mean, you were in the area? This is enemy-occupied territory. You're a British journalist. The Germans will have more than one reason to shoot you if they catch you.'

He couldn't have come all this way just to see her. He was too angry with her for betraying him to take the risk. There must be another reason. As her nerves steadied, she didn't know whether to thank him for coming, or curse him for putting himself in danger.

'They shot Eva.'

The words burst from her before she could find a way to soften them. Now, saying them for the first time, it was all she could do to hold herself together. Of all the people in the world, Jack was the one she'd always run to for comfort. Now, he was no longer someone she could count on.

'I'm sorry, Iris. You didn't deserve to lose her.'

Was this all he was going to say? It wasn't only Iris's loss, but his too. Eva had loved him like a son. Had her betrayal killed his every emotion, or was it the war that had done this to him? She held her breath, clenching the muscles in her stomach to keep back the tears. She couldn't let Jack see her cry. She wouldn't make a fool of herself in front of him, and she wouldn't let him know how broken she was.

He followed her into the sitting room and watched her light a fire, rubbing his hands in front of the first faltering flames as the news of Eva's death sank in. She wondered how long he'd been standing outside in the cool night-time air, risking his life coming to see her.

The fire lit up the room, prompting another stab of grief as she looked at him, seeing him as the man he was now rather than the man he used to be. His hair had begun to turn grey during the time they'd been apart, the skin on his face was weathered from prolonged exposure to the sun, and he was thinner than she'd ever known him. His teeth had yellowed and there were dark patches beneath his eyes. Yet somewhere beyond the hollowed-out look was the man she loved.

Where had he picked up that blue shirt that suited him so well and where had the trousers come from? Had he bought them on his travels, or in London when she wasn't with him? Had another woman helped him to choose them, the way Iris always used to, or had he managed alone, trusting the mirror and his own judgement to give an honest appraisal?

It was the strangeness the clothes gave him that hurt the most, the way they demonstrated how separate their lives had become. She must have looked different too, but she didn't want to know. After so many years of war, this was who they were now.

At one time, they'd known every crevice of each other's lives intimately; now, she didn't suppose he recognised the pyjamas she was wearing or remember them as her favourites from before the war, and it mattered beyond vanity that he wouldn't notice what she had on, that he couldn't bring himself to consider her as the same woman she used to be.

The fighting couldn't go on forever; if only this moment could mark the beginning of the rest of their lives. She'd never believed in the idea of soul mates until she met Jack. At eighteen, she thought long marriages were due to people simply rubbing along together, or becoming so used to one another that it was too much trouble to look for anyone else. Observing her parents' amicable marriage had taught her that settling for someone decent who wouldn't do you any harm was the right thing to do. But then she met Jack and instantly everything she'd ever understood or believed changed.

She'd read romantic novels, where love was described as striking like a thunderbolt, and laughed them off, but with Jack it had been more than thunder, it had been lightning too, and beneath it all, absolute stillness, and so much quietness that she heard her heart whisper to his, *I know you. We are the same.*

At eighteen, she'd only meant to spend a year in London, studying to improve her English, but when Jack asked her to marry him, she didn't think twice about staying. Twenty years on, the feeling hadn't changed; it had simply grown stronger and more assured. And even now, the power of it terrified her. France would always be her homeland, but her true home would always be with Jack.

Noticing he was shivering, she gathered up the throw Eva kept on the back of the sofa and placed it around his shoulders. The love she felt at his nearness was so intense she wanted to cry. Having him here reminded her how he'd always been her haven, the place she ran to when nowhere else would do.

'Would you like me to make you one of Eva's tisanes? It'll warm you up.'

'This isn't a social call.'

He pushed his hand into his jacket pocket and pulled out an envelope. 'I had our divorce papers drawn up before I left London. All you have to do is sign them.'

So this was why he'd come so far, why he'd taken such a risk. Not to try again with her, but to finish it, once and for all.

He refused to meet her eye as he thrust the envelope at her. This cruelty wasn't Jack's style. How could she make it clear without betraying Ambrose's orders, that she was his and always would be?

'People don't get divorced, Jack. Not people like us, anyway.'

'You were unfaithful. The evidence appeared on the front page of every newspaper in Britain. You can't expect me to stay married to you and pretend everything's all right.'

Tears were stinging her eyes, but she refused to let him see them. He couldn't have risked his life just to do this. She held up her hands, refusing to take the envelope.

'I won't accept the papers and I won't agree to a divorce.'

'You should have considered the consequences before you took up with Mason.' He threw the envelope at her feet, where she let it lie as an unacknowledged recrimination between them.

'The thought of coming home to you was the thing that kept me alive during all the time I was reporting from the front line. Knowing you were waiting for me, that we had a life ahead of us, is what made me brave, but you humiliated me in the most public way possible.' He paused to take a breath, trying to control his bitterness, his anger. 'You can't expect me to forgive you for it.'

Even if she hadn't been bound by secrecy, she doubted Jack would accept that in cultivating a relationship with Mason she'd been following orders, fighting the war in the way she'd been asked, even though she'd been revolted by him and everything he stood for, even though she'd cried every time she'd allowed him to touch her, and that it was still going on today.

'If you'd seen Albert at Eva's funeral, crying for their lost years as he said goodbye to her, you'd understand why we'd be fools to waste our love. It won't simply fade and die if you insist on denying it, because it never does. It will endure, and if you don't believe me, ask Albert.'

'You're wrong, Iris. Nothing lasts forever. Even the strongest hearts eventually die of the cruelty inflicted on them.'

The hurt had altered every aspect of his face. She'd wounded him more than any bullet, more than any bomb blast.

'Why are you really here? I don't believe you've risked your life just to deliver the divorce papers.'

'Mason should never have been allowed to get away with treason. After he was forced to leave the country, I decided to follow him and find out his secrets. If the British government won't expose him for what he is, then I will. I've discovered his uncle owns an armaments factory in Germany. Mason has made a fortune from the manufacture of German weaponry. The British public have a right to know who he really is, what deals the government made with him behind closed doors to save their embarrassment. They'd rather allow him to leave the country and let his crimes go unpunished than admit they'd harboured a German spy in their midst. I'm not going to let him off that easily.'

He was wrong about Mason escaping his punishment, but she couldn't tell him that she was the one ordered to administer it.

'His Bavarian cousin remains close to Hitler. The war has been a great boost for the family engineering company, which shifted all its production to making German armaments as early as 1936. As a shareholder in his cousin's company, Mason's cut of the profits is sitting in a Swiss bank and growing fatter by the day. Mason passed on British military secrets to ensure his cousin kept favour with Hitler to gain preferential treatment when it came to awarding lucrative contracts.'

Iris already knew all this, because she'd been the one to discover it. She tried not to let the thought show on her face.

'It was cowardly of the British government to let him go.'

'I'm determined to report the truth of what happened, to find out what he does next.'

Jack wasn't only out to right the wrong served against his country, but also the wrong served against himself. Even if he wouldn't admit it, his need for revenge against Mason was personal and went right to his heart.

'It's not worth putting yourself in danger over him.'

'There you go, protecting him. Do you expect me to believe it's a coincidence that he came straight here, straight to you?'

'You know why I'm here, Jack, and it has nothing to do with Mason.'

'You've seen him though?'

She nodded, not wanting to give too much away. 'I don't know how he managed to find me.'

It was unlikely that Jack would believe her, even if he wanted to. He was silent for a long time, staring at the flames dancing fiercely in the grate.

'It's not my concern who you see anymore.'

'I don't see anyone. Not in the way you mean.'

She tried to keep the rage out of her voice, knowing it would leave her only one step away from tears, and she wouldn't let Jack see how hurt and scared she was.

'It's not safe for you to be here on your own, Iris. You should go back to England. There are people who could escort you across the border to Switzerland or Spain. They're the same people who supplied me with false papers and helped me to get in.'

'Eva left me this house and everything in it, and there's her literary estate to consider. I can't leave, not now.'

'You should give it up and go home.'

'I won't abandon my country in its hour of need.'

For a second, she thought he was going to congratulate her on her fortitude, but the look in his eyes told her he didn't trust himself. He was too broken, too weak to risk even the smallest kindness towards her and there could be no going back.

She put another log on the fire, making the room cosy, so he wouldn't want to leave. 'Where are you staying?'

'I'm living with a group of resistance fighters in the hills, outside the town. They've offered me protection, and in return I cook their meals and act as their lookout.'

He got to his feet and pulled Eva's throw from his shoulders, folding it carefully so the corners aligned before returning it to the back of the sofa. 'I should go. They'll be worried in case I've been stopped for questioning. It's a risk, being out after curfew.'

'Won't you stay? You look like you could do with a bath and decent bed for the night.' She gave him an intent look, allowing him to interpret the offer in whatever way he wished.

He held her gaze a moment longer than necessary before looking away. 'I don't think that would be a good idea.'

He couldn't stand that she'd been with Mason; that was what it came down to. His heart was broken, and it could only be because he still loved her. This was the thought she had to hang on to. If there was love, then there was always hope that she could win him back.

'There's nothing between me and Guy Mason. I suppose it's too much to expect you to take my word for it.'

'It's too much to expect from a straightforward man like me.'

She hated herself for the way she'd hurt him, for the way Mason's presence continued to damage them both, but Ambrose was right; Mason couldn't be allowed to get away with his treachery. It was her duty to make sure he paid for it, whatever the cost might be to her and Jack.

Chapter 14

It was still early when Mason appeared. His propensity to turn up unannounced meant Iris was constantly on her guard. She forced a smile as she opened the door to him.

'Mason, this is a surprise. I wasn't expecting you.'

'I didn't realise I was required to make an appointment.' He forced a kiss on her lips, pushing her off balance and causing her to stumble backwards. 'Not another dizzy spell?' He laughed, mocking her. 'I didn't realise I had the power to make you swoon.'

'You caught me off balance, that's all.'

He marched into the kitchen without waiting to be invited, as if he owned the place, his German officer's uniform giving him an even greater sense of self-importance than he'd displayed in London. 'I've brought this.'

He dropped a brown paper package on the table. 'It's coffee. I don't want you offering me any more strange concoctions made from whatever's growing in your garden.'

'Let's make you some now. I prefer a tisane though, if you don't mind.'

She grabbed the kettle and began to fill it from the tap, ready to boil the water for her tisane. There had to be a simpler, cleverer way to kill Mason that didn't involve waving a knife at him. If she tried anything like that again, he'd be sure to suspect something. She glanced around the room. Domestic accidents happened all the time. The kitchen was potentially a death trap. She placed the kettle on the stove and lit a match before reaching to turn on the gas. And that was when the idea struck her.

She blew out the match without igniting the gas and dropped it on the work surface. 'I'm popping into the garden to pick some mint for my tisane. I won't be a minute.' She retrieved Eva's coffee grinder from the cupboard and handed it to him. 'You can grind some beans while I'm gone. The coffee pot is on the dresser.'

She fled the kitchen without waiting for a reply, closing the door firmly behind her, taking deep breaths of fresh air as soon as she reached the garden.

It wasn't uncommon for people to die from carbon monoxide poisoning due to gas leaking from an unlit stove. The gas was odourless and impossible to detect. Once it was in the bloodstream, it only took a few minutes to saturate the blood and starve the brain and the nervous system of oxygen. Mason would be dead before he'd finished grinding the coffee beans. There was a reason the gas stove was known as the execution chamber in everyone's kitchen.

Iris took her time picking the mint for her tisane, checking for overgrown herbs that needed trimming, and any other produce that might be ready for collecting along the way. This harvest, hastily gathered in Eva's trug, would be her alibi if she later had to explain why she'd been away from the kitchen for so long, why she hadn't been there to succumb to the same poisoning as Mason, and why she hadn't noticed in time that the gas had failed to light. After all, there was a spent match beside it, which proved it was thought to have been lit.

She'd report the incident to the authorities as a tragic accident, admitting that Mason must have failed to ignite the gas when he turned it on. It was an old stove and he hadn't used it before. It was a simple mistake that anyone could have made. He'd have been distracted, grinding the coffee beans. At the time, she'd been in the garden, picking the mint, trimming back the overgrown chamomile and harvesting the best of the tomatoes.

Given these circumstances, she'd have no trouble disposing of Mason's body, because they'd take it away for her, while offering sympathy for her loss. What a terrible tragedy it would seem.

She pulled up a clump of chamomile and held it to her nose, absorbing its scent. Five minutes had already passed. Was it safe to rush back in and turn off the gas, holding her breath as she opened the windows to let in the fresh air?

In her statement to the police, she could say she returned to the kitchen and found Mason slumped over the coffee grinder, unconscious. Remembering his intention to boil the kettle for her tisane, she checked the stove and realised in a second what had happened. She turned off the gas and opened the windows straight away, but when she checked on Mason, it was too late. He'd already breathed in too much of the gas.

It was the perfect plan. Not murder, but a bloodless accidental death. How had she not thought of it before?

She picked up the trug, bracing herself to venture into the house to make the horrifying discovery. She hadn't gone far when she heard a familiar footfall, an irritable voice calling from the back doorstep.

'Iris. Are you still out there? What are you up to?'

It was Mason, in all his living glory, his arms folded across his chest as he hollered at her to come inside.

'You forgot to light the gas. You could have killed me.'

She gripped the trug as it threatened to fall from her trembling hands. Her attempt to assassinate him had failed again. She thought fast, desperate to recover the situation without incriminating herself.

'Of course I lit the gas. You saw me with the match. There must have been a problem with the supply or the valve. Is it all right now?' She tried to sound calm, as if the problem were not of her making, masking her frustration that Mason was still alive.

'I happened to look up at the stove after you left and noticed there wasn't a flame.' He turned to go back inside. Despite his bravado, she could see he was shaken. 'I made the coffee. Do you want a tisane or not?'

He'd flung open the doors and the windows. The new locks she'd attached hadn't prevented him from doing this quickly or delayed the influx of fresh air long enough to kill him. The scent of the coffee, bubbling in the pot, was drifting out through the open windows, leaving her vulnerable to the accusation that she shopped on the black market if anyone happened to smell it.

She placed the trug on the table and sank into a chair, trying to hide her disappointment. Killing Mason had been almost in reach. For a moment, she'd allowed herself to believe she was capable of committing the perfect murder and that she'd planned it cleverly enough not to arouse suspicion.

It was important to act normally, so he didn't guess what she'd tried to do. 'Would you like something to eat while you're here?' It was a half-hearted offer, but at least he couldn't accuse her of not making the gesture.

He poured himself a cup of coffee and gulped it down. 'I can't stay. You shouldn't have wasted so much time in the garden if you wanted my company.'

He dropped a rough kiss on her forehead on his way out, the force of it destabilising her once again. As soon as he'd gone, she emptied the remaining contents of the coffee pot down the sink and rinsed away the grounds, as if she were destroying the evidence of attempted murder. It was the second time she'd failed to complete her mission. It was vital she succeeded next time. There wouldn't be many more chances before he guessed what she was up to.

Chapter 15

It was a couple of hours into the curfew; the moon was hidden behind the clouds, adding an extra layer of density to the blackout. Iris was in the kitchen when she heard a crash at the bottom of the garden, as if someone had tripped over a watering can. She ran out of the house, not thinking about the danger when she called out, demanding to know who was there, her eyes narrowing on the dark shapes of the shrubs and the overhanging trees as she made her way along the brick path that twisted around the vegetable beds towards the shed.

Whoever it was she'd caught in the garden before must have returned. The bolt she'd put on the gate couldn't have been strong enough to keep them out. How many times had they been back since, or had they been there all along?

'Who's there?'

The gate slammed as the intruder fled from the property. Iris went after them, darting along the narrow alleyway that ran parallel to the back of the garden. And there he was, in the near distance, his body no more than a thin shadow, a spade waving like a paddle in his hand as he ran at full speed, swerving to turn the corner, before disappearing out of sight.

Iris picked up her pace, following him along the alley to the turning, but she was too late. Already, he'd vanished into an adjoining street, or slipped into another garden, his feet silent in soft-soled shoes. She stopped to catch her breath, not considering what could have happened if she'd caught him, that he might have used the spade as a weapon.

If he was keeping out of sight in a nearby garden, he'd eventually have to show himself, and so she continued searching around the back of the houses and in the surrounding streets, peering over high walls and fences, listening for the sound of his ragged breath, the disturbance of leaves as he took cover in a shrub, but there was nothing, only the echo of an owl's hoot, and the soft swoop of the starlings passing overhead as they put themselves to bed.

Conscious of the risk she was taking by breaking the curfew, Iris eventually returned to the house. She checked behind every door, peering into the cupboards and under each piece of furniture, in case whoever it was had stolen inside while her back was turned. Adrenalin had made her brave during the chase, but now she'd had time to consider it, she realised how reckless she'd been. She couldn't allow herself to forget that Eva had been murdered in the garden. Yet, she'd swear to it that the intruder wasn't a German soldier.

Still unable to settle, and against her better judgement, she returned to the garden, continuing her search for clues in the dark, all the while rationalising her fear, telling herself she'd seen off the intruder, that there was no one there. But what had he been doing, and was he planning on coming back?

After checking the shed, she took the long way back to the house, skirting the perimeter of the garden. The intruder had taken his spade, but he might have left something else behind in his hurry to leave. It was then the thought struck her; why would he have a spade unless he was digging something up?

What was he searching for? She hadn't seen any disturbance to the soil the last time she'd caught him, but that was because she hadn't known to look for it.

The bats flipped and swooped in tangential shapes above her head, encouraging her on, until she found a patch of disturbed soil directly beneath one of the old ash trees, the ground sliced away by the sharp edge of a spade. Iris's assumption had been correct. The intruder had been visiting for a purpose. What would he be prepared to do if she continued to get in his way?

Iris pushed the thoughts from her mind as she filled in the hole, nudging the soil back in place with the side of her foot before double-checking she'd closed the gate, cursing herself for not having fitted a stronger bolt. She couldn't afford to be careless when her life might be at stake.

Chapter 16

It would have been Nathalie's thirty-fifth birthday, if she hadn't been gunned down by an enemy plane as she fled Paris after the fall of France. Iris went to see Paul to ask if there was somewhere he'd like to lay flowers in her memory. She wanted him to know she hadn't forgotten how much the three of them had meant to one another when they were younger, how those bonds still held, no matter how much time had passed.

The things he'd said while they were sitting on the bench after Eva's funeral had disturbed her. She needed to reassure herself that the old Paul was still there, that the war hadn't destroyed him. She also wanted him to know she was supporting him as he mourned his sister. She couldn't bear to lose anyone else.

He was standing by the gate when she arrived at the vineyard, looking up at the sky as if he expected an attack from the air at any moment, preparing to be subjected to the same death as Nathalie.

'Paul.'

She called his name three times before he responded. The crevices around his eyes grew deeper when he finally looked at her. 'How was the rabbit?' There was a cruel slant to his mouth as he asked the question.

'It was good, thank you.' She hesitated, not knowing how to raise the subject of Mason. 'The German officer who was at the house when you arrived. It wasn't what it looked like, he . . .'

'What did it look like, Iris? You tell me.'

'He's just someone I knew . . . from before.'

'A friend of Jack's too, is he?'

He used to tease her about any male attention she attracted, as a brother would. Now, there was a cocky edge to his voice that reeked of contempt. She needed to know he wouldn't spread rumours about her fraternising with the enemy while she attempted to assassinate Mason.

She showed him the bunch of Michaelmas daisies she'd cut from Eva's garden. 'I thought we could lay these flowers somewhere in memory of Nathalie.'

Nathalie's body had never been recovered and so there was no grave, no place to mark the spot where she lay, only a hollow in everyone's heart where she used to be.

The suggestion seemed to calm him. 'We'll go to the top of the ravine. She loved it there.'

It had been their favourite haunt as children, a place where they'd picnicked and climbed trees or simply daydreamed, hiding from real life, planning trips to the moon and under the sea, because at that age, nothing seemed impossible, and so far above the town, it made them feel as though they were standing on the top of the world.

She waited while he picked a dozen of Nathalie's favourite roses, struggling to negotiate the thorny stems as he tied them with a length of twine, his lack of coordination indicating he hadn't slept. After years of hard labour in the German prison camp, he didn't appear to have enough strength to cope with the ordeal he was about to put himself through.

She squeezed his hand, letting go more quickly than she'd intended. His bones felt so brittle, she thought she might crush them.

'Are you sure you want to do this, Paul? We could just sit quietly and remember her. We don't have to climb all the way to the top of the ravine.'

It seemed a challenge too far, and not so much a tribute to Nathalie, who wouldn't have expected it, but self-punishment for being the one who'd survived.

'You don't have to come if you don't want to, but I'm going.'

She struggled to keep up as he marched through the town, trying to show he was stronger than he looked, that the enemy hadn't destroyed him, despite their best attempt. It wasn't determination that fuelled him, but fury. She could see it in his eyes, in the way he clutched the roses, no matter how deeply the thorns dug into his flesh.

He didn't slow down until they reached the outskirts of the town. The air was keener without the shelter of the buildings and a shudder ran through her as she paused for breath. The cold wind, tumbling from the higher ground, was surely meant as a warning to keep them in check.

From this point, it was a steep walk up through the wooded hills to the place their childhood hearts had claimed as theirs.

The three of them had been inseparable during those magical summers. It all started when Paul saw Iris playing alone in the square outside Eva's house one day and invited her to visit their camp in the woods. He said no little girl should be made to play alone, because it wasn't any fun that way. At the time, seven-year-old Iris couldn't have known that an innocent invitation to play would lead to a decade of summers of joy and adventure.

Paul placed the roses in a circle around the ancient beech tree at the edge of the ravine they'd adopted as their favourite all that time ago. Year after year, it had been their protector, sheltering them from the midday sun and the sudden rain, from thunderstorms and chilling winds.

'I came here as soon as I was released from the labour camp. I had to explain to the tree why none of us had visited for so long, why Nathalie wouldn't be coming back.'

He rubbed his hand across his face, banishing his tears. His grief had grown over him like a hard shell, as impenetrable as the bark of the ancient tree. Iris placed the Michaelmas daisies under the dense canopy of leaves, propping them against the roots knuckling though the parched ground. Already the petals had begun to wilt, their delicate white tips nodding gracefully in sorrow.

They'd only been standing there a minute when a sudden breeze swept through the trees, rustling the leaves and sending another shiver through her. Alert to the danger, she stepped back from the ravine. Until that moment, she hadn't realised how close she was to the edge. The thought of the sheer drop made her stomach turn over. She'd heard the local stories of the tragedies that had happened in this place, of people falling to their deaths, of the sightings of their lost spirits hiding in the trees. In safer times, the human heart demanded to be pricked by horror stories and as a child, she'd revelled in the second-hand fables. Now, making the spot a shrine to Nathalie would only add to the mysticism of the place.

With the flowers laid, they started to make their way back, taking a detour through the densest part of the woodland, so the overhanging canopy of trees would shelter them from the afternoon sun. Iris was regretting taking such an unreasonably long route when a young man dashed across their path, swift and flighty as a stag, a Sten gun strapped to his back. He was gone before she could take in his face, to work out if she knew him, only the distant crack of twigs underfoot giving him away as he ran towards a cluster of trees.

Paul gripped her arm and dragged her in another direction. 'Let's go back to the main path. It's not safe here.'

Iris shook him off, refusing to be herded. 'Do you know who that was?'

'One of the local resistance fighters. They're living rough in the hills and the woods around here. Who do you think has been sabotaging the roads and the railway lines, disrupting the German supplies between Paris and Lyon?'

It must be the people Jack was hiding out with. Most were young men, on the run from the forced labour camps. Their aim was to sabotage German movements using guerrilla warfare, aided by the British government, who supplied them with arms and money through their network of agents.

Paul's reaction suggested he was uncomfortable with their presence. She wouldn't judge him for not joining them. Nor would she criticise him for still working the vineyard, even though it was largely for the benefit of the enemy. War had forced difficult choices on all of them and there was no right way to survive.

By the time they'd reached the town, Iris was ready to go home. Her head ached from the heat and she was unused to the physical demands of the climb. She was about to say goodbye to Paul when a blast of gunshots shattered the afternoon silence. She ran through the streets, following the direction of the sound, ignoring Paul as he ordered her to come back.

A lone German soldier was standing outside the café when she reached the square, his pistol aimed at the sky. The shattered corpse of a pigeon lay on the ground, a mass of blood and feathers. All around, women, children and old men had stopped what they were doing, not daring to move in case they became the next target.

The soldier waved his pistol manically in all directions, spinning on his heels and pointing it at everyone before pushing it into the holster on his belt.

'Next time you refuse to serve me coffee, it won't be a bird I shoot. It will be every one of you miserable creatures.'

He turned to Adele, standing beside one of the tables outside the café, gripping Georges to her chest.

'That brat of yours will be the first to die.'

'You'll have to kill me first, and every other woman in the town who'll stand beside me. What would your Führer think of that?'

Adele's words were loaded with enough venom to kill. The soldier bunched his fists, but it was a feeble attempt to intimidate. Georges must have sensed the danger, because he let out a fierce cry. Adele lowered her eyes from the soldier's glare to comfort him and the tension was broken without anyone having to back down. The soldier clicked his heels, his eyes shifting from Adele's face to Georges's and back again, before spitting through his teeth.

'Whore.'

Iris remained out of his line of sight so as not to draw attention to herself, but she needn't have worried because he barely raised his eyes from the ground as he left the square.

Once he was gone, she ran to Adele. 'Are you all right?'

'I'm fine.' Her hands were shaking, despite her brave face. 'How did the idiot expect me to serve him real coffee when we don't have any?'

The Grey Mouse was sitting at one of the tables, her face partly obscured by the café's awning.

'You must forgive him. These young soldiers don't understand the situation here.'

'Don't try to justify the brutality of your men. We'll never forgive them for what they're doing to us.'

The words came out with more venom than Iris had intended. Adele squeezed her arm, warning her not to overstep the mark. The Grey Mouse might speak fluent French but she was still the enemy.

The Grey Mouse got up from the table and smoothed down her uniform that everybody hated, leaving a generous tip on the table as she prepared to leave. 'There was no need to worry. He wouldn't have shot Georges or Adele unless he'd been given orders to do so.'

The words held no reassurance for Iris. She knew what the enemy was capable of and it was always the women and children who suffered, just as it was always the men who began the wars.

'Iris.'

Paul was loitering around the corner, out of sight. She'd forgotten he was there until he called her.

'Don't run away from me like that again. Come for a drink. We both need one after the day we've had.'

Adele had already gone back inside the café. Through the window, Iris could see her sitting at a table in the far corner, rocking Georges backwards and forwards as she cried. Where had Paul been when Adele stood face-to-face with an armed soldier?

'Not now. I'm tired. I want to go home.'

'I'll walk you there.'

She pushed him away as he slid his arm around her waist. 'The house is only across the square. I don't need an escort.'

Irritated by her tone, Paul straightened to his full height. 'You never used to be this unfriendly. I suppose it's because of Jack.'

'You seem to forget he's my husband.'

'Then why aren't you in England with him? If you were mine, I'd never let you out of my sight.'

There was a difference between love and possession, but there was no point trying to explain it to Paul, because he wouldn't understand. Control was all some men understood. It was the reason the world was at war.

'Something happened between us. I've hurt him very deeply.'

Paul's tone was softer when he spoke, as if he'd spotted the crack in her heart and was determined to infiltrate it. 'If he loved you, he'd have forgiven you. None of us are innocent in this world. Whatever it is you've done, I'd never hold it against you.'

She ignored his comment and said goodbye, dashing across the square before he could detain her any longer, holding back the words she was tempted to say because she didn't want to risk his fury. *But you're not Jack. You're not Jack.*

Chapter 17

Mason was waiting on the doorstep when Iris returned home. She looked around as she approached him, hoping no one had noticed him loitering outside the house. She wondered if he'd witnessed the incident with the pigeon. And if he had, did it make him ashamed of the uniform he was wearing?

Before she could ask what he was doing, he thrust a bottle of wine into her hand. 'Iris, there you are. Do you know how long I've been waiting for you?'

'Did you see what happened in the square?'

'Unless you want to get into trouble, you'll turn a blind eye to such things.'

The warning sounded like a threat. His mood was darker than when he first arrived, as if he'd been brooding on the lukewarm welcome she'd given him, and was disturbed by the conclusions he'd come to over it. He'd expected to walk into her life and be welcomed without question. Now, he didn't seem so certain she'd have him. The volatility of his moods made him dangerous. Iris had seen his temper before, and knew how it could flare up from nowhere, and without warning.

Back in London, there'd been a barman called Tom, who worked in one of the West End nightclubs where Mason used to take her dancing. He was an out-of-work actor, and couldn't shake off the idea that he was there to entertain, and not simply to mix cocktails. Iris had seen him in a play before the war, and he was flattered that she remembered him, that she said she'd enjoyed his performance. Mason became upset when Tom came over to their table one night to continue their conversation, and there was a terrible row. She'd learned then that he didn't like her talking to other men.

After the scene in the club, Mason had had Tom sacked for imposing on them and ruining their evening. Mason was a big spender and the owner wasn't prepared to lose his custom over a spat with a jumped-up barman. Later, Tom waited outside the club for Mason. He was angry and drunk and threatened to blackmail him, though over what, he didn't say.

The next time they went dancing, one of the waitresses told her Tom's body had been found in a back alley just off the Strand. Someone had plunged a knife into his back and left him for dead. There was no proof that Mason had anything to do with his killing, but it had stayed in Iris's mind that he wasn't a man to be crossed.

During those critical weeks leading up to his arrest, she and Mason had spent a lot of time in clubs and restaurants, where he'd played the part of a sophisticated man about town. It was the fate of the barman that made Iris first realise what he was truly capable of. As time went on, alone with him in his London flat, as Ambrose had ordered, she'd suffered enough of his brutality to confirm her worst fears. No man who mistook violence for love could ever be trusted.

Now, the thought of what he might do if he discovered she'd crossed him truly frightened her. If she was going to carry out her assignment, she had to make sure he didn't suspect her role in the honey trap.

Before she let him in, she glanced at the pot of lavender by the front door, checking it hadn't been moved, reassuring herself that Yvette hadn't arrived while she was out. When Mason looked the other way, she nudged it out of place with her foot, so if she appeared while he was there, she'd know not to enter the house.

As she reached in her bag for her key, Mason grabbed her and pulled her to him, kissing her fully, openly on the mouth.

'Where were you this afternoon?'

His question lacked the upward inflection of general conversation and sounded more like an interrogation. She steadied herself against the assault, fighting to appear calm.

'I went to lay some flowers in memory of a friend.'

'You were with that man again. The one who gave you the dead rabbit.'

'I told you, he's an old friend. We were laying flowers in memory of his sister.'

Her hands shook as she unlocked the door and went inside. Mason followed her without waiting for an invitation, his hand in the small of her back, pushing her forward with enough force to make her stumble.

'I don't want you seeing him again.'

He dashed to the window next to the stove and forced it wide open. 'Don't close this again. You need to let the fresh air in. You can't be too careful with that old gas stove.'

She nodded, hardly daring to disagree. He might have been concerned for her safety, but by making sure she always kept the window open, he'd also removed all hope she had of killing him with gas poisoning.

It was too early in the day for wine, but he insisted she open the bottle anyway. By the time she'd poured the first glass, he'd wandered out of the kitchen and begun to explore the rest of the house. Iris fought the urge to stop him. It wouldn't do to rile him and it would only make him suspicious if he thought she was trying to hide something.

He was frowning when he finally joined her in the sitting room, undoing the top two buttons on his uniform jacket with a haste that suggested the whole thing was soon to come off.

'So this all belongs to you now?'

Iris nodded. She still couldn't think of the house as hers. It had always been Eva's and always would be.

'You'd better sell it before it starts to fall down. You'll never get a decent price for it otherwise.'

She hadn't asked for his advice and certainly wouldn't act on it. The house was sound. It had stood for three hundred years and was one of the glories of the town. She couldn't imagine selling it, not if she didn't have to. The place was too full of memories. Eva's enduring spirit rang out in every room. These things meant more to her than any amount of money she could make from it. She set her face to make it look as if she was considering his advice. 'I'll give it some thought.'

She sipped the wine, struggling to appear comfortable in his presence, the violence of his kiss still smarting on her lips. She couldn't keep up the pretence for long. She needed to kill him as soon as possible. As far as she could tell, he didn't suspect her previous attempts, and she had to make sure it stayed that way.

Mason raised his glass, offering a toast. 'To the future.'

The word *future* had a deadly ring to it. She forced herself to raise her glass. 'No more looking back.'

'I'm still determined to find out who betrayed me. I won't rest until they've paid for it. No one crosses me and gets away with it.'

Iris steadied her glass against her lap so he wouldn't see her hand shaking. 'You're here now. Isn't that enough?'

'It must have been someone I trusted. Someone I allowed to get close to me, who then exploited their position, bugging my home and searching for papers when my back was turned. Whoever it was, they'll suffer for it.'

'It might not have been someone you know. It could have been a stranger. They might have broken into your home when you weren't there to plant a listening device or to search for papers. Some people will do anything for money.'

If she was going to disarm him, she had to convince him his assumptions were wrong. She watched his reaction as he took another mouthful of wine. Did she have the power to influence his thinking?

'Whether I knew them or not, my associates will root them out, and then God help them.'

'The British let you go. Surely that's all that matters.'

'They let me go to save the government embarrassment. They'd rather pretend it hadn't happened than let it be known there'd been a spy in the heart of the establishment, passing military secrets to Germany.'

'It must have been humiliating for them, having you outwit them like that.'

'I'm finished in England, if that's what you mean. If I return now, I'm likely to find myself swinging from the end of a rope.'

'So you can never go back.'

'Not until Germany wins the war. There'll be plenty of opportunities there for a man like me then. I made a fortune exploiting corrupt British institutions in the past and intend to do so again.'

There was no doubt that he put money before principle. His conspicuous spending was one of the things that had led British Intelligence to suspect him in the first place. When Ambrose approached her about the job, it had been with the remit of finding out who his contacts were, who he was passing top secret documents to. She'd been shocked when she'd worked out the links: the names he'd dropped during his alcohol-fuelled bragging, the telephone conversations she'd overheard late at night behind closed doors in his London flat. Now, she relied on him not remembering most of the things he'd revealed to her.

The wine had begun to relax him. The heat from the fire she'd taken pains to light had made him drowsy and brought a glow to his cheeks. It was enough to encourage the slip of his weakest defences. It was the first hint that she might be able to pull off this trick after all.

He patted the seat on the sofa and beckoned her to sit next to him. 'Tell me, Iris. What's happening with this husband of yours? Should I be worried that you're married?'

She slipped into the seat beside him, making sure their thighs didn't touch. 'He knows what went on between us, and he's not the forgiving type. Our marriage is over.'

She tried not to choke on the words as she made them sound matter of fact, as if her heart wasn't broken. If Mason didn't believe her, she'd fail in her assignment.

'My wife wants nothing to do with me either, so we're in the same boat.'

Iris tried not to tense as his hand strayed onto her leg. 'Does she know you're with me now?'

'It's the treachery I'm guilty of that bothers her more than my infidelity. She worried about being tainted by it. She's English born and bred, and will remain loyal to her country until her dying day. She'll go quietly, as long as there's a decent enough payout as part of the divorce settlement.'

'Are you sad to lose her?'

'Do you think I'd have come all this way to find you if I were?'

She allowed a silence to settle between them, trying not to think too much about his hand resting on her leg. She had to give him enough hope to keep him dangling, but not too much. She couldn't stand to think that he might lean over and kiss her again, when all she could think about was Jack.

'I'm going to look for a house. This one won't do. It's too dark and too conspicuous in the corner of the busy square. When I find the right place, I want you to come and live with me. You'll have to not object to being my mistress until we're both free to marry.'

If that was a proposal, she hadn't seen it coming. She had to think quickly, to put him off without him realising that was what she was doing. 'Is it the right time to be settling down? What if the Third Reich decides to send you somewhere else?'

His eye twitched, betraying his anger at her response, his fingers tightening around her leg, digging into her muscle.

'Will you say yes, or no?'

It was better to seem indecisive rather than reluctant, if she was to buy herself time.

'I'm flattered by your offer, but Eva's death came as a shock. I still haven't come to terms with it. I don't think I should make any big decisions yet.'

He must have expected her to jump at the idea of setting up home with him, of one day marrying him, and her coolness had unsettled him. He knocked back the last of the wine and stood up to leave, doing up the buttons on his jacket to reassert his authority.

'I won't wait forever. Women like you are two a penny to a man like me.'

If he thought she was going to crawl to him, he was mistaken. 'I need some time, that's all.'

'Don't take too long.'

He grabbed her jaw after she'd shown him to the door, his thumb stroking her cheek as he promised to come back soon, the words whispered as a threat more than a promise. Just when she thought that was all it was going to be, he lunged forward and kissed her again, pushing her against the wall and holding her by the shoulders, until every part of her went rigid with panic. There was no passion in his assault. It was simply a ruse to prove his dominance.

'We'll discuss our future next time.'

After he'd gone, she locked the door, wiping the remains of the kiss from her lips, as she tried to shake off the sensation of his body pressed up against her. He'd intruded upon her too many times.

While he lived, every nerve in her body would remain on high alert. Mason already had plenty of blood on his hands from betraying the movements of British soldiers to the enemy, opening them up to ambush and attack. Now, the next person to die had to be him.

Chapter 18

The day hadn't yet broken when Iris heard the crack of a tiny stone against the window shutter. She crept out of bed and opened it just wide enough to see who was there. Even in the fading dark she recognised his figure; it was slighter now than it was before, but it was definitely Jack. Her heart beat a little faster at the sight of him. The fact that he'd taken the risk of returning to her was a good sign. She crept downstairs and let him in, conscious that it was still a few hours until the end of the curfew.

He looked as if he hadn't slept, the clandestine life he was living was clearly exhausting him. He followed her through to the kitchen and sat in his favourite chair beside the fire, as he always used to. She was pleased to see that he did it without thinking, because it meant he still had the capacity to feel at home there.

Eva had adored him from the moment Iris had taken him to meet her. Iris had desperately wanted the two people she loved most in the world to love each other with the same devoted spirit, and she'd been granted her wish. Eva had seen in Jack exactly what Iris saw in him herself. She said she could see the love they shared, as ingrained in their hearts as rings in the bark of a tree and was convinced they could weather any storm if it ever came to it. If only Eva had been there now to help them through this, to remind them both how much they loved each other, because one of them seemed to have forgotten.

Iris leaned against the dresser, trying to seem casual, wishing she'd had time to put on a smart dress and tidy her hair, even though such things didn't matter to Jack. For him, love had never been about appearances, but something deeper.

'Would you like a drink?'

Jack stared at his grubby fingernails. 'No thanks. I'm trying to give it up.'

'I wasn't offering you alcohol.'

'This isn't a social call. I've come to collect the divorce papers. You've had plenty of time to sign them.'

'If you want them, they're in there.' She pointed to the fireplace. 'They made excellent kindling.'

His lips twitched, and for a moment, she thought he was going to smile at her act of defiance, but the solid wall of his defence remained intact. 'You can't avoid it that easily.'

When she asked how he was, he squeezed the bridge of his nose with his finger and thumb, just as he always did when he was tired.

'Let me make you a tisane like the ones Eva used to make for you.'

Before he could say no, she put the water on to boil and slipped into the garden to pick a handful of mint, choosing the leaves most vibrant with the morning dew. Once the drink was made, she stirred in a spoon of honey, as Eva used to. She tried not to cry as she remembered Eva's method, her heart hollow because Eva wasn't there to check she'd used the right amount of mint, that she'd left it the right length of time to infuse in the hot water, checking it was just how Jack liked it.

Jack wrapped his hands around the cup for warmth as she handed it to him and for a moment, it felt as if Eva was working her magic after all. Food and drink, she always insisted, were the greatest comfort, the greatest way to bring people together.

Iris studied Jack's face as he took his first sip, waiting for a nod of approval.

'How is it?'

He ran his tongue over his lips where the honey had made them glisten. 'Fine, thank you.'

Praise had been too much to expect for such a simple thing, but that wasn't what she'd been hoping for. It was the connection she'd wanted, the slightest clue that there might still be a chance for them.

Perhaps it was the heat from the fire, or the restorative properties of the mint, but after a few minutes, Jack seemed to relax. She asked which newspaper had commissioned his investigation into Mason, and how long the editor was prepared to leave him out in France, risking his life.

'I'm not working for a newspaper. Since *The Daily News* fired me for kicking up a fuss over the inhumane bombing raids on Hamburg, nobody will give me a job. I've become too much of a liability. They say I'm damaging the country's morale.'

It explained why Jack was there alone, determined to carry out his vendetta against Mason.

'You should go back to England. It's not safe for you to be in France.'

'I could say the same about you.'

'You know why I'm here, Jack.'

'To be with Mason.'

'I'm here to help us win the war.' He looked at her curiously and she realised she'd said too much. 'People are different since the Occupation. Everyone is suspicious of everyone else.'

He ran his finger along the edge of the cup, gathering the honey where it had begun to run, not allowing a drop of its magic to be wasted. 'I caught sight of Paul the other day as I passed by his vineyard. I made sure he didn't see me. I didn't recognise him at first. He's half the man he used to be.'

'He's not the same person he once was. I don't suppose any

of us are.'

Jack nodded, or perhaps he was just swallowing the last of the tisane.

'Do you miss me, Jack?'

'I miss the people we used to be. But there's no going back to who we were. Look at me. A few months ago, I was reporting from the front line for a national newspaper. Now I'm reduced to stalking an enemy in occupied territory, determined to destroy him for tearing my heart out.'

'You'll find your feet again. You're a great journalist.'

'I can't do it anymore. I saw too much and was powerless to stop any of it. What kind of a man does that make me? Observing the atrocities felt voyeuristic. I shouldn't have stood there and taken pictures. I should have done something about it.'

'You risked your life bringing the realities of the war to the attention of the world. Britain hung on every word of your dispatches. You were brave and unflinching in the face of unimaginable horrors, and you reported on them with humanity. Your work matters, Jack. You made a difference, and you will again.'

'I was on board with one of the bomber crews when they bombed Hamburg. It was worse than any form of hell you can imagine. We flew over again the following day to take a look at the carnage once the dust had settled. It was the smell of it I can't shake off, the stillness and the silence. Even the birds stayed away. I couldn't find the words to express it the way it truly was, or do justice to the suffering of the victims. They deserved better from me.'

'Your reports made sure the world knew about it. The Allies will think twice before they inflict such suffering on civilians again.'

'But it happened, and there's no getting over it.'

'Justice has to be served for every unnecessary death, for every ounce of suffering brought upon us by the enemy.'

'You can't carry the world's troubles, Iris. You need to let them go.'

It was all well and good for Jack to say that, but the atrocities he'd witnessed still haunted him, and she expected they always would. She'd give anything to be able to wipe his memory clean of them, to take them both back to being the people they used to be, if only it was that simple.

'When you talk of justice, Iris, you sound like the woman I fell in love with, but you still betrayed me with a traitor.'

The words stung all the more because of the truth in them. 'That's the thing about war. We end up doing things we regret, things we could never imagine doing in normal life. It demands different rules.'

She reached out her hand, hoping he'd take it, but he was so lost, he didn't even see it. It was as if he could no longer see anything beyond the images that were locked inside his mind.

'What if I were to help you with Mason?'

Jack leaned back in his chair, suddenly suspicious. 'In what way?'

'You want information on him. I'm the best person to get it for you.'

'Why would you do that?'

'Because he's the enemy.'

'He's also your lover. And he'd kill you if he found out.'

'Didn't you hear what I said about justice?'

He couldn't look at her. Once again, it was as if he didn't know her. By mentioning his name, she'd brought Mason into the room and he couldn't stand it. Nor did she know if he'd trust her. She'd do anything to win back Jack's heart, and if this was the only way to do it, then she'd take the risk. It would be a dangerous double game, but it was worth it, if it kept Jack coming back to see her.

'What do you want to know?'

Jack shook his head, confused, bewildered. 'I can't use you like this.'

'You're not using me. I'm offering to help.'

'It's too dangerous.'

'I know what I'm doing.'

There was a long silence as their eyes locked. Silently she pleaded with him to read her thoughts, to work out the full story. She wasn't breaking her vow of secrecy to Ambrose, if she didn't actually reveal her mission. All she needed was for Jack to guess what she'd really been up to with Mason. To suspect there was more to her actions than met the eye, to trust her enough to not give up on her.

He looked away, focusing on the torn leaves at the bottom of his tisane. 'How does he come to be wearing the uniform of a German officer?'

'He was given the honorary rank in return for the British military secrets he passed on to the German high command.'

'Goddammit.'

'What else would you like to know?'

'What's he going to do next?'

'He's looking for a house. As soon as he finds one, I'll let you know.'

Jack's mouth hardened at the realisation of what she was offering to do. 'Pillow talk?'

'I won't let Mason anywhere near my bed. I give you my word.'

There was no reason for him to trust her, but she had no other way of pledging herself. Feeding information to Jack was a means of proving her loyalty, the only way to keep him coming back to her, whatever danger it might put her in with Mason.

Jack stood up to leave, his eyes travelling here and there around the room, as if he didn't know what to make of what had just happened.

'Would you like something to eat before you go?'

'I've already stayed too long. I only came to collect the divorce papers. I'll have copies made as soon as I return to England.'

It was as if she hadn't spoken. 'I wish you wouldn't.'

He was gone, even as she said the words, closing the door silently behind him, and heading back to the maquis camp, somewhere in the hills. But at least he'd been to visit her and that had to count for something. She could only hope she'd given him a reason to keep coming back.

Chapter 19

Today should have been Eva's wedding day. Iris baked a cake for Albert using some of the almonds she'd harvested from the garden, and an egg from one of Clemence's hens. It was no replacement for the marriage that was supposed to have taken place, but Iris wanted him to know she was thinking of him.

He was sitting at the kitchen table when she arrived, helping Fabrice to shell the last of the season's peas. His beard was untrimmed, but his eyes were brighter than on the day of the funeral. He made room for her to sit next to him and set her to work, demonstrating with his thumb the optimum place to squeeze the pod, so it would split open without damaging the peas. Eva had taught her the same trick years ago, but she didn't want to admit it, seeing the delight he took in showing her the simple skill.

'Eva said she expected me to cook most of the meals after we were married.'

Iris slipped a pea into her mouth, its sweetness bursting on her tongue as she bit into it. Food had never tasted this fresh in London. After years of rationing, she'd begun to think she'd never eat anything decent again.

'You're a great chef, Albert. That's why Eva would have wanted you to cook for her.'

He smiled, acknowledging her tribute. 'Fabrice does the cooking these days. The restaurant is doing better than ever since he took over.'

Fabrice looked fondly at his father. Albert had spent over three decades building the business before passing the day-to-day running of it to Fabrice. 'I'm only doing what you taught me, Papa.'

Albert caught Iris examining his face and smiled. 'Never mind about me. How are you, Iris?'

She fumbled with the peas. 'I miss Eva very much.'

'It's hard to accept she's gone, or that those brutes murdered her.'

'It's sad that so few people felt able to come to her funeral.'

Albert dropped the last of the peas into the bowl and pushed it away, his mind returning to the circumstances of her death. 'Our lives are ruled by monsters. People are too scared to demonstrate what they really feel.'

Fabrice lowered his voice, as if the fear of being overheard was ingrained in him. After all, there were enemies at every door. 'There were rumours about her and Schiller, that German officer she billeted. Some said they were as thick as thieves. But if you start accusing people of collaborating, where do you draw the line on what's acceptable? People have to do what they can to survive. I allow German soldiers to eat in the restaurant because the business wouldn't continue to exist otherwise. I do what's necessary to feed my family. You could say that makes me a collaborator. Scratch below the surface and you'll find very few people aren't compromised in some way by the war.'

Iris only had to consider her own position to recognise the truth in Fabrice's words, even if she couldn't acknowledge it.

Albert got to his feet and stumbled towards the door, his words swelling under a burst of emotion. 'You must excuse me, Iris.'

Once Albert had left the room, Fabrice took the bowl of shelled peas from the table and carried it to the sink. 'I know Eva was very dear to you, but she brought my father nothing but heartache. Even now, he cries for her every day. It's hard for me to think fondly of a woman who caused so much sadness. I made no secret that I was against the marriage. You only have to look at the misery in my father's face to understand why.'

'You don't believe in happy endings?'

'Look around you, Iris. What do you think?'

'I think everyone deserves the right to be loved.'

Iris left the untouched cake on the table and said goodbye. All she could think about was Albert and how his love for Eva had lasted a lifetime, how he never gave up believing they were meant to be together. If only she could convince Jack to think the same way.

It was getting close to curfew and the streets were already deserted as Iris made her way home, slipping along the quiet roads to avoid the scrutiny of the German soldiers who constantly patrolled the main streets. Every time she left the house, she was stopped and asked the same questions over and over again. *Where have you come from? When are you going back?*

Word had spread among the enemy that she was newly arrived in the town and they were curious. Each time she was questioned, she gave the same answers, hoping they were too lazy to check her story with the authorities in Paris. It wouldn't take much for them to discover the address where she claimed to have been living before arriving in Dijon was false.

Taking a shortcut past the cemetery, she spotted Madame Legrand, the widow of the Mayor, standing in front of the war memorial, her eyes trained on the names of those who'd fallen in the Great War. One day, when all this was over, the stonemasons would return to add the names of those lost in this conflict. Monsieur Legrand's name would be carved alongside them.

Iris had never seen her without lipstick and face powder, or with her hair uncombed as it was now, with the grey leaking though the colour where it had grown out. Most women showed their resistance to the enemy by keeping themselves immaculate. Madame Legrand appeared to be the exception.

'I hope you're well, madame. I was sorry to hear about your husband's death.'

Madame Legrand's eyes were glassy, as if she'd been staring at the names on the monument for a long time.

'Go back to Paris where you belong. We have enough filthy outsiders cluttering up our streets.'

It was the first time Iris had been called an outsider. Before the war, she'd always been made to feel at home. When she was seventeen, they'd crowned her the queen of the flowers for the annual summer carnival. Clemence had made her a turquoise satin dress, and she'd led the parade. Everyone had cheered and applauded. Now people wouldn't even catch her eye in the street.

'Have I done something to upset you, madame?'

Madame Legrand continued to stare at the memorial. 'You remind me too much of Eva.'

'What did she do to you that you hate her so much?' Hate was a strong word, but it was the only one that fully described Madame Legrand's attitude.

'Don't think you can treat this town as your home, or come and go as you please. Nobody wants you here.'

She batted Iris away as she moved closer, her once perfectly manicured nails, now ragged and bitten-down. 'Thanks to Eva, I've become one of those embittered widows who litter France, redundant now I no longer have a man to take care of.'

Iris froze at the vehemence of Madame Legrand's words. The accusation was unthinkable. 'What did Eva have to do with it?'

'I didn't deserve to lose my husband.'

'No, you didn't, and I'm sorry for it.' Iris tried again, desperate for an answer to her question. 'What did Eva have to do with your husband's death?'

'I suppose yours is still alive?'

Iris nodded, even though she no longer had the right to call Jack hers.

'The German soldiers dragged mine out of the Mayor's office while he was innocently going about his daily business. They forced him into the square, and they pushed him to his knees and made him beg for his life. Everyone in the town was summoned to watch. I begged them not to shoot him, but they wouldn't listen. And so they shot him. They shot the man I loved.'

'I'm so sorry.'

'It was a just punishment that Eva was shot before her wedding. Why should she have been allowed to enjoy the happiness of marriage after she'd made me a widow? She didn't deserve a husband's love.'

'Have you considered what you're saying?'

'Why would I wish her anything but the very worst?'

'Please tell me why you think Eva was to blame for your husband's death.'

Madame Legrand turned her back, refusing to say another word. Propelled by her grief and anger, she disappeared into the dusk, ignoring Iris's repeated pleas for her to explain herself.

Shaken by the cruel words, Iris made her way home. Her accusations against Eva couldn't be true. They were simply the barbs of a grieving widow. Her beloved aunt Eva couldn't have been responsible for the Germans shooting the Mayor. And yet it would explain why so few people attended her funeral, and why even her dearest friends were reluctant to talk about her.

Chapter 20

Iris was on her way back from the market when Clemence came up to her, insisting she join her at the café.

'Come quickly. Schiller's body has been found. It seems he was served a just punishment for being such a brute after all. Let's see what we can find out.'

Despite the beautiful weather, everyone was huddled inside the café. With the windows closed, the air was hot, the atmosphere overcooked. Iris recognised the regulars sitting alongside the occasional customers and those she'd never seen before.

Christophe got to his feet and offered Clemence his seat. Solange, who was standing in the only available space beside the counter, beckoned him to join her. Iris was too distracted to notice his response. Everywhere, people were murmuring under their breath, discussing the discovery in depth, desperately trying to keep it quiet, while wanting to know everything there was to know.

Iris recognised a familiar figure sitting at one of the tables. She didn't know his name, but she'd have known him anywhere. It was her intruder. The man she'd chased out of the garden. Even now, he was holding his spade as if it were some kind of trophy, his weasel face wide-eyed, like a nocturnal animal flushed out into the daylight.

Clemence put on her spectacles and looked at him intently. 'Emile, tell us what happened.'

Adele handed him a shot of brandy, which he drank in one gulp, his hand shaking as he gripped the glass.

'I was digging near the ash trees in the empty plot of land at the bottom of the cemetery when I felt the spade hit some resistance. At first, I thought it was a tree root, but it was softer than that. I took a closer look and realised it was a boot with the foot still in it. I dug a bit more and discovered the foot was attached to a leg, and so on, until I recovered the whole body.'

'How could you be sure it was Schiller?'

Iris hadn't realised Monsieur Vallery was sitting at the edge of the group until he asked the question, his eyes narrowed on Emile, examining his face for truth.

'He was still in his uniform. The worms hadn't got to his wallet or his identification and his gun was still in its holster.' Emile shuddered as if someone had walked over his grave. 'Even death hadn't managed to wipe that sneer off his face.'

Perhaps it was the shock of the discovery, but nobody asked why Emile was digging in the cemetery.

'What should we do with him now?' Clemence looked at Monsieur Vallery, as if she expected him to know the answer.

Monsieur Vallery's eyes were still fixed on Emile. 'Did you rebury him where you found him?'

Emile nodded, turning the empty glass in his fingers. 'I didn't want to risk the Germans coming across him, so I covered him back up and replaced the turf, disguising the area with a pile of leaves, broken branches and stones. You'd never know the ground had been disturbed.' He pulled a black leather wallet out of his pocket and tossed it onto the table. 'I kept this to prove it was him.'

Monsieur Vallery reached for the wallet, turning it over in his hands, as if it were an ancient artefact with no connection to a recently living human being. 'This needs to be disposed of. I'll take care of it. I suggest we leave the body where it is.'

The following silence implied no one disagreed. Madame Legrand, who'd been sitting quietly beside Monsieur Vallery, suddenly spoke up. 'Perhaps now, Emile, you'll stop digging wherever takes your fancy.'

'I dig only under ash trees. I didn't know anyone had been buried in that part of the cemetery. I thought it was an untouched piece of land. I wouldn't have gone near it otherwise.'

There were no known graves in that part of the cemetery, yet someone had buried Schiller there and decided to keep it a secret. If Emile was digging under all the ash trees in the town, it explained why Iris had caught him in Eva's garden. She raised her hand to catch his attention.

'What are you searching for, Emile?'

Emile rubbed nervously at the calluses on his hands. 'Sorry if I gave you a fright, madame. I didn't know anyone was living in Eva's house since she'd gone.'

This didn't answer Iris's question. 'What were you digging for under the ash trees?'

'My mother's jewellery. Papa buried it under an ash tree somewhere in the town to keep it from the Germans when they invaded, but he didn't say which one. After they shot him, he took the secret to his grave.'

'The jewellery doesn't exist, Emile.' Clemence's voice was full of frustration. 'I've told you this a hundred times. Your mother sold it before the war. None of it was real in any case. It was all paste.'

Emile ran his hands across his face, not wanting to believe it. 'The jewellery was all I had left. The war has taken everything else.'

It was another cruel irony of war, that in searching for hidden treasure, all Emile had unearthed was the rotting corpse of the German soldier who'd terrorised them.

Clemence put her arm around him, shaking him out of his self-pity with a brusque hug.

'Go home to your wife, Emile. Tell her you love her. Make the most of the life you have. Don't go searching for what's lost to the past, because you won't find it.'

People were beginning to drift away. No one wanted to dwell on the fact that Schiller had reappeared among them, even if he was no longer in a state to do them harm, and no one raised the question of who'd killed him. Perhaps it was because they already knew the answer. Perhaps whoever it was had been sitting in the café with them.

It was only after the place had emptied that Iris noticed the Grey Mouse sitting at a table in the corner, picking over the last of her breakfast, an empty cup on the table beside her. She'd swopped her uniform for a floral tea dress, which she must have bought in one of the local shops. At a glance, she could pass as French. Iris felt a twitch of unease stirring in her stomach. No one had noticed she was there. There was a good chance she'd overheard them discussing the discovery of Schiller's body. If she reported it to her superiors, they were all as good as dead.

She must have sensed Iris's eye on her, because she suddenly sat up a little straighter and brushed the crumbs from her lips with her handkerchief. After acknowledging Iris with a brief nod, she slipped silently out of the café.

Adele had retreated to behind the counter and was perched on a stool, hugging Georges, her face buried in the blankets she'd used to swaddle him as she quietly cried. Iris didn't notice her until the Grey Mouse had left the café.

'Are you all right?'

'What am I supposed to do now?'

'Don't cry. You'll upset the baby.'

The words only made Adele cry harder. 'I should be thankful that he's too young to understand.'

She was sobbing too much to make any sense. 'What is it, Adele?'

'Max Schiller was the enemy and a terrible man, but he was still the father of my son.'

This was the first Iris had heard of it. These days, she was considered too much of an outsider for anyone to share such secrets. Adele having a child by an enemy would have caused a scandal, as well as bringing shame on her. It explained why she'd claimed not to know the whereabouts of Georges's father when Iris asked about him. She must have assumed he'd abandoned her and Georges. Now it turned out to be something much worse.

'I didn't love him the way you'd hope to love the father of your child, but what other choice did I have when the best of our men are dead or imprisoned? I assumed he'd come back once all this was over. Georges is his son, after all. And what man wouldn't want to meet his son? There was even a small part of me that thought he might marry me, that we could be a real family. Now, at least I know that'll never happen. It's not the disappointment as much as the shock. All hope of a husband and a father for Georges has gone and I have to get used to it.'

Unsettled by Adele's tears, Georges started to fight against the restraint of his blankets. Iris offered to take him, but Adele refused, clinging to him in a way Iris had never seen her do before. Of course there was love there, beyond the despair. Iris only had to look at Adele to wonder how she ever could have doubted it.

Chapter 21

Paul was leaning against the wall on the corner of the street, smoking a cigarette. Iris noticed him as soon as she stepped out of the bakery, the soft crust of the freshly baked bread still warm in her hand. He caught her eye and ran to meet her, thrusting a bunch of flowers against her body.

'I thought it was you I saw entering the bakery.'

She took the flowers, not quite understanding why he'd given them to her. 'Have you been waiting for me to come out?'

'I went to buy you the flowers and came back.'

She looked at the sunflowers, their heads nodding under their own weight. Already the yellow petals were dropping. Any self-respecting flower seller would have put them on his compost heap rather than on his stall.

'There was no need to buy me flowers.'

'I wanted to apologise for how I behaved the last time I saw you. I'm finding it hard to accept Nathalie's death. Everywhere I turn, I'm faced with her German murderers. It's a difficult time for me. You're still upset about Eva. I should have respected that.'

'Think no more of it.'

She tried to turn the corner onto the main street, stumbling as he wrong-footed her and barred her way. There was no time for his games. She was due to meet Mason for lunch and didn't want to be late. 'Thank you for the flowers, but I have to go now.'

'I'll walk with you.'

'There's no need.' She quickened her pace, her anger brewing as he stuck to her side, matching her strides.

'I want to make sure everything's all right between us.'

'Everything's fine.'

'You told me you'd hurt Jack. Does it mean you're no longer together?'

'I'm not discussing my marriage with you.'

He grabbed her arm, pulling her out of the way of a woman with a pram. Why did men assume the right to manhandle her these days?

'Your separation puts a completely different light on things.'

Iris pushed him away, straightening the line of her dress where his rough treatment had disturbed it. 'The state of my marriage has nothing to do with you.'

He stared at her, refusing to acknowledge her point. 'With Jack out of the way and Eva no longer here to disapprove, there's nothing to stop us being together.'

What did she have to do to make him understand she didn't want him? She was sorry for the way he was suffering, but that was all.

'Not now, Paul. I have to go.'

When she tried to move, he blocked her way. 'I don't think you understand. Let me explain it to you.'

'It's a friend I need right now, Paul, someone to behave like a brother, not a possessive lover.'

She thrust the flowers back at him, hoping the gesture would make him understand the message, but even as she walked away, feeling the heat of his eyes burning into her back, she knew she hadn't got through to him.

Mason was pacing up and down outside Eva's house when Iris returned from the bakery. He tapped his finger against his watch.

'What time do you call this?'

Thank God she'd rejected Paul's flowers, because she was in no mood to explain them. 'I'm sorry to have kept you waiting.' She pasted on a false smile. 'Shall we go and find somewhere to eat or do you have somewhere in mind?'

'Why are you so late?'

It was only three minutes. It seemed an overreaction for three minutes of waiting. 'I met an old friend in the street after I left the bakery.' She waved her baguette as if to strengthen the point that she'd been to buy bread. 'We stopped to talk and I didn't notice the time.'

His eyes narrowed on the bread. 'Will it always be like this?'

'Like what?'

'Will you always put others before me?'

Iris had blundered. She was supposed to be winning his trust. To do this, she had to let him think he was in charge, because that was the kind of man he was.

'I'm sorry, Mason. It won't happen again.'

He pulled out his pipe and began filling it with tobacco, stringing out the silence until she felt obliged to speak.

'There's a lovely bistro not far from here. Their poached trout with olives and white wine is delicious.'

The square was busy with lunchtime shoppers and Mason's display of petulance was beginning to draw attention. The soldier who'd shot the pigeon was there again, leaning against the fountain, smoking a cigarette and missing nothing of what went on. If people got used to seeing Mason in her company, not only would they consider her a collaborator, but they'd question her if he suddenly disappeared.

'Shall we go?'

Discretion was the key to a successful assassination. She raised her eyebrows, trying to urge him on, but still he didn't budge.

'I'm not a great one for fish. I can't stand the way it stares back at you from the plate as you eat it.'

He was behaving like a child, but she didn't dare say it. 'Then we'll have something else. What would you like to eat?'

'It's too late now. All this fuss has made me lose my appetite.'

This was all because she'd kept him waiting for three minutes. 'Then we'll do it another time.'

It was a fine line between standing up to him and letting him think he was in control. By keeping him waiting for three minutes, she'd overstepped the mark, but there was no going back. He wouldn't respect her if she didn't assert herself from time to time, and it wasn't in Iris's nature to be subservient to anyone.

He held his unlit pipe in the air like a prop that had suddenly become redundant. He'd made himself look a fool and he knew it.

'I don't like to be kept waiting, Iris. If we're to get on, you need to learn that now.'

She watched him cross the square, his bluster making him ridiculous as he disappeared down a side street, where she guessed he'd be looking for the bistro that promised the poached trout with olives and white wine, even though she hadn't mentioned the name of it or the street where he'd find it. The meeting hadn't gone the way she'd planned and she needed to work out what to do next.

As she turned to go inside the house, Clemence leaned out of her bedroom window, gripping the corner of a duster, as if she were about to shake it. The position gave her a perfect view of everything that went on in the square. She couldn't have missed the scene with Mason.

'I found a bottle of cherry brandy at the back of the cupboard. I'll bring it round. It looks like you could do with a drop.'

Iris had only been in the house a few minutes when Clemence appeared with the cherry brandy, the cobwebs on the bottle suggesting it had been sitting around since long before the war. She glanced over her shoulder at something in the square when Iris invited her in.

'What's caught your eye?'

'That German soldier who shot the pigeon. He keeps loitering outside the café and pestering Adele. He's been there for most of the morning and he's still there now.'

'Why is he back? She told him she doesn't have any coffee to serve him.'

'It's not coffee he's after. He's heard that Georges's father was a German. Now he thinks she'll sleep with any soldier who asks.'

'Is he asking or demanding?'

'Adele stood up to him before. She can take care of herself.'

There was a question Iris had been meaning to ask. 'Why does Adele blame Eva for the fact that she has Georges?'

'If he hadn't insisted on being billeted with Eva, he wouldn't have been living here, and Adele wouldn't have fallen pregnant by him. She has to blame someone for allowing herself to be seduced by him. She was naive to think he'd marry her.'

'She acts as if she's thrown her life away.'

'Everyone in the town was angry with her at first for being stupid enough to get involved with him, but after he disappeared, most began to pity her. The only anger now is with herself, and her family, who still refuse to have anything to do with her. Thanks to the war there's a shortage of young men in the town and it's unlikely any who survive will want to marry her when all this is over, not now she has a child by the enemy. It's little Georges you have to feel sorry for. He didn't ask to be born and he must sense his mother's resentment.'

She helped herself to a couple of glasses and poured them both a large measure of cherry brandy. 'Never mind about Adele. You've got enough to worry about with your own filthy German.'

'He's not as bad as he seems.'

'That's what Eva used to say about Schiller. If you take my advice, you'll stop seeing him. Jack would never treat you roughly. No one in the town will look kindly on you for entertaining him.'

The cherry brandy burned the back of Iris's throat as she knocked it back, the surface layer of sweetness sticking to her lips. 'Did the town turn against Eva because she was forced to billet Schiller?'

'Some did, but not everyone.'

'I met Madame Legrand by the war memorial the other evening. She blames Eva for her husband's death.'

'Don't take too much notice of her. Grief does terrible things to people's hearts and minds.'

'But she was adamant it was Eva's fault.'

'Eva was stuck with Schiller whether she liked it or not, so none of the blame for what he did should be put on her.'

Iris topped up Clemence's glass and pushed it across the table, encouraging her to drink. 'You'd better tell me what happened.'

Clemence took a small sip, running her fingers along the surface of the bottle to remove the cobwebs. 'Schiller was a vile, bullish man. In his last few weeks, his behaviour became even more strange and unpredictable. He went around the town, raving at all hours of the day and night, convinced someone was trying to kill him. He claimed to see attackers on every corner. Nobody risked getting in his way in case he shot them. If you ask me, he was hallucinating.'

'It must have been terrifying for Eva, having him in the house.'

'She lived in fear of her life. Feeding him well was the thing that saved her. One day, he came across a group of women working in a field outside the town. They weren't doing any harm, just turning over the soil ready for planting a fresh crop of salad. He took against that fact that they had hoes, claiming they were weapons and that they were planning an attack. It was the biggest load of nonsense you've ever heard. When one of the women tried to put him right, he pulled out his pistol and shot every one of them, leaving them for dead in the field.

'It was dusk before the bodies were found. One of the young women had enough breath still in her to be able to say what had happened. When Schiller didn't show up for duty the next morning, the Germans were convinced he'd been killed in a revenge attack. They dragged Monsieur Legrand from his office and shot him in retaliation.'

'Do you think the Germans executed Eva for the same reason they killed Monsieur Legrand?'

'I can only guess they went to question her about Schiller's disappearance and ended up shooting her when they didn't get the answers they wanted.'

Iris didn't need convincing that this could be the case. 'I've seen these soldiers on the streets. Some of them are out of control.'

'Schiller was one of the worst. Now his body has been discovered, at least people know he received a just punishment for his brutality.'

'I don't suppose we'll ever know who killed him.'

'The job was done. That's all that matters. It doesn't do to ask questions.'

'But if they'd admitted to it at the time and revealed where Schiller's body was buried, both Eva and Monsieur Legrand might have been spared.'

'The Germans are a law unto themselves. No one could have anticipated what would happen to either of them. There's no point trying to think of ways in which they could have been saved.'

'Why do you think so few people came to Eva's funeral?'

'Some stayed away because they thought she'd shielded Schiller and helped him to escape after he shot the women in the field.'

'Madame Legrand must believe this. It's why she revelled in Eva's death.'

Clemence refilled Iris's glass. 'As I said, my love, grief can do terrible things to people's hearts and minds.'

'Does everyone think Eva was a collaborator?'

'I don't think so. Most people stayed away from the funeral out of fear. Life is hard enough, without showing sympathy to someone the occupying enemy has chosen to execute. You've seen the terror in the faces of the people in the streets when a German soldier walks by. It doesn't mean people aren't mourning Eva in their own way, and it doesn't mean they think what happened to her is right.'

Iris sipped the cherry brandy, but it did nothing to steady her from the shock of what she'd heard. 'Why didn't you tell me about this when I first arrived?'

'It was too cruel what happened to Eva. I wanted to spare you the worst of it. I didn't expect you to stay. I thought you'd go home after the funeral and put it all behind you. But now you've taken up with that filthy German, you need to know what these monsters are like, and what you're getting yourself into. If you take my advice, you'll stop seeing him. If nothing else, you don't want people to think you're a collaborator.'

Clemence had a point. Iris already sensed the critical eyes of those in the town on her when she visited the market and the bakery every morning, but she wouldn't let their suspicions put her off. She had a job to do, and the fact that her beloved Eva had died at the hands of the Germans made her even more determined to carry it out.

Chapter 22

Iris made mushroom soup using the dried ceps she found in the pantry, thickening it with yesterday's stale bread and flavouring it with garlic, parsley and nutmeg. It was one of the recipes Eva used to make for her when she was unwell. After everything she'd learned from Clemence, Iris longed for the comfort of Eva's embrace more than ever, and eating her food was the closest she'd come to it.

She'd just put the soup on to simmer when she saw Christophe approaching the house, his mournful face peering into the distance as he walked up the path and stood awkwardly on the doorstep, his arm strapped to his chest in a way that made him stoop.

He removed his cap after she invited him, his eyes darting everywhere as she led him to the sitting room as if he expected Eva to appear at any minute, as Iris did a dozen times a day, forgetting herself for a moment until she remembered she wasn't coming back.

'I'm sorry to bother you. I've come to see if there's any honey. Eva used to let me have a jar whenever I wanted one.' He thrust his good hand into his coat pocket with intent. 'I'll pay for it.'

'There are a few jars left in the cellar. I'll fetch one for you. I won't be a minute.'

When she returned, Christophe was sitting in Eva's favourite armchair by the window, looking out onto the square. She was glad to see him a little more relaxed. It was the atmosphere Eva had left behind that did it. Iris wasn't taking any credit for it.

He thanked her for the honey, curling his fingers around the jar as if to extract its sweetness through the glass. 'Eva used to make me a tisane whenever I had a headache or when my arm ached. I don't know what she put in it, but it helped a lot.'

It was a familiar story. Everyone used to go to Eva for a herbal remedy now and then, even if it was only for a dose of honey and lemon when they had a cold. Unlike the doctor, Eva didn't make anyone pay for it.

'Would you like me to make one for you? Eva would have written down the recipe. I can go and look for it. It's probably in one of her notebooks.'

Christophe shifted in his seat as if the idea made him uncomfortable. Iris would never be Eva and she couldn't pretend to take her place.

'No, thank you. How much for the honey?'

'It's a gift.'

'Don't tell Maman. She'd be angry if she knew I'd taken it.'

She remembered what Clemence had said about grief twisting people's hearts and minds. 'Everyone is angry these days. You mustn't blame yourself for it.'

'She's angry because of Papa. All he did was say the wrong thing to a group of soldiers. The next thing we knew, he was dead.'

He pressed the palm of his good hand against his temple. 'It's getting worse all the time. Now, the nightmares are as bad as the headaches. It's like I'm being attacked from the inside. The war has made me useless and I can't stand it. Maman doesn't understand. All she cares about is that I can't do the work Papa used to do in the shop. She says I'm no replacement for him, that I'm not a real man.'

'She probably doesn't mean to be that way.'

'She can't forgive Papa for dying and she can't forgive me for being the one who's still alive.'

'I'm sure she loves you.'

'There's no future for me like this. I should have been the one who died, not Papa.'

'Have you tried to tell her how you feel?'

'She's only interested in the locks and bolts she sells in the hardware shop. If Papa was still alive, if I hadn't been made useless by the war, everything would be different.'

Iris offered him a bowl of soup, but he wouldn't take it. The way he flinched suggested he was still troubled by the pain in his arm.

'Has a doctor taken a look at your injury? It shouldn't still be hurting you after all this time.'

'There's nothing to be done about it. The doctor says I have to learn to live with the pain.'

He stood up to leave, gripping the jar of honey to his chest. 'I'm sorry. I shouldn't have told you all that about Maman. She'd be angry if she knew.'

'Anything you want to tell me will always remain our secret. You can come and talk to me any time you want to.'

He lowered his head as he left, wiping his tears on his sleeve, and she wondered how long it had been since he'd allowed anyone to see him cry.

Chapter 23

It had been a mistake to drink the cherry brandy. Its years of being tucked away in the back of Clemence's cupboard must have increased its potency. The headache it had brought on the night before was not only still with her, but was steadily getting worse. Iris pressed her cool palm against her forehead, but it did nothing to soothe the pounding behind her eyes, or the nausea that was slowly building inside her.

If Eva had been here, she'd have made her a special tisane, not a simple pick-me-up, which was only mint and hot water, like she'd made for Jack, but something more complex and soothing that would attack the source of the pain. Something more like the tisanes she used to make for Christophe. His visit had reminded her that the recipe must be somewhere in the cellar, tucked away in one of her notebooks.

The cellar had the same smell it had always had: distilled lavender with a darker undertone that Iris had never been able to identify, which she suspected was a blend of bitter herbs. Whenever she'd asked Eva what the distinctive aroma was, she'd always replied with an enigmatic, *Oh, this and that.* After decades of Eva distilling aromatic plants, the oils had embedded themselves into the walls and the floor, until it was impossible to separate one scent from another beyond the top notes of the lavender.

The notebook containing the recipes was tucked at the back of a cupboard. Eva had never been one for expensive stationery, believing she'd only spoil the fine paper with her scrawling ink, and this one was just as unassuming, with its simple cardboard cover, which had been knocked about from years of use. Iris flipped through the dog-eared pages until she found what she was looking for.

Remedy for Christophe's headaches and anxiety. Strictly bruised mint leaves with a hint of chamomile steeped in hot water for five minutes. Add a teaspoon of honey to mask the bitterness of the chamomile.

It's the care and attention that goes with serving the tisane that soothes as much as the herbs themselves. All he really needs is someone to listen to him and offer sympathy and understanding.

There was nothing more to the treatment than a little love and kindness. That was all Christophe really needed. Iris scanned further down the page.

Note – replace the chamomile with lemon balm for Monsieur Janot. It appears to have a more soothing effect on him than the chamomile and he prefers the flavour.

Iris hadn't known that Eva had also treated Christophe's father. *Treated* was the wrong word, rather she'd offered him comfort in the same way she'd offered it to Christophe and to Jack when they were tired and overwrought. The same remedy Iris now craved to soothe her headache.

She turned over the pages. Nothing appeared to be in date order, and soon another name jumped out at her. *Adele.*

Pennyroyal tea – do not use essential oil, which is very potent and could lead to organ failure. Three cups of pennyroyal tea a day will encourage the womb to contract and should do no harm. Add only a pinch of dried pennyroyal leaves and flowers to each cup to encourage menstrual bleeding. Use sparingly. Add honey to taste.

Iris had seen advertisements on the back pages of the women's magazines for similar remedies. Pills or herbal teas to remove *internal blockages* were as common and as ancient as the hills. They never actually mentioned the words *unwanted pregnancies*, but they were abortifacients in everything but name. Now Iris understood why Adele blamed Eva for her having Georges. It wasn't just that she'd attracted Schiller to their community, as Clemence had suggested. She must have gone to her for help in ending her pregnancy, but Eva's potion had failed.

The rest of the book was filled with similar remedies, all of them traditional herbal teas that were simple to make using local plants. It was Eva's kindness that held the magic ingredient as much as the healing properties of the herbs.

Iris looked up from the notebook. The usual glass jars were set out on the shelves, just as they'd always been, filled with dried seeds, nuts and mushrooms; jar upon jar, labelled to differentiate between sage and marjoram, hyssop and thyme, which in their dehydrated form, looked so similar.

Some of the almonds Iris had brought in remained in the basket where she'd left them, alongside the bags of sugar Eva had stockpiled. Another basket, forgotten under the table, contained courgettes, peppers and tomatoes, which must have been harvested by Eva for a ratatouille before she died, their once-firm flesh already soft, the skins withered and beginning to fur with mould.

As a child, Iris had been taught never to touch anything in the cellar without Eva's permission, and she was never allowed to go down there alone. Everything Iris did, from helping to scrape the honey from the combs into the jars, to preparing the flower heads for the still, was always done under Eva's watchful eye. Now Iris couldn't shake off the feeling that she was trespassing.

Inside the tall cupboard in the corner, she found more large glass jars filled with dried plants and seeds: the labels, each marked with a red dot, indicating tomato and rhubarb leaves, hydrangea and tansy, oleander and brugmansia, wolfsbane and larkspur. She recognised some of them as having been collected from the plants in the flowerbed behind the shed.

She retrieved Eva's copy of *Frossard's Herbal* from the shelf and looked up each of the plants. They all contained toxic properties. It was the thing they all had in common. It explained the warning red dots on the labels, and why they'd been set aside from the edible ingredients in the cellar.

The solution to Iris's problem was right in front of her. The idea rolled around her head like a loose marble. It was unthinkable, but it might just work. A slow drip of these toxic ingredients might not only heal certain types of sickness in moderation, but they might be enough to kill Mason without anyone suspecting foul play. Presenting him with good home-cooked meals would lull him into a false sense of security and prove her devotion to him. He wasn't usually finicky about what he ate. He'd only turned down her suggestion of the poached trout for lunch to be difficult. If she filled him up with the right food, he'd keep coming back. With any luck, the poisons would build up in his system and be enough to kill him.

There was no one close enough to him to suspect poisoning, and his death could easily be put down to years of high living. His bloated features and ruddy complexion were enough to point to a man of a certain age used to an excess that had finally caught up with him. It was a risk, but less of a risk than attempting to kill him with a knife or a gun. Thanks to Eva, everything she needed to accomplish her mission was at hand.

Chapter 24

The chestnut cake, made to Eva's recipe, with added tomato stems and rhubarb leaves, was still warm when Iris brought a fresh jar of honey up from the cellar and drizzled it lavishly over the top, allowing the thick syrup to run down the sides and pool around the bottom of the plate. There could never be too much sweetness where this recipe was concerned. She considered the cake, breathing in the earthy smell of the chestnut flour and the butter she'd bought on the black market, the honey with its lavender and heather undertones striking the strongest note. She could only hope the same could be said for the flavour.

Once it had cooled, she took it to Mason's hotel. It was mid-morning when he opened the door to her, stiff-backed in his officer's uniform.

She stood in the corridor, hoping he wouldn't invite her in. The stale air escaping from the room, redolent of unwashed clothes and stale tobacco, had already wiped the carefully prepared smile from her face.

She held the cake at arm's length, gesturing for him to take it. 'This was one of Eva's special recipes. It wasn't published in any of her books. I hope you enjoy it.'

He grabbed her arm and pulled her into the room, closing the door behind them. Once they were alone, his eyes narrowed on the cake, his nose twitching as the aroma of the crumb reached him. She'd judged him well. He was a glutton.

'Eva left you the recipe?'

He was wondering if he could make money out of it. She could read him as easily as an open book. Bad men were predictable. It was the good ones, like Jack, who constantly surprised her. She glanced around the room, looking for an escape route in case he started tearing at her clothes.

'She taught me how to make it during one of the summers I spent with her before the war. The recipe isn't written down.'

'This could be quite special. Make sure you don't forget it.'

He grabbed the cake and ripped off the brown paper she'd used to cover it, his fingers digging into the top and clawing at a chunk, the honey running down his fingers as he shovelled a handful into his mouth.

She wanted to scream at him to respect the cake, which deserved to be cut into slices and served on china plates, but she held it in. If he gorged on it, all the better.

He nodded his approval, his cheeks bulging as he bit down on the cake, the effects of the honey already softening the sharpness behind his eyes. Taking another mouthful, he moved around the hotel room and sat on the bed, beckoning her to join him.

'Take off your clothes.'

Her mind worked at double speed, searching for an excuse that wouldn't leave him suspicious. Nothing would induce her to get into bed with him. She'd made the promise to herself, for Jack's sake, and she wouldn't break it.

'I can't stay. I've left something in the oven. I only came to bring the cake and to invite you for lunch.'

'If you want to show me how sorry you are for keeping me waiting the other day, you'll take off your clothes and get into bed.'

He stared at her while she searched for an answer, his jaw working up and down. Another lump of cake had been pulled from its centre. What was left sat in a collapsed heap on the plate. She couldn't let him see how appalled she was at the sight of it.

'I'm cooking one of Eva's special meals, just for you. If I don't go back and check on it, it'll be ruined.' She tilted her head to one side, trying to appear thoughtful, innocent, contrite, whatever he wanted to read into it, as long as it wasn't the contempt she was attempting to hide.

He ran the back of his hand across his lips to wipe away the honey and dropped the plate on the bed, a satisfied look smeared across his face. 'If the lunch is as good as the cake, I'm in for a treat. I'll be there at one o'clock.' He looked her up and down, his tongue interrogating the corner of his mouth where a crumb must have lodged itself. 'I don't have to tell you what I'll be expecting afterwards.'

Iris dashed towards the door before he changed his mind and grabbed her. She'd worry about what would happen after lunch when it came to it.

As she left the hotel, she noticed a familiar figure standing outside the nearby *tabac*, his face shadowed by the hat he'd pulled low over his brow. Jack. He must have seen her leaving the hotel, because he fell into step with her as she crossed the street.

She brushed her arm against his to let him know she'd recognised him, her heart beating faster at his closeness, at the danger of having him so near and what the consequences would be if they were caught.

She kept her voice low as she spoke, her eyes scanning for any signs of approaching German soldiers. 'It's not safe for you to be on the streets.'

'I have to stay close to Mason. I can't lose track of him now.'

His eyes were thick with a lack of sleep and he smelled as if he hadn't washed for days, his body odour mixing with the smell of stale tobacco and alcohol.

It was all Iris could do not to cry at the sight of him. 'You must take better care of yourself. Come to the house for a bath and a good night's sleep any time you want.'

They wandered into a nearby park, neither wanting to relinquish the other's company, despite the risks they were taking.

'I saw you enter the hotel. I suppose you went to see Mason. Do have any information on what he's planning to do next?'

'Nothing yet. If I'm too curious, he'll get suspicious. We'd had a misunderstanding. I took him a cake as an apology.'

'You never used to bake cakes for me.'

He'd never needed appeasing, that was the reason. He wasn't the kind of man who needed bribery to bring him round from an argument. Crossed words had always been soothed with empathy and kisses.

'I'll bake one for you, if you want.'

'This isn't you, Iris. Don't let him turn you into a housewife. You're so much more than that. If he doesn't value you for who you really are, then he doesn't deserve you. You're a lioness. Don't let him tame you.'

She'd changed. He could see it and he didn't like it. But Jack had changed too. The only difference was that she was pretending. All she wanted was the old Jack restored to her, and to be the woman she'd always been to him.

'Come for supper later. I'll cook for you.' She tried to sound bright, as if her heart wasn't breaking under the weight of all the lies, as if she wasn't begging him.

'No, thanks. If you don't have any information on Mason to give me, there's no point coming.'

'Then let me know where I can contact you.'

'I'm sorry, Iris. It doesn't work like that. Not anymore.'

Jack picked up his pace, shaking her off as he negotiated the narrow paths of the park. He'd grown faster, leaner in the time they'd spent apart, and he used this now to break free of her. He'd gone before she could stop him, and without looking back, and based on everything he'd seen of her, she couldn't blame him.

Chapter 25

Lunch was ready long before Mason was due to arrive. Iris had slow-cooked the mutton with the last of Clemence's cherry brandy and six whole cloves of garlic, until it was tender enough to cut with a spoon. Now, the house was filled with its dense aroma, the accompanying roasted vegetables, glazed with honey, adding a sweet top note to the air.

By one o'clock, Iris was ready and waiting. She'd reapplied her make-up and pinned her hair in a chignon at the nape of her neck, in a way that appeared chic, but slightly unravelled. She knew better than to strive for perfection if she wanted Mason to underestimate her. She'd tried hard with her clothes, but not too hard, opting to wear a simple tea dress with a sweetheart neckline. The plan was to leave him uncertain as to whether she would take him to her bed or not. If there was to be a game of cat and mouse, all the traps and exits had to be prepared in advance.

He arrived fifteen minutes late. Iris didn't comment on it as he staggered through the door, bouncing off the walls in the narrow hallway. For a minute, she thought he was drunk, until she noticed his face was paler than uncooked pastry, his eyes red-rimmed, as if something had got into them that couldn't be rubbed out.

'Are you all right?'

She fetched him a glass of water, but the sight of it made his chest heave and he pushed it away. She wondered how he'd managed to stagger all the way here, given the state he was in.

'You need to sit down.'

She bundled him into the sitting room, where he dropped onto the sofa, not a moment before his legs went from under him.

'What's brought this on?'

She tried to sound sympathetic, burying the shocking realisation that she could actually have done this to him. She'd never truly believed that a few simple ingredients added to the cake mixture could have this effect. She was beginning to understand why it was said poison was the murder weapon of choice for women.

Mason grunted. 'It's nothing. A headache, that's all.'

He tried to sound unconcerned, covering his eyes with his hand as he spoke, as if to shield them from the light.

'Poor you. Is it very bad?'

'Blinding. All I can see is flashing lights. And my stomach's not too good either. I need to rest. I'll be all right in a minute.'

She closed the window shutters, shading him from the sunlight, hinting that perhaps he'd drunk too much wine the night before. 'I'll make one of Eva's tisanes for you. It's just the thing to put you right.'

He shook his head, gripping his face as if he thought his skull might shatter with the movement, but she slipped into the kitchen and made it anyway, piling the bruised mint leaves into a cup and steeping them in boiling water.

When she returned to the sitting room with the tisane, Mason was lying on the sofa, his knees tucked up to his stomach, a trembling hand still covering his face.

'Would you like a spoon of honey stirred in, or would your stomach not stand it?'

After he failed to answer, she pushed the tisane under his nose. 'Sip this. It'll make you feel better.'

He took it from her without opening his eyes and gulped the first few mouthfuls, seemingly insensible to the fact that it had been made with boiling water. The way he trusted her was a small victory. All it had taken was a headache and a bit of sickness, and he was as vulnerable as a child.

'I'll give you a few minutes and then I'll serve lunch. I followed Eva's recipe to the letter. The mutton will melt in your mouth. Can you smell it cooking?'

'Not now, Iris.'

She sat with him, encouraging him every few minutes to take another sip of the tisane until he'd finished it. All the while, she talked to him about how she'd prepared the mutton, trying to distract him from his symptoms while tempting him to the lunch she'd prepared.

'It was a stroke of luck that there was mutton available.'

She didn't admit that she'd resorted to the black market, buying from one of Eva's old friends who kept a small farm outside the town, and who for the right price, could always lay his hands on a little meat and dairy. It wasn't for feeding herself that she did this, it was for Mason. She only hoped he appreciated the trouble she'd gone to.

He winced as he took a breath to speak. 'I can't stand mutton. I'll bring us a couple of steaks next time. You can get anything if you throw enough money around.'

Iris felt sick when she thought of where his money came from, how countless soldiers had died because of the secrets he'd betrayed to the enemy, all to secure lucrative contracts for the German armaments company he had a stake in.

He must have sensed the change in the atmosphere, because he opened one eye. 'What is it? You're not ill as well, are you? I thought it must have been something I'd eaten in that blasted hotel, but if you're feeling it too, then it must be a virus we picked up somewhere.'

Iris placed her hand on her forehead, pretending to test her temperature. 'Now I think of it, I have been a little under the weather. Maybe there's something in the air.' If she appeared to be ill too, he wouldn't suspect that his symptoms were of her making.

After he'd closed his eyes again, she lit the fire and placed a blanket over him, determined to make him sweat, double-checking the shutters to make sure not a chink of light could get in. Once he was settled, she studied his breathing. Would it take more than this to finish him off? She'd guessed the dose, not knowing how much would do the job, or how the cooking would affect the properties of the ingredients, or even if he'd detect them. If this wasn't enough to kill him, she'd have to learn how the poisons behaved through trial and error.

When she was sure he was asleep, she slipped her hand under the blanket to retrieve his tobacco pouch from his pocket, and crept downstairs to the cellar with it, quickly adding dried brugmansia leaves, crumbling them to a similar size and shape as his usual blend of tobacco. He was so practised at filling his pipe, he barely paid attention as he did it, allowing his fingers to feel their way as he transferred it, pinch by pinch from pouch to bowl before tamping it down. Unless he gave it more than a cursory glance, he was unlikely to spot the rogue leaves among the strands and curls of those he was accustomed to.

The brugmansia leaves wouldn't kill him, but the hallucinations it induced would be enough to confuse him, and the more debilitated he became, the easier it would be to finish him off.

Back upstairs, she returned the tobacco pouch to his pocket. The soft pressure of her hands on his body must have disturbed him, because he opened his eyes. Startled by his sudden attention, she jumped back, the guilt of her interference written all over her face.

'Sorry, Mason. I didn't mean to disturb you. I was repositioning the blanket to make you more comfortable.'

It was a second or two before he realised where he was. He threw off the blanket and sat up, patting his pockets, as if to check everything was still where it should be. Iris prayed that she'd slipped the tobacco pouch back into the right place, that he wouldn't notice if it was positioned incorrectly.

'Are you ready for the mutton? Or perhaps you'd like another mint tisane?'

He shook his head, and then grabbed it with both hands, as if instantly regretting the movement. 'I'd better go back to the hotel and see if I can sleep off this blasted headache.'

She acquiesced, noting how the effects of what she'd fed him lingered, sorry the mutton would be wasted, disappointed that she hadn't managed to kill him with it. It would keep for a day or two on the coldest shelf in the pantry. Perhaps there'd be another chance to feed it to him before then, that was if she could convince him to eat what he considered inferior meat. If she was to finish him off before he guessed what she was up to, she'd have to make sure he ate everything she offered him.

Chapter 26

The Grey Mouse was sitting at a table outside the café again, her drink untouched as she watched people come and go in the square. Iris had planned to stop off for breakfast, but this woman in her German uniform, with the questioning eyes that seemed to track everyone's movements, had put her off. Instead, she walked past, hoping to remain unnoticed, rummaging in her handbag to demonstrate her distraction, but these days it wasn't so easy to appear invisible.

'Iris. May I call you that?'

The Grey Mouse was looking up at her and smiling. 'My name is Frieda. I introduced myself to you recently. I was a friend of Eva's.'

No one occupying a country by force could ever be considered a friend. Before Iris could think of a civil response, Adele appeared from inside the café, saving Iris from having to make conversation with someone who stood for everything she despised.

'Iris, there you are. Would you take a look at Georges for me?'

'Of course.'

She nodded to the Grey Mouse, forcing herself to be polite. It wasn't wise to snub the enemy, however great the temptation. 'Please excuse me.'

Everyone was sitting outside in the sunshine and the café was empty, but for Georges, who was sleeping in his crib beside the counter. Iris leaned over him, envious of his peace.

'What is it?'

Adele rubbed her hands nervously down her apron, her eyes shifting to the spot outside the café where the German soldier who shot the pigeon had stopped to light a cigarette, taking more time over it than was necessary.

'Is he bothering you?'

Adele shook her head a little too vehemently, her eyes shifting to the Grey Mouse. 'No. It's that woman. She comes to the café at the same time every morning and stays for an hour, sometimes two, lingering over her breakfast and trying to make conversation. Every time I look up, she's watching me.'

'Perhaps she has no friends.'

'If she thinks I'm going to be her friend, she can forget it.'

The Grey Mouse had been in the café the day they discussed the discovery of Schiller's body. If she was as alert as she always seemed, she must have heard everything that was said. If she suspected the café was a meeting place for the Resistance, it would explain why she kept coming back. She had too much curiosity to be anything other than a spy.

Adele's attention had returned to Georges, her eyes taking on a faraway look as she stared at his sleeping form. Iris hadn't forgotten how she'd blamed Eva for being burdened with him.

'I was going through some of Eva's notebooks and found a reference to some herbs she'd given you when you discovered you were carrying Georges.'

She didn't have to be any more direct for Adele to understand she was referring to the abortifacients she'd requested to end her pregnancy.

'She supplied them because I begged her to. She advised me not to take them, even as she handed them to me, and I didn't. She was right. For all the shame I felt at finding myself carrying

Schiller's child, he was my child too, and when it came to it, I couldn't face the prospect of losing him.

'When I told you I blamed Eva for the fact that I have Georges, I didn't mean it. I slept with Schiller out of my own free will. I shouldn't have spoken ill of her.' She forced a smile which spoke more of her bravery that it did of her contentment. 'What would you like to drink?'

Adele was taking Iris's order when Solange came into the café. Her eyes lit up when she saw Solange was carrying a dress.

'Did you manage to repair it?'

Solange held the dress up to the light, pointing to the invisible stitching at the waist. 'I had to cut back the fabric where the tear had frayed. If you look closely, you can see it.'

Adele smoothed the dress against her body, trying to get an impression of the fit. 'I'll go upstairs and try it on. Keep an eye on Georges for me.'

Solange wandered over to the crib where Georges was still sleeping, unmoved by his mother's burst of excitement. She glanced at Iris, as if she had something to say, but didn't know how to say it.

It was Iris who finally broke the silence. 'Did you make that dress for Adele?'

'No. She caught it on something and tore it, so I offered to repair it. There wasn't much fabric to spare. I hope it still fits.' Her eyes drifted back to Georges. 'Can I ask you something?'

'Of course.'

'You know Christophe. We both know he's troubled, but underneath, he's kind and decent, and only wants to be loved. How can I make him understand that I want to be the woman to do that?'

'Have you tried telling him?'

'He runs away like a scared rabbit whenever I go near him.'

'Don't take it personally. I think he does that with everyone.'

'He doesn't believe he's worthy of being loved, but he's wrong. How do I prove it to him?'

Adele returned before Iris had time to consider the question, twirling around the café in her dress, the repair invisible unless you knew to look for it.

'It fits even better than it did before. Solange, you're a genius. The couture houses in Paris don't know what they're missing.'

Solange inspected the reconfigured seam, making sure it sat smoothly on Adele's waist, but her mind was still on the previous conversation.

'Tell me, Iris. How did you make Jack love you?'

If Iris knew the secret of winning love, she'd have used it to win Jack back. Lost for an answer, she remembered what Eva had written about Christophe in her notebooks next to the recipe for his tisane.

'Try kindness and a listening ear. That's what he needs more than anything.'

The conversation was interrupted by a commotion in the square. Iris dashed outside, to where a crowd had quickly gathered. Through the gaps of vying elbows and shoulders, she spotted two women on their knees, their faces buried in their hands. Paul was among the crowd, his face blank with shock. Iris worked her way towards him, touching his arm to get his attention.

'What's happened?'

'The camp in the woods where the maquis have been hiding out was discovered by the Germans. They set fire to it last night. The flames tore through their makeshift shelters as they slept. The ones who tried to get away were shot. No one survived.'

It was the camp where Jack was hiding. He couldn't be dead. It couldn't be true. It had to be a mistake.

'Are you sure?'

'The smoke carried as far as the vineyard. I saw it from my bedroom window when I opened the shutters first thing this morning. I thought it was a wildfire in the hills. There's been such little rain, the earth is parched up there. It wouldn't have taken much for it to set alight. I was on my way to help put it out when I was stopped by a group of German soldiers. They laughed in my face as they told me what had happened.'

Jack couldn't have been killed. She wasn't prepared to let him go. His name was on her lips, but she couldn't say it. She couldn't risk anyone knowing he was here, alive or dead.

She needed air and space. She moved away from the crowd. No one must see how distressed she was. She had to find out what had happened to Jack. Someone must know. Someone must be able to tell her. Knowing if he was dead or alive was all that mattered.

'Iris, are you all right?'

She hadn't realised Paul had followed her until she felt the weight of his arm around her shoulders. She tried to shake him off, but his grip only grew tighter.

'You've had a shock. Let me take you home.'

'How many?'

Paul frowned at her question. 'How many what?'

'How many died? Do we know their names?'

He squeezed her shoulder, his fingers digging into her flesh, as if such pain could relieve the shock.

'It's too soon to say. It'll be a while before they recover the bodies, that's if the Germans don't remove them first. I wouldn't put it past them to deny people the right to bury their dead.'

The sound of leather boots ringing on the cobbles announced the arrival of the German soldiers, shouting insults and laughing, as the people in the square clung to one another, supporting friends and neighbours in their grief. One or two at least had the decency to look shame-faced as they waved their guns to disperse the crowd, turning a blind eye to the old man who risked his life by calling them murderers. His grandson had disappeared six months ago after being summoned to join a forced labour camp in Germany. It didn't take much to guess he'd joined the maquis as a resistance fighter.

Paul pulled Iris closer, constraining her in his grip. 'I'll take you home. You don't need to see this.'

It was easier to let him lead her back to the house than to fight him. She needed all her strength for Jack. How long would it be before she had news of him? Before she was forced to resign herself to his fate?

Chapter 27

Hour upon hour, Iris paced the house, keeping one eye on the square. If there was news, this was where it would be posted. And yet there was no news. The town remained as silent as the grave. Everyone was already in mourning for those who'd been murdered. They didn't need to know their names to feel their loss. The victims had been warriors, fighting for the freedom of France, and that was all anyone needed to know.

But how about Jack? He'd been living with the maquis clandestinely. The men he lived alongside might not have known his real name. If he'd died, she might never hear of it. Instead, she'd be forced to rely on the slow-growing certainty of it, until one day, she'd have no choice but to accept he was gone. But today was not that day. She wouldn't give up on him. Not now, not ever.

Iris hadn't slept when Mason appeared just before lunchtime the following day. She greeted him at the door, pretending to be pleased to see him, bracing herself for another encounter, when all she really wanted to do was cry for Jack.

The effects of the poisoned cake seemed to have worn off, and so she offered him the slow-cooked mutton she'd previously made. It was past its best, but it would hardly make any difference, given the dried larkspur and foxglove leaves she'd added to the recipe.

'I ate most of it last night, but I set some aside for you, because I knew you'd want to try it. Did I tell you it was one of Eva's special recipes and not one she shared widely?'

He gave a slight twitch, his eyes moving backwards and forwards, as if he were scanning the pages of a book somewhere in the distance.

'Did you see that?'

She traced the line of his eyes. 'What?'

'The bat. The huge green bat, flapping its wings as if it were drowning.'

'Are you sure?'

There were no bats at this time of the day, green or otherwise. He must have been smoking the tobacco she'd laced with brugmansia leaves. They were well known to cause hallucinations.

'It couldn't have escaped.' His eyes darted around the sitting room, scanning the rug and the backs of the chairs. 'It must have landed somewhere. Don't let it near you. It might bite.'

'I'll warm up the mutton. It won't take long. Come through to the kitchen.'

He didn't appear to be listening as his eyes tracked nothing in the air. 'There it is. Can't you see it?'

'It's probably a trick of the light. Come and eat the mutton.'

He grabbed the top of her arm where the last set of bruises, round and dark as damsons, had only now begun to fade.

'I said, can you see it?'

'Whatever it was, it must have gone. Now, will you eat the food or not?'

She made her voice high-pitched, trying to sound cheerful, as if her world hadn't collapsed around her. 'The flavours will have infused deep into the meat by now. It should taste better than ever.'

He insisted on her opening the window before he entered the kitchen. Despite his confused state, he was still conscious of the risk of gas poisoning.

By the time she served the food, he was finally seated at the table. He looked up at her, his eyes still wild and flitting, like the wings of the imagined green bat itself.

'Aren't you having any?'

'I ate my share last night. I saved this especially for you.'

She trusted he wouldn't check in the pantry, where the rest of the dish remained untouched. Nothing on earth would make her eat her own poison.

The mutton gave way like warm butter under the pressure of Mason's knife. He shovelled it into his mouth, his fork piled high with the meat, glistening with the extra honey she'd dribbled over as a last-minute glaze before serving.

'I'm no fan of mutton, but I can taste the merit in this.'

Once he'd cleared his plate, he slumped in the chair, sated. His eyes had begun to lose their wild, unfocused look and would remain that way until he lit his pipe again. She'd need to have her wits about her if she was to top up his tobacco pouch without him noticing.

He pushed his fingernail between his front teeth, digging out a string of mutton that had lodged itself there. 'You heard about the attack on the camp of those resistance fighters.'

It wasn't a question, but a statement, and she refused to be led into giving an opinion on it. 'I didn't offer you any wine with your mutton. Would you like some?'

He placed his hand on his forehead, as if remembering the headache he'd recently suffered, and she wondered if the last traces of it still remained, whether he was hiding the effects of the slow poisoning, or whether they weren't bothering him that much. She had to tread carefully, to make sure he didn't connect feeling ill with the food she was giving him.

'Not now.' He sat up a little straighter and she realised he was finally getting round to the real purpose of his visit.

'One of the junior officers told me you were in the square when the news came through about the attack on the maquis camp. He broke up the ensuing scuffle.'

It wasn't a scuffle. People had gathered to comfort the two

women who'd lost their men in the attack. Iris bit back everything she was tempted to say. She'd learn more by listening than by correcting him.

'I happened to be in the café at the time.'

'The young officer reported to me you were with a man, that he embraced you and kissed you. Then he came back to the house with you.' His eyes had suddenly grown wild. Once again, he was seeing things that didn't exist.

'That would have been Paul. You know about him. He's an old friend.'

'It's not the first time you've been seen with him.'

Was he having her watched? If he was, then she was under more scrutiny than she'd realised.

'I've known him since I was seven. He's the brother I never had.'

His empty plate clattered as he banged his fist on the table. 'Don't lie to me.'

'Why would I lie to you, Mason?'

'You call him *the brother you never had*, but you have a brother. The night we met. You were sitting alone in the bar in Claridge's. You said you were waiting for your brother. When he didn't turn up, I offered to buy you a drink.'

This was Iris's first blunder. Ambrose had planted her in the bar purposely to meet Mason. She'd used the excuse of her brother failing to turn up to meet her as a reason for being alone. It didn't seem to matter at the time that she'd lied to him about having a brother. She hadn't expected to have to see him more than once or twice. She'd never imagined the mission would go on this long, or that it would come to this.

She cleared his plate from the table, grasping the used cutlery to stop her hands shaking. Suddenly, it felt as if she were fighting for her life. 'It was a cousin I referred to, not a brother. It was noisy in the bar that night. We were trying to talk over the sound of the piano. You must have misheard me.'

He wasn't clear-headed enough to dispute her answer. 'The fact remains that you were seen with this man in the square. You're far too intimate with him. People are commenting on it. You're making a fool of me.'

'That wasn't my intention. It's all perfectly innocent. If I had anything to hide, I wouldn't be seen with him in a public place. You know how closely I guard my reputation here for the sake of Eva's memory.'

His expression told her his mind was too addled to combat her logic. He rubbed his hand over his stomach. It was either indigestion or the effects of the poisons stirring.

'It's time to get a few things straight between us. If you're going to be associated with me, you need to start behaving accordingly.'

Iris dreaded what was coming next. So far, she'd managed to avoid any real physical intimacy with him, largely because the poisons had left him incapacitated with headaches and nausea.

'I've been invited to dinner at the house of Commander Frisch and his wife tomorrow evening. I want you there as my companion. I trust you won't let me down.'

'I'd be honoured to join you.'

Frisch was one of the highest-ranking officers in the town and wielded a lot of power. According to Clemence, he'd been the one tasked with investigating Schiller's disappearance. It meant she'd be walking into the lion's den. If she did anything to make him suspect she was a British agent, he'd have her arrested and shot.

Mason got up from the table, unsteady on his feet as he moved about the kitchen, blindly searching for the door as if he'd forgotten the way out.

'Are you all right?'

He grunted, full of bravado. 'Fine. I must have overdone it, that's all. I'll be as right as rain after a good sleep. Watch out for those green bats. You don't want any more of them flying in.'

She passed him his officer's cap and saw him out, bolting the door behind him, glad to be rid of him, and bracing herself for the challenge that lay ahead.

Chapter 28

It was almost dark when Iris heard Yvette's familiar footfall coming up the path. It wasn't her usual light step, but something heavier and more hurried. She dashed to open the front door and let her in, saving her the precious seconds of fiddling with the unaccustomed lock.

'Are you all right?'

Yvette carried the suitcase through to the sitting room and hid it behind Eva's favourite armchair before collapsing onto the sofa.

Iris closed the window shutters in case anyone happened to be watching, and gave her a minute to catch her breath. 'Would you like something to eat?' Without realising it, she was practising Eva's belief that food could solve all the evils of the world.

'In a minute.'

'What happened?'

'I was stopped by a couple of German soldiers as I stepped off the train from Lyon. It was just a routine check of my papers and travel pass. I've been stopped before. They've always let me go after a cursory glance. No one's interested in an ugly schoolgirl like me, but this time it was different. They kept asking questions, wanting to know what school I went to and whether I had a boyfriend.'

'You had satisfactory answers for all their questions?'

Despite the fear, there was still a look of triumph in her eyes. 'Of course, just as you taught me.'

'Do you think they were simply flirting with you?'

'It's possible. I'm sure they followed me as I left the station. I didn't dare look back, but I could hear their laughter and their boot-steps on the cobbles close behind.'

'But you managed to shake them off?'

'I went to the library and played the part of the studious schoolgirl, browsing the shelves of history books. They didn't follow me inside, but I stayed for half an hour, in case they were waiting in the street. It was dusk when I finally left, and there was no sign of them, but it didn't stop me looking over my shoulder all the way here, checking every turning and corner.'

Damn Ambrose for sending such a young and inexperienced girl into the field. How could he have been so reckless? If anything happened to Yvette, Iris would never forgive him.

'You'd recognise them if you saw them again?'

'Without a doubt.'

'Then you must stay at least one step ahead of them.' Now Iris had reassured herself that Yvette was safe, there was something she was desperate to ask.

'The maquis camp that was razed to the ground by the Germans. Do you know if any of the men who were trapped in the fire survived?'

'I've heard nothing. Everyone has gone to ground since the attack. It's the safest way.'

Yvette had distanced herself from the tragedy, as Iris had taught her. It was vital to remain clear-headed while in the field if you were to avoid making mistakes.

It was wrong to have put the question to her, wrong to have suggested she might have any kind of connection to the victims or their associates. She shuddered. The chill she felt whenever she thought of Jack went bone deep. 'Forget I asked. I'll make you some food.'

While Yvette had a bath, Iris made onion soup, adding fresh parsley and garlic for fortitude. It was the quickest and most nourishing meal she could think of. It was also the easiest thing for Yvette to digest, given the little she appeared to have eaten during the last few days.

Yvette appeared much calmer once she'd eaten. 'I know you advised me not to come back, but Ambrose ordered me to deliver a message to you.'

There hadn't been time for Iris to learn Morse code or how to operate a wireless before setting out on her mission, and Yvette was the only channel of communication she had with London. 'What is it?'

'If you've completed your task, I'm to let him know. If you haven't, he says you need to hurry up and get on with it.'

'I've tried a couple of times, but both attempts failed.'

'Ambrose said to remind you that even though Mason's a traitor, he's not a fool. Don't string him along for too long, because sooner or later, he'll work out what you're up to.'

Ambrose was right. Iris had already made a mistake. It had been careless to refer to Paul as the brother she'd never had, when it was just a lazy figure of speech. Her carelessness had put her at risk. If Mason realised it was a lie, rather than a misunderstanding, or if he discovered she worked for British Intelligence, her cover would be blown. She had to step up the poisoning, and she had to do it in such a way as to make his death not appear suspicious if there weren't to be any reprisals.

Chapter 29

Mason collected Iris at seven thirty, just as he said he would. It wouldn't do to be late for dinner at the house of Commander Frisch and his wife. It wasn't his house of course, but one that had been requisitioned.

Iris clapped her hand over her mouth, stifling her reaction as Mason turned off the road onto the gravel drive that led to the beautiful fin-de-siècle property that had taken Monsieur Hoffman, a local respected surgeon, most of his working life to afford. Like all the Jewish families in the area, Monsieur Hoffman, his wife, mother-in-law and two grown-up sons had been rounded up and sent to a prison camp in 1940. None of them had been heard of since. Allowing senior German officers to claim their homes only added further injury to the crime.

Mason must have noticed her reaction as he stopped the car in front of the house, straightening his cap in the rear-view mirror.

'Are you all right? You're not going to be sick, are you?'

'I didn't realise this was where we were coming.'

Eva had been great friends with Madame Hoffman. They'd shared a passion for kitchen gardening. Over the years, they'd planted potagers together, swopped cuttings and shared seeds. Iris glanced at the strawberry beds, tucked up against the high stone wall, wondering how many spoonfuls of jam she'd eaten from their fruits during the endless summers she'd spent with Eva. In those days, life had revolved around the simple pleasures of food and spending time with the people you loved. Even after the war, there'd be no going back to how things once were. Not only had lives been lost and the love taken away, but the innocence had gone too.

'Did you bring Frisch's wife a gift?'

Iris showed him a small pink box, tied with a cream ribbon. Inside were a dozen squares of quince paste, made with the first ripe fruits from Eva's tree.

Mason's eyes grew wide. 'Is it sweet?'

'Very.'

Iris would be forever thankful for the sugar Eva had stashed in the cellar. She had no idea how long she'd been stockpiling it, or whether Schiller had provided it, but it was turning out to be a major weapon in her armoury.

'It's made to a Spanish recipe and quite plain. Yours are different.' She handed him a similar box, this time without a ribbon. 'These are made to a recipe adapted to include local herbs. I made them especially for you.'

She couldn't say what the herbs were exactly, because it was her secret. Now she'd seen the house the Frisches were living in, she regretted not making the special recipe for them too.

It was a substantial house with nine bedrooms spread over four floors. During the summer, the sun slanted on the honey-coloured stone until it glowed. There was a heavy oak front door and balustrades at every window. When the Hoffmans had lived there, each one had frothed with trailing red pelargoniums.

The door was opened by a flustered-looking maid, who disappeared as soon as she heard Frisch approaching along the hallway. Despite having swopped his uniform for a formal suit, he clicked his heels and offered a curt nod, while his wife stood behind him, keeping one eye on the mirror as she patted her hair in place.

The house no longer smelled of beeswax and lavender as Iris remembered it, but of something bitter, although the hallway floor was still highly polished. The table where Madame Hoffman used to lay out the letters to be posted was still free of dust and the china ornaments of cats she collected were still arranged in their artful clusters.

It surprised Iris to see the reminders of the family at every turn: the pictures on the walls, the cheerful umbrellas in the antique stand. If she ran upstairs and checked the wardrobes, she suspected Madame Hoffman's summer dresses would still be hanging on the rails, her matching shoes neatly lined up beneath.

The Hoffmans had been usurped, and these enemy invaders had slipped into their lives like ghosts. And yet, the spirit of the place could never be the same. The warm family atmosphere had gone and in its place stood two German monoliths, their hearts as cold as stone.

'I see you're admiring the house. Would you like me to give you a tour of the rooms?'

The offer came from Madame Frisch. There was no, *pleased to meet you* in her greeting, but simply, *look at our beautiful home*, as if she'd been responsible for every brick and carpet of it, rather than being the brazen thief who'd claimed it.

Her tailored dress, with its narrow belt, emphasised the fact that she was all bosom and hips, although Iris imagined there must be a heart beating beneath it all, if not a conscience. She clearly hadn't suffered from the food rationing during the past four years. Although broad, she was shorter than Iris imagined most German women to be, certainly more diminutive than the Grey Mouse. She'd probably never done a day's work in the fifty-odd years of her life beyond ordering around the cook. Her hair, steel grey to match her expression, was pinned in curls around the vicinity of her face, the diamond clips on her ears bringing a sparkle that distracted from the lack of life behind her eyes. Iris inspected the earrings, suspecting that they too belonged to

Madame Hoffman.

Iris declined the offer of a tour, putting on the best smile she could manage for the sake of her country.

'The previous owners were friends of my family. I've been visiting this house since I was a child. I'm probably better acquainted with the rooms than you are.'

When Iris said, *the previous owners*, she actually meant, *the owners*. The enemy invaders could snatch the house from the Hoffmans, but it would never be theirs.

The smile froze on Madame Frisch's mouth. 'You probably know all the best people in the town. I do miss good society. You must introduce me to everyone worth knowing.'

Judging who was worth knowing was highly subjective, especially during wartime, but Iris knew better than to say as much. It would be a mistake to get on the wrong side of her so early in the game.

'I don't think any of the old families are still here. They're all in Paris.' *Or fled*, she wanted to add, *or imprisoned*.

Madame Frisch tilted her chin at an odd angle, as if she were the epitome of chic. 'All the best people are in Paris. That's where I should be. I'm not suited to this provincial life.'

By now they were in the sitting room, sipping an unnamed cocktail of a strength Iris had never before encountered. It had been thrust upon her by Frisch without being given the opportunity to refuse it.

Commander Frisch was exactly what his title suggested, commanding and overbearing: a stiff shirt hidden behind the barricade of his rank. Beneath that, she doubted there was any substance to him. Certainly, there was no heart. His veins ran with the bluster of a bully, and the ingrained fear that at any moment, he'd be exposed for the coward he was. He was tall and lean, as unyielding as a poker, his face chiselled from granite with eyes to match. He believed he'd been put on this earth to conquer, and every gesture he made reinforced that fact. One day, he'd be proven wrong.

But for now, it was Iris's job to put on an amenable face. She mustn't forget Frisch had been Schiller's superior. The Grey Mouse had been in the café the day Emile announced he'd discovered his body while searching for his mother's jewellery. She must have reported it back to him, which meant Frisch knew Schiller was dead, even if he hadn't publicly admitted it. The fact that he'd chosen not to act on the knowledge suggested he was laying a trap for a longer game.

Iris had to watch her step. Once Frisch realised her connection to Eva, there would be awkward questions. If she was going to disarm him, she must appear completely open and defenceless.

'Sweets.'

She retrieved the box of quince paste from her handbag and handed it to Madame Frisch, smiling sweetly through the word. 'They're made to my dear Aunt Eva's recipe. I hope you enjoy them.'

A light seemed to switch on in Frisch's head as he made the connection. 'You're a relative of Eva Fournier, the famous cookery writer.'

Iris nodded, trying not to flinch at the sound of Eva's name on the lips of the man who'd ordered her murder. 'I'm her niece.'

Frisch nodded, pleased with himself for making the link. 'Shame about her death.'

Anger boiled in Iris's veins at his disrespect for Eva's memory, at his lack of sensitivity for her grief. At the fact that she was dead because of him.

'You've inherited her house?'

She hated his tone as he asked the question. Her inheritance was no victory and it was no compensation for the fact that one of his men had shot Eva. She nodded, not trusting herself to speak.

His eyes remained on her face. 'Not all bad news then, eh?'

Before Iris could summon an answer, the maid called them through to dinner.

The wine they were served was the best quality Iris had tasted since before the war. Frisch bragged about the fact that it had come from a local vineyard, and she wondered if Paul had been altogether honest about his dealings with the Germans. There was no saying it was his wine, of course, and there was no checking the label, because it had been poured into Madame Hoffman's crystal decanter before it reached the table.

The food was more substantial than anything Iris had seen since rationing began. They started with artichoke hearts, drowning in a mousseline sauce, the unaccustomed richness of the whipped cream coating Iris's mouth until her tongue was thick with it. This was followed by chicken, roasted in butter, stuffed with olives and tarragon, served with yet another cream sauce, potato gratin, honey-glazed carrots, creamed spinach and peas stewed in even more butter. The Frisches tucked in as if they ate that way every day. Knowing the Germans took most of the French produce for themselves, Iris was quite certain they did.

Mason, who'd been surprisingly quiet all evening, pushed the food around his plate, cutting the chicken into increasingly smaller pieces with barely any of it reaching his mouth.

'Is it not to your taste?'

Frisch appeared more annoyed than concerned for his guest, taking Mason's reluctance to gorge himself on the food as a snub. He'd put on a good show and he liked to see his efforts appreciated.

Mason rubbed his stomach. 'It's excellent.'

He'd gulped down a couple of the quince paste sweets from the box Iris had given him on the short walk from the car to the house, and she suspected the wolfsbane she'd added might be having an effect. Already his eyes were looking red around the rims, and the way he held himself suggested he was battling stomach cramps.

'I'm a bit out of sorts. It must be something I ate before I came.'

Iris presented a sympathetic face. 'He hasn't been well for days.'

She placed her hand on top of his, lowering her voice and

speaking slowly, as if he were a half-wit. 'You haven't been well since you arrived in Dijon. I wonder if the local water doesn't suit you, or perhaps it's the climate.'

Madame Frisch helped herself to more potatoes. 'I'll never get used to this French food. There are too many vegetables. It's unsophisticated.'

Frisch lifted his plate, gesturing to his wife to serve him another helping of creamed spinach. 'Mason told me the two of you met in London.'

What else had Mason told him? What did he suspect? Iris swallowed, trying to dislodge the stewed peas that had stuck in her throat.

'That's right.'

She stabbed a piece of chicken with her fork and pushed it into her mouth, hoping it would dislodge the peas on its way down.

'You're a journalist, married to an Englishman.'

It wasn't a question, but a statement. He'd obviously done his homework on her. Iris used the excuse of her mouth being too full of chicken to answer.

Frisch pushed his fork into a honey-glazed carrot. 'And a spy, too, from what I hear.'

Every bone in Iris's body turned to liquid. She tried not to gag on the chicken, which had finally begun to work its way down the back of her throat, taking the peas with it. She shot a look at Mason. Did he believe the accusation levelled against her?

Mason's hand shook as he lifted one of Madame Hoffman's prized crystal glasses to his lips and gulped the wine, placing it back on the table a little too heavily.

'I never said she was a spy. I only said she'd been a useful associate during my last few months in London.' His lips trembled from the effects of the wolfsbane. 'She was very pleasurable company too.'

Iris finally allowed herself to breathe. They'd mistaken which side she was on. Mason had led them to believe she'd helped him in London, probably to save face after his wife refused to leave England when he was expelled. She forced another piece of chicken into her mouth and commented on its succulence. It was best to say nothing about London.

'Are you happy to be back in France?'

Iris nodded at Madame Frisch's question, nervous of where it might be leading. 'I'm very glad to be home.'

Frisch leaned forward, his breath sweet from the wine and so much cream. 'And it's quite a home you have. I've heard the house your aunt left you is very special, that she made it famous in her books.'

'I didn't know she was planning to leave me such a generous legacy.' She knew where he was driving the conversation and there was nothing she could do to avert it.

'Max Schiller was billeted with her until his disappearance.' He raised his eyebrows, and leaned in closer, proving to Iris that you didn't have to be arrested to face questioning. It could take place under any circumstances, even across a dinner table. 'Have you heard his name before?'

'I've heard it mentioned about the town.'

Is this why she'd been invited to dinner, so he could find out what she knew about Schiller's death?

Mason patted his lips with his napkin. Iris realised he'd begun to dribble. It was the perfect excuse to get away. She slid him a sideways look.

'You don't look well. Would you like to go home?'

Madame Frisch looked affronted. 'You haven't had dessert yet. It's coffee ice cream with raspberries.'

Mason shifted uncomfortably in his seat, as if he were about to run from the room. 'I'm fine. It'll pass in a minute. I wouldn't want to miss dessert.'

Iris took a sip of wine, still feeling the heat of Frisch's attention on her. She raised her glass and smiled, her stomach clenching as their eyes locked. 'Delicious.'

The maid came in to clear the plates, and as if by unspoken agreement, they each fell silent. Iris recognised the woman as one of the regular customers at Adele's café. She tried to catch her eye, but she refused to look up as she balanced the greasy plates on top of one another and carried them away.

The pause in the conversation seemed to highlight the artificiality of the situation. This wasn't the occupiers' home or their country. They were here by brute force and they had no moral right to entertain in a house that didn't belong to them. And Iris was here because she had no choice, because Frisch wanted to observe her at close quarters.

While they waited for the dessert, Frisch lit a cigar, puffing great clouds of fragrant smoke across the table.

'Now Schiller isn't here to occupy that fine house of yours, perhaps it's time it was requisitioned. I can think of plenty of German officers who'd appreciate it. I hear the garden is something special.'

Iris froze, her fingers threatening to snap the stem on Madame Hoffman's crystal wineglass as she gripped it. 'The garden is a labour of love. It takes a lot of upkeep and whoever took it on would have to know how to manage the bees. They're a menace if you get on the wrong side of them.'

Mason leaned back in his chair, avoiding the cigar smoke as it wafted across the table. 'I've already inspected the house. It's no place for a German officer. It's dark and draughty and too overlooked from the square. You can't come and go without everyone knowing your business.'

Was this what Mason really thought, or was he trying to save it for her? 'It's not the easiest of houses to live in, but I've always considered it my home, for all its faults.'

Frisch grinned. 'I wouldn't throw you out after you've been such a loyal ally. Mason would never forgive me.'

This was how they played with people, threatening to turn their lives on end, then pretending it was a joke. If it hadn't been for

Mason's intervention, Frisch would almost certainly have gone ahead with his intentions and taken Eva's house from her. Or else, she'd have been forced to share it with a German officer, as Eva had done.

Frisch took another puff on his cigar, his eyes narrowing on Mason. 'Talking of houses, it's time you were settled somewhere decent. You might walk and talk like an Englishman, but you've proved you're a German at heart. I don't like to see you roughing it in a hotel. A man needs his privacy and his comforts. Come and see me tomorrow. There's a list of properties we're looking to requisition. One of them might suit you.'

'That's very good of you. I'll take you up on it.'

They fell silent again, as the maid returned with dessert. Mason's eyes followed her movements, his face betraying his growing panic as she placed a large bowl of ice cream in front of him. He took a deep breath, his Adam's apple shifting as he swallowed, forcing down whatever was rising in his throat.

'It looks delicious.'

He only managed a couple of mouthfuls before he got up from the table, swaying as he dropped his linen napkin on the floor. 'You must forgive me for cutting the evening short. I must have a fever coming on.'

Despite the chill of the dessert, a sweat had broken out on his brow. Frisch gave him an unsympathetic look before reluctantly showing him and Iris to the door. Madame Frisch remained two steps behind, making weak noises and rubbing her hands together as if she were witnessing a tragedy. Iris could only hope she was. With any luck, Mason would be dead by morning.

The fresh evening breeze took the heat out of Iris's cheeks as they left the house, crunching their way along the gravel drive to the car. Her stomach hurt from eating so much food, an unsettled feeling of nausea hanging somewhere between her chest and her throat. She hated herself for having eaten at the table of the enemy, but to have refused the invitation would have caused suspicion.

They drove back into the town in silence, Iris trying, now and then, to make polite conversation. 'It was good of you to talk Commander Frisch out of requisitioning Eva's house. It would break my heart to lose it.'

He took his eyes off the road and turned to her. For a moment, she thought he was going to force a kiss on her. She took a deep breath, bracing herself, as he leaned forward and opened his mouth, his vast stomach suddenly retching uncontrollably. Trapped in the moving car there was no escape from the cascade of vomit as it poured from him, covering her arms and her thighs and soaking her dress.

'Damn.'

He stopped the car and rushed out, doubled-over with convulsions, as he staggered to the side of the road.

Iris climbed out of the car, desperate to get away from the stench, her handkerchief useless against the slime of the warm vomit as she tried to wipe it off.

She stood at a distance, her stomach heaving at the mess, as Mason emptied the last remains of his stomach into the gutter, the curdled cream and butter he'd regurgitated plastered around his mouth. She buried her revulsion deep in an attempt to show concern.

'Are you all right?'

'That maid of Frisch's must have poisoned the food.'

'If that were the case, we'd both be ill. It must be a virus.'

It was almost curfew. She couldn't risk being caught on the streets, even with Mason, and she was desperate to get out of her soiled dress.

'It's getting late. You don't mind if I leave, do you?'

At a brisk pace, she could be home in ten minutes. She couldn't stand another second of looking at Mason. Just the smell of him was enough to make her retch.

He nodded, dismissing her with his hand, as another wave of convulsions overtook him. She didn't need telling twice. If he had a seizure and died in the street, she had the excuse of the curfew for abandoning him. She couldn't be held to blame for any of it.

Chapter 30

Iris had been wearing her favourite green silk dress, the one with the sweetheart neckline, a neat waist and a flared skirt that brushed her calves as she walked. She'd bought it in Paris before the war. It had worn well because she kept it for best, folding it away in tissue paper, with sprigs of lavender to deter the moths. Jack had called it her Rita Hayworth dress because of the way it made her walk, as if she were the most sensual woman alive. Now, the stains and the sour smell of Mason's vomit embedded in the fabric had ruined it for good.

It was a miracle that the Hermès scarf she'd been wearing had remained unscathed. Eva had given it to her for her birthday only months before the outbreak of the war. Neither of them could have known it would be Eva's final gift, or that it would be the last time they'd see each other. Now, the fine silk square with its distinctive pattern of horse-drawn buses, and young people sitting at a table in the centre was more precious to her than anything.

It had been two days since the dinner party and she'd heard nothing from Mason. He must have been too ill to leave his bed. If he'd died like a dog on the side of the road, she'd have heard about it by now.

The late summer sun was warm on Iris's face as she sat in the garden, the nearby cluster of apple trees shielding her from the breeze as she thought of Jack. She still had no way of knowing if he was dead or alive. Thoughts of him filled her every waking minute. Every time she closed her eyes, he appeared before her, his troubled face turning away as she reached her hand out to him.

The last of the jasmine flowers were still holding on, filling the air with their bitter fragrance and beckoning the bees to come hither as the down-looking trumpets of the brugmansia flowers played their silent song. This was the only place where Iris could think clearly. It was here she felt closest to Eva, where everything she'd nurtured conspired to give her a hug.

Eva was no longer there to offer comfort, but the bulbs she'd planted before she died would still flower in the spring, and the fruit trees she'd pruned would blossom and fruit. Eva used to say that gardening was about the continuation of life; that those with the most defiant spirits made the best gardeners, because those were the ones who refused to believe in death. Here, in the paradise Eva had created, it was possible to believe life would go on forever, that Jack would return, and that one day everything would be right with the world.

The spell was broken by the gentle rattle of the gate. 'Iris, are you there? It's me, Clemence. I tried the front door, but there was no answer.'

Iris undid the bolt and Clemence strolled in carrying a small basket. 'I've brought some eggs. My girls are laying so well these days, I can hardly keep up with them.' She sat on a garden bench and looked around at the vegetable beds, the flowers and the trees with satisfaction. 'Eva was famous for her cookery books, but this was where her real work took place. It was her best-kept secret, and it's a privilege to be able to sit here and enjoy it.'

'She once told me she put all her passion into the soil, and in return it gave her the kind of love that never lets you down.' Iris didn't know if this was the saddest thing Eva had ever told her, or the most positive.

Clemence placed the basket of eggs beside her on the bench and settled in for a chat. 'Talking of love, why aren't you in England with Jack? Don't tell me it's the war keeping you apart. I know you weren't living in Paris before you came here, because Eva told me you were in London. It's the reason she wasn't expecting you at her wedding.'

Where to start with the story of her and Jack? How much was she prepared to confess?

'Jack and I aren't together anymore.'

She couldn't admit that he might have died at the hands of the Germans when they set fire to the maquis camp, or that it wouldn't have happened if he hadn't followed her to France to settle a score with Mason. If she hadn't agreed to act as bait in a honey trap to catch a traitor, her marriage would still be intact and Jack would still be safe. But that wasn't how wars were won.

Sworn to secrecy, she couldn't disclose any of these things. And if she did, it would make them real. As long as they remained unspoken, there was still a chance that Jack was alive, that he'd come back to her.

'Your falling out with Jack. Is it something to do with that German officer I've seen visiting the house?'

Iris nodded.

Clemence sucked her teeth. 'Filthy German. What were you thinking?'

'It's complicated. There's a war on. I don't have to tell you about the kind of compromises we're all forced to make.'

'Poor Jack.'

Iris held her breath, refusing to let the tears come. Not only tears for Jack this time, but because she'd disappointed Clemence.

'You didn't expect the brute to turn up here, did you?'

Iris shook her head.

'I saw the way he grabbed you when you ran out of the house after Paul the other day. That was no gesture of love on his part; that was possession.'

'It was a misunderstanding, that's all.'

'You must have broken Jack's heart.'

If she'd been harsh, Iris could have withstood it, but the words were spoken with love and a level of understanding Clemence couldn't possibly have, given that she knew nothing of the situation.

'Sometimes it feels as if the war will never end.'

'Given the right amount of determination, most battles can be fought and won.'

The tears were coming now anyway. Iris couldn't help them. She didn't deserve Clemence's understanding. 'It's a bit of a mess.'

'Do you want that filthy German gone?'

'He's not that easy to shake off.'

'Some men are like that.'

Suddenly the breeze got up, bringing with it a rush of scent from the late roses and sending the heavy blooms nodding on their stems. Clemence pointed to the nearest shrub, which was still carrying a mass of ruby flowers.

'Eva planted that in honour of you. She called you her English rose; so full of beauty and elegance, but resilient, and not without thorns. She cursed it every time she pruned it. However careful she was, she always ended up scratched and bleeding. We all need to display our weapons now and then. Eva knew that better than anybody.'

Iris glanced at the rose bush, its stems bowing under the weight of the flowers. 'She said the cuts were worth it, because of the blooms that always came the following year.'

'This filthy officer of yours reminds me of the other German. He turned up when he wasn't wanted.'

'You mean Schiller?'

'They have the same overbearing manner, the same capacity to ruin lives and not turn a hair as they do it. Of course, Eva had no choice but to put up with him.'

'I suppose she'd have been punished if she hadn't looked after him the way he demanded.'

'She wasn't doing it out of the goodness of her heart, that's for certain. She was doing it to survive. I know the battle she fought, and it's not all that different to yours. It's all well and good trying to keep on side with the Germans, but all that compromise counts for nothing if you happen to displease them, whether you meant to or not. If you take my advice, you'll get him out of your life before he starts treating you any worse than he already has. You know what happened to Eva. Don't let the same happen to you, my love.'

Chapter 31

'Seeing Commander Frisch's house the other evening set me thinking.'

It wasn't Frisch's house. It belonged to the Hoffmans. Iris bit back the correction. She was finding it increasingly difficult to humour Mason, but she couldn't risk losing his trust or making him suspicious.

This was the first time she'd seen him for days. He'd looked pasty when he appeared at Eva's front door, and had dropped a little weight, the trousers of his officer's uniform sliding off his stomach at an unsightly angle. He claimed to have recovered from whatever it was that had affected him and insisted he was fighting fit. It wasn't a seizure he'd suffered at the side of the road when she'd left him that night, but simply a bout of vomiting. He didn't seem concerned that she hadn't stayed with him, and nor did he apologise for throwing up on her favourite dress. He didn't appear to recognise the concept of understanding or empathy. This was what made him the man he was. Now, she was disappointed to hear he was feeling better.

'Would you like a slice of carrot cake? I made it especially for you.'

'Is it one of Eva's recipes?'

'It's a war cake recipe. From the Ministry of Food in England. I've added ground ginger, almonds and honey to make it more lavish.'

He didn't need any more convincing, and he pounced on it as soon as she offered him the larger of the two slices she'd already cut, slathered in honey, and with the addition of white hemlock, which thanks to its distinctive carrot flavour, she hoped he wouldn't detect. It had been a chore, baking two separate cakes, but she didn't want him to become suspicious of her not eating the food she gave him if he fell ill afterwards.

According to *Frossard's Herbal*, white hemlock had the capacity to deliver a cardiovascular collapse. So far, all Iris had managed to inflict on Mason was sickness, headache and hallucinations. She needed to finish him off, but he was proving resilient to everything she fed him. The problem was getting enough of the poisons into him without him detecting it. Too much and he'd taste it, not enough and it was ineffective. She also suspected that cooking was killing off the toxic properties of the ingredients.

She watched him wolf down cake, the honey glazing his lips and masking the poison. 'Would you like a second slice?'

He nodded, brushing the crumbs from his chest onto her freshly swept floor. 'Then I'll take you out. There's a place I want to show you.'

It was risky to be seen with him in public, with the critical eyes of the town on her. She put a second large slice of cake in front of him and drizzled extra honey over it.

'Where are we going?'

'To look at a house. You heard what Frisch said the other night. I've done my bit for the Third Reich and now they're rewarding me with a place of my own. An officer of my rank can't be expected to stay in a hotel forever.'

She looked away as he shovelled the second slice of cake into his mouth. Mason's rank was purely honorary, bestowed on him because of the British military secrets he'd betrayed and because his cousin was part of Hitler's inner circle. Deserving didn't come into it.

'Is the house for sale?'

'We're the conquerors. We have the right to take anything we please.' He swallowed the last of the cake and picked up his officer's cap, spinning it in his clumsy fingers. 'It was on the list of recommendations Frisch gave me. Let's take a look.'

There was little traffic on the roads these days, and Iris kept her head down, hoping not to be recognised, as people peered through the windows of Mason's black Citroën to see who was inside.

'How far is it?'

She tried not to sound uneasy as he drove through the centre of the town, wondering what the Grand Dukes of Burgundy, who'd once ruled the region, would have thought of the swastikas that now adorned the public buildings, certain they'd have fought the occupying enemy to the death rather than acquiesce to them.

Mason suddenly stopped the car. She glanced at him, wondering if the white hemlock had begun to have its murderous effect, and braced herself for more vomit.

'Is something wrong?'

'What do you think?'

His face was as bright as she'd ever seen it and displaying no signs of poisoning. He gestured towards the house on the corner as if he were enacting a magic trick.

'I think I deserve this, don't you?'

The half-timbered merchant's house dated back to the fifteenth century and was one of the most notable buildings in Dijon. Like many houses of this stature, the descendants of the original owner still lived in it. Requisitioning it would amount to theft on the grandest scale and the crime would be taking place in broad daylight. Iris held her nerve, preparing herself for whatever was about to unfold.

'What will happen to the family who live here?'

'They'll be made to leave.'

How far would this once seeming Englishman go to make sure he was accepted as one of the victors? He'd already sacrificed his British connections, his wife and his original allegiances to assimilate himself with what he perceived to be the winning side. If he'd been brought up in Germany, she might have understood it, but the fact that he'd been part of the British establishment made it all the more despicable.

He climbed out of the car and hammered on the front door, clicking his heels and saluting when the owner of the house answered.

Madame Beauchamp was a little older than Iris and already a widow, her husband having been shot by a drunken German soldier who accosted him in the street one night, accusing him of breaking the curfew.

Iris waited on the pavement, reluctant to be part of the conversation, until Mason summoned her to join him. To avoid suspicion, she had no choice but to appear an accessory to his crime.

Madame Beauchamp watched Mason swagger into the house as if he already owned it, her shoulders tensed as she forced herself to stand tall. Her shabby dress and slippers, the novel upturned on the armchair in the sitting room, suggested she hadn't been expecting visitors.

'What can I do for you?'

Her eyes, sharp as cut-glass, snatched a look at Iris, the accusation behind it needing no more than a split second to make itself felt.

Iris looked away, glancing at the family photographs on the bureau, the bundle of knitting in the basket beside the sofa. This wasn't simply a grand house, it was a family home.

Mason explained in his stumbling French that he'd come to take a look around the house. It wasn't a request, but an order. If he liked it, he'd requisition it.

Madame Beauchamp's slim figure appeared to grow even taller in the face of his command, her hands curling into fists.

'But this is my home. It's where I live with my daughter.'

'It's up to me to decide who lives here.'

There was a look of the snake in Mason's eyes, a determination to dominate and humiliate that Iris had seen too often. It made her want to run from the house and never set foot in it again, but if she was going to save the situation, she had to dig in and fight. He couldn't get away with throwing Madame Beauchamp and her daughter out of their home and claiming it for himself, even if the regime they were living under assumed the right to do just that. Somehow, she had to find a way to prevent it happening.

The smell of violets gave every room they explored an atmosphere of fragile gentility, while the Aubusson rugs on the polished oak floors, the crystal chandeliers and the silk wallpaper, suggested nothing had changed in thirty years or more. Damask curtains hung in swags at every window, the Belgian lace dappling the fierce afternoon light as it forced its way in. If only the invaders could be weakened so easily, the Allies would already be well on their way to liberating France.

Madame Beauchamp followed them around the house, answering Mason's questions about the temperature of the rooms in the winter and the upkeep of the garden. All the while, Iris stared at her feet, refusing to be a part of the conversation. Invading a country was bad enough, but invading a home was the lowest act of an oppressor.

While Mason inspected the pantry, Iris crept over to Madame Beauchamp, who stood on the threshold of her own kitchen, reluctant to step inside, as if she knew in her heart she'd already lost it. She looked the other way when Iris spoke.

'If he makes you leave, do you have somewhere else to go?'

'The Germans took over my husband's business after they murdered him. We have nothing left. This house is all I have.'

The gaps where large pieces of furniture had once stood, the shadows on the walls, where paintings had once hung, suggested their personal possessions were being sold off, one by one. How else were they to find the money to eat?

Iris stood a little closer to Madame Beauchamp, angling her back to Mason, in case he suddenly appeared from the pantry, mouthing her promise, so it would be seen rather than heard. 'I'll do what I can to stop this. I'll . . .'

She was interrupted by the sound of the front door opening. Madame Beauchamp glanced over her shoulder. 'That's my daughter, Helene. I beg you not to tell her why you're here.'

'Please, trust me to help you.'

'I'll die before I'll turn to a collaborator for help.'

This couldn't go on a moment longer. Iris called to Mason, telling him it was time to leave.

He was on his knees in the pantry, checking for mouse-droppings. He swayed, gasping for breath as he got to his feet and staggered towards her, grabbing his head with both hands to steady himself.

Iris's heart swelled with hope. 'Are you all right? You must have stood up too quickly.'

She helped him into a chair, while Madame Beauchamp watched from a distance, her lips pressed together with contempt. The scene was so thick with possibility that Iris failed to notice the heavy tread of approaching feet until Helene appeared with a basket of shopping.

'What's going on?'

Madame Beauchamp seemed more alarmed that her daughter was about to find out about the requisition than the fact that a German officer might be dying in her kitchen.

Iris grabbed Mason's shoulder, trying to keep him upright in the chair as his body slumped forward, his face turning blue as he fought for breath.

'Could someone get him some water?'

She had to be seen to be doing something. Water was no

antidote to poison and if he couldn't swallow it, perhaps he'd choke on it. None of them could be expected to know what to do to save him under such conditions.

When Madame Beauchamp didn't move, Helene put down her shopping and grabbed a glass, filling it with water from the tap and thrusting it at Iris.

Madame Beauchamp shifted her weight as she leaned against the kitchen doorway.

'Should I go for a doctor?'

There was nothing genuine about her offer and no trace of concern in her voice. Iris guessed the gesture had been made to avoid later accusations. Nobody wanted to be blamed for standing by and doing nothing while an officer of the Third Reich died in front of you, even if they were part of the regime responsible for your husband's murder.

Iris pushed her face close up to Mason, shaking him to attention. 'Would you like a doctor?'

It was the last thing she wanted, but like Madame Beauchamp, she couldn't risk being accused of denying him medical attention if he requested it.

He pushed the glass away as she pressed it towards him. 'No. I'll be fine. Help me to get up.'

'Don't try to move. Wait until you feel better.'

But already Mason was struggling to his feet, leaning heavily on her arm and almost bringing her to her knees. 'I need some air. Get me outside. Quickly.'

She pulled him towards the door, dragging his dead weight as he struggled for breath. 'Please excuse us.'

Madame Beauchamp moved out of the doorway, allowing just enough space for them to stumble through. Helene remained by the sink, her arms folded across her chest, unmoved by Mason's suffering.

As they left the kitchen, Madame Beauchamp spat out a single word, aiming it at the back of Iris's head.

'Traitor.'

Indignation burned in Iris's heart, but it would have been too dangerous to correct Madame Beauchamp's assumption.

Mason seemed to rally a little once he was on the pavement. The heat of the late summer air must have relaxed his lungs, because his breathing became easier and the trembling in his hands steadied.

'Are you in any pain?'

He looked at her, his face now having turned from blue to livid from the strain of trying to breathe. 'What do you mean?'

She shrugged, making it up as she went along. 'Your heart, for instance. Is it beating normally? Do you have stiffness in your limbs, or stomach cramps like before?'

She had to make it seem like an ongoing problem. He couldn't be allowed to consider his symptoms in terms of simple cause and effect.

He leaned against the car, his face clouding with worry while he thought about it. 'You think there might be something wrong with me?'

'I'm only asking. You seem to have had a few turns lately.'

He put his hands in front of his face and stared at them, and she wondered if he could see properly. 'You're not fit to drive. Shall we sit for a few minutes?'

Meek as a puppy he climbed into the car, staring out of the window at the road ahead. 'It must be the heat. I'm not used to this kind of weather.'

'It's humid today. There's a storm brewing.'

Something had to give. She couldn't go on like this indefinitely. The pressure was enormous. She longed for thunder, for the crack of lightning. There was always the hope that it would find him and strike him dead, but she couldn't leave it to chance.

'What did you think of the house?' He sank lower in the seat and looked at her from the corner of one eye. 'It's one of the best there is.'

'It's a bit gloomy, don't you think? And draughty.'

Mason blinked, second thoughts rattling inside his head. 'Really?'

'It gets quite cold here in the winter. You'd notice the draughts then. Not only from the windows and the doors, but coming up through the floors. There are only thin rugs between your feet and the floorboards. Beneath that, there's nothing but the foundations of the house and good old-fashioned dirt.'

'But it looks so grand.'

'I guarantee that if you take that house, you won't have a decent night's sleep ever again.'

It was a promise she made to herself, the promise she owed to Madame Beauchamp and Helene.

Mason appeared to be recovering from his turn. The white hemlock she'd fed him was still having an effect somewhere in his system, but it wasn't enough to be fatal.

'I wouldn't rush into making a decision, not while you're feeling unwell. You're fine at the hotel for now.'

He was quiet for a moment; his breathing still disturbed, which she took to be a good sign.

'Tell me, Iris. What kind of house do you think we should have? Where is it you'd like to live?'

She hesitated, making a great play of thinking about it. 'We should take our time choosing somewhere. Wherever we settle, it'll be for life, so we shouldn't rush into it.'

He nodded, his lips pursed. 'Together, until death parts us. I like that.'

'So you'll wait before deciding on a house?'

Her plan was to put him off every one he suggested, so there'd be no more victims created by his sense of entitlement.

'We should widen our search.' He grabbed her hand, squeezing it with a force that proved his strength was coming back. 'We have a good life ahead of us. I'll make you the queen of this town. You'll be the envy of every other woman in Dijon.'

As he started the car, she knew better than to remind him what had happened to the last queen of France. And as for being the envy of every woman in Dijon, suspicion was already building against her. The longer her pretence went on, the more chance there was that Mason would see through it, and the more likely she was to be condemned as a collaborator by the people in the town. It was more important than ever to deal with Mason as quickly as possible.

Chapter 32

Iris was impatient for the poisons she was feeding Mason to have a more immediate and deadly effect. Desperate to find something that would work quickly, she returned to the flowerbed behind the shed to see if anything else there might be useful. And there it was, a rogue plant that had no rightful place in a kitchen garden: deadly nightshade.

She waited until dusk to collect the lethal harvest, whispering *good evening* to the bees on her way to picking twenty glossy black berries, pulling them one by one from their green star-shaped cuffs, careful not to spill the juice, before returning to the kitchen with a handful of death that could easily be mistaken for blackcurrants.

It was worth using some of her precious stash of sugar to find out if a poisonous jam would work. She only needed a small amount, enough to dollop on an English baked scone. Mason wouldn't be able to resist it.

She'd just put the berries on a low heat on the stove when Clemence appeared at the kitchen window, waving to catch her attention. Iris let her in, setting her expression to cheerful to hide what she was really up to. Lately, there was a coolness in Clemence's manner that Iris regretted. It was all because of Mason.

After what had happened to Eva, it must have been difficult for her to witness another filthy German being welcomed into the house.

'Look who I found outside.'

Christophe was standing behind Clemence, his figure hunched as he cradled his injured arm. It was impossible to tell if he was in pain or whether the gesture had become a habit.

'Christophe, would you like a tisane?'

'No, thank you. I didn't mean to intrude. That soldier is back in the square, the one who shot the pigeon. I was keeping an eye on him.'

Iris gave Clemence a nervous glance. 'You don't want to let him know you're watching him, Christophe. He won't need much of an excuse to arrest you.'

Christophe twitched at the accusation. 'I wasn't watching him. If anyone asks, I was resting against the wall while I got my breath back.'

'Have you been making deliveries for your mother?'

'It's hard to steer the bicycle with only one hand. I have to take it slowly.'

There was no sign of his bicycle outside, but he appeared too anxious for Iris to question him about it. If he'd come to talk about his troubles, he was unlikely to do so with Clemence scrutinising him.

'If you don't have time for a tisane, let me fetch you a jar of honey to take away with you.'

When she came back from the cellar, the two of them were sitting at the kitchen table. If anyone could encourage someone as introverted as Christophe into conversation, it was Clemence.

She grinned at Iris, as if a small victory had been won. 'I've been telling Christophe that he should make more effort to see his old friends. It doesn't do any good to go around moping all the time.'

'Maman says I should stop feeling sorry for myself.'

Clemence tapped her knuckles on the table as if to mark the

scoring of points. 'Well, there you go.'

'Nobody wants to know me.'

Iris forced a smile, trying to jolly him along. 'There must be lots of girls who'd be glad of your company.'

'Like who?'

'There's Solange. She's been trying to get your attention for a while. You must have noticed.'

Clemence chuckled. 'Now there's a catch. She's one of the prettiest girls in the town and the best dressed. You'd never be missing a button with her to look after you.'

'She's only doing it because she works for Maman.'

'She's doing it because she likes you.'

'Look at me. What's there to like?'

Tears were brimming in his eyes. Iris wanted to take them away, to cry on his behalf. 'You're a beautiful young man, Christophe. You're the only one who can't see it.'

The legs of his chair scraped across the stone floor as he pushed it back from the table and left the room. Iris had gone too far. In trying to help, she'd upset him. She went after him as he stormed out of the house, waving the jar of honey.

'Don't forget this.'

He stopped at the front gate to take it from her, stuffing it in his jacket pocket. 'Thank you.' His eyes ranged across the square, as if to check to see if anyone was watching. 'You won't tell Maman I accepted it, will you?'

It was a ridiculous concern and not even worth remarking on. 'I meant what I said about Solange. She told me herself how much she likes you.'

'It's only because there's no one else to catch her eye. What kind of future could a one-armed man give her?'

Back in the house, Iris offered Clemence a drink, but she didn't seem inclined to stay. 'What Christophe said about watching the soldier was a lie. He'd been sitting on your garden wall for at least twenty minutes before the German appeared.'

This didn't come as a surprise. Iris regularly saw him loitering around the town and the market. Sometimes, she'd see him in the square or near the churchyard, hunched over a book, or staring into the distance. She'd even spotted him near Madame Beauchamp's house the day she visited with Mason. After everything he'd been through, Christophe was a young man who didn't know what to do with himself.

Clemence retrieved something from her apron pocket and pushed it into Iris's hand. 'I came to give you this. I thought you might like it.'

It was a photograph of Eva, Jack and Iris. It must have been taken in the garden sometime in the early 1930s, during one of Iris and Jack's regular summer visits. The three of them were sitting on the bench in the shade of the apple tree, squeezed in shoulder to shoulder, hip to hip, where there was only room for two. All three of them were laughing. Love came off the picture in waves. It was so overwhelming she could hardly breathe.

Clemence studied the reaction on Iris's face. 'It was Eva's birthday. We'd just drunk a bottle of her homemade elderflower wine when I took the picture.'

It was a reminder of everything that was lost. Iris stroked the photograph, soothing it as if it were a restless cat. If only she could show it to Jack, to remind him what they were missing, but it was probably too late.

'Can I keep it?'

'Of course.'

Clemence's attention was suddenly drawn to the berries, which were still warming gently in a copper pan on the stove. Her eyes lingered on the bowl of sugar beside them.

'You're making jam. Is it one of Eva's recipes?'

Iris nodded, hoping Clemence didn't ask for any once it was made. It was impossible to buy sugar these days, which meant jam had become a rare luxury, and it would be awkward to refuse her request.

Clemence walked over to the stove and sniffed, turning her nose up at the glossy black skins. 'Eva made the same jam a few weeks before she died. I recognise the smell of the berries. I happened to visit as she was spooning it into the jars. She tried to hide them from me. Sugar is so precious these days I don't suppose she wanted to share it.'

'Judging by the smell, I don't imagine it'll taste all that good. Maybe Eva felt the same way.'

'She said it was for Schiller. A special recipe just for him. It was unlike her to be so ungenerous.'

The realisation struck Iris like a body blow. If these were the same berries, as Clemence claimed, then Eva must have been using them to poison Schiller, just as Iris was trying to poison Mason.

It couldn't be a coincidence, when everything Eva had left behind pointed to the same action. The flowerbed behind the shed where she'd cultivated the poisonous plants, the jars full of toxic leaves, seeds and flowers stored in the cellar, the bags of sugar she'd stockpiled and the jars of honey. All the clues were there.

'Did Eva cook a lot of special recipes for Schiller?'

'The brute demanded it. No one else was offered so much as a taste of them.'

The pan had begun to overheat. Already the air was acrid with the stench of deadly nightshade. Iris opened the window, letting in a blast of fresh air to dispel the odour.

Iris recalled what Clemence had told her about Schiller's behaviour before he shot the women in the field, how he'd become wild and unpredictable, and even more aggressive than his uniform sanctioned. How he thought his mind and body were under attack, but he couldn't work out what was causing it.

'Can you remember how Eva reacted to the news that Schiller had shot the women in the field?'

If Clemence thought the sudden change in the conversation was strange, she didn't show it. 'She was devastated. She felt responsible for their deaths, but I don't know why, when it was all him. I suppose she blamed herself for him living in the town.'

Whatever it was Eva had fed him must have affected his behaviour. This would have been why Eva blamed herself for the women's deaths. It must have been after the murder of the women in the field that Eva decided to put a stop to him, once and for all.

Everything was beginning to make sense. Eva had played the same game as Iris and ended up dead. If Iris was found out, she'd undoubtedly suffer the same fate. Her eyes drifted to the photograph of her, Eva and Jack, and the image of their three laughing faces. When the picture was taken, none of them had any idea how much tragedy was lurking. Even if she could turn back time; go back to that day and start again, it wouldn't change things. It was never in their power to control the events. Still, Iris couldn't give up now. Everyone in the photograph was lost to her. She had nothing else to lose.

'How do you think Schiller ended up in an unmarked grave in an unused part of the cemetery?'

Clemence shrugged. 'You shouldn't ask so many questions, Iris. No good will come of it.'

'Never mind that. Who do you think buried him there?'

'It would have been the local Resistance. They bury anything they don't want the Germans to know about in false graves in the main part of the cemetery, which they mark with wooden crosses to distinguish them from the real graves.

'That empty part of the cemetery isn't expected to be needed for a generation or more. You can see why it made sense for whoever killed Schiller to bury his body there and leave it unmarked. They relied on the fact that by the time anyone came to dig there, it would have decomposed beyond recognition. They couldn't have known about Emile's mission to dig under every ash tree in the town.'

'You say, *the Resistance*, but who specifically would have done this? Can you give me a name?'

Clemence sniffed, her nose wrinkling at the lingering smell of the deadly nightshade berries.

'Who was it, Clemence?'

'If you want to know about the Resistance, you need to talk to Monsieur Vallery. He's in charge of it all.'

This was the last name Iris expected to hear. Monsieur Vallery gave the impression that the world was passing him by. He behaved as if there wasn't a war on. Yet all the while, he was the head of the local Resistance. Iris thought she could always spot a lie, but he'd fooled her. She'd been taken in by his distracted manner. How cleverly he'd hidden his true nature.

Clemence folded her hands in front her chest, beseeching. 'You won't tell him it was me who gave him away, will you?'

Iris rushed over and gave her a hug, her heart almost breaking as she encompassed her tiny frame, her bones, brittle as eggshells. 'We're all on the same side, Clemence. Please don't ever forget that.'

Chapter 33

Before working out her next move, Iris wanted to know how Schiller had ended up in an unmarked grave in the cemetery. However efficiently he might have been killed, mistakes had been made and Iris was determined to learn from them. She couldn't risk the town suffering reprisals over Mason's death the way they had over Schiller's, and there was only one man who could answer her questions.

Monsieur Vallery stuck his pencil behind his ear and stood up as his assistant showed Iris into his office, greeting her in an unflustered manner that suggested his work was interrupted all the time.

'How can I help you, madame?'

Iris handed him a jar of Eva's honey. Seeing the papers scattered across his desk, she regretted not making an appointment. It had been wrong to appear unannounced when he was so busy. The gift she'd brought would hardly make up for the inconvenience.

He invited her to sit down, turning the jar over in his hands, admiring the toffee-coloured honey as it slipped against the glass. Hoping to catch him off guard, Iris came straight to the point.

'Schiller's death led to terrible reprisals. It's important such mistakes don't happen again.'

Monsieur Vallery set aside the jar. 'It doesn't do any good to dwell on such things, madame. You should leave it in the past where it belongs. If we're to survive the enemy occupation, we have to concentrate on the present. All we can do is live from day to day. There's nothing to be gained from looking back, because we cannot change what has passed.'

'But it's only by learning from the past that we can hope to be more successful in the future.'

He shifted his weight in the chair, demonstrating his impatience. 'I'm sorry, madame. I cannot help you.' He gestured once more to the papers on his desk. 'I'm a busy man. Now, if you'll excuse me. I have a client due any minute and I need to prepare.'

'Colette sends her good wishes.'

Colette was the code name used by Yvette. If Monsieur Vallery was as high up in the Resistance as Clemence suggested, she'd have delivered messages to him from the intelligence service in London who supported the network in this part of France. The fact that Iris knew Colette would prove she was connected to the same people.

'These are dark and troubling times, madame. There is suspicion everywhere and many are nursing wounds that will never heal. You cannot expect people to reveal what may be uncomfortable truths.'

Behind his irritation he was hiding a broken heart. She could hear it in his voice, see it in his eyes, as he avoided looking at her. She mustn't forget how fond he was of Eva. Her death had shaken him more than she'd first realised.

'It's a matter of justice, monsieur. A matter of honour.'

He was silent for a moment. The mention of Colette was making him think again. 'I was surprised to see you at Eva's funeral. She'd told me you would be unable to attend her wedding, because you were in London, not Paris as you claimed when you first arrived.'

'What she told you was correct. I haven't been in France since before the war.'

Her words were enough to indicate she'd travelled from an allied country into enemy-occupied territory when such movement was not only banned, but also highly dangerous.

'Were you Eva's accomplice, monsieur?'

He leaned forward in his chair and lowered his voice. 'Something had to be done to avenge the murder of those women who were shot in the field, but I cannot take the credit for it. Eva blamed herself for the atrocity and was determined to act alone.'

'Why did she blame herself for Schiller's actions?'

'I couldn't say, madame, but it lay heavily on her heart, and she was prepared to risk her own life to avenge their deaths.'

He cleared his throat, a flicker of grief misting his eyes. 'The news that Schiller had murdered the women in the field spread through the town like wildfire. You could smell the shock and anger in the air. The best of the men set to roaming the streets and the back alleys, hunting for him with any weapons they could lay their hands on.

'Eva had a visit from the maquis, who insisted on searching the house. When they didn't find him, she was warned to let them know as soon as he appeared. The maquis were as threatening as the Germans. Eva was shaken by their visit, but not enough to put her off her plan.

'It was gone midnight when Schiller finally appeared, stumbling over his own feet and out of his mind. He knew the maquis were after him, that they'd kill him if they got hold of him. A couple of them were in the square, watching the house, but they hadn't counted on him coming in through the back gate.'

'Did Eva tell the maquis he'd returned?'

'Eva wasn't about to let them finish Schiller off. It was her job. She'd been waiting for him all night, watching and planning. As soon as she heard the gate rattle, she slipped into the garden, warning him not to enter the house, because the maquis were waiting for him. He begged her to hide him. Now he was under threat, the murderer was suddenly a coward. She told him there was no hiding place in her home. Wherever she concealed him, they'd find him.

'She then told him not to worry, because she had a plan to save him from the maquis, but he had to remain silent and do exactly as she said. He knew if he didn't obey her, his death was imminent. The maquis would see to it. And so the fool trusted her.'

'What was the plan?'

'Eva offered to take him to someone who, for a fee, would lead him through the woodland trails beyond the town and safely out of the area. If he was prepared for the hard trek, they could eventually get him across the French border into Switzerland.

'He didn't think twice about the consequences if he was caught deserting the German army and begged Eva to take him to her contact straight away. Eva was already prepared for the next part of the plan, dressed from head to toe in black, with a shawl draped over her head, so she was less likely to be seen moving around the streets in the blackout.

'She led him through the town, taking the main streets, knowing the maquis would be searching down the back alleys and the quieter roads. So many hours into the curfew, there was no one to see them as they headed into the hills and the dense woodland, where anything was possible.

'Eva knew the area intimately and could anticipate every dip and curve of the landscape, even in the dark. She'd played there as a child, and as an adult, she'd foraged for mushrooms and wild herbs. This was her kingdom.'

'It's hard to believe Schiller followed her without question.'

'She didn't know if the plan would work, but he was scared and on the run. He was also wild and unpredictable. She had no idea what he might do at any given moment. She had a knife tucked in her belt in case he turned on her, but it was only to be used as a last resort. It was vital his death didn't look suspicious.'

'Where did she lead him?'

'Round in circles to begin with, weaving through the trees in the darkest part of the woods. She wanted to disorientate him, so he wouldn't know where he was, but she knew exactly where she was taking him, and when it came to it, he was too confused to realise he was on the edge of the ravine, his feet only one step away from the edge.'

Iris knew exactly where he meant. It was the same spot where they'd played as children all those years ago. The place that had since become a shrine to Nathalie.

'She pushed him over the cliff?'

'By now, he was raving, as if he'd suddenly realised he was a mass-murderer. Eva suggested he take a moment to catch his breath. In such an isolated place, there was no one to hear him screaming.

'As he claimed to be a good Catholic, Eva told him to get on his knees and pray to God for forgiveness. He couldn't have known how close he was to the edge as he stepped forward, preparing to fall to his knees.'

Monsieur Vallery paused, imaging the moment when Schiller went tumbling over the cliff, falling onto the rocks below.

'What happened after she'd killed him?'

'He wasn't dead. She could hear him screaming, his voice echoing around the ravine. It was as if he was too mad to die, as if whatever insanity was inside him was now keeping him alive.'

'What did she do?'

'It was too dangerous to leave him there half-alive. If the Germans found him, the whole town would face reprisals. If he'd been dead, his fall would have looked like an accident or suicide. But if he survived, Eva couldn't risk him working out that she'd sent him over the edge.

'Having abandoned him at the bottom of the ravine, Eva came to my door and told me everything that had happened. We agreed she should go home and get into bed. If anyone came looking for her or asking questions, she could say she'd been there all night.'

'What happened then?'

'I instructed my men to collect him from the ravine. If he was still alive, they were to finish him off and dispose of the body where it wouldn't be discovered.'

'Which is how he ended up in the unmarked grave?'

'When my men arrived, the body was nowhere to be found. It wouldn't have been possible to walk away from such a fall, and so I can only assume the maquis found him and disposed of his body. Eva had led Schiller to a place very close to their camp. It's possible that one of them heard him cursing after his fall and made sure he was dead before disposing of the body.'

'And no one from the maquis has ever admitted to anything?'

Monsieur Vallery lowered his head. 'No, and now they never will. Every one of them died when the Germans set fire to their camp.'

It was the camp where Jack had been. The men he'd called comrades were implicated in Eva's death. Each tragedy seemed to trip blindly over another's heels. She swallowed back her tears. It wouldn't do to think about Jack now.

'What happened next?'

'When Schiller failed to appear for duty the following morning, the Germans turned the town upside down searching for him. They wanted to question him over the shooting of the women in the field. Even by their standards it was an atrocity and he had to answer for it.

'When he couldn't be found, they assumed he'd been killed in a revenge attack. To prove their displeasure, they dragged Monsieur Legrand out of his office and shot him in cold blood.

'Eva was distraught, blaming herself for the Mayor's death. If she'd been able to kill Schiller outright, and make it look like an accident or suicide, then the Germans wouldn't have carried out the reprisals.

'Killing the Mayor wasn't enough to satisfy them, and they came for Eva the next day. They interrogated her for hours, but she told them nothing. She didn't know where Schiller was, or even if he was dead or alive, and thanks to the intervention of the maquis, neither did I. It tortured me that I had no information to offer to save her.'

'And so they shot her.'

'They released her from questioning and we thought she'd got away with it. It was the following day when one of them stole into her garden and shot her. It was the cruellest blow. I'll never forgive myself for it.'

The tears were running down Monsieur Vallery's cheeks. He wasn't to blame for any of it, but her words, however many times she tried to comfort him, meant nothing. His heart was broken, like so many others, and there was nothing Iris could do to mend it.

Chapter 34

Mushrooms
Deadly Web Cap – often mistaken for the chanterelle. Found among heather from August to November. A long-lasting poison which only begins to work two or three days after ingestion. Causes flu-like symptoms, including headache and vomiting. Also kidney failure. Potentially deadly.
Death Cap – found in woodland from August to November. Causes vomiting, diarrhoea and severe abdominal pain from 6–24 hours after ingestion. Also causes kidney and liver failure. Half a cap can kill.
Destroying Angel – pure white and deadly. Found in woodland, usually near birch trees during July to November. Effects are seen 8–24 hours after ingestion. Causes vomiting, diarrhoea and severe stomach pains. There may be a deceiving period of improvement before the effects of liver and kidney poisoning appear.
Funeral Bell – grows in clusters on tree stumps and bark – also on dead and decaying wood from August to November. Causes vomiting, liver damage and death.
Fool's Funnel – found in meadows. Causes excessive salivating and sweating in large doses – also abdominal pain, sickness,

diarrhoea, blurred vision and difficulty breathing – not usually fatal in healthy people.
Panther Cap – found in beech and oak woods from July to November. Causes intense sickness, hallucinations, confusion, a feeling of greater strength, delusions and convulsions. Not usually fatal.

It was Monsieur Vallery reminding her how Eva used to forage for mushrooms that sent Iris searching through *Frossard's Herbal* to check which types were safe to eat and which were not. If she was to debilitate Mason enough to assassinate him without it looking like murder, or without sending him on a paranoid killing spree, as had happened with Schiller, she needed a poison that would do more than simply upset his stomach in the small quantities she was able to disguise in her cooking.

The jars of mushrooms were lined up on a high shelf at the back of a cupboard in the cellar, the contents looking like dried chips of leaves, and harmless. The poisonous specimens, which Eva must have picked specifically for Schiller, had a tell-tale red dot in the corner of their label. The Destroying Angel seemed the most promising. The fact that it had a deceiving period of improvement before the effects of liver and kidney poisoning became evident would avoid the suspicion that the poisoning was directly due to anything she'd fed him. As the effects could take a while to manifest themselves, she had to plan ahead.

When Mason came for dinner that night, she served white mushroom risotto, strictly made to Eva's recipe, using locally sourced dried mushrooms. She only had to mention that it was one of Eva's recipes and he was guaranteed to gorge on the food, as if he knew he was being given something special and didn't want anyone else to have a share of it. Fame was a powerful thing when it came to influence.

He tucked into the first mouthful, his eyes gleaming with greed rather than pleasure. 'I've decided to stay the night. It's time you showed me how pleased you are to see me.'

Nothing in the world would induce Iris to sleep with him. With Jack still missing, her pledge held stronger than ever. So far, she'd kept Mason at bay with a combination of excuses and poison, but she couldn't hold him off forever without making him suspicious. She lowered her eyes, straightening her napkin on her lap, the butter from the risotto glistening on his lips too revolting to look at.

'You've been very patient. Losing Eva has affected me in all sorts of ways.'

He lifted his fork, holding it midway between the plate and his mouth. 'I don't want any more excuses. You've agreed to be my wife. I have rights. I won't take no for an answer.'

She had to think fast. She couldn't betray Jack again, not knowing the pain she'd caused him. She simply couldn't bring herself to do it.

Having recovered from his recent stomach troubles, Mason wolfed down the risotto without bothering to taste it. *Frossard's Herbal* said it would take between eight and twenty-four hours for the Destroying Angel to have an effect, which meant she couldn't rely on it to incapacitate him quickly enough to stop him forcing himself on her that evening. She needed something to work much faster if she wanted to keep him out of her bed.

'Is there enough parsley in the risotto, do you think?'

She doubted he'd noticed it, even though she'd used it lavishly as a garnish. Not everyone was keen on the strong taste of mushrooms, and the herb was meant to add freshness to the dish and cut through the garlic, among other things, which might have been a little heavy-handed.

He looked up, wiping away a grain of rice that had escaped from the corner of his mouth, eyeing her untouched plate. She'd deliberately served him a small portion, knowing it would leave him demanding more.

'Aren't you going to eat that?'

She pushed her plate towards him. 'The flavour of the mushrooms is too strong for me.'

He gave her a superior look. Even if it wasn't poisonous, she wouldn't have been able to stomach it, knowing what he expected from her later.

'They're an acquired taste. Your palette isn't sophisticated enough.'

'That must be it.'

His eyes roved around the dining room to see what else there was to eat. Already his mind had moved on to dessert, wondering which other recipes of Eva's Iris had conjured up.

'There are peaches poached in a little wine to follow.'

'Fruit? Is that all?'

'I didn't think you'd want anything too heavy on top of the risotto.'

'And tomorrow's picnic? You haven't forgotten about that.'

Mason had invited her to visit the Château Guillard, to see if it would make a suitable home for them. It was one of the largest houses in the area, with twelve acres of formal gardens and woodland, the surrounding vineyards and farmland having been sold off two generations ago. It had been unoccupied since the family fled to Switzerland at the start of the Occupation. As far as Mason was concerned, he had the right to claim it as his own.

They were to make a day of it. Iris had said she'd bring the picnic if Mason brought the wine. She planned to make sure he was taken ill in the vast grounds, where there was no one to come to his rescue, where his death could be made to look like an accident. Things couldn't go on like this any longer. She had to finish the job before he realised what she was up to, and the mushroom risotto was just the start of it.

Excusing herself from the table, she went to prepare the peaches, her mind spinning as she tried to figure out a way to avoid sleeping with him that wouldn't ruin her plans for tomorrow. If Mason was too ill, or upset with her, he'd cancel the trip to the château.

She put a saucepan on a low heat, adding a little wine and the peaches, while she tried to work out a plan to keep him out of her bed, but based on everything she'd already given him, there was nothing that would do the trick. While he waited for his dessert, she poured him a large glass of brandy, hoping he didn't notice her hand shaking as she gave it to him. Having pacified him with the drink, she slipped next door to ask Clemence if she had any ideas.

Clemence chewed her bottom lip while she thought about it. 'Eva didn't have this problem with Schiller. Any woman over twenty-five was of no interest to him.'

'How old was he?'

'Nearer to Eva's age than he was to twenty-five, let's put it that way.'

They were getting off the point and Iris didn't have much time. If Mason wandered into the kitchen and realised she was missing, she'd have even more questions to answer.

'Do you have any idea what I can do to knock Mason out? He'll get suspicious if I try plying him with too much alcohol and there's no guarantee it'll work.'

Clemence nodded, her eyes sparkling with an idea. 'Send him to Verona.'

Flippant answers weren't helpful. Didn't Clemence realise how serious this was, and how dangerous it could become if she didn't handle Mason properly? 'I'm sorry, Clemence, I don't understand what you mean.'

Already Clemence was rummaging in her handbag. 'I'm sure I have one left. I kept it for just this kind of emergency.' She pulled out a tiny leather purse, her fingers undoing the clasp and digging to the bottom.

'Here it is.' She presented a small tablet on her upturned palm, her face full of triumph. 'I knew there was one left.'

'What is it?'

'Veronal. Before the war, Doctor Bisset used to hand them out like sweets to anyone who couldn't sleep. Get this into his stomach and it's guaranteed to knock him out for the night. He might be a bit sluggish in the morning, but there shouldn't be any other effects.'

Iris gave Clemence a hug. It was a mistake to have doubted her. 'Thank you. I can't tell you how much you've saved me tonight.'

There was leftover carrot cake in the pantry. Iris cut a large slice and broke the pill into tiny pieces, tucking them deep into the sponge. She then made custard, using an egg from one of Clemence's hens, and poured it over the cake. If Mason gobbled it down quickly enough, he'd swallow all traces of the pill without detecting it.

He raised his eyebrows when she placed the pudding in front of him. 'This isn't peaches.'

'You didn't fancy them, so I made you this instead. It's a proper English pudding with custard, like you used to have at boarding school.'

He stabbed the edge of his spoon into the cake and began shovelling it into his mouth. Iris sat with a bowl of poached peaches in front of her, watching as each mouthful slithered down his throat, hoping the pill was still potent and counting the minutes, wondering how long it would need to take effect. He'd drunk plenty of wine and brandy over dinner, surely that should help.

Playing for time, she poured him another brandy and started clearing away the plates. 'I'll wash up and tidy the kitchen before we go to bed, so I won't have to do it in the morning.'

'Leave it. It can wait.'

'But . . .'

He grabbed her wrist, forcing her to put the dirty crockery back on the table and led her through to the sitting room.

'The washing-up can wait. I can't.'

He pulled her to him, kissing her roughly, his hands digging into her shoulders as he held her against her will. She tasted the sweetness of the vanilla on his breath, felt the smear of custard on his tongue as his kiss grew more insistent. How long would it take for the barbiturate to work? How far would she have to go with this charade? How long until the drug knocked him out and he released his grip?

Coming up for air, she angled her face as far away from him as she could get, playing for time. 'Would you like coffee?'

Coffee was probably the wrong thing to give him if she wanted him to sleep, but it was too late, she'd offered it to him now. Hopefully, the Veronal would already have knocked him out by the time it was made.

'Not now. Let's go to bed.'

He grabbed her arm, dragging her through the sitting room and up the stairs. She gripped the handrail, stumbling as they went, hardly able to catch her breath, her legs turning to liquid with fear.

'Don't you want to digest your dinner first?'

'Don't tease me, Iris. Not now you've got me all worked up.'

The plan wasn't working, the pill was taking too long to knock him out, or it had lost its potency. She had no idea how many years Clemence had been keeping it.

He kissed her again at the top of the stairs, his hands pulling at the buttons on her blouse. 'Which is your bedroom?'

There had to be a way out of this. 'You need to give me a minute.'

Ignoring her words, he rushed at the nearest door, lifting her off her feet and throwing her onto the bed. Already, he was forcing off his shoes, undoing the buckle on his belt. She tried to move away, but he grabbed her wrists, forcing himself on top of her and pinning her down. His weight was too much, the feel of him like razors on her skin. It was all she could do to stop herself from crying out and begging him to stop.

She had to think quickly, before he took off any more of his clothes, before he started to remove hers. She began to cough, acting as if she was choking, forcing him to let her sit up, doubling-over as he let go of her wrists, coughing as if she were about to be sick.

Knowing any kind of illness revolted him, she played to his phobia, relieved as he moved away, inching towards the edge of the bed. Now she was free of him, she slid off the mattress, straightening her clothes and not bothering to cover her mouth as she forced out another spluttering cough.

'I'm so sorry, Mason. I'll be fine in a minute. Take your clothes off and make yourself comfortable in bed while I fetch a glass of water and wash my face.'

He nodded, his manner suddenly more subdued. Had her violent fit of coughing dampened his passion, or had the Veronal begun to take effect?

She slipped downstairs to the kitchen for a glass of water, taking her time, wondering how long it would be before he fell asleep. She gave it five minutes and then ten. The fact that he hadn't come looking for her was a good sign. Quietly, she crept upstairs, holding her breath as she slowly pushed open her bedroom door and peered inside. The evening light had gone and the room was almost in darkness. Mason was flat on his back in bed, perfectly still, but for the regular up and down of his chest, and the grunting snore that escaped every now and then.

She'd done it. She'd staved him off, at least for now. But this couldn't go on. This had to be the last time she put herself at risk. Tomorrow would be the day. Tomorrow would be the end of Mason.

Chapter 35

Iris was already packing the picnic when Mason got up the next morning, claiming to have slept well, and too embarrassed to mention that he'd been overcome by sleep rather than passion the night before. Much to Iris's dismay, he seemed perfectly well, despite the Destroying Angel he'd digested in the risotto.

She wondered if the mushroom had lost some of its potency. There was no way of knowing how long ago it had been collected and dried, or even if Eva had labelled the jar correctly. For all she knew, she might actually have fed him chanterelles. She had to put her trust in its delayed reaction, and hope that when combined with the picnic, the poison would finally have its effect.

It was one of those still, late summer days where the heat hangs heavily and there's hardly any air. Mason appeared uncomfortable in his uniform when they set out for the Château Guillard, but since he'd arrived in France, Iris hadn't seen him wearing anything else. The fear of being mistaken for an Englishman must have weighed heavily on him. Knowing who he really was, she couldn't see it as anything other than a form of fancy dress, a barrier to hide behind. She even questioned whether he knew how to fire the pistol that was permanently strapped to his side.

The Château Guillard was only a few kilometres outside the

town, but it could have been another world. It was mid-morning when Mason swung the car through the tall iron gates, which had been propped open at an unruly angle, as if someone were expecting them. As they passed through, Iris noticed the lock had been broken by previous hands, and she wondered if Mason had visited before, and whether the house had already been ransacked, not only for its objects, but for its soul, as France itself had been.

When she asked him if it was his first visit, he seemed agitated, and cursed the humidity as he wiped a smear of perspiration from his forehead.

'I came to look around a few days ago, why do you ask?'

She'd asked because she wanted to know if she should list housebreaker and vandal alongside his other crimes, but she couldn't say it. The day needed to go smoothly if things were to work out the way she'd planned.

His knuckles were white where he gripped the steering wheel, guiding the car along the gentle curve of the driveway that led to the château, and she wondered if he was feeling quite himself.

'I wanted to see it for myself before I showed it to you. Did I need your permission for that?'

Iris took his irritability to be a good sign. Somewhere deep inside, the Destroying Angel was bothering him.

'You're serious about living here?'

He parked in front of the château and climbed out of the car, waving his arm expansively at the front of the grand building.

'Take a look and tell me why anyone wouldn't want to live here.'

Despite having been unoccupied since the fall of France, the château was as beautiful as ever, the sunlight reflecting off the local honeyed stone, creating a halo of golden light around it, the rows of slender windows designed to welcome the sun into every room.

Ivy clung to the front in fits and bursts, muffling the fairy-tale turrets that stood as sentinels on each corner of the building. The lavender that had been planted in a formal arrangement in front of the house was shaggy and overgrown from its years of neglect, the box hedging, once cut in elegant swirls, had blurred at the edges, but the underlying shapes were still there.

'It'll take a while to get the garden back to how it once was.'

Mason shrugged off the comment. The detail was unimportant. Only the glory of possessing the place mattered.

'Let me show you inside. You can choose our master bedroom.'

She expected him to have keys, but she'd overestimated him. Instead, the lock on the front door had been broken where he'd forced his way in on his previous visit, just as the gates had been forced. Iris silently apologised to the owners as she stepped over the threshold, reminding herself she was there to make sure he didn't take possession of the place, that they'd forgive her intrusion for that reason alone. This was the one thing she could do. It was the one crime in this terrible war she could strive to avert.

Already Mason was climbing the grand staircase that swirled its way up through the centre of the house, his boots, heavy on the thick carpet, throwing up clouds of dust.

'You won't believe how many rooms there are.'

The air was sweet where the dried rose petals in the potpourri had gone to ruin, while the wall-hangings on the first-floor landing had been attacked by moths, the fine silk threads of tapestry unlaced where the grubs had fed. It was a house left to decay, because the family who loved it had been forced to flee, and the greedy oppressor who coveted it could see nothing wrong.

Mason threw open the doors of room after room, showing off the spaces, the furniture and the decoration, without leaving time for her to take it in before moving on to the next. She kept her eyes averted from the family photographs that adorned every side-table and cabinet, unwilling to meet the gaze of the smiling faces looking out from the tarnished silver frames, just as she blinked away the sight of the children's toys scattered on the nursery floor, trying not to consider what had caused the tiny suitcase, half-packed with baby clothes, to be abandoned.

Iris quickly built up a picture of the once happy family that had been forced to run for their lives. The coffee set on the dining-room table, the plates laid out for a breakfast that was never enjoyed, the wardrobes full of clothes and shoes, the hairbrushes and the lipsticks on the dressing table, the tangle of glass beads, bracelets and coral necklaces dangling from the mirror: talcum powder and eyebrow pencils, satin dressing gowns and silk slippers. The disarray pointed to a family who'd left in a hurry, with only what they stood up in.

She kept one eye on Mason, who chose to see nothing of what had passed, of what had brought the house to its current condition. All he saw was gain. Having seen the upper house, they continued downstairs to explore the lower floors, examining the kitchen and the scullery and the housekeeper's study. The more Iris saw, the more the atmosphere crowded in. The rooms, shut up for so long, were airless, the dust clawing at her throat until she could stand it no longer. She had to get out before she started screaming, before the sorrow and the suffering associated with the abandoned house overwhelmed her.

'It's hot in here. Shall we explore outside for a bit?'

By now, Mason was sweating heavily. He clenched his fists, betraying his annoyance at her response to the house. Any minute now, she expected one of his punches to come flying her way.

'Don't you like it? It's all for you.'

It wasn't really for her. That was just the excuse he made. It was all for him, but it didn't belong to either of them and it never would.

'I made lemonade. I'll fetch it from the car.'

She stepped away from him before she revealed her disgust at his physical presence, her fear that she might not be able to carry out what she'd come here to do. How could he appear this well, this strong? The Destroying Angel should have begun to debilitate him by now. Why was he not showing its effects? She remembered what Clemence had said about Schiller, how he'd become violent and unpredictable. It must have been the poisons affecting his mind and his personality more than his body. She mustn't forget that it was Schiller's paranoia that had led to him killing the innocent women in the field.

The crunch of Mason's boots on the gravel told Iris he was following her to the car. Did he think she was going to drive away and leave him? Is that what it was? His presence was as oppressive as the heat, his mood darkening by the minute, and he wasn't letting her out of his sight. She lifted the picnic basket from the back seat, forcing herself to sound happier than she felt.

'Shall we eat now or later?'

He rubbed his stomach with irritable hands. 'What have you got?'

'Salad and potatoes, fresh bread and cheese.'

She'd kept the food simple, knowing it was going to be a hot day. 'There are English scones to follow and a little jam.'

'Did you make it?'

'It's one of Eva's recipes, using the blackcurrants from her garden.' She swung the basket onto her arm and slammed the car door. 'Let's find a nice spot, somewhere in the shade. You'll feel better once you've cooled down a bit.'

She led him away from the château, through the formal gardens at the back, skirting the wooded area to the lake beyond. In the house, there'd been photographs of children bathing on sunny days, of rowing boats bobbing in the centre, parasols propped at angles to save the passengers from the sun. Now, she looked out across its still water and wondered how deep it was.

It was early afternoon by the time she laid out the picnic blanket at the edge of the lake, the water lapping at their feet, as if it were intent on soothing the atmosphere which had become increasingly tense with the darkening of Mason's mood. The sky had clouded over and the increased humidity had created a sultry heat that appeared to have drained him of energy.

He took off his officer's cap and his jacket and threw them

aside as she set out the potatoes and sprinkled them with chives, freshly picked that morning from Eva's garden. She didn't ask how he was feeling in case he questioned why, but kept one eye on his pistol.

He stared at the cold potatoes, boiled to the point of crumbling, his nose wrinkling at the accompanying salad.

'Is this the kind of food you usually feed the men in your family?'

Jack had never criticised the food she put in front of him, but then she'd never set out to poison him.

'When the weather's hot, yes.'

He waved his hand dismissively at the salad. 'So you'd serve this to your brother?'

Once again, he'd dragged her onto uncertain ground. She cursed herself for making such a blunder.

'I don't have a brother. You must have misheard me.'

'Never trust the word of a woman. That's what my father used to say.'

'Why would I lie to you about having a brother?'

The question must have been too difficult to answer. Mason picked up a potato and threw it into the lake. It dropped silently into the water like a soft pebble, hardly breaking the surface. The clouds rolled above their heads, prophesying thunder, the inescapable heat pressing like a heavy weight against their skin. Now there was even less air to breathe.

Mason shot her a look. 'The picnic was a stupid idea.'

'I thought it was going to be a nice day.'

He leaned back on his elbows, raising his face to the sky as if to summon the rain, just so he could punish her for it. Her eyes shifted once more to his pistol, which he'd discarded with his belt when he removed his jacket. If his mood grew any worse, would he use it against her?

She handed him a glass of lemonade, not bothering to ask if he wanted it. She'd added hardly any sugar, keeping her precious stock back in case she needed it for something more important. He gulped it down, shuddering as the sour taste hit his tongue and flung the glass into the lake to join the potato. Now he really was behaving like a spoiled child.

'Are you trying to poison me?'

The call was too close to home. Iris sat up a little straighter on the picnic blanket tucking her feet beneath her, imitating the pose of a perfect wife.

'There's little sugar to be had anywhere. It's the best I could manage.'

'Then you shouldn't have bothered.'

The sneer on his face was enough to make her want to kill him. 'Why don't you try the salad? I made one of Eva's special dressings to go with it.'

'Salad is no food for a man.' He pushed away the plate of cheese as she passed it to him. 'It's too hot for cheese. It's probably gone off.'

Iris was running out of options. 'How about a scone? There's sugar in the jam. It'll take away the sourness of the lemonade.'

Mason rubbed his chest. The acid in the lemons must have accelerated the work of the Destroying Angel. *Frossard's Herbal* said the effects could take between eight and twenty-four hours to ignite. Having fed him the deadly mushroom the evening before, she was hoping for a reaction any time now, and it finally seemed to be happening.

'Are you all right, Mason? You've gone pale.'

He rolled over onto his side and grabbed his stomach. 'That blasted drink is attacking my insides. What else did you put in it?'

'It's just the juice of a few lemons from Eva's tree and a little sugar.'

She watched as he brought his knees up to his stomach and groaned. 'It's probably indigestion. It'll pass in a minute.'

She tore off a piece of bread and pushed it into her mouth, chewing slowly as if nothing was wrong. The next time she looked at him, his eyes were closed, his breathing laboured. She couldn't risk not appearing to help him in case he survived.

'You look awfully hot. Would you like me to fetch you some water?' She put aside the bread, shaking the crumbs from her dress. 'I'll go up to the house and see if the taps are still working in the kitchen.'

Without waiting for a reply, she ran towards the château, desperate to get away from him, hoping he'd think she was acting quickly to help him, hoping when she returned, the delayed effects of the Destroying Angel would have worked on his internal organs and he'd be dead.

Once she was out of his sight, she slowed down, taking her time to wander into the château and make her way to the kitchen, whose location she couldn't instantly recall. Once she'd found it, she spent a few minutes searching the cupboards for a suitable jug. Only after this did she start looking for a tap in the scullery, running off the water until the rust had gone and it was clear. It wouldn't do to offer him the water that had sat in the pipes for the last few years. It wouldn't taste right and she couldn't allow him any reason to suspect she'd given him something that would harm him.

By the time she returned, he was sitting up, staring with distrust at the lake. He turned to look at her when he heard her coming, accusation written all over his face, and she wondered if this was the same look the women in the field had seen on Schiller's face before he shot them in cold blood.

'Are you feeling better?'

The effects of the lemon juice on his stomach seemed to have passed. She tried to sound pleased, trying to work out what she should do now.

He snatched the water from her and gulped it, taking deep breaths as it went down. 'There's going to be a storm. Pack up the picnic. It's time to go.'

She'd vowed he wouldn't leave this place alive. She wasn't about to go back on her promise now.

'I haven't finished eating yet.'

His eyes were wild and unfocused. Whatever symptoms he was suffering, he was trying to hide them from her.

'Do you always intend to disobey me?'

'I didn't realise I was under your rule.'

It came without warning, the hard slap across her face. He was in pain and he was out of control. And he was also a monster.

She looked him dead in the eye. His act of brutality against her wouldn't go unpunished. 'That was unnecessary.'

'What's your game, Iris?'

'You can't blame me for the change in the weather.'

'Tell me again why you left London so suddenly?'

She thought she'd put this one to rest, but he must have been mulling it over. 'I wanted to come back to Dijon, to be in my country during its hour of need.'

He hit her again, this time knocking her backwards. 'I don't believe you.'

'I wrote and told you of my plan before I left. I invited you to join me, and here we are.'

She took a breath, refusing to show her pain, her cheek already tender with the emerging bruise. It was time to try a different approach.

'What's brought this on, Mason? I thought we were getting on so well.'

The first spots of rain were already landing, dropping into the lake like tiny pins. She didn't have much time left before the storm broke and he insisted on leaving.

'You left England while I was in custody, expecting to go to trial. You abandoned me when I needed you.'

'You didn't need me. You had everything under control. I never doubted you'd be released. The fact that we're here together now proves I was right.'

'You're lying. You lie to me every day. You lied to me about your brother.'

'For the last time, I don't have a brother. You must have misheard me that night in the bar.'

'I heard from one of my contacts in London. Not everyone in the civil service has abandoned their loyalty to me.'

There was a sudden crack of lightning, the clouds crashing above their heads. 'He said British Intelligence have sent an assassin to finish me.'

There it went again, another roll of thunder. 'Why do you imagine they'd go to so much trouble? You left the country. That's punishment enough, surely?'

Her tone must have infuriated him. He lunged at her from his place on the ground, his arms waving wildly. Iris scrambled to her feet, holding his gaze as he struggled to stand up, an invisible force gripping him and holding him back. Finally making it onto his knees, he let out a groan and grabbed his stomach, struggling to fight off his invisible attacker, his face screwed up in pain. Finally, the Destroying Angel had come to get him.

Iris stood over him as he lay on the ground. 'You're not well. Take deep breaths. Everything will seem clearer when your indigestion passes.'

The lemonade, suddenly rejected by his stomach, came out of his mouth in rapid bursts, the convulsions sending his arms and legs twitching in all directions.

'You've poisoned me, you bitch. What did you put in that lemonade?'

'You drank it on an empty stomach. It'll be the acid in the lemon juice upsetting you.'

The one thing she hadn't poisoned was the thing he thought was killing him. She stepped back as his whole body went into spasm. The power of the Destroying Angel had arrived just in time to save her.

'Why don't you help me?'

'What do you want me to do?'

He rolled onto his stomach and crawled towards his jacket, grabbing his belt, which he'd discarded alongside it, and pulled it towards him. It was a second before Iris realised his intention. His pistol was in the holster attached to his belt. As she ran forward to reach it, he grabbed her ankle and pulled her to the ground. Rather than weakening him, his fight for life seemed to have given him more strength. He pushed his hand into her face, twisting her neck at a breaking angle until she could hardly breathe.

His gun was just out of her reach. Even if she could get hold of it, she couldn't use it against him. It had to be a bloodless kill if it was to look like an accident.

It was impossible to overpower him from this position. 'Mason, please.' She whispered the words though clenched teeth, trying to make it sound as if she were pleading; his fingers still tight around her jaw. When he refused to release her, she changed her tone. 'You're hurting me.' Without warning, she brought up her hand and slapped his face. 'Let go of me.'

The shock of the sting made him loosen his grip, just long enough for her to break free. She clambered to her feet, grasping the moral high ground.

'What do you think you're doing?'

He got to his hands and knees, shaking his head like a dog, his stomach retching, a pool of bile stringing from his mouth. He was in no state to answer her question.

'Drink some water. It'll make you feel better.' She had a terrible feeling he was going to live.

Mason sat up, wiping the drool from his lips with the back of his hand. 'Pack everything up. We're leaving.'

'You're in no state to drive. Sit quietly for a few minutes and take deep breaths.' She wrapped up the salad and the potatoes, keeping herself at a distance. When he closed his eyes, she took his pistol and dropped it in the picnic basket out of sight. She was burying it under the napkins when he suddenly opened his eyes.

'What are you doing?'

'I'm putting the food away, like you told me to. Have some jam.' She tossed the jar to him, knowing he wouldn't be able to resist catching it.

His hand shook as he held it up to the light, turning it to inspect the contents. The jar was less than a quarter full. He blinked at it in distaste. 'Is this all there is?'

'I ate the rest. I couldn't resist it. Why don't you try it? It's one of Eva's special recipes.'

He'd broken into a sweat and seemed not to notice that the rain was growing heavier. She tossed him a spoon, not daring to get too close in case he lashed out again.

'The sugar in it will make you feel better.'

Despite whatever was going on inside him, he was unable to resist. After a couple of attempts he managed to unscrew the lid, which he cast aside before digging the spoon into the soft jam.

Iris sat back on her heels and watched as he took the first mouthful, willing him to swallow it before he registered the flavour. Something as toxic as deadly nightshade couldn't possibly be palatable, even with the addition of sugar, and she was relying on him swallowing at least some of it before he spat it out. According to *Frossard's Herbal*, four berries were enough to kill.

She looked away, busying herself with packing up the last of the picnic and not appearing to take any notice of him when she heard the splutter. Suddenly, he was back on all fours, coughing and struggling for breath. She finished packing away the plates before she went over to him.

'What's wrong? Did it go down the wrong way?'

He shook his head, a dog once more, spitting at the ground. 'It's foul.'

She'd overdone it. He was already made wretched by the Destroying Angel and she'd made him angry again. Without warning, his stomach went into convulsions, rejecting the jam that spewed from him in one long arc.

'Take deep breaths.'

She faked her concern, revolted by the stench of his breath, the look of his eyes as they rolled wildly in their sockets. Surely, this couldn't go on for much longer?

Desperate now, he crawled towards the edge of the lake and dipped his face in the water, as if the shock of the cold could restore his senses. Thunder cracked overhead, the rain now coming down in sheets.

'Let me help you.'

She knelt beside him and ran her fingers through his hair, pretending to soothe him before pushing his face into the water. Expecting him to resist, she lodged her knee in the back of his neck, using the full weight of her body to hold him under. And then she counted: *one, two, three . . . seventy-four, seventy-five*, until all the fight had gone out of him, until he could do no more harm.

Lightning flashed over the lake as if to mark his last breath, lighting her up as a murderer, but there was no time to think about that now. It was vital she removed any evidence that she'd been there. So far, everything had gone to plan. Mason was dead. Now she had to make it look like an accident.

She dragged his head from the water and turned him over on the bank. Working at double speed, she put his jacket back on him and fastened his belt, before retrieving his pistol from the picnic basket and returning it to its holster. She worked quickly and efficiently, making sure every scrap of picnic was put away, tightening the lid back on the jam and gathering the discarded spoon, securing the top on the lemonade bottle and wrapping it in the napkins in case it leaked.

There was only one thing left to do. She kicked off her sandals, pulled her dress over her head and waded into the lake, dragging Mason's body along with her, a dead weight, until the water buoyed it up. Leaving nothing to chance, she swam out to the centre, pulling him by the arm until he was far enough to be out of his depth, then without giving him a second look, she let go and swam back to the bank, leaving his body floating face down, a prone starfish made of flesh for the fish to feed on.

She pulled her dress over her head, forcing it over her wet skin, and pushed her feet into her sandals, ready to leave. It was only then she noticed Mason's cap, abandoned near the place where they'd picnicked. Cursing her carelessness, she picked it up and flung it as far into the lake as her strength would carry it.

That was the last of him. Finally, she allowed herself a sigh of relief. He'd been made to pay for his treason, for the deaths of the countless soldiers who'd been sent into a trap because of the military secrets he'd revealed to the Germans. It was all over. Mason was finally gone.

It was a long walk home in the rain but not impossible. The most important thing was not to be seen. Before setting out, she'd checked one of Eva's maps and committed a route to memory that avoided the main roads, following an old walking trail through the vineyards and the local farms. Given the rain and the storm, she gambled on few people being outside. And if anyone stopped her, she'd say she'd been for a picnic and got caught in the storm, because it wasn't a lie.

There was plenty of time before the curfew as she walked through the town. By now, the rain had cleared and her clothes were almost dry. She adopted an air of dejection, shivering from catching a chill, as she moved through the streets. Given the state of her, no one would take her for a murderer.

Once home, she took a hot bath, in an attempt to wash off her sins, crying big tears of revulsion at the crime she'd committed, at the person she'd become, the weight of Mason trying to force his head out of the water still heavy on her hands. Exhausted with crying, she went to bed, summoning the sleep that would never come. All she had to do was hold her nerve when the Gestapo came knocking, as they were bound to do when they realised Mason was missing. Killing him was the easy bit. The consequences would prove much harder to evade.

Chapter 36

The knocking began in the early hours, the clenched fist repeatedly beating on the front door until the blood came. They couldn't have found Mason's body already. It was too soon for them to realise he was missing, too soon to work out she was guilty of his murder.

She climbed out of bed and peered through the shutters, her eyes squinting in the dark for signs of a black Citroën, the slick shadows of the Gestapo. It was impossible to make anything out, but who else would be reckless enough to break the curfew and cause such a racket?

She ran down the stairs, her nerves shattered by the repeated knocking, and determined to make it stop. If they'd come for her, there'd be no escape and there was no point even trying, so she might as well get it over with.

'Who's there?'

The clenched fist met the door with another determined thud. 'Let us in, please, before someone sees us.'

It was Adele, her voice high-pitched with panic. She wasn't alone. Paul was with her. Iris opened the door and she stumbled into the hallway, staggering under Paul's weight, his arm, slumped around her shoulders, pulling her off balance.

'I saw him lying on the bench in the square when I went downstairs to check I'd locked the door to the café. Can you take him in? I hardly know him.'

'I don't need women fussing over me.'

Paul's voice was slurred from too much wine, his clothes covered in dirt, as if he'd crawled through a ditch. Adele pushed him away, forcing him to lean against the wall.

'I couldn't leave you there. If you'd been caught by a German patrol, you'd be in all sorts of trouble.'

Paul threw back his head, bashing it against the wall, his eyes rolling. 'You shouldn't have disturbed me, God damn you.'

Despite the slurred words, his tone was vicious, his fists clenching and unclenching with the rapidity of his breath.

'You'd better get back to Georges. I'll take care of Paul. Thank you for coming to his rescue.'

Iris kept her eye on Adele as she dashed across the square and let herself into the café, satisfying herself she was safe before closing the door. Paul must have been pretending to be drunker than he was, because he seemed more sober now they were alone.

'So here we are, Iris. You and me together in the middle of the night. What shall we do now?' He leaned into her, the alcohol fumes acrid on his breath.

'You're drunk. You can either sleep it off on the sofa or go home.'

If she sent him back out onto the streets, she could be sending him to his death. The Germans weren't beyond shooting anyone they caught breaking the curfew.

'It's up to you, Paul. What do you want to do?'

'You know what I want. The same thing I've always wanted.'

She tried to push him away as he moved towards her, but he was quicker, grabbing her wrists and pushing her against the wall.

'What do you say, Iris? Haven't you ever wondered what it would be like?'

She turned her face away, as his mouth searched for hers in

the dark, his fingers crushing the small bones in her wrists. Even in his drunken state he was stronger than her, angrier.

'You can sleep on the sofa or take your chances on the streets. It's up to you.'

'You don't mean that.'

'Let me go, Paul.'

When he refused to move, she thrust the full weight of her body forward, knocking him off balance as her forehead struck his nose. Instantly he let go, cursing and grabbing his face as the blood began to pour from his nostrils.

'You should know better than to mess with me, Paul.'

He followed her through to the sitting room, pressing his forearm against his nose to stem the blood. 'There was no need for that.'

'Why are you in such a state? What have you been up to?'

'Drinking. What does it look like?'

'You can't have been out drinking until this time. The bars closed hours ago.'

He collapsed onto the sofa and threw his head back to stop the flow of blood. If his nose was broken, it would teach him a lesson.

'I fell asleep on the bench in the square. Our bench. The one where we used to sit, before the world turned against us.'

She looked at him, sprawled on the sofa, every part of him wired like a wild animal, ready to leap to violence.

'What made you drink so much?'

'I had a visit this afternoon from our German overseers. They came to check the quality of the grapes on the vines, to judge what kind of harvest they could expect.'

'And what did they conclude from it?'

'They *concluded* it's going to be a bumper harvest, that the weather has created the perfect conditions for a vintage wine, with no consideration for the work I've put into the soil and the vines, or my skill as a winemaker that can make the difference between an average and a superior wine.'

'That goes without saying, surely.'

The rage had returned to his eyes. These days, it was as if there were two sides to him, his personality shifting from light to dark at the whim of circumstance.

'I'm going back to bed. Try to get some sleep. And don't bleed on the sofa.'

He grabbed her wrist to detain her as she tried to leave. 'You know what the worst of it is? They're sending their own men to pick the grapes. Then, when the wine is in its barrels, they're coming for that too. Not for eighty per cent of it, which is their usual take, but for all of it.'

She twisted her arm, releasing herself from his grip. 'How are you supposed to live?'

'As if they care. They're the conquerors. They own us now, in case you hadn't noticed.'

'It can't go on like this forever. The war has to end. Things will change.'

'Fine words from the woman who has chosen collaboration over resistance.'

'I don't see any evidence of you standing up to them, Paul.'

He examined his sleeve, smeared with the blood that would never come out. Already his nose was swelling, the tender skin around it beginning to marble. Even if it wasn't broken there'd be a lot of bruising to answer for in the coming days.

'I'm going back to bed. I don't want to hear any more noise from you.'

'Don't worry. I'll be gone before you wake up in the morning. You can forget I was ever here.'

If only it was that easy. She returned to bed, her forehead tender where she'd smashed it against Paul's nose as she fought him off. Her senses were still on high alert after killing Mason. Her response to his clumsy advance had been instinctive, but an overreaction. It was lucky he'd been too drunk or too shocked to retaliate against her violence.

She lay awake, staring at the ceiling, counting down the hours until sunrise, listening for Paul to start moving around the house, bracing herself in case he decided to follow her upstairs, but either he'd learned his lesson or had sobered up enough to know better than to try it.

It was the sound of the shopkeepers, opening their shutters in the square the next morning that finally caused him to stir, and it was with a sigh of relief that she heard him open the front door and close it quietly behind him, the controlled sound indicating a more sober mind.

As soon as he'd gone, she climbed out of bed and put on a fresh dress, not the one she'd worn the day before, but something clean and untainted by the memory of what had happened at the lake with Mason, as if the consequences of murder could be cast off as easily as yesterday's clothes, as if the memory of the act could be forgotten with the start of a new day. A day during which she'd have to watch her back and hope that nobody worked out she was a murderer.

Chapter 37

Despite her determination to carry on as normal, Iris spent the following three days sitting at Eva's kitchen table, replaying in her mind everything that had happened. Until it came to it, she wasn't sure she'd be capable of killing Mason, but she'd done it. And it was all thanks to Eva. She couldn't have managed it without the poisons she'd gathered around her, transforming the cellar into the devil's larder. Now she had to make sure she didn't end up paying for his murder the way Eva had paid for Schiller's. But then, was Iris really guilty of murder when she'd just been following orders?

Rumours were already spreading about Mason's disappearance. Clemence had warned her that the police were stopping people in the street and questioning them; that the Gestapo were going from door to door, demanding to know if anyone had seen him or spotted anything suspicious.

It was late afternoon on the fourth day when the knock Iris had been expecting finally came. Her heart was racing, but she had to answer it. It was important to act normally. If she hid now, people would wonder why.

It wasn't the Gestapo, as Iris had feared, but Madame Frisch, her fake smile and air of false pretence a sure sign that she'd been sent by her husband.

'Madame Frisch, please come in. I was about to make a mint tisane. Would you like one?'

She followed Iris into the kitchen, her eyes searching every nook and crevice of the narrow hallway.

'So this is the famous house.'

It was famous only in the imagination of Eva's readers. In reality, they knew nothing of the truth of it.

'Yes, although I think of it only as my home.'

'I suppose you would.'

Madame Frisch sat at the kitchen table while the water boiled for the tisane, her eyes tracking Iris's every movement as she tore the mint leaves from their stalks and dropped them into the cups.

'I've read all Eva's books. They're very popular in Germany.'

She seemed to have forgotten that, the last time they met, she'd expressed her dislike of French food.

'Which of Eva's recipes is your favourite?'

Madame Frisch's bottom lip quivered while she tried to make up an answer. 'There are too many to choose just one.' She placed the paper bag she'd been holding on the table. 'I brought you some strawberries from the garden. They're the last of the season.'

Iris opened the bag to admire the bulging red fruits and sniffed. Instantly, the memories of summer days spent in the Hoffmans' garden were reawakened, reminding her that the life she and Eva had shared was lost and could never be regained. What good was Mason's death when there were plenty more like him to take his place? As she handed Madame Frisch the tisane, her efforts for the war seemed futile, the stain the murder had left on her soul, indelible. She was no better than the man she'd killed.

Madame Frisch took a sip of the tisane before discarding it. 'Will you show me around the house?'

It sounded more like an order than a request. Thank God Yvette wasn't here with her wireless equipment. If she was discovered, they'd both be finished.

Iris put on a hostess's smile. 'Of course. Everyone who visits wants to see where Eva worked.'

'You should open the house as a museum. There are plenty of Germans who'd pay to see where Eva wrote her books, especially the cellar where she kept her still.'

There was no doubt that Madame Frisch had been sent by her husband to search the house. More worryingly, she knew about the cellar. For now, Frisch was taking a soft approach, but it was a house search nevertheless.

'It's only really the kitchen and the garden that are of interest. They're the places she mostly describes in her books.'

As they passed through the sitting room, Iris pointed out Eva's favourite armchair. Madame Frisch shot across the room and threw herself into it, bouncing on the cushions and testing the springs to their limits with her large behind. Iris could almost hear Eva laughing at the ridiculous sight.

'Has Mason recovered from whatever it was that made him ill the night you came to dinner at our house?'

Iris kept her tone casual. 'He seemed fine the last time I saw him.'

'When was that exactly?'

'Saturday evening. Shall we go into the garden?'

Iris helped her out of the chair and led her outside, taking time to show her every tree and shrub, hoping she'd grow bored and forget about the cellar, but Madame Frisch was under orders and not to be put off. Brushing aside the splendour of the apple trees and the herb beds, she headed back into the house.

'The cellar's down those stairs, is it? Can I take a look?'

Iris led the way, hoping the lack of interest she'd shown in the garden would extend to the dried specimens in the jars.

'This is the still where Eva made her essential oils. The jars you can see contain the usual ingredients you'd find in any kitchen: dried herbs and edible flowers for garnishing salads and soups. The baskets under the bench are where the fruit and vegetables and the nuts from the garden are stored.'

Madame Frisch's eyes scanned the shelves, her nostrils twitching at the mix of bitter herbs that scented the air. She didn't know what she was looking for, that much was clear. Still, Iris needed to get her out before she started poking around in the cupboards.

'It's chilly down here. Shall we go back to the kitchen?'

Madame Frisch was silent. Her limited imagination seemed unable to summon any further indirect questions to help the search for Mason.

'He doesn't stay here with you, then?'

Iris looked confused. 'Who?'

'Mason.'

'He has a room in one of the local hotels. I only see him from time to time. I think he's more interested in Eva than he is in me.'

'I can understand that.'

As a personal slight, it was as heavy-handed as they come, but it was an insight into the limits of Madame Frisch's mind. Iris rose above it, thanking her for the strawberries and reminding her she hadn't finished her tisane which she'd left on the kitchen table. It was the prompt Madame Frisch needed to find an excuse to leave. Iris hadn't added any honey to sweeten it, and going by the way she'd shuddered at it, Iris guessed nothing would induce her to take another mouthful.

Iris said goodbye to her at the front door, closing it quickly behind her, hoping no one had seen them together. Madame Frisch's visit would only add to the suspicion that she was a collaborator.

Frisch wouldn't be fool enough to believe it was a coincidence that Mason had now disappeared as well as Schiller. No wonder he was interested in the house, in Eva and herself. Lightning didn't strike twice in the same place and he knew it. He'd be looking for patterns, connections to link the disappearances. If the Grey Mouse had reported what she'd overheard in the café the day Emile dug up Schiller's body, then he'd be pretty sure that Mason was also dead. Sending his wife to search the house was all part of his trap to catch her.

It had been a mistake to use the same methods as Eva, however inadvertently she'd stumbled upon them. She'd been noticed by those who were watching. Eva had ended up dead. Now Iris had to make sure history didn't repeat itself.

Frisch knew Iris was married to an Englishman, that she'd spent most of the war in London. This was reason enough for him to question what she was doing here and why she'd chosen to come back when the borders were closed and the journey into Occupied France was dangerous.

There'd been no sign of Yvette for some time, and without her, Iris had no way of contacting Ambrose to let him know she'd completed her mission, or that she was under suspicion over Mason's disappearance, even before his body had been found. All she could do was wait for further instructions and hope that whatever Madame Frisch reported back to her husband, it wouldn't feed the suspicion that was already building against her.

Chapter 38

Iris didn't know they'd discovered Mason's car until the following day when two Gestapo officers came to inform her. They'd broadened their search for him beyond the town after Frisch had recalled his conversation with Mason regarding his interest in acquiring a château. This had prompted a search of all the grand houses on the list of properties ripe for requisition. It hadn't taken long for them to find the car parked in front of the Château Guillard. There had, however, been no sign of Mason himself.

'When did you last see him?'

The two officers insisted on coming into the house. Iris stood with her back to the stove as their eyes roved the kitchen, their curiosity fuelled by the fact that they too were familiar with Eva's books.

'He came for dinner on Saturday night.'

'What time did he leave?'

What he meant was did he stay the night? Did you sleep with him?

'He left early, so as not to break the curfew.'

'Did he say where he was going?'

'No.'

'What did you do after he left?'

'I went to bed.'

'Were you alone?'

'Yes.'

The second officer wrote down her answers as the first one fired the questions. It felt as if everything had been rehearsed before they came, the outcome a foregone conclusion.

'You must come with us for further questioning.'

She expected to be driven to the backstreet hotel where the Gestapo had set up their headquarters and was surprised to find herself being taken along the quiet roads outside the town, to the house that belonged to the Hoffmans, where she and Mason had dinner with Commander Frisch and his wife not all that long ago.

It was the same maid who answered the door, her head turned away to avoid catching Iris's eye. If she'd allied herself with the occupying enemy to keep herself safe, then Iris couldn't blame her for it. There was no right or wrong way of conducting yourself in this life, only survival. For many people, morality didn't come into it.

As the front door closed behind her, Iris saw the Grey Mouse hurrying along the hallway, a bundle of files tucked under one arm. She gave Iris a brief nod before disappearing into what had once been Madame Hoffman's sitting room. Iris wondered if the walls were still painted a cheerful yellow, or whether they'd been covered up with something more austere to reflect the forbidding mood of the Third Reich.

The Grey Mouse had given nothing away in her expression and it was impossible for Iris to judge whether she was surprised to see her there. Rather than being reassured by a familiar face, Iris found the Grey Mouse's presence unsettling.

Commander Frisch was sitting behind the desk in Monsieur Hoffman's study when Iris was shown in. He gestured for her to take a seat and ordered the two accompanying Gestapo officers to leave them.

'So, here we are.'

He poured himself a coffee from Madame Hoffman's silver

coffee pot and dribbled in a glug of cream, sipping it slowly in front of her before he continued.

'You know what this is about?'

'No, you're going to have to tell me.' She tried to sound matter of fact, as if the life wasn't being terrified out of her.

'Mason has disappeared. No one has seen him since he left his hotel on Saturday afternoon. My wife said you told her he came to your house for dinner on Saturday night. You must have been one of the last people to see him.'

'Oh, yes. Please thank your wife for the strawberries. They were delicious.'

Frisch twitched and she knew she'd hit a nerve. He wasn't completely certain that she wasn't one of them and he wouldn't want to make himself look a fool by misjudging her. For all her prying, it seemed Madame Frisch hadn't found anything in Eva's house to report against her.

He drummed his fingers on the desk. 'Do you have any idea where Mason is?'

Iris gave it some thought. 'He stayed for dinner and left early, before the curfew. He seemed rather tired. We didn't talk of anything much beyond the food. I'd made a white mushroom risotto. It was one of my aunt's recipes.'

'The food he ate is of no consequence. His car has been found parked outside the Château Guillard. Did you know he was intending to visit?'

'Does he have friends living there?'

'The château has been empty since the fall of France.'

'Yes, of course. I knew the family had left. I wasn't sure if anyone else had moved in.'

Frisch gave her a dubious look. Her implied criticism hadn't been lost on him. 'Mason was looking for a house. Did he mention this château to you?'

'He took me to see the house owned by Madame Beauchamp recently. He was taken ill while we were there.' Iris paused, as if she'd suddenly had a terrible thought. 'Do you think he could have taken ill again?'

'Was he well when you saw him on Saturday night?'

'He hasn't been right since he arrived in Dijon. Sometimes I think he's hiding his symptoms from me and pretending to be well when he really isn't. No man likes to appear weak in front of a woman.'

'We've searched the château and there's no sign of him. If he'd been taken ill and collapsed, we'd have found him.'

'Perhaps he was never at the château. Could someone have stolen his car and driven it there? I hope nothing's happened to him. Have you checked the local hospitals?'

She was offering Frisch a new line of thought, but wasn't sure he was taken in. With his eyes focused on pouring a second cup of coffee, he was impossible to read.

'Didn't it seem strange to you that you hadn't seen him for so many days?'

'Not really.' She shuffled in her seat, displaying an awkwardness that she trusted him not to miss. 'I suspect he might have led you to think we're closer than we actually are.'

'You're his mistress, yes?'

'Yes.'

'You're planning to live with him in his new residence?'

'We hadn't really discussed it.'

Frisch lit a cigarette, giving himself time to collect his thoughts. 'Do you have any idea where he might have gone?'

Iris stared at Madame Hoffman's silver coffee pot. It had been a wedding present from her sister and had been her pride and joy. She must have been heartbroken when she was forced to flee, leaving all her domestic treasures behind.

'If he didn't want any of us to know he was ill, he might have taken himself off to a clinic somewhere for treatment.'

Frisch took a long drag on his cigarette, blowing the smoke out through his nostrils like a feeble dragon. 'It doesn't explain why his car was parked outside the Château Guillard.'

Iris shrugged, as if the whole thing were a mystery. 'Which brings us back to the idea that his car might have been stolen and later abandoned.'

He flicked his cigarette ash into one of Madame Hoffman's best china saucers. Heaven only knew what had happened to the matching cup.

'Something isn't right.'

He took another drag on his cigarette, his irritation visibly growing with each unsatisfactory answer Iris offered. This was the second officer who'd disappeared under his command and it was making him edgy.

'Did Eva ever mention Max Schiller to you?'

'I hadn't spoken to Eva since before the fall of France.'

'You know he was a high-ranking German officer and that he was billeted with her?'

'People in the town have mentioned it.'

'Then you'll know he also disappeared.'

'I don't see what this has to do with Mason.'

'It seems too much of a coincidence that both men had a connection to the house you're living in, a connection to both you and Eva.'

'I wasn't here when Schiller was here and Eva's dead. I've inherited her house. I can't see any connection beyond tragedy and circumstance.'

He kept his eyes trained on her, stubbing out his cigarette in the china saucer with more force than was necessary. 'You don't seem too upset about Mason's disappearance.'

'Mason is a resourceful man. I have faith in him, but I also know he's been unwell. I expect he's in a clinic somewhere or taking a rest cure. I don't understand why his car was found at the château unless somebody stole it and later abandoned it. He'll probably return next week, fighting fit and furious that someone has stolen his car. He'll be grateful to you for finding it.'

Frisch leaned back in Monsieur Hoffman's chair, dropping his head to one side as he considered her argument.

'You might be right. Nevertheless, if he was taken ill at the château, he might still be there. I'll have the place searched again, more thoroughly this time. I've been told there's a lake. Perhaps we should dredge it.' He nodded, reaching for a second cigarette. 'You can go.'

She stood up to leave, trying to behave as if it had been a social call, as if her legs weren't threatening to collapse under her. It was vital Frisch didn't see she how frightened she was.

'Please say hello to your wife for me. I'm sorry not to have seen her today.'

He nodded, lighting his second cigarette with Monsieur Hoffman's lighter. 'Don't leave the town without my permission.'

Iris gave him a small nod, as if it were nothing, still presenting herself as a friend rather than someone under interrogation. 'I wouldn't worry about Mason. I'm sure he'll turn up sooner or later.'

Chapter 39

It was a long walk home after her interrogation. The air had turned cooler and Iris shivered in her light cotton tea dress. The Gestapo hadn't allowed her to take a cardigan or a coat when they forced her out of Eva's house and into their waiting car.

In spite of the cold and the fear, she held her head high, giving the appearance of someone untroubled. The German soldiers would be watching her from the street corners and the cafés where they loitered, looking the women up and down for their own amusement. For her, their attention would be different. She'd been called in for questioning. Her card had been marked.

Seeing the Grey Mouse working alongside Frisch had made her more nervous than ever. Now she couldn't even visit the café without knowing his eyes were on her by default. She must have been sent to spy on her. Why else would she spend so much time there?

From now on, she'd have to be more careful. If only she had a way of warning Yvette to stay away from the house. Much as she needed to contact Ambrose, it was too dangerous for them to risk being seen together.

Now the decision had been made to dredge the lake at the château, it was only a matter of time before Mason's body was found. She was certain Frisch had made up his mind to do this before he called her in for questioning and had mentioned it to see how she'd react. She couldn't be sure if he'd believed what she'd told him. She might have given herself away a hundred times and not realised it. When it came to interrogation, she was used to being on the other side of the questioning.

Still, she was confident she'd covered her tracks, that the circumstances of Mason's death couldn't be traced back to her. And yet someone might have seen her climb into his car with the picnic basket on that fateful Sunday morning, or noticed her sitting in the passenger seat as they drove through the town to the château. There'd always be someone willing to come forward for the right price. It would take only one person in the town to be suspicious of her, one grievance to give them the justification they needed to denounce her.

Clemence dashed out of the café as soon as Iris entered the square, her face white with shock. 'Something terrible has happened. Come quickly.'

The square was eerily quiet for the time of day, the windows of all the surrounding houses shuttered. Clemence lowered her eyes as she led Iris into the empty café, ignoring the *closed* sign on the door.

'It's Georges. Adele is distraught. She's refusing to speak to anyone. I don't know what to do. Perhaps you can help her.'

Adele was sitting on a high stool beside the counter, her back as straight as a post as she stared into space. If there was life behind her eyes, she didn't show it and she gave no indication that she knew they were there. Iris placed her hand lightly on her shoulder, so as not to startle her. She flinched at Iris's touch, her movements as stiff as an automaton.

'Georges is dead. They shot him.'

It couldn't be true. Iris's eyes scanned the café. Georges was never out of Adele's sight, but now he wasn't anywhere. He wasn't in her arms or wrapped in the shawl she used to secure him to her chest, and the crib that usually sat beside the counter had gone.

'What happened?'

Having made an effort to speak, Adele had now crawled back inside herself, to the place where none of this was real. Iris tried to hug her but there was no response. Cold to the touch, it was as if she'd turned to stone.

Iris looked to Clemence, her eyes begging her to tell her what had happened, because she couldn't bring herself to say the words.

'I was cleaning my windows when I heard two gunshots ring out across the square. I saw the German soldier who shot the pigeon running from the café, pushing his gun into his belt. Adele came out after him, screaming and holding Georges to her chest. Despite all the fuss, he was still and silent.' Clemence cast her eyes across the floor, reliving the moment. 'There was so much blood.'

'When did this happen?'

'Not long after the Gestapo took you away.'

Iris looked around the empty café, searching for signs of the tragedy. It was as if it had never happened, but for the fact that Georges was no longer there.

'The police came and removed Georges's body and the crib and cleared up the blood. They forced Adele to put on a clean dress and took the other one away for burning.'

The soldier had been pestering Adele for weeks. Iris should have taken more notice of him. She should have done something about him, but when it came to it, he was just one of many, put there to terrorise them and determined to blight their lives.

'Have they arrested him?'

Clemence shrugged. 'Why would they? Soldiers are trained to kill. It's what they do.'

'Were there any witnesses?'

'The café was full, but everyone fled when they realised what was happening. I couldn't leave Adele alone, but now I don't know what to do.'

Adele moved from beside the counter and stood with her back

against the wall, her movements stiff and uncoordinated as if she were learning to navigate a new world.

'Why did they take Georges away? I begged them not to take him away.'

Iris bit back her rage. It wouldn't do Adele any good to see it. 'I'm so sorry, my love.'

The conversation must have carried on in Adele's head because it was a moment before she spoke again, her thoughts having moved on, but not very far.

'Georges was sleeping quietly in his crib beside the counter, just as he always did. He wasn't hurting anyone. I begged the soldier not to shoot. He knew he'd be spilling German blood but he did it anyway.'

'Why did he do it?'

'Because there's no coffee and no sugar. Because I wouldn't allow him into my bed. Because he is full of hatred. Because he is too stupid to understand the value of life. Because he doesn't know what it is to love.'

What could Iris offer that would make any difference to Adele? She only had words and gestures, and they were no comfort at all.

'Will you go upstairs and rest?'

Adele shook her head, refusing to move. 'I have to stay here, where Georges was. If I go, he'll be gone too. Then I'll have to come back to him not being here.'

Clemence whispered to Iris. 'I've sent word to Adele's mother, begging her to come. They haven't spoken since she found out she was pregnant with Georges, but surely this horror is greater than her shame.'

She'd hardly finished speaking when Madame Blanchet appeared, pushing past them as she entered the café and pulling her daughter into a stiff embrace. Not wishing to intrude on their privacy, Iris drew the blinds and slipped away with Clemence, closing the door quietly behind them.

Neither of them spoke until they'd crossed the square. Stopping at Eva's front door, Clemence let go of her arm. Until that moment, Iris hadn't been sure which of one of them was holding the other up.

'Are you all right?'

Clemence nodded, but the gesture was too emphatic to be genuine. 'I saw the Gestapo take you away. I hope they didn't hurt you.'

Compared to what Adele was suffering, it was nothing. 'I'm fine. They asked me a few questions, that's all.' She felt the pockets in her dress, searching for her door key, forcing herself to recall what had happened earlier in the day, before the shock of Georges's murder made everything else inconsequential.

'Can you let me into the house? They refused to let me carry anything when they took me away.'

'You won't need a key to get in.'

It was only when Clemence pointed it out that she realised the door had been forced open in her absence. Iris suppressed a cry. She couldn't face anything else, not today.

'The soldiers appeared as soon as you'd gone. They must have been waiting for you to leave. They were in there a long time.'

'Were they here when the gunshots went off in the café?'

Clemence nodded. 'I can only guess they chose to ignore them.'

Every room in the house had been turned upside down, the kitchen dresser and the pantry ransacked, the chairs in the sitting room upturned and the sheets torn from the beds. In the cellar, the still had been dismantled and the cupboards emptied, the jars tumbled here and there and the contents scattered. They didn't appear to have taken anything away when they left, they'd simply created chaos. They hadn't known what they were looking for and hadn't been aware that the dried plants and mushrooms they'd discarded on the cellar floor were Iris's and Eva's murder weapons.

Iris and Clemence set about putting everything straight, sweeping up the mess and salvaging what they could of the food in the pantry and the cellar, straightening the furniture and making the beds, scrubbing away every scuff made by the soldiers' boots, every dirty fingerprint and smear they'd left behind, until nothing remained of their uninvited presence. They worked in silence, not allowing themselves to think, channelling their rage into the work, and exhaling it through every breath. If only it had been enough to bring Georges back, to undo life's tragedies and make everyone whole again.

They didn't stop until every trespass had been washed away, until Iris could feel the home was hers again. But it would never be the same, not until the enemy had been driven out of France, until the nation could call itself free.

Frisch's questioning and the coordinated ransacking of Eva's house proved the enemy was closing in, while the murder of Georges in cold blood showed the brutality they were capable of. Under suspicion, and with no means of contacting Ambrose, Iris was completely alone. All she could do was watch and wait and keep her wits about her. It was only a matter of time before Mason's body was found and she had nowhere to hide but in plain sight.

Chapter 40

It was late afternoon when Iris heard the rattle of the back gate. She ran outside and through the garden, heart in mouth, as she threw back the bolt. And there he was. Jack, his eyes red-rimmed, the tender skin on his face scorched, but he was alive.

'Thank God. I thought you were dead.'

The tears wouldn't stop coming as she ushered him through the gate, fighting her instinct to touch him, to verify he was real and not a fantasy. 'I heard the camp where you were hiding had been burned to the ground. I had no way of knowing if you'd been caught in the fire, whether you were living there under an assumed name. And if you were, how would I ever know it?'

'I came as soon as I could.'

His voice was hoarse from the smoke damage, his vowels indistinct as if they'd been burned away at the edges. It was a miracle he'd been so close to the fire and survived.

'You're safe. That's all that matters. You'd better come inside.'

He waited while she picked a handful of mint for his tisane from the herb patch, his breath labouring over every small step as they made their way to the kitchen, where he lowered himself into his favourite chair, as if every part of him was damaged.

'I wasn't there when the fire was started. I was in Lyon, meeting a contact from a Swiss newspaper. He'd been finding information for me on Mason's financial activities. I travelled back through the night to avoid being seen and arrived at the camp just after daybreak. I couldn't believe what I was seeing.' He covered his face with his hands, reliving the horrors in his mind. 'I did everything I could to drag the bodies of the young men from the flames. If only I'd been there that night, acting as a lookout, it would never have happened. I could have warned them. I could have extinguished the fire before it got out of control.'

'You couldn't have known it was going to happen.'

'Those young men were my comrades and I let them down.'

His hands were singed where he'd pulled the bodies from the embers, his lips cracked from the heat of the flames.

'Where have you been all this time?'

'I must have passed out from inhaling too much smoke as I fought to retrieve the bodies. By some miracle, a member of the Resistance spotted me and managed to get me to safety.'

He paused to cough, his chest rattling like pebbles in a zinc bucket. He bent over, as he struggled for the breath to carry on. He'd lost more weight, and his eyes had reduced to dark pools in his shadowed face.

'Someone in the network was good enough to take me in and look after me. You'll understand why I can't give you their names. Today's the first day I've been strong enough to get out of bed.'

'Let me put something on your burns.'

She cleaned his hands with cool water and dabbed honey on the enflamed skin, as Eva had done when Iris burned herself on the stove as a child. Jack looked into the distance as she tended him. He was still on the burning hillside with his lost comrades, fighting back the flames that had killed them, and a part of him would never return.

She insisted he put on a pair of thin cotton gloves to keep the honey from rubbing off his hands and placed butterfly kisses on the inside of his wrists. If he sensed the tenderness in her care, he didn't comment on it, accepting her touch as a healer rather than a lover.

'You must thank Eva's bees for the treatment before you leave.'

He looked away at the mention of Eva's name, as if the memory of her was too much to consider. The hollow she'd left in their lives echoed in every room and he couldn't have failed to feel it. It was another thing that neither of them was ready to talk about.

'What will you do now?'

'The fire won't deter the maquis from continuing their fight. A new camp is already up and running again. I'm on my way to join them.'

'Won't you go back to England instead?'

'No, won't you?'

With her mission complete, the safest thing for Iris would be to return to London, but until she saw Yvette, she had no way of contacting Ambrose to make the arrangements to get her out. Having been called in for questioning by Frisch, it wouldn't be safe for her to continue working in Dijon as an agent, as she'd originally hoped. She cleared her throat, fighting the temptation to tell him everything. 'This is my home now.'

'Do you have any information on Mason? He seems to have disappeared.'

Iris busied herself at the sink. One look at her face and Jack would know she was lying.

'If I hear from him, I'll let you know.'

Clemence had left four freshly laid eggs on her windowsill, and she was desperate to feed them to him. 'I'll make you something to eat.' She smiled, as if they weren't at war. 'How about an omelette?'

He wriggled his fingers, testing the flexibility in his hands inside the gloves, as if her simple care had made a difference.

'Those omelettes of yours. Do they still turn out like scrambled eggs?'

It was the joke he always made, his gentle teasing, reminding her of how he'd once loved her, taking her back to the endless weekend breakfasts and lazy lunches they'd cooked together before the war. At the time, she'd taken them for granted, assuming they'd last a lifetime. Now, every moment spent with Jack was precious, knowing it could be the last one.

She touched his arm, her voice straining with mock indignation, as she encouraged him out of the chair.

'If you're going to criticise my cooking, you can make it yourself. I'll fetch some tarragon from the garden. There's butter in the pantry and fresh goat's cheese from Monsieur Roubert. It cost me three large potatoes and a bunch of sweet peas, so treat it well.'

Having banned the sale of home-grown produce, the Germans authorities were unaware that Monsieur Roubert had created an underground market in his cellar, where people who were used to living off the land brought goods to exchange. There, you could find large hams cured in ash, jars of clarified butter, dried sausages and countless other edible treasures that made life worth living.

Jack's mood seemed to improve as he slowly beat the eggs and poured them into the pan, nudging the edges softly as they began to set. For a fleeting moment, she could almost imagine things were back to how they used to be, that Eva would wander in from the garden, tugging off her gardening gloves and demanding coffee. But those days were gone, and no amount of wishing could bring them back.

After they'd eaten, Jack carried the empty plates to the sink, ready for washing, just as he used to, but the air of false brightness Iris had tried to cultivate over a simple meal was too brittle to last.

'Would you like to rest for a while? You look like you could do with some sleep.'

There was a bed freshly made up in the attic. And there was her bed, which was always ready for him, although she left the invitation to it unspoken.

'I've stayed too long already. It wasn't meant to be a social call.'

'Stay as long as you like. Stay forever if you want to.'

He looked away, his eyes bleeding love as they scanned the

room, and she knew he was thinking about Mason, looking for traces of his presence, and if he looked hard enough, he was bound to find something. If nothing else, there was her guilt. She was suffocating in it, and it was deep enough and thick enough to be visible.

'You'll be safe here, Jack. It's better than sleeping with strangers.'

After everything he'd been through, Jack didn't take much persuading to stay. She made him another tisane and ran him a bath before showing him up to the bed in the attic. If he thought it odd that she was prepared for a guest, he didn't comment on it.

She sat on the floor beside the bed while he slept, crying silent tears of loss as she watched over him, his dream-filled cries a testament to the atrocities he'd witnessed and been unable to prevent. In between his nightmares, in the deepest part of his sleep, his face relaxed and she glimpsed the traces of the Jack she loved.

He was still there, locked inside the shell of his suffering. It would take time and peace for him to return to himself. And love. If all else failed, there was always love, whether she could convince him to believe in it or not. She couldn't stop the war, but here, in Eva's house, she could offer him a respite from it, and if she looked after him well enough, perhaps he'd stay forever.

Chapter 41

Jack left early, slipping out of the house before Iris was awake, leaving nothing behind but an empty bed, and the dent in the pillow where his head had lain. Despite her disappointment at his departure and his failure to say goodbye, at least now she knew he was alive, and that mattered more than anything.

When she finally ventured out, she was surprised to find the café open and even more surprised to see the Grey Mouse sitting at her favourite table outside.

The place was busier than usual, each customer sending a message of solidarity to Adele and one of defiance to the Germans. Among the clusters of people, Iris noticed Solange and Christophe sitting at a table in the corner, their heads bowed as they leaned into one another. Solange's dark hair was loose around her shoulders, her fingers close to Christophe's hand as she whispered in his ear.

The only available table was next to the Grey Mouse, who struck a cruel figure, putting herself where she wasn't wanted. Her quickness to engage in conversation, her eyes that missed nothing, suggested she was under orders to observe everything that went on in the café and the square.

Iris had only just sat down when the Grey Mouse raised her

hand to catch her attention. Iris wondered if she was going to mention Georges's murder, or whether she intended to brazen it out by pretending it hadn't happened.

'I heard you're in charge of managing Eva's literary estate.'

She spoke as if it were part of an ongoing conversation, as if that German gun had never been fired at Georges.

'Yes. It's an honour to have been trusted with it.'

Iris kept her rage under control. It was important not to seem unfriendly. If the Grey Mouse was working as Frisch's eyes and ears, she didn't want to give him a reason to take her in for questioning again.

'Will you be publishing more of Eva's recipes? When I visited her house, she told me she was working on another book. Do you plan to finish it on her behalf?'

'I can't think about it yet. Her death was a great shock. We were very close. She was like a mother to me.'

'My question was too intrusive. Forgive me.'

Of all the things she needed to beg forgiveness for, this was far from the worst, but it wouldn't do to say it. It was important to keep the conversation light. 'Not at all. It makes me happy to know Eva's work was admired by so many.'

'Good food, books: these are the things that unite us, no matter what our differences, don't you think?'

Her sentiments didn't fit with her army uniform. Since the rise of Hitler, the Third Reich was only interested in promoting its own culture. They'd set out to destroy everyone else's. Iris tried to hide her distrust. She couldn't be sure the Grey Mouse hadn't set a trap.

As they spoke, Adele appeared from inside the café and began working her way towards the table with a tray. Iris had assumed someone else was running the place. She couldn't possibly be in any state to work.

'Adele, why aren't you resting?'

Her face was still set with the same blank look it had presented the last time Iris had seen her, her eyes reduced to thin slits of misery as she placed a drink on the table. It was impossible to tell what it was without tasting it, and judging by the bitter smell, Iris was inclined to leave it alone.

'I can't leave the café. You know why that is.'

Adele stared at the Grey Mouse, as if seeing her for the first time, registering her uniform that condemned her as a killer, before dropping the tray, allowing it to clatter to the ground and letting out a scream.

'What are you doing here? I don't want you here. Leave now. Go, before I kill you.'

She flew at the Grey Mouse, her dry-eyed agony finally finding a release and a target. Iris shot out of her seat and took Adele gently by both arms, restraining her fury before she gave anyone a reason to arrest her. She turned to the Grey Mouse, struggling to contain Adele's need for violence, fighting the temptation to allow its release. At that moment, revenge would taste very sweet, no matter what the consequences.

'Perhaps you should go now.'

The Grey Mouse stood up, pushing the strap of her bag onto her shoulder. If she was shaken by Adele's threat, she made a good job of not showing it.

'I have enjoyed our chat, Iris. I hope we can speak again soon.'

No one turned to look as Adele leaned against Iris and sobbed. They were willing to support her by visiting the café, but no one was brave enough to look her agony directly in the face.

Iris took Adele's hand, intending to take her back inside, when her mother appeared, her face registering the same despair as Adele's.

'Thank you, Iris. I'll take care of her.'

Iris had only just sat down again when Madame Janot walked up to her, eyeing the empty seat at the table. 'Do you mind if I join you? Solange is inside with Christophe. She's trying to persuade him to take her dancing and I don't want to intrude.'

She slid into the chair, keeping one eye on the Grey Mouse's retreating figure as she left the square.

'Are you all right? I heard you were taken in for questioning by the Gestapo.'

'I think so, for now. It was Frisch himself who questioned me.'

'People say he's a monster. He's the one who ordered the Mayor to be shot when Schiller went missing. God knows what he'll do now a second one of his officers has disappeared.' Madame Janot leaned in closer and lowered her voice. 'Mason, the man they're looking for. He's been seen coming and going from your house.'

'I knew him from before. I didn't know he was part of the Third Reich when I first met him. I was as surprised as anyone when he turned up here. It's all been rather awkward, to tell you the truth.'

'No wonder you came to me for new locks and bolts for Eva's house. None of us sleep safely in our beds anymore, but you seem to have made yourself an enemy of both sides.'

When Iris didn't react, she tried again. 'You know what people are saying about you?'

'Frisch wouldn't have called me in for questioning if I was a collaborator.'

'Appearances can be deceptive. People haven't forgotten that the Mayor was shot right here in this very square after Schiller disappeared. Now Mason is missing, they see history repeating itself. It's not only Madame Legrand who blames Eva for her husband's death.'

This explained why so few people attended Eva's funeral, why people were reluctant to talk about her.

'Schiller's body has been found. It proves Eva didn't hide him or help him to escape.'

'Watch yourself, Iris. That's all I'll say.'

'You think I'm a collaborator?'

'It makes no difference what I think. The Mayor is still dead and the war carries on.'

'People shouldn't be so quick to judge.'

'You've been seen courting a German officer. He was spotted entering your house on a number of occasions. It's going to take a lot for anyone in this town to trust you. People are sore over the fact that Georges was murdered in cold blood. Someone has to suffer for the terrible things that are happening. If there are reprisals over Mason's disappearance, you'd better watch out.'

Chapter 42

Eva's house wasn't the same since the German soldiers had ransacked it. Despite Iris's and Clemence's efforts to put everything back as it had once been, the rooms still felt as if they'd been violated. The stamp of heavy boots, the abuse of enquiring hands and prying eyes, could be felt everywhere. Each time the breeze got up, Iris threw back the shutters and opened the windows, welcoming it in, hoping it would blow away the sense of intrusion that filled the place up like a bad smell. It was a fanciful notion when only time would remove the traces of the trespassers, softening the sharp edges of the memory, just as she hoped it would soften the pain of every other hurt she endured.

After Madame Janot's warning, Iris stayed close to home, avoiding the curious eyes that were waiting for her on the streets. It wasn't only the attention of the German soldiers who'd been set to watch her that she avoided, but that of the townspeople too. She couldn't blame them for being suspicious when the fact that she was a murderer was ingrained in her soul.

If Frisch had instructed the lake at the Château Guillard to be dredged as he'd threatened, it would only be a matter of time before Mason's body was found. What then? Would they come for her again with more questions? Had she cleaned away the evidence that she'd been there with him at the time of his death, or had she left behind something of herself that would be enough to incriminate her?

Someone would have seen her leaving the house with Mason on the morning of his death, just as they'd have seen her returning home alone after the storm. The question was, would anyone hate her enough to come forward and denounce her, or would they spare her for the very fact that she'd killed one of the enemy? In the eyes of most people in the town, this should make her a hero.

With her bed no longer feeling her own, Iris sat up late, listening to the hushed sounds of the curfewed night, where even the moon took refuge behind the clouds and refused to show itself, as if to do so would have been an affront to the occupying forces. Nothing stirred, not even the breeze, however much she tried to summon it. Even the bats were still, the trees and the shrubs in Eva's garden like frozen images slipped from the pages of a book.

And so the sound of movement when it came was even more distinct: the self-conscious shuffle of feet in heavy boots, the shift of an arm in a cumbersome jacket. A German soldier would never appear so apologetic in his movements. It had to be Jack. He must have come to see if she was all right. She was desperate to see him again, to check his burns were healing and to know that he was safe.

Careful not to say his name out loud, she crept to the window, angling her head to look between the slats in the shutters where the dark shadow of a man lingered. Iris's heart turned over. It wasn't Jack. The figure was too tall, the body too broad. He didn't hold himself the way Jack did, as if the world and all its troubles were on his shoulders, waiting for him to fix them.

She backed away from the window, hoping whoever it was hadn't seen her. What was he waiting for? Why was he standing on her doorstep in the middle of the night? If he was caught breaking the curfew, he'd risk being shot. Whatever had brought him here, he must have been desperate.

By being awake, she'd made herself vulnerable. She should have forced herself to go to bed, even if only to use it as a hiding place from the demons of the night. She crept along the hallway, avoiding the floorboards that gave the loudest groan, but it was too late. The quiet tap of knuckles on the door told her she'd given herself away.

'Iris, please let me in.'

It was an English voice. She froze, listening for more clues. Whoever it was, he knew her name. She needed to know she could trust him before she considered opening the door. A full minute passed and still the stranger gave no hints as to his identity. She began to think she'd imagined him, but his figure was too imprinted on her mind for her to question whether he was real or not.

Tap, tap. There it went again. 'I was told this was a safe house.'

Had Ambrose put the word out that she was able to offer a haven to any British agent who needed it? Would he have done such a thing without warning her first? She thought of Yvette, so vulnerable out in the field, her wits and her schoolgirl figure her only defence against a brutish enemy. And then there was Jack, living in the hills with the maquis. How would she feel if either of them was denied help when they were in danger?

She crept towards the door and undid the bolt, hearing the sigh of relief escape from the man waiting on the step. Still cautious, she opened the door no more than the width of an eye and peered out.

The stranger raised his hands, showing himself to be unarmed. 'Thank God. I was beginning to think I'd got the wrong place.'

Beneath his coat, he was wearing the rough clothes of a farm labourer. Iris remained silent, the full weight of her body pressed against the door in case he tried to force it open.

'The plane that was supposed to take me back to England wasn't able to land. I was told this was the place to come to if I needed to hide.'

She stared at him through one eye, the other half of her face still hidden behind the door. He had the muddy complexion of so many Englishmen, his hair not fair enough to be blond, or brown enough to be dark, but somewhere in between, his eyes, grey rather than blue. His skin was the colour you'd expect from someone who'd spent the summer in a dull climate and his hands shook as he struggled to know what to do with them.

Would Ambrose have been foolish enough to advise him to come here if he was in trouble? Surely, he couldn't consider this to be a safe house, given what she'd come here to do? And yet times were desperate.

The stranger looked nervously over his shoulder at the square. 'Can I come in?'

Iris closed the door another fraction as he took a step forward. If she let him in, there was no saying what might happen.

'Who told you to come here?'

'Ambrose.'

Ambrose would never have used his real name. It was all she needed to confirm her suspicion. 'Whoever told you this was a safe house was mistaken. You must leave now and never come back. I won't help you.'

'I'm an Englishman in trouble. I'm on your side. What do you mean, you won't help me?'

'If you don't leave now, I'll betray you to the Gestapo.'

She closed the door, dragging the bolt to secure it and turning the key in the lock, while the stranger stood outside and quietly raved, ordering her to open up.

'You're a traitor to the cause.'

He was still there when she crept upstairs to bed, climbing beneath the covers without bothering to undress.

It was a trap. Ambrose hadn't sent him. She knew every agent who had passed through his hands. She'd helped to train most of them. And even if this hadn't been the case, he'd failed to give the password that was used for recognition in the field.

'I order you to let me in.'

Her whole body tensed as he hammered the door with his fist, his voice travelling up from the street. If she ignored him for long enough, he'd eventually go away.

'Ambrose will make you answer for this. I swear to God.' He slammed the flat of his hand repeatedly against the door to emphasise each word.

Someone had betrayed her. There was no other way he could have known Ambrose's name. Frisch must have sent him. But how did he know about Ambrose? The only person who knew of their connection was Yvette. Iris hadn't seen her lately and she had no way of knowing if she was safe. If she'd been captured, there was every chance she'd given Iris away during interrogation.

If only she could have stopped Ambrose sending Yvette over to France. She was too young, too inexperienced, despite the training she'd been given. Without a good dose of luck, she was unlikely to survive.

Iris pulled the bed covers under her chin and closed her eyes, waiting for whoever was outside to exhaust himself. Eventually, the shouting stopped and he retreated across the square, returning to whoever had sent him.

From now on, Iris would have to assume her cover had been broken and be more careful than ever. All she could do was keep her head down and her wits about her. It was only a matter of time before Mason's body was dragged from the lake, before Frisch decided on his next move, and whatever it turned out to be, she had to be ready for it.

Chapter 43

Iris lay awake for most of the night, expecting the return of the man who'd tried to trick her into hiding him. She'd been right not to be taken in by his story. In these dangerous times, trust had to be double-checked and when that failed she had to rely on her instincts.

It was almost morning before she allowed herself to relax. She'd only been asleep for a few minutes when she was woken by a disturbance outside. Peering through a gap in the bedroom shutters, she looked down into the square where the busy hum of voices told her a crowd had gathered. Something wasn't right. She could tell by the low pitch of the sound, by the way people huddled together, as if an ill-wind had blown in, chilling them to the bone. After reassuring herself there were no soldiers in attendance, she went to find out what was going on.

Clemence met her at the door, her hand trembling as she pointed to a notice nailed to a cross in the centre of the square. 'It's happening again.'

Reprisals. Iris had guessed it was coming, but it was still a shock. She forced her way to the front of the crowd to get a clear view of the sign, desperate to know what cruelty Frisch was preparing to inflict this time.

Missing
Guy Mason
If information is not received regarding his whereabouts within 72 hours, the people on the hostage list will be rounded up and shot.

Iris had done this. Innocent people were under the threat of execution and it was all her fault. How had it come to this? She'd only set out to punish Mason for passing military secrets to the enemy. How could she have ended up putting so many lives in danger? She considered the people in the square, the old men and the young mothers, each one living in terror. Which of them were facing death because of her? She turned to Clemence, fighting to keep her voice steady.

'Whose names are on the hostage list?'

'They won't tell us. We have to wait to see who they drag from their homes after the seventy-two hours have passed, wait and see who they place in front of the firing squad, ready to shoot in cold blood, just as they did with the Mayor. Until then, each of us is living under the threat of a death sentence. That's the fun of it for them, don't you see?'

'I can't let this happen. I have to find out whose names are on the list. They need to be warned.'

'If they flee, the Gestapo will know the list has been leaked and it will only lead to more reprisals.'

Iris couldn't worry about what might or might not happen. She could only deal with the matter in hand. 'Whoever is on the list has to be given the opportunity to escape.'

The notice implied the Gestapo still hadn't found Mason's body. Had they searched the lake and failed to find him, or had they not attempted it yet? If they could persuade someone to come forward with information, it would save them the trouble.

The temptation to return to the scene of the crime was almost overwhelming, but it would be a mistake. The Gestapo was watching her. They'd already tested her, trying to trick her into taking in someone posing as a British agent. They'd failed to catch her that time, but it didn't mean they wouldn't try again. The whole point of the hostage list was to draw her out, to force her to make a mistake and give herself away, but they'd underestimated her if they thought she'd play into their hands. Now, the most important thing was to make sure those on the list weren't made to die as a consequence of her actions.

Chapter 44

Iris put on her soft-soled shoes and set out across the town, retracing the route she'd taken with Paul to the top of the ravine the day they laid the flowers for Nathalie, the same place Eva had lured Schiller, intending him to fall to his death. Today, there wasn't time to stop and pay her respects to the memory of her lost childhood friend. Instead, she carried on into the dense woodland that lay beyond, searching for signs of a maquis camp. The Germans might have burned the original hideout to the ground, but Jack had mentioned it had already been rebuilt. There would always be more freedom fighters to replace those who were lost, men living on their wits, made wild by circumstance and determined to win the war. Brutal acts of destruction wouldn't stop them.

Jack had inadvertently revealed something about the lie of the land where they'd built the camp when she last saw him. Iris had recognised the rocks he described from when she used to forage for wild garlic with Eva. Now, if she could find the exact place, it might lead her directly to him.

Someone must have been looking out from the camp and seen her approaching because before she'd even reached the clearing where she suspected Jack would be, he came striding towards her.

'What are you doing here?'

He had a British gun slung over his shoulder and was walking tall, his eyes alive with purpose and danger. His lungs had begun to recover from the smoke damage and he was breathing more freely. Thanks to the honey from Eva's bees, the skin on his hands and face already appeared less scorched.

'I need your help.'

He beckoned her to follow him to the darkest part of the woods where the sun never reached, their faces shadowed by the dense canopy of leaves above them.

'Were you followed?'

'No.'

This was the old Jack, the man full of vigour and honour that she'd fallen in love with. Here, living alongside the maquis, he'd found a purpose and despite the terrible things that were happening, it had brought him back to life.

'You've heard about the hostage list?'

He nodded, keeping his eyes focused on the ground as if he didn't trust himself to look at her.

'I need to know whose names are on it, so I can warn them and give them a chance to escape. Is there anyone in the maquis who could help me to get the information?'

'Why do you want to help the people of the town all of a sudden?'

'They can't be allowed to suffer for the actions of a British agent. I'm already being watched. I can't risk being caught trying to get hold of the information that could save them.'

She'd considered breaking into the Hoffmans' house to search for the hostage list, which was probably in the study Frisch had claimed as his office, but it was too risky. If she was caught, she'd be arrested.

Jack finally looked at her, his eyes searching her face as he slowly worked the whole thing out in his mind. 'It was you, wasn't it? You're the one responsible for Mason's disappearance.'

Iris couldn't lie to him and she wasn't going against Ambrose's orders not to tell him, because he'd already guessed. Surely, Jack couldn't think any less of her for admitting the truth.

'I was ordered to assassinate him by British Intelligence.'

A burst of air escaped from his chest as if she'd winded him. 'And you've carried out your orders.'

'I came here to complete the mission I began in London, to make sure he was punished for his treachery. Who do you think gathered the evidence that proved he was passing military secrets on to the enemy?'

'They used you as a honey trap to catch him.'

'He was known to have a weakness for French women. I was only meant to engineer a meeting with him in a bar, maybe have dinner with him once or twice to assess his character, and find out what he was up to. It was never meant to go on the way it did. When I began to suspect he was passing military secrets to Germany, they asked me to continue the mission. I couldn't say no. Too many Allied soldiers had been led to their deaths because of the intelligence he'd betrayed. He had to be stopped.'

Jack leaned against the trunk of an ancient tree as if to draw strength from it. 'All this time and I never knew.'

'I was refused permission to tell you and so I relied on you not finding out. They promised to keep me out of it when the story went public, but they went back on it. They said allowing my photograph to be seen in the newspapers would prevent Mason suspecting I'd been involved in the plot to trap him. I would never have accepted the mission if I'd known it would destroy our marriage.'

'And yet it did.'

'When the British government dismissed the spying case against him to save their embarrassment, I was tasked with luring him here to assassinate him. Whatever you and the rest of the British public were led to believe, it was never the intention to let him go unpunished.'

He nodded at her words, but said nothing. The spark that had lit his eyes had gone. The pain of her betrayal had come back with all its force and it was her fault. Her confession was too much for him to take in and whatever her motivation, she'd still been unfaithful and no attempt at justifying it would change the fact that it had happened.

The sudden rustling of a bird in a nearby tree brought them back to their present danger. Iris touched Jack gently on the arm, a comrade's goodbye. 'I'd better go before someone sees us. Keep yourself safe.'

He made no effort to stop her as she started to leave. His mind was still working through everything she'd told him, his eyes fixed on the ground.

'I'll see what I can do to get you the names. I might know someone.'

'Thank you.' She threw a parting look over her shoulder. 'Come to the house if you need anything.'

If you need me, she wanted to add, *if there's anything I can do to make things right, to heal the pain I've caused*, but there was no use saying any of it because it was too late, and she had to accept there was no way back for them. The problem with loving an idealist is that sooner or later, you're bound to let them down.

She took a winding route back into town to avoid leaving an obvious trail. Jack had been too stunned by her revelation to show any kind of reaction to her confession but finally, he knew the truth. Whatever his opinion of her, at least now it would be based on facts.

Chapter 45

Time was ticking by, but there was no one else Iris could trust to ask for help in finding out the names on the hostage list. As the head of the Resistance, Monsieur Vallery had proven too slippery for her taste. She hadn't completely believed him when he claimed to have had no hand in the removal of Schiller from the bottom of the ravine, or in the disposal of his body, and because information about Schiller's fate had been withheld, the Mayor's life had been sacrificed.

In Vallery's defence, nothing he could have said or done would have stopped the killing in the name of reprisals. It might, however, have removed the suspicion from Eva and possibly saved her life. With war, there were no boundaries to define morality. Winning was all that counted, no matter what the consequential damage. Iris and Jack were living proof of this.

And so with no one else to trust, Iris waited out the following few hours, hoping Jack could help her to get the information she needed. Despite the heartbreak she'd caused him, there was no one else she could turn to.

She was picking the last of the apricots when she heard the rattle of the gate. *Jack*? His name burst into her mind, hope exploding like a firework. She rushed to the bottom of the garden, while whoever was there waited to be admitted.

He must have heard her footsteps approaching on the path and risked calling out.

'Iris, it's me, Jack.'

Her instinct hadn't been wrong. She slid back the bolt and opened the gate, her pleasure at seeing him quietened by the question of whether he was able to help her or not.

'Come inside. I'll make you something to eat.'

He glanced around the garden. 'Are you alone?'

She nodded.

He ran his fingers through his hair, rubbing at his three days' growth of beard. She wanted to tell him how much his rugged look suited him, but it wasn't what he'd come for. Instead, she tossed him an apricot and led him inside, thankful for the eggs Clemence had left on her windowsill again that morning.

'Can I tempt you to an omelette?'

He rolled up his sleeves and washed his hands in the kitchen sink, as if he'd never been away, as if the war hadn't stepped in and broken them.

'Only if you let me cook.' He turned his hands over to show her the palms. 'Look. The skin has nearly healed.'

It was all she could do not to cry. She could almost hear Eva's murmur at the sign of a small victory won as she handed him the eggs. 'I'll pick some herbs for garnishing.'

It was too much to hope that one day he'd forgive her, that he'd want to give their marriage another try. He'd offered to cook the eggs. It was nothing more than that.

When she returned to the kitchen, he'd already laid the table. The jug of Michaelmas daisies she'd put on the windowsill now sat between the two place settings. He washed and chopped the herbs, sprinkling them over the omelette before placing it in front of her, then sat down, his fork poised over her plate, and she realised he'd made it for them to share, just as he always used to.

He closed his eyes as the first mouthful slipped down his

throat. 'Why does the food cooked in Eva's kitchen taste better than anything made anywhere else?'

Eva was still working her magic. She didn't have to be there for it to be felt. 'It's the love. However hard I try to scrub it away, it just won't budge.'

It was ingrained in the walls and the stone floor, in the beaten-up wood of the table and the chairs, and it would be there forever. During her darkest times, it was its endurance that kept Iris going.

She waited until he'd finished eating before she mentioned the hostage list. He hesitated, helping himself to one of the apricots she'd placed in a bowl in front of him.

'Are you sure you want to go ahead with this?'

'Of course.'

He seemed to have forgotten she was an assassin, that she was capable of more than he could ever consider.

'Go to the café in the square tomorrow morning. Someone will contact you there.'

He got up from the table, nervously turning the apricot in his fingers, and she regretted bringing the war back into the room when everything had been going so well. She had to pull it back round. The old Jack had shown himself. She couldn't let him get away again.

'Would you like a tisane? I've finally mastered the recipe Eva used to make for you.' Iris didn't care how desperate she sounded. She didn't want the magic to disappear.

He bit into the apricot and settled in his favourite chair beside the fire. The return of the hollowed-out expression behind his eyes told her it was the only answer she was going to get, and yet it was enough. The fact that he was here with her now was enough.

She fought her instinct to make conversation as she tore the mint leaves and put the water on to boil, forcing herself to leave the silence unbroken until he was ready to begin.

'You didn't tell me you'd been arrested by the Gestapo, that they'd questioned you.'

'I wasn't formally arrested, but they did question me.'

He stared at the drink as she handed it to him. The smell of the tisane filled the room, the mint heady in the air between them 'You've taken such risks. What were you thinking, leaving London and entering occupied territory?'

'The British government banished Mason from Britain to save their embarrassment. If he was to be punished, it had to take place on foreign soil. There was no longer anything to keep me in London. Mason didn't take much convincing to follow me to France.'

He took a sip of the tisane, the sweetness of the honey she'd added softening his expression. She took the opportunity to take another risk.

'Would you like a bath? You can stay if you want to. A good night's sleep will make you feel better.'

For a moment, she thought he was tempted. He finished the rest of his tisane, running his tongue over his lips, savouring the last of the honey. 'I can't stay. I'm on lookout duty tonight. After the Germans set fire to the previous camp, we can't be too careful.'

'You came here to investigate Mason. Now he's dead, will you go back to England?'

'Mason's no longer the reason I'm here.'

'Then what's keeping you?'

She wanted him to say it was her, but of course, he never would. The days when he was committed to her, when he hated to be apart from her were gone.

'The maquis have welcomed me like a brother. They're the bravest men I've ever met, risking their lives, fighting for the freedom of their country. I can't abandon them now, not when there's still so much to fight for.'

'When all this is over, you'll be able to tell their story to the world. Make sure their bravery is recognised.'

He smiled at her optimism, at her assurance that they'd survive to tell the tale. 'Perhaps.'

He leaned into her as he stood up to leave, kissing her lightly on the forehead. 'Don't forget your appointment at the café tomorrow. And remember, these are dangerous times. Don't take any more risks than you have to.'

'I can't promise you that.'

Iris's world had taken her beyond the point of needing to stay safe. It was others she needed to protect now. The people on the hostage list couldn't die because she'd killed Mason. She had to stop this terrible thing happening and it meant everything that Jack was the one helping her to do it.

Chapter 46

Adele was still working in the café when Iris arrived the following morning. Her blank expression, as she went through the motions of clearing the tables, was a testament to the barrier she'd put up as protection against her acceptance of Georges's death. While she didn't have to acknowledge it, it didn't have to be real. She'd been wearing the same dress for days and she looked as if she hadn't slept. The shawl she'd once used to secure Georges to her chest was tied loosely around her shoulders.

She presented Iris with a drink before she could place her order, dropping it on the table without acknowledging her. She wasn't in the mood to talk, and so for now, people would get whatever she chose to serve them.

The sun was shining and most of the tables outside the café were busy. Iris scanned the faces of the customers, wondering if one of them might be her contact. Most were regulars. Others were women she recognised from around the town, each one there to offer her unspoken support to Adele and trying to behave as if nothing was wrong.

The absence of men was still something Iris couldn't get used to. It was impossible to accept that a whole generation of husbands, sons and fathers had been swept away by the war, and there was no knowing how many would come back, or what state the survivors would be in when they eventually returned. She only had to look at Christophe and Paul and Jack to see the toll it was taking. The people left to suffer at home weren't doing any better. Adele's grief was enough to show that tragedy was taking place on all fronts.

Her thoughts were interrupted by a flurry of activity in one corner, as three separate tables emptied at the same time, the customers simultaneously paying their bills and straightening their hats in their hurry to leave.

'Iris, may I join you?'

It was the Grey Mouse, her tall figure standing over her and blocking out the sun. It explained why the other tables had emptied so suddenly. The presence of a German uniform was too awful to stand after what had happened to Georges, and while the threat of reprisals hung over everyone.

How could this woman be so insensitive? Did she not understand how much distress her presence caused?

'I wasn't planning to stay long.'

The Grey Mouse ignored the hint and assumed the seat anyway. 'Then we'll enjoy the little time we have to spend together.'

Adele must have seen the Grey Mouse arrive because she appeared from inside the café and placed a drink in front of her. Iris braced herself to intervene the moment Adele turned on her, but she barely gave her a look. Whatever was going on in Adele's heart and mind, she was broken. The shift in her behaviour was monumental, but if the Grey Mouse noticed the change, she didn't show it.

Iris stared at her drink, quietly seething at the interruption. Her contact couldn't risk handing over the names on the hostage list while she was sitting with the enemy. She could only trust that whoever it was would have the patience to wait. The Grey Mouse couldn't have made things more difficult if she'd tried.

'Have you given any thought to Eva's new recipe book?'

'I'm sorry?'

'Have you decided whether to finish writing it?'

Once again, the Grey Mouse had picked up the conversation where they'd previously left off. 'It's still too soon to think about it.'

'Of course. The future is hard to consider when everything is so uncertain. I feel that too.'

'Will you be going back to Germany soon?'

'I have to go where I'm sent. But I hope not. I like it here very much. Before the war I taught French in a school in Berlin. I have a great love of the culture.'

And yet you've come to destroy it. Iris bit back the words. She couldn't risk making an enemy of the enemy. Instead, she talked about the weather, before attempting to close down the conversation, hoping the Grey Mouse would leave, but rather than taking the hint, she opened it up again, indulging in a lengthy description of the novel she was reading.

Forty-five minutes passed and still the Grey Mouse made no effort to leave. Adele stayed inside the café, as one by one, the other customers finished their drinks and departed. Iris was beginning to think the Grey Mouse would never go. Her contact couldn't be expected to wait this long, and Iris was getting restless.

The last customers had just gone when they heard a loud crash coming from the café. Iris rushed inside to find Adele on her knees, surrounded by broken glass, her face buried in her hands as she made herself small.

Iris helped her to her feet and guided her to the nearest chair. 'It's only a few smashed glasses. It's nothing to worry about.'

Adele remained silent, seemingly unaware of the tiny cuts on her legs where she'd knelt on the splinters, all the while staring at the broken glass, its sharp edges glinting in the morning light as Iris began to clear it up.

'Can I help?'

A dark shadow clouded the doorway as the Grey Mouse appeared. Iris shot her a nervous glance, worried how Adele might react.

'We don't need you here, everything's fine.'

Pain sliced through the skin on Iris's finger as she caught it on a piece of broken glass. She flinched, pressing the wound against her lips. The Grey Mouse stepped forward and pushed a handkerchief into Iris's hand.

'Take this to stem the blood.'

Iris recoiled from the enemy's touch, trying to refuse the handkerchief, but the gesture had been so quick, it was in her grasp before she could pull away. She gave a grudging nod of thanks, risking a glance at Adele, who seemed oblivious to the whole scene.

'It's probably best if you leave now.'

It was the first time the Grey Mouse had looked contrite. 'Yes, of course. Thank you for your company this morning. I hope I haven't detained you too long.'

The moment she'd gone, Madame Blanchet appeared from the kitchen, her manner almost as stiff as Adele's, as if the shock of Georges's death had spread between them, the grief doubling in its intensity rather than halving as they shared it.

'Thank you, Iris. You can go now. I'll take care of Adele and clear up the mess.'

'Are you sure there's nothing I can do?'

'Please turn the sign to *Closed* on your way out. My daughter has done enough for today.'

With the café closed, Iris had no choice but to leave. Thanks to the Grey Mouse, she'd missed her contact and the opportunity to receive the names on the hostage list had been lost. Frustrated, she pressed the handkerchief against the wound as she crossed the square on her way back to Eva's house. Despite the sharp pain, it was little more than a scratch and the bleeding had already stopped. The shock of it had been worse than the injury itself.

Once home, she stood at the sink to wash the cut, putting the handkerchief aside until something familiar about it caught her attention. His name faltered on her lips as she read it. *Jack*. The handkerchief belonged to Jack. It was one of a dozen she'd given him for Christmas before the war. The woman in the shop where she'd bought them had arranged for his name to be embroidered in one corner. And there it was, quite visible where the square had begun to unfold at the edge.

There was only one reason the Grey Mouse would have one of Jack's handkerchiefs. Iris went rigid at the thought of his betrayal, but it was none of her business what Jack got up to these days. After what she'd done with Mason, she had no right to feel hurt if he'd found someone else. She'd return the handkerchief to him the next time she saw him. He might be glad to have it back. It was only when she shook it out, preparing to rinse the blood from it that she saw the names written in tiny letters in the centre of the linen. The hostage list.

The truth slowly dawned on her. The Grey Mouse had been her contact. She'd taken the risk to secure the names and pass them on. All this time, she'd been helping the cause while Iris could barely bring herself to be civil.

Passing on the information via Jack's handkerchief proved he'd had a hand in it. It was his way of making sure Iris knew she could trust her. She checked the names, her heart in her mouth as she read each one.

At the top of the list was Christophe. What did the Gestapo hope to achieve by murdering a young man who'd already been invalided in both body and mind by the war, and what would his widowed mother do without him?

The second name was Albert's. Poor tender-hearted Albert, who'd wanted nothing more than to spend his final years living quietly with Eva. How could they be so cruel when he'd already suffered so much?

Paul was next on the list. Iris's legs were shaking so much she had to sit down. She was beginning to see a pattern. They'd picked all the people closest to her. If they wanted to punish her for Mason's death, then they knew how to go about it. What had

Paul ever done to them? They'd already broken him during the years he'd worked as forced labour in a German factory. Now all he was trying to do was keep the family vineyard going against all their efforts to bleed it dry.

The fourth name was the greatest shock of all. Clemence. How was she ever going to break the news to her?

The final name on the list came as no surprise. It was the one she'd expected to see all along. If any name deserved to be there, it was hers, and there it was, spelled out in the Grey Mouse's neat hand. She was condemned along with the rest of them.

She took a deep breath, steadying her nerves while she worked out a plan. There wasn't a minute to waste. The people on the list had to be given time to decide what to do. If they wanted to escape, they needed to be informed of their fate right away.

She was about to leave the house when Jack arrived, rattling the garden gate and not seeming to care if the neighbours heard as he called her name. She let him in, putting her fingers to her lips to quieten him as she led him into the kitchen, where they were least likely to be seen or overheard.

Still out of breath, he threw himself into his favourite chair. 'Frieda has just got word to me that your name is on the hostage list. Pack a bag quickly. We have to get you out.'

He called her Frieda, not the Grey Mouse. 'You gave her your handkerchief.' She couldn't help her accusing tone.

'I knew if you saw it, you'd make the connection to me. It was the only way I could be sure you'd trust her.'

Iris had suspected the Grey Mouse was a spy because of how much time she spent at the café, but she'd misjudged which side she was on. She'd failed to see beyond her uniform and allowed her prejudice to get in the way of her usual clear-sightedness.

Jack dropped his voice to a whisper. 'She came to the camp one day, asking how she could help the cause. Working as a translator, she has access to all kinds of useful information.'

'You trust her?'

'Her mother's side of the family is French. Her cousin was one of the maquis who was killed when the Germans set fire to the camp. Not every German wants to see Hitler win. Not even those forced to wear the uniform of the Third Reich. Appearances and loyalties can be deceptive. You of all people should understand that.'

Iris had been blinded by her uniform. Despite her friendly overtures, she'd seen her only as a Grey Mouse and had judged her accordingly. The experiences of the war had taken away her ability to trust anyone.

'I can't worry about myself, Jack. People have to be told they're on the list so they have a chance to flee.'

'If they disappear, the Germans will know the list was leaked.'

'I'll worry about that if it happens. For now, all I can do is save the people who have been condemned.'

'You have to get out as well. The danger is too close. You can hide in the maquis camp until we get word to London to send a plane to take you back to England. I'll go to Lyon. I know how to reach the British agent coordinating the network there. He can put me in touch with a wireless operator who can send a message.'

'I can't run away while innocent people are at risk of being put to death for the murder I've committed.'

'You've completed your mission. We have to get you out.'

'I can't simply abandon what I started here.'

'I'm begging you to leave. I'm still your husband. That has to count for something.'

It was a stalemate of the most loving kind, but Iris was determined to make sure no one died because she'd killed Mason.

'There has to be another way. There's still time to work something out. Will you trust me, Jack?'

Love and trust were different things. After everything that had happened, she couldn't assume the right to either one.

'You haven't got long. It's getting more dangerous by the minute. I can't lose you again, Iris.'

He hadn't answered her question, but he was prepared to go along with her for the time being. Whether he trusted her or not was another matter. Now all she had to do was come up with a plan that would save everyone on the list and prevent any further reprisals.

Chapter 47

Five minutes later, Iris was sitting with Clemence, gripping her hand to stop it shaking, as the news that her name was on the hostage list sank in.

'I'm sorry, Clemence. It's all my fault. You didn't deserve this after you'd been such a loyal friend to Eva.'

'You mustn't think like that. I'm proud to have been a friend to both you and Eva. I don't know what you've done to Mason, just as I don't know what happened with Schiller, but I know you've done us proud. We can't leave it to the young men to fight our wars for us.'

Iris hadn't mentioned that her own name was also on the list. It didn't seem right to burden Clemence with that too.

'There's still time to get you out of town. Is there someone you could stay with in another part of France? Or we could try to get you across the border to Switzerland. The maquis might be able to help.'

'I'm going nowhere. If they want to shoot me, I'll stand up straight and look them in the eye as they do it.' She got to her feet, urging Iris towards the door. 'Go. Whoever else is on the list needs to be told.'

Iris was reluctant to leave her, but time was short and she had to speak to the others on the list if they were to have time to plan their escape. She gave Clemence a hug, her heart breaking at her tiny frame. When had she become so small, so brave?

'I'll come back soon.'

'Don't worry about me. Go and do what you have to do.'

Fabrice was eating his lunch when Iris arrived. He stood at the front door, spoon in hand, making the point that she'd interrupted at a sacred time.

'May I speak to Albert?'

His face contorted as he pushed the tip of his tongue into the crevices of his back teeth, working free whatever part of his lunch had lodged itself there. 'Go on up.' He stepped aside, making room for her to pass and nodded towards the stairs. 'He's taken to his bed. It's the second door on the left.'

The smell of bean stew and garlic followed Iris up the stairs. Fabrice hadn't mentioned that Albert was ill, so why was he in bed in the middle of the day? She knocked quietly on the door, not wanting to startle him if he was asleep.

'Albert. It's Iris. May I come in?'

She heard his rough cough from the other side of the door, the sound of him clearing his throat.

'One moment please.'

He was still straightening his pyjama top when she entered. The curtains were pulled back to let in the light and Albert was sitting up in bed, propped up by half a dozen pillows. The room smelled of camphor and brandy, of a man who'd lain too long in one place.

'Are you all right? Nobody told me you were ill.'

He shrugged off her concern, smoothing his hair down with his fingers where the pillows had ruffled it. His beard was untrimmed, the spark gone from his eyes.

'There's nothing wrong with me that winning the war won't cure.'

Iris opened the window, allowing the mild midday breeze to blow in. 'Don't tell me you've given up.'

'Not given up, just tired. I won't go to the restaurant now Fabrice has encouraged the Germans to eat there, and without Eva, there seems little to get out of bed for.'

'Eva would want you to carry on with your life, to make the best of it.'

'If she were here, that's exactly what I'd be doing.'

Iris sat on the edge of the bed and took his hand. 'Then do it for her memory. You can't lie in bed all day. It's time to act.'

'What is it? What's happened?'

There was no easy way to break it to him. She just had to come straight out with it. He nodded as the news sank in.

'I should've guessed. They're coming for me because they can no longer get at Eva. That's it, isn't it?'

Iris wasn't brave enough to tell him it was because of her, because they suspected she'd killed Mason.

'Is there somewhere you can hide where the Germans won't find you?'

Albert gave a bitter laugh. 'So much for Fabrice welcoming the enemy to our restaurant. He said it would protect us from threats such as this. How wrong he was.'

'Shall I ask him to join us? He might know of somewhere you can go.'

He touched her arm, making her stay as she attempted to get up. 'I don't want him to know about this. It won't do any good to implicate him.'

'Then what will you do?'

'I'll lie in my bed and wait. And if they come for me, I'll let them take me. It's better for an old man like me to be sacrificed rather than anyone younger.'

'But they'll shoot you. Eva wouldn't want you to die like that. Your life is as valuable as anyone else's in this town.'

'It'll be the work of a moment and soon forgotten. And then I'll be with my beloved Eva. She'll be waiting for me on the other side.'

His eyes were set with determination. There was no convincing him to change his mind. It seemed wrong, not warning Fabrice of his father's impeding fate, and yet Albert had the right to decide for himself.

'There's still time to change your mind. If you decide to leave, tell Fabrice. He'll be able to arrange it for you. And if he needs help, tell him to come to me.'

'Thank you, but my mind is made up.'

He looked up at her from the pillows as she prepared to leave, his eyes blazing with any number of emotions, but it was his determination that burned the brightest.

'I'll give Eva your love when I see her.'

Iris crept down the stairs and slipped quietly out of the house, avoiding Fabrice so she didn't have to lie to him or evade his questions. It was the only way to respect Albert's wishes. And if she could stop the shooting of those on the hostage list, then there was no need for him to have been told.

Chapter 48

Paul was checking the vines when she arrived. It was almost time for the harvest and he was testing the grapes for ripeness, just as he'd done at this time every year for as long as he could remember. As soon as he was old enough to walk, his father had begun to teach him how to assess the grapes, using touch, taste and smell to judge if they were ready for harvesting. His sense of duty to the land bordered on reverence, just like his father's and his grandfather's before. Nothing was more important than the soil and the vines it nurtured. Nothing mattered more than producing the best wine in the region. Invaders would come and go, but the land would endure.

He wiped his hands down the front of his trousers to remove the grape juice when he saw her approach.

'Iris, what are you doing here?'

It was the first time she'd seen him since Adele had rescued him from the square in the middle of the night after he'd drunk too much. She didn't know if he'd kept away out of embarrassment, or because she'd made it clear there was no future for them. None of that was of any consequence now. It was only survival that mattered.

He was carrying a little more weight and his muscles had

regained some of their definition from the physical effort he'd put into the land. With labour in short supply, he was doing the work of the three other men he'd usually employ.

Her eyes scanned the landscape, checking she wouldn't be overheard. 'There's something I have to tell you.'

He listened without comment, his shoulders rising as he realised the consequences of what she was saying.

'Why me? What have I ever done to deserve this? I worked for them, didn't I? I let them take the best of my wine.'

She wasn't going to admit it was because of his association with her. That they'd been watching her and probably seen them together.

'You can make it across the border to Switzerland if you're quick about it.'

The afternoon sun was still high in the sky as he looked at her, his eyes narrowing against the glare.

'I can't leave my mother to run the vineyard again. She's not capable. The quality of the wine dropped immensely while she was in charge.'

'If you stay, you risk being shot.'

'Then I'll hide. There are cellars on the estate the Germans don't know about. I won't leave my land again. The occupiers will be driven out sooner or later, and when that day comes, I'll still be here, protecting what's mine.'

She wanted to believe it was possible for him to remain safe. 'You should at least get your mother to leave. She'll be terrified if they come looking for you. Is there anywhere she can go?'

'She has to stay here. If I'm hiding, we'll have to make it look as if she's running the vineyard in my place. Whatever happens, they'll still demand the wine.'

'You should discuss it with her first.'

He looked at her with contempt, his teeth bared like a wild animal's. She hated how much the war had damaged him. She could imagine him bullying his mother into obeying him, just as he'd tried to bully his way into her bed.

'You have to do whatever you think is best. It might not come to it anyway.'

'You think you can find a way stop these men having their sport? You think because you gave yourself to one of them, that they'll listen to you. Well, let me tell you this. They have more contempt for you than the rest of the town.'

There was nothing he could say that would hurt her, nothing she didn't already know. She began to retrace her steps back to the road, throwing her parting words over her shoulder.

'You can think what you like, Paul. I've warned you what might happen. It's up to you how you act on the information. I don't expect you to thank me for it.'

The afternoon had grown overcast by the time Iris reached Madame Janot's hardware shop, where she hoped to find Christophe. The fact that his injury prevented him doing any hard physical work was probably one of the reasons his name had been added to the hostage list. He was no use to the Third Reich and so he was disposable. His connection to Iris, however slight, was yet another reason for him to be condemned to death.

Madame Janot looked up from her ledger and frowned when Iris walked into the shop and asked if she could speak to him.

'Christophe isn't here. He's at home writing more of his terrible poems. You'll find him in the shed at the bottom of the garden. I blame you for encouraging his literary endeavours.'

She wasn't in the mood to take the blame for Christophe's poetry when she was responsible for something far worse. She cut the conversation short, nor caring how rude she appeared as she set out to find him.

It was a short walk across the town to where Christophe lived with his mother. Remembering what Madame Janot had said about finding him in his shed, she went straight to the back of the house and pushed open the garden gate.

'Christophe, it's Iris. Are you there?'

The small patch of land was a mass of weeds. No one had tended it for years.

'Christophe?'

She fought her way through the brambles as they snatched at her feet, following the path trodden in the long grass that led to the shed. When she tried the handle, the door was unlocked. She was reluctant to walk in without an invitation.

'Christophe. Christophe.'

After the fourth time of calling, he still hadn't responded. She knocked loudly, giving him further seconds to answer before she opened the door and stepped inside, blinking at the sight that confronted her as her eyes grew accustomed to the dim light.

The desk and the floor were piled with volumes of Eva's cookery books, the walls covered with copies of her obituary collected from numerous newspapers and magazines, alongside interviews she'd given over the years, reviews and samples of her recipes. Whichever way Iris looked, Eva's face stared back at her.

She was still struggling to take it all in when she heard the crash of the garden gate. It had to be Christophe. Conscious that she was intruding, she stepped out of the shed, ready to explain what she was doing there. As soon he saw her, he started to run away.

'Wait, Christophe. Please, I need to talk to you. It's urgent.'

He turned to look at her, cradling his injured arm like a wounded animal, and she wondered why it hadn't healed, whether he was doing something to make sure it never would.

'What were you doing in my shed? I didn't give you permission to go inside.' His voice was high-pitched and cracked, a trapped animal crying out.

'I know and I'm sorry. I was looking for you; that's all.'

He stared at her, unmoving, his feet caught in the brambles. 'What do you want?'

'I want to talk to you. Shall we go into the house?'

She couldn't face entering the shed again, knowing Eva's image would be bearing down at her from every angle.

Still Christophe refused to move. 'You can say what you have to say here.'

'I saw Eva's pictures in your shed and the articles that were written about her. I didn't know you had so many of her books.'

'I didn't steal them.'

'I didn't think you did.'

His whole body was hunched as he nursed his damaged arm. 'I miss her very much.'

'So do I. She was taken from us so cruelly. It's hard to understand it.'

He sank to his knees and began to cry like a child, unmindful of the brambles that snagged his trousers, the sharp points pushing through his skin. How could she warn him that his name was on the hostage list when his mind was already so troubled? But she had to. She couldn't abandon him to his fate.

'Are you sure you wouldn't like to go inside?'

He shook his head, wiping his nose on the back of his hand, like the eight-year-old boy he suddenly appeared to be, scared and alone in a frightening world.

'I miss my papa too.'

'I know you do.'

'What those soldiers did to him, beating him like that. It wasn't that bad. He shouldn't have died.'

Iris thought of the young boy she'd witnessed being beaten by the soldiers the day she arrived in Dijon, the way the army boots repeatedly thrust into his stomach and his kidneys. She remembered the sound of the air being knocked out of him every time the blows landed. For all his bravado, he hadn't stood a chance against the combined force of the soldiers. No one could be expected to survive such brutality.

She sidled up to Christophe, working her way around the brambles, and sat beside him. 'Your father must have had internal injuries from the beating. If he was bleeding inside, no one would have known it. There would have been nothing anyone could do.'

'Eva gave him potions. They were supposed to make him better, but they didn't.'

'She wouldn't have been able to heal his unseen injuries.'

'Before that, when the Germans sent me back from the prison camp, Eva gave me potions and urged me to drink them. She said they'd make me feel better, but the headaches and the pains got worse and the nightmares carried on.'

'The herbal teas she gave you and your papa were only designed to soothe. There was nothing more to them than that.'

'Maman was angry after Papa died. She said the same thing would happen to me if I didn't stop visiting Eva. She blamed her for every bad thing that had happened to us. She said she poisoned Papa, gradually weakening him over years and years, and that was why he died. It couldn't have been those few cuts and bruises from the soldiers' beating that did it. She said she was slowly poisoning me too, and that was why my arm wouldn't heal.

'Mama went on and on, blaming Eva for our miserable lives. I wanted to make it stop. I had to make her proud of me again, show her I wasn't good for nothing, that I could do something to make things better. So I picked up the German pistol, left by a soldier outside a bar when he was too drunk to know what he was doing, and the next morning I went to see Eva. She was in her garden picking almonds. When she saw I was upset, she offered to make me a tisane, and that was when I knew Maman was right. Seeing her surrounded by all her fruits and her flowers, I knew what she was doing with her potions. She'd poisoned Papa and now she was poisoning me too.

'And so I pulled the pistol from the inside of my jacket, and I shot her through the heart, breaking it in two, just as Maman's heart had been broken when Eva killed Papa.'

Christophe had murdered Eva. The realisation splintered every part of Iris's soul. If Eva had died at the hands of the enemy, it would have made more sense, but this . . .

Christophe's sobs were coming thick and fast, his face buried in his one good hand as he fought for breath. 'Only Eva didn't kill Papa, did she?'

'No, she didn't.'

'Then why did Maman say she did?'

'Because she wanted someone to blame. When you lose a loved one, the grief can be unbearable.'

'I knew it was a mistake as soon as I'd shot her, but it was too late. And now the headaches and the nightmares are killing me from the inside until I can't stand it anymore.'

Slowly, Iris withdrew from him, as one would back away from a deadly snake, all sympathy for his plight gone. She'd silently blamed every German soldier she'd ever laid eyes on for murdering Eva. She'd never once considered it might have been Christophe.

He'd shot her in cold blood, even as she'd tried to help him. What was Iris supposed to say to that, and what was she supposed to do now?

Christophe scrambled to his feet and ran towards the shed, slamming the door behind him and locking himself in.

'Don't look at me, Iris. I can't stand it.'

She followed him to the shed, her arms folded across her chest, her back rigid as she tried to hold herself up, forcing herself to take deep breaths.

What would Eva tell her to do? She wouldn't want revenge for her murder. It would only perpetuate more suffering. Christophe wasn't in his right mind; she had to remember that as her thoughts drifted to the Destroying Angel sitting in the jar at the back of the cupboard in Eva's cellar. How easy it would be to dispense it, and Christophe wouldn't even know he'd been poisoned.

She forced the thoughts out of her mind and focused on what she'd come to do. 'I have to tell you something, Christophe. It's important. Are you listening?'

'I'm so sorry. You must never forgive me.'

She could hear the trauma in his voice, the suffering and

the self-recrimination. 'Your name is on the hostage list. They'll come for you tomorrow afternoon, and they'll shoot you. You need to get away before they find you. Do you understand? You can't let them take you. Your mother needs you. Solange needs you.' Iris leaned forward, putting her ear to the shed. 'Did you hear what I said?'

'Yes.'

His voice was steadier now. The reality of what she'd told him hadn't sunk in.

'Do you understand what you have to do?'

'Yes.'

'Is there anything you want me to do to help? Perhaps I could pass a message to your mother or Solange?'

'No. Please go away and leave me alone.'

Iris couldn't just leave him, even if he was Eva's killer. Everyone else on the list knew exactly what they must do, but Christophe was different. The brutality he'd endured at the hands of the Germans and his mother had taken away any sense of his self-worth and damaged his understanding of right and wrong.

'Shall we talk about what you should do? You don't have long to work it out.'

'I don't need your help. Please go.'

Reluctant to leave, she stayed a few more minutes, hoping he might emerge from the shed. If he did, she didn't know what she'd say to him, but it didn't seem right to simply abandon him and it wasn't what Eva would have wanted.

The shock of learning he was Eva's killer was beginning to have its effect. Suddenly cold, she was unable to stop shaking. The world was shifting beneath her feet. She couldn't stay here any longer in an overgrown garden, staring at a shed, because if she did, she didn't trust herself not to tear it down, to destroy every picture of Eva that was pasted on its walls, so Eva wouldn't see her as she ripped Christophe limb from limb.

Chapter 49

Iris had only just returned home when Clemence appeared, struggling under the weight of the large square basket she was carrying.

'Can I come in? I have something to give you.'

Inside the basket were three hens, their beaks and wings pushing in all directions in the limited space. Clemence bundled them through to the kitchen and placed them carefully on the table.

'I want you to have my girls. I trust you to take care of them after I've gone and I know you'll make use of the eggs. Make sure you keep them hidden. They're good little layers.'

Iris looked in the basket. Three sets of enquiring eyes peered back at her. How could she explain to Clemence that she wasn't able to keep the birds?

'Hold on to them for a bit longer. We don't know what's going to happen yet.' Clemence couldn't be forced to face a firing squad because Iris had killed Mason. And she didn't have the heart to tell her that her own name was also on the list.

Clemence placed her hand on the basket to settle the hens. 'We know what's going to happen. The Gestapo will come for me tomorrow afternoon. They'll drag me out into the square and they'll shoot me, just as they shot the Mayor and just as they shot

Eva. And I'll be brave. My only concern is for the hens. Please say you'll take them.'

She was more resolute and dry-eyed, than Iris would have expected. There was nobility in her courage that made Iris honoured to know her. This wouldn't be the end for Clemence, not if Iris had anything to do with it.

Jack was waiting at the back gate when Iris carried the basket into the garden, releasing the hens so they could peck at the soil. Clemence had refused to leave until Iris had agreed to take them. If things went to plan, they'd be returned to her tomorrow.

She let Jack in, speaking in hushed tones. 'What are you doing here? If you're seen on the streets, you'll be arrested.'

'The camp is no place for you to hide, so I've found a safe house. It'll only be for a short while, until we can contact London to send a plane to get you out. I'll take you there now. The Gestapo could come for you at any minute.'

This wasn't in Iris's plan. 'They won't come for me until tomorrow afternoon. There's another twenty-four hours before they start to round up the people on the hostage list. The others have all been warned and given the chance to hide or get away.'

'What if they come for you before then?'

'They won't. Frisch will gain more satisfaction from publicly flushing people out. Everyone in the town knows what's going to happen. By four o'clock, there'll be a crowd in the square. Frisch won't pass up the opportunity to put on a public spectacle. Trust me. We still have time.'

'Then will you let me stay with you?'

This was the last thing she expected him to say after everything that had happened between them. 'You don't have to do that.'

'Why do you think I came to France, if not for you? Why do you think I'm still here?'

She'd longed for him to come back to her, but it was too much to expect of him. 'I'm not your responsibility anymore, Jack. You don't have to put yourself in danger for me. You should leave.'

She couldn't let him suspect that she was planning to give herself up. Even if Clemence, Paul, Albert and Christophe managed to evade capture, there were plenty other innocent people to take their place. It was knowledge of Mason's fate the Gestapo wanted, and she was the only one who could give it to them. And they wouldn't stop killing until they'd got it.

'I'm your husband, Iris. If you're in danger, then we're in it together. I'm not going anywhere without you.'

Chapter 50

They were woken at dawn by the sound of a single gunshot echoing around the square. Jack jumped out of bed, his eyes narrowing as he peered through the gap in the window shutters.

Iris followed him out of bed, pulling on her dressing gown and joining him at the window.

'What is it?'

He tried to protect her view, but she was determined to see what the trouble was. It was only just daybreak. No one of sense would be out this early. Jack put his arms around her and held her tight as she took in the scene.

'Christophe.'

His body was slumped on the ground, his hands tied behind his back, the blood dripping from the single gunshot wound at his temple. Beside him stood the unyielding figure of Commander Frisch, his pistol still held at arm's length, pointing at the place where the bullet entered Christophe's head before he collapsed.

Jack clung to her as she tried to break free from his embrace. 'Don't go down there, Iris. There's nothing you can do.'

Christophe should have left town while he had the chance. She'd given him enough warning to get away.

'They weren't supposed to round up the hostages until this afternoon.'

'When have you ever known the Germans to play fair?' Jack released her from his embrace and started to dress. 'We have to get you out of here right away. They'll be coming for you next.'

It wasn't supposed to be like this. This wasn't in the plan. She threw on a dress and ran downstairs. She had to catch up with Frisch before he left the square. She had to give herself up before anyone else was shot in her place.

'Iris, wait.'

She hesitated at the sound of Jack's voice. She couldn't stand the sound of his distress. The pause was long enough for her to spot the letter that had been pushed under the door. She recognised Christophe's handwriting from the poem he'd sent her.

Iris,

By the time you read this letter, I will already be dead. Please don't hate me for what I've done, but don't thank me either. Once this letter is written and delivered I will hand myself in to the Gestapo and confess to killing Guy Mason. This is the only way I can atone for killing Eva. The only way I can make it up to you.

Don't worry that my plan will fail. I can tell them where to find Mason's body. I saw you get into Mason's car on the day of the thunderstorm, and followed you on my bicycle to the Château Guillard. I waited outside while you were in the house, and I trailed you as you explored the grounds. I watched you lay out the picnic and I saw what you did afterwards.

I shouldn't have believed Maman when she said Eva had poisoned Papa, but it was easier to think she'd killed him than to accept he'd died because he couldn't be saved after what those soldiers did to him. Now, I realise Eva had only given him tisanes to comfort him, just as she did with me.

When you arrived in the town, you said you'd been living

in Paris, but it wasn't true. Eva had told me you were in London and that was why you couldn't go to her wedding. I guessed you'd returned for a purpose. When I saw you kill Mason, I realised what that purpose was.

You could have had me arrested when I confessed to killing Eva. Instead, you told me to flee for my own safety. I don't deserve your compassion, but I thank you for it. In return, I will free you from the threat of the Gestapo. They will dredge the lake at the Château Guillard and find Mason's body. The people on the hostage list will no longer be punished.

I can't bring Eva back, but I can save the lives of whoever else is on the hostage list.

Christophe.

After Iris had read the note, she handed it to Jack. Outside, the square was quiet and empty, but for Christophe's body, which would be left there as a warning for everyone to see. It would only be a matter of time before the town woke up and his murder was discovered, before Madame Janot was woken with the news that her world had come to an end, not for the first time, but for the second.

Christophe's sacrifice amounted to a tragedy on the grandest scale. It was the war that had damaged him, war that had driven him to murder and to seek his own death.

The letter dropped from Jack's hand after he finished reading it. 'Why didn't you tell me it was Christophe who killed Eva?'

'It would only have broken your heart and there's been too much of that already.'

Jack began packing Iris a small bag. 'This only goes to prove you're not safe from anyone. You need to leave, right now.'

Before they could debate it, someone rattled the back gate. It was too early for visitors and it couldn't be the Gestapo. If they were still coming for her, they'd come to the front door when the square was full of people, to make sure everyone saw them take her. She ran into the garden and opened the gate, her heart thumping at the sight of the enemy uniform.

'I'm sorry to disturb you. May I come in?'

It was the Grey Mouse, her face pale in the early morning light. Iris ushered her through to the kitchen and invited her to sit down. She hadn't forgotten the risk she'd taken procuring the names on the hostage list.

The Grey Mouse didn't seem surprised to see Jack, who'd already put on his jacket and was all set to take Iris to the prearranged safe house.

'You know what happened in the square this morning.' She dropped her inflection at the end of the sentence. It wasn't a question but a statement.

Iris was still struggling to take it all in. 'I can't believe Christophe sacrificed himself like that.'

'He will be a hero in the eyes of the town. Thanks to his actions, the rest of the people on the hostage list will be spared. Their lives are no longer under threat, but it's not enough to save you, Iris.'

This didn't make any sense. With Christophe taking the blame for Mason's death, the Gestapo had nothing else on her.

Jack's voice shook as he spoke. 'What is it, Frieda? What do you know?'

'The young girl, the wireless operator you sheltered here.'

She was referring to Yvette. 'What's happened to her?'

'She was captured. I'm sorry. She betrayed you when she was questioned.'

Not questioned, but tortured. And it wouldn't have been a betrayal, but a desperate bid to stop her own suffering. Yvette was too strong to have given in easily, and even if she had, Iris couldn't blame her for it.

'Is she alive?'

The Grey Mouse nodded. 'They're still holding her.'

Yvette was too young to have been caught up in all of this. Iris thought of the weeks she'd spent with her in London, preparing her for being questioned. There must have been something she could have done better, something she could have taught her to evade capture. She should have talked Ambrose out of sending her into the field, but if it hadn't been Yvette, it would have been someone else.

Iris braced herself to ask the question. 'What do they know about me?'

'They know you're an agent working for British Intelligence.'

'Are you sure it wasn't Mason who betrayed me?'

'No, he was too taken with you to see anything beyond his attraction.'

Iris cast a glance at Jack to see how he reacted, but there was nothing, only the gentle pressure of his hand on hers, telling her he understood that what she'd done, she'd done in the name of war.

The Grey Mouse was still talking. 'Commander Frisch has been suspicious of you for some time. He was the one who forced the English prisoner of war to approach you in the middle of the night, posing as a British agent needing somewhere to hide. The fact that you didn't fall for it only served to make him more suspicious. It told him you must know all the agents working in the area.'

'What happened to the prisoner of war?'

'He was shot for failing to convince you he was genuine.'

Jack gripped Iris's hand even tighter. 'Christophe confessed to killing Mason. Surely that's enough to remove the suspicion from Iris.'

'They've already dredged the lake and recovered Mason's body based on what Christophe told them, but Yvette admitted you'd been tasked with assassinating him. Her denunciation is all they need to charge you with killing him. I doubt they believed Christophe's confession. There's no evidence that a weapon was used against Mason, and a one-armed man could never overpower someone of Mason's strength, certainly not enough to drown him.'

'They have no evidence I killed him beyond Yvette's confession.'

'It hadn't escaped Frisch's notice that Mason had become ill and begun to behave strangely, just as Schiller did before he disappeared. Both men were connected to this house. Mason has now turned up dead, and as far as Frisch is concerned, Schiller's fate is still a mystery, but he doubts he is still alive.'

So the Grey Mouse hadn't informed Frisch that Emile had dug up Schiller's body. By choosing to keep their secret, she'd saved the town from further reprisals.

'When Frisch has you arrested, he'll want to know what both men were given in this house that affected them so badly. He won't stop asking until you provide him with the answers.'

Jack had heard enough. He fastened Iris's bag and hitched it onto his shoulder. 'There's no time to discuss this any longer. Come on. We need to get you out of here.'

'Jack's right. You must go quickly. I must also leave now. If I'm caught here, it will look suspicious.'

The Grey Mouse wished them luck and was gone, slipping through the back gate before Iris could thank her. Already the square was getting busy, the noise and confusion growing ever louder now Christophe's body had been discovered.

'If they knew Christophe had given a false confession, why did they execute him?'

'Because they've taken it upon themselves to claim the right, and if you start questioning that, you'll go mad.'

Iris grabbed Eva's straw hat that still hung on a peg by the door, and pulled on one of her oversized coats. It wasn't only an attempt at disguise, but a way of taking a part of her beloved Eva with her. There was no way of knowing how long it would be before she could return to the place that still held so much of her. She hesitated as she closed the back door, turning the key in the lock for the last time.

'I need to say goodbye to Clemence.'

'There isn't time. They could come for you at any minute.'

'She needs to know to collect the hens.'

Jack grabbed her hand, leading her to the back gate. 'She can work that out for herself.'

Jack was right, there was no time for sentiment when her life was at stake, no time to say goodbye to Clemence or to the house or the garden, or to pick the last ripening apricot from the tree as she pulled Eva's straw hat low over her face and fled for her life.

Chapter 51

'Where are you taking me?'

'You'll see when we get there.'

Already there was a buzz on the early morning streets, a sense of alarm in the air as, house by house, the people of the town were waking up to the news that Christophe had been executed.

Iris kept her head down as Jack led her by the hand through the quietest alleyways and along the back roads of the town. She could tell he was fighting the temptation to increase his pace, but eyes were everywhere even if minds were distracted. It would only take one person to notice them and recall their unusual behaviour when later questioned and it would all be over.

They'd just taken a shortcut around the edge of the park when Iris heard a familiar voice call her name. Jack gripped her hand, encouraging her to keep going as she faltered. Now wasn't the time to stop when crossing the wrong path could be fatal. Before she could decide whether to ignore it, there was a tug on her shoulder as strong fingers dug into her flesh and pulled her off balance.

Iris spun around, finding herself confronted by Solange, the tears running down her face. Her nightdress was creased where she'd bunched it in her fingers, her naked feet raw from running through the streets.

'Murderer.'

She lunged at Iris, her fingers clawing as they went for her eyes, her sharp nails primed to blind. Iris ducked, grabbing Solange's wrists and pushing them away from her face.

'I'm sorry, Solange. I warned Christophe what was coming. He should have left while he had the chance.'

'Don't blame Christophe. You did this, Iris. This is your fault. He left me a note, explaining what he was going to do. He sacrificed himself for you. Why would he do that? What hold did you have over him?'

'It wasn't meant to go like this.'

'An innocent man is dead because of you.'

A murderer has paid the price for killing Eva. That was what Iris wanted to say, but it wouldn't do any good to break Solange's heart more than it already had been. It would never heal if she knew the reason Christophe had sacrificed himself.

'It's not as simple as that, Solange. In wartime, nothing ever is.'

'Nothing is more black and white than death. Don't try to tell me anything different. Christophe gave himself up when it was you they wanted. It's still you they want, and they won't stop until they have you.'

Jack grabbed Iris's arm, pulling her away before Solange lashed out again.

'Come on, Iris. We have to go.'

Solange spat at the widening ground between them. 'Go on, run away, but you won't get far. I'll tell them I've seen you. They'll set the dogs after you and they'll sniff you out like the vermin you are.'

They picked up their pace, slipping down a narrow alley to shake off Solange. 'Christophe should never have sacrificed himself for me.' Even as Iris said the words, she was grateful to him for saving the lives of Clemence, Albert and Paul.

'You can't blame yourself, Iris. You gave him the opportunity to leave. He chose his own fate, which was more than he allowed Eva.'

Jack was right, but it didn't take away the fact that Solange's future had been laid to waste.

They steadied their pace, trying not to look conspicuous as they made their way through the streets. Everything around them seemed to be closing in. Even the sky felt lower, as if it would come crashing down on them at any minute. It was Solange's threat that had done it. If she informed on them, it wouldn't take long for the dogs to track them down, for the soldiers patrolling on foot or motorcycle to find them.

By now, they'd reached the oldest part of the town, where the grand merchants' houses lined the streets. Iris blanched when Jack stopped outside Madame Beauchamp's house and knocked discreetly on the door.

'I can't go in there, Jack. I visited with Mason when he was searching for a home to requisition. Madame Beauchamp accused me of being a traitor. She'll report me to the Gestapo.'

It was too late. The front door had already opened and Iris found herself face-to-face with Madame Beauchamp. Before she could back away, Jack nudged her gently by the arm, encouraging her inside before she was seen.

Madame Beauchamp moved back into the shadows, her voice an impatient whisper. 'Come in, quickly.'

Iris followed her into the sitting room, where a bundle of knitting sat in its basket on the floor, where a novel remained upturned on the arm of a chair, the window shutters closed against the early morning light. She hovered beside the desk just inside the door, ready to make a run for it.

'Forgive the intrusion, madame. I won't take up any more of your time. I'm sorry to have disturbed you at such an early hour.'

Jack blocked her way as she tried to leave. 'Don't be a fool, Iris. It's certain death for you out there.'

'Please take a seat.'

Madame Beauchamp behaved as if everything that had gone before had never happened. 'Jack explained to my daughter,

Helene, that you needed somewhere to hide for a few days.'

Iris remained standing, distrustful of the offer. 'I must be the last person you want in your home.'

'I was furious that day you came to the house with that awful Englishman who was pretending to be a German officer, I won't deny it. But you were as good as your word. You told me you'd try to stop him requisitioning the house, and you did. And for that I'm grateful.'

'How do you know it was me who stopped him?'

'Because he came back two days later and told me of all the faults you'd found with it. I accepted the criticisms with good grace, because every one of them was unfounded, but I'm sure you know that.'

'You have a lovely home. I refused to stand by and let him take it from you.'

'And in return, I open its doors to you for as long as you need it.'

Jack rubbed his hands together, trying to contain his restlessness. 'It won't be for long. I'll catch a train to Lyon this morning. There's someone there who can contact London and ask them to send a plane. Iris won't be safe until she's out of France.'

The conversation was interrupted by the sound of the door crashing open as Helene burst into the room.

'It's too dangerous for you to be seen, Jack, and you're still not fully fit after the fire. I'll go in your place.'

Helene's expression was as fierce as it had been on the day she'd stood in the kitchen, watching Mason suffer the attack from the hemlock.

Madame Beauchamp barely turned a hair. 'Don't crash about so much, Helene. You'll have the devil down upon us.' She waved her hand casually in Iris's direction. 'You remember Iris. She saved the house from that half-baked Nazi.'

'Of course.' She turned to Iris, the same hard stare still in place. 'The least we can do is help you to get out of France.'

'You mustn't put yourself at risk.'

It wasn't that Iris didn't trust Helene, but after what had happened to Yvette, she was worried for her safety.

Helene flicked her hair, which sat around her shoulders in perfect waves. 'I'm a travelling hairdresser. The German patrols are used to seeing me move around the area. It's what makes me such an effective courier for the maquis.'

So this was how Jack had made the connection with the Beauchamp family. Helene was using her perfect hair and make-up as a disguise in the same way that Yvette had used her youth and her school uniform to fool the enemy into overlooking her. In her smart heels and tight-fitting skirt, no one would guess Helene was an active member of the maquis.

'Then that's settled.' Madame Beauchamp's manner was matter of fact, as if she risked her life for the cause every day. 'Come upstairs. I'll show you to your room.'

The room was at the top of the house, the yellow-painted walls lit up by the sun as it shone through the floor-to-ceiling windows. Iris recognised it from when she'd visited with Mason. It was elegant and comfortable, but it was hardly a suitable hiding place. Iris did her best not to appear ungrateful.

'I remember thinking how beautiful this room was when I first saw it.'

'You won't have noticed this.'

Madame Beauchamp gripped one edge of the dressing table, with its triptych of mirrors, and dragged it aside to reveal a small door, its outline disguised in the decorative wooden panelling. Behind it was a set of narrow stairs which led to an attic.

'Please go up. I've made it as comfortable as the space will allow.'

There was a bed and two easy chairs, a small table and a lamp. The daylight broke in through a small window, the single square of glass giving them a view of the street below. For now, it was everything they needed.

'I'll bring you some food shortly. First I must open the shutters and the curtains in all the rooms, so no one suspects anything.'

The following hours passed slowly. For all the time they'd spent apart, or perhaps because of it, Iris and Jack found little to say to one another. There was no point in discussing the past when the present was vital, so perilous, and the idea of a future was still too brittle to consider. And so they did what their instincts told them to do, sitting beside one another on the bed and holding each other close, not daring to move or speak, but simply being, living in the moment of the in and out of each breath while they had the luxury to do so.

Iris must have drifted off to sleep because she was woken some time later by a gentle knock on the door.

'It's only me.'

Madame Beauchamp's expression was set to deliver bad news. 'Another notice has gone up in the square. I saw it when I went to buy the bread.'

Iris swallowed the hard lump of fear gathering in her throat. 'It's about me, isn't it?'

'There's a ten-thousand franc reward for your capture. I'm sorry, Iris. There'll be a lot of desperate people out there searching for you right now.'

It was more important than ever to get away quickly. 'Are you sure you want to take the risk of hiding me? If you're worried about being caught, I'll leave straight away.'

'Helene will be back tonight. Let's wait until then. She'll have news of when there'll be a plane to take you to London. It won't be long.'

Together, Iris and Jack watched the sun move across the sky, the shadows shifting as the day passed, until the moon rose, casting its cool light into the room. Rather than risk the lamp, they sat in the dark, counting the stars through the tiny square of glass, marvelling at the size of the sky in contrast to the space in which they found themselves. It was easier to look up, to look out at the great expanse, than to consider the danger they were in.

Daylight woke Iris from her restless sleep, the reassuring pressure of Jack's body lying against hers bringing back the joy of his presence before she remembered where she was and the fear struck. If she was discovered, then Jack would be, too. The Gestapo would put him through hell when they realised who he was and what he'd been up to.

Madame Beauchamp appeared with breakfast, her face set to disguise her concern that Helene hadn't returned from Lyon. It was a worry to have her gone all night. She offered a tight smile as she passed the bread.

'Helene should be back today. Then we'll have news. It would have been the curfew preventing her from returning, that's all.'

That's what they wanted to believe, and so they told themselves it was the case. The fact that she might have been arrested was unthinkable, as were the repercussions they'd all face if they broke her under interrogation.

The morning dragged into afternoon and still there was no news of Helene. The sun was at its peak when they heard a car pull up outside the house. Jack went rigid. Only German officers had petrol for cars.

Through the window, he watched a woman climb out of a black Citroën, her handbag swinging from her arm like a corpse from the gallows. After Jack described her, Iris risked a quick glance at the street.

'It's Frisch's wife.'

'It could be a coincidence that she's here.'

Madame Frisch was a social climber and desperate to be accepted by the people she considered worth knowing, and Madame Beauchamp, respected for her charity work and a descendant of one of the old merchant families, would have come under that category. She also wasn't above using the pretext of a social call to carry out a house search on her husband's behalf.

Iris gripped Jack's hand, straining to hear the conversation going on below, as Madame Beauchamp opened the door and let her in. The rhythm of the voices made it sound like a spur-of-the-moment social call, but given the situation, it could never be just that.

Jack gave Iris's hand a squeeze. 'She'll never find us, even if she searches the house from top to bottom.'

Iris remembered how Madame Frisch had gone through Eva's house, forcing her vast behind into her aunt's favourite armchair and poking her nose into every corner, not even bothering to conceal her curiosity, as if she thought Iris should take it as a compliment to be so intruded upon. She'd have to move the dressing table to discover the door to the attic, and Madame Frisch was unlikely to find an excuse to do such a thing, even if she could justify exploring as far as the bedrooms on the fourth floor.

They sat in silence, listening to the sounds of the house, trying to track any movements on the stairs, but the building was solid and unyielding and betrayed nothing of what was going on below.

How long was it acceptable to stay for a social call? Was there anything to give Iris and Jack away? Would Madame Beauchamp be able to remain calm enough to avoid suspicion?

Jack kept an eye on the street, watching for her to leave, angling his body so if anyone happened to look up, they wouldn't see him. After twenty minutes, he spotted Helene approaching the house, her bag containing her hairdressing tools slung over her shoulder, her manner unflinching as she saw the black Citroën parked outside the house, warning her that something was going on inside.

Her arrival must have been enough to disrupt Madame Frisch's visit, because five minutes later, she left the house, hurrying to her car as if she had a purpose. The front door had barely closed behind her when they heard Madame Beauchamp's gentle knock on the attic door.

'Get your things together. You have to leave now, quickly.'

Iris pushed her feet into her shoes and grabbed her bag. 'What's happened?'

'She spotted your scarf. It was on the chair by the desk. You must have dropped it when you arrived. I told her it was mine, but I don't think she believed me. She commented on how unusual it was and that you had one just like it.'

Madame Beauchamp pushed her hand into her pocket and pulled out the silk Hermès scarf Eva had given Iris before the war, now neatly folded into a small square. It was the last gift from her aunt and Iris carried it everywhere. When she wasn't wearing it, it was tied to the handle of her bag. It must have slipped its knot and landed on the chair when she arrived at the Beauchamps'.

'Madame Frisch said she recognised the bold design, with the horse-drawn buses and the young people sitting at a table in the centre. It's very distinctive. She said you were wearing it when you had dinner with them. The colours complemented the green silk dress you wore.'

How could Iris not have realised she'd dropped it, especially here and now, when it was most dangerous. 'I'm sorry. It was unforgivable of me to be so careless.'

'It's not your fault. Madame Frisch caught me off guard with her visit. I wasn't expecting her. I should have checked the room more carefully for clues that you'd been there. The chair had been pushed under the desk. The scarf was on the seat and out of sight of any but the most enquiring eyes.'

By now, they'd made their way out of the attic. Helene was waiting in the yellow bedroom, sitting on the corner of the bed, massaging her feet which were swollen from covering too many miles in high heels. Beyond her make-up she looked tired, her dress crumpled from two days of uninterrupted wear.

'There'll be a plane tonight. It will land in the clearing on the north boundary of Duplantier's farm.' She looked up from her feet and met Iris's eye. 'You know where I mean?'

It wasn't far from the Château Guillard. A brisk walk would get them there in an hour as long as they weren't intercepted. Iris pulled on Eva's broad-brimmed straw hat and tied it under her chin.

'We'll go straight there now and hide in the nearby woods until nightfall. If we hurry, we should be able to get there before the patrols are alerted to come looking for us.'

Madame Beauchamp ushered them down the stairs. 'Even as we speak, Madame Frisch will be on her way to tell her husband she's found a clue to where you're hiding.'

Iris handed her the scarf, even though it broke her heart to part with it. 'You'd better keep this. If they search the house and can't find it, it'll look suspicious.'

Madame Beauchamp nodded, her hand gentle on Iris's as she took the scarf. 'I'll keep it safe until it can be returned to you.'

Jack and Iris kept their heads down as they made their way out of the town, taking the quiet lanes and the back roads, hoping not to be seen, trying not to appear in a hurry. It wouldn't only be the German patrols who were looking for Iris, but anyone chasing the reward for handing her in, which meant she was at risk not only from the enemy, but from anyone who might recognise her.

Now they had the scarf to go on, it was only a matter of time before the Gestapo searched the house where they'd been hiding and it was inevitable that Madame Beauchamp and Helene would be questioned. But the scarf wasn't unique. It was perfectly reasonable that Madame Beauchamp could have owned the same one. She could easily have bought it during a trip to Paris; her husband could have given it to her as a gift before he was shot by a drunken German soldier. If Madame Beauchamp followed this line of argument, perhaps she'd get away with it, if only she could be convincing enough, and if only they would believe her.

As they took the quiet lanes that circuited the vineyards and the farms, Iris was reminded of the day of the storm when she'd fled the grounds of the Château Guillard in the rain. The memory of it would haunt her forever. Her plan had seemed perfect at the time; now she felt she'd never be free of the consequences.

'You there. What are you doing?'

Iris and Jack stalled at the sound of the rough voice calling from the other side of the hedge. They weren't trespassing. They'd taken great care to stay on the public paths to avoid drawing attention to themselves.

Jack pulled Iris close to his body, shielding her so she wouldn't be recognised. 'We're just passing. We didn't mean to disturb you.'

Iris was relieved to discover how much Jack's French had improved. Since living with the maquis, he'd even begun to use the local dialect. If he didn't say too much, he might get away with passing as someone who'd lived in the area for most of his life.

She could feel the man's eyes on her. They needed to move on quickly. The longer they stayed, the more likely she was to be recognised.

Jack cleared his throat, betraying his nervousness. 'If you'll excuse us . . .'

'Wait.'

It was too late. The man had already guessed something. If they made a run for it, it would make him suspicious. Lingering would only make him more so. Iris stared at her feet, wishing for the ground to open up beneath her, hoping Jack had the sense not to say too much and risk giving them both away.

'I know you, don't I?'

The words were aimed at Iris. She felt Jack's grip on her tighten. 'You might have seen me around the town.'

Jack stepped forward, indicating their intention to leave. 'We won't disturb you any longer. We'll be on our way.'

'It's Iris, isn't it? Eva Fournier's niece.'

She could feel the heat of his eyes on her, his curiosity burning through the wide brim of Eva's straw hat she'd used to hide her face. If she didn't look up and admit it, it would seem suspicious. She had no choice but to brave it out.

'Yes, it is.' She looked him dead in the eye and forced a smile. 'You must have been a friend of Eva's.'

He had the sun-grained skin of someone who'd spent his life

working the land and could have been any one of the men who visited the bars in the town or sat in the square drinking beer at the end of a hot day.

He took his time in responding, his eyes searching her face. It was impossible to tell if he was looking for traces of Eva or considering the reward he could collect for denouncing her.

'My wife has one of her books on the shelf in the kitchen. It's always a celebration day when she cooks one of the recipes.'

Iris smiled, despite her growing anxiety and her desperation to get away. 'Eva would have been glad to know that.'

'What are you doing so far out of town?'

By keeping her talking he was delaying them, buying time for his wife to alert the German patrols.

'We're taking a walk. It's lovely at this time of year, just before the grape harvest.'

He raised his eyebrows, as if he didn't understand her reasoning. Those who worked the land often failed to see the beauty in it.

'I'll let you get on then.'

They tried not to run as they continued along the path, stumbling over the loose stones, their shoes throwing clouds of dust up at their heels. It wouldn't do for the stranger to see they were frightened out of their wits and desperate to get away.

Iris waited until they'd cleared the edge of his land and were safely in the shelter of the woods before she dared to ask the question.

'Do you think he'll tell anyone he saw us?'

Jack shrugged, tugging at the lace of his boots where it had come undone. 'I don't know. It's ill-luck that he recognised you. We'd better find somewhere to hide in case anyone comes searching.'

His eyes scanned the dense woodland. They were close to the clearing where the plane would land, but it was still hours until it was due and they couldn't risk being seen in the meantime. The sun was already beginning to set and it would soon be dark, which would make it easier for them to disappear in the shadows.

There was a disused barn nearby. Iris remembered passing it the day she'd walked back from the Château Guillard. If they hid inside, it might put them at risk of missing the plane. They hadn't been given the exact time of its landing, so they had to keep a lookout.

Already the temperature had begun to drop as the early autumn damp crept in. They'd eaten nothing since breakfast. Madame Beauchamp had been in too much of a hurry to get them out of the house to think of offering them any food to take with them and they couldn't risk stopping along the way in case they were recognised. Iris listened to the growl of Jack's stomach as he put his arms around her to keep her warm.

'I'm sorry you've been dragged into all this. I never intended any of it to happen.'

He kissed the top of her head. 'You're not responsible for the war. I don't blame you for trying to do what you could to fight it.'

'Jack, I . . .'

Before she could continue, the peace was disturbed by the sound of heavy boots stalking through the woods, brittle twigs snapping under several pairs of feet.

Iris froze, not knowing whether to stay still or to run, her heart thumping as she locked eyes with Jack, and sensing he was asking himself the same question. Already the feet were getting nearer. They could hear the German voices calling to one another, sending each other in various directions. It wouldn't be long before they were encircled.

Jack grabbed her hand. They had no choice but to run. Their only hope was the disused barn. With any luck, the soldiers wouldn't know the area well enough to go looking for it.

They weaved their way through the trees, light-footed and as nimble as their nerves would allow and sticking to the shadows, increasing their speed when they finally left the shelter of the trees, sprinting across the open land until they reached the barn.

Iris pulled at the wooden door, using all her weight to drag it open just wide enough for them to slip inside. Breathless now, her eyes strained to adjust to the dim light as they scoured the empty space, checking the walls and the roof. There was nowhere to hide. Even the shadows weren't dense enough to disguise them.

'Is there a cellar? Some old barns have a cellar.'

Together they searched the floor, pushing aside rotting sheets of old canvas and straw, their eyes stinging from the years of dust that came flying up, but there was nothing to suggest an opening. If they were caught here, there was no hiding place and no way out.

The soldiers were getting closer. The sound of their rough voices, tossed here and there on the breeze, was becoming more distinct. Iris knew enough German to understand the instruction to enter the barn. The soldiers knew they were in there.

The excitement in the young officer's voice was unmistakeable as he ordered them to come out with their hands up. They were trapped. Once again, Iris checked the walls and the roof. The only escape was through the door and the Germans were already lined up outside. Jack reached for Iris's hand as it burst open and three soldiers entered.

'Whatever happens, you have to believe I love you, Jack. I always have.'

Without warning, three shots were fired. Jack and Iris dropped to the floor, but they weren't the only ones who fell.

Iris opened her eyes, desperate to check on Jack. The air was thick with the smell of blood as it spread across the barn floor. Not her and Jack's blood, but the blood of the three soldiers, their faces now buried in the dirt and the rotting straw.

'Are you all right?'

There was the sound of more heavy feet. This time it was accompanied by a familiar voice as Helene stormed into the barn, pushing her pistol into the waistband of her trousers.

'I shot each one in the back. They deserved nothing better.' She stared at the bodies on the ground. 'This was how they murdered my father, shooting him from behind as he hurried home in time for the curfew. If I kill enough of these bastards, I might get the one who did it.'

'You got here just in time.'

Iris could hardly get the words out. She scrambled to her feet, brushing off the dirt from the barn floor and avoiding the expanding pool of German blood as she stepped forward to greet Helene.

Jack wasn't far behind. 'I don't mean to sound ungrateful, but what are you doing here?'

'The British have promised to drop off more ammunition when they collect Iris. I'm here with some of the others from the maquis camp to receive it.'

Helene checked the soldiers on the ground, turning each one over with her foot. A set of eyelids flickered, betraying that one of them still had a little life in him. She pulled out her pistol and shot each one in the head, just to be sure, before she looked at her watch, angling it at the moon to catch its light.

'We'd better go to the clearing. The plane could arrive any time now. You don't want to miss it.'

Iris touched her gently on the arm. 'You saved our lives. I don't know how to thank you.'

Helene shrugged as if it were nothing, when they both knew it was everything. She pulled something from her pocket and thrust it into Iris's hand. 'Maman asked me to return this.'

It was the Hermès scarf Eva had given her. Iris's heart almost burst at the sight of it. 'Your mother should have kept it. What if the Gestapo demand to see it?'

'They won't. She's on her way to Switzerland. I convinced her to flee to safety as soon as you left. She'll be across the border by this time tomorrow. My uncle can give her a home until it's safe for her to return to France.'

'You should have gone with her. If they catch you . . .'

'My duty is here, fighting alongside the maquis for a free France. The house is locked up. If the Gestapo come calling, they'll find it empty.'

Half a dozen members of the maquis appeared out of the shadows as they left the barn and returned to the cover of the woods, their stealthy figures obscured by the fading light. Each one greeted Jack not only as a friend, but as a comrade. There was a familiar figure among them, her stature no more than that of a child, despite her determination to stand tall.

'Yvette?'

The name burst from Iris's lips before she could stop it. 'How did you escape?'

'A member of the German auxiliary staff visited me in my cell this afternoon. She spoke to me in fluent French, instructing me to follow her and telling me not to make any fuss. I thought I was being taken for more questioning, until she showed me the papers she'd arranged for my release. She led me to a side-gate and unlocked it. Helene was waiting for me on the other side.'

'Your rescuer, did she give you her name?'

'No, but she said to tell you that she looks forward to reading Eva's last cookery book when you finally get around to finish writing it.'

Iris threw her arms around Yvette, grateful for her life, grateful once more to the Grey Mouse for risking her own safety to save her.

They crouched on the edge of the woodland, keeping out of sight, until the distant rumble of the Lysander engine grew closer and more distinct. Iris signalled to Yvette, instructing her to get ready to board. They had to be quick. The turnaround would be so rapid the pilot would be preparing to take off almost before the landing wheels had touched the ground. The cargo of ammunition would be unloaded within an instant; dispersed and hidden before the hour had passed.

Iris grabbed Jack's hand as the plane touched down. 'This is it.'

She tried to pull him to his feet but he resisted. Iris tried harder. 'If we don't hurry, the pilot will go without us.'

Jack took his knapsack from his shoulders and offered it to her. 'You go. Take this with you.'

She paused, staring at him in the moonlight. 'We have to go now, together.'

He got to his feet and pulled her close. 'I'm staying here to fight for the cause.'

'It's not safe. I can't lose you again.'

'Here, alongside the maquis, I have a purpose. What I do counts for something.' He stepped back and pushed his knapsack into her arms. 'This bag contains articles I've written, highlighting the work of the resistance fighters. Take them to every newspaper editor in London until one of them agrees to publish them. Help the people in Britain to understand how the French are fighting to win their country back.'

'If you're staying, then I will too. We've already spent too long apart.'

'You can't do any more here, Iris. If you stay, they'll hunt you down and kill you.'

He was right; if she remained in France, she'd have to go into hiding. It would be too dangerous for her to play an active role in the Resistance. She could do much more in London, training French agents to send into the field.

Helene ran up to them, pushing Jack roughly by the shoulder towards the plane. 'Go with her, Jack. Show the British agents what the maquis are doing. You've lived the life. Teach them the kind of sabotage we're using to win the war.'

Iris grabbed Jack's arm, determined never to let go. 'Helene's right. Think of the difference we can make if we work together.'

He was still for a moment, his heart torn between love and duty, until he realised they were in perfect accord. And with this thought, Iris saw the look in his eyes change, reflecting the old Jack, the one who loved her without compromise or justification.

The engines were roaring; the plane bursting to take off. Yvette was already on board when Jack took Iris's hand, and together they climbed into the plane. As they strapped themselves in, the pilot informed them they'd be home before sunrise, but Iris was already there. Anywhere with Jack was home, and now he was by her side, it was exactly where she intended him to stay.

A Letter from Theresa Howes

Wars are fought and won on many fronts and in any number of ways. When I came to write *The French Affair*, I wanted to consider once again the roles women played in the Second World War. Perhaps the biggest asset women had was the way they were, and often continue to be, underestimated by men.

This idea was the starting point for the development of my characters. It wouldn't be difficult for a female agent to present herself as a bored housewife, embarking on an affair with a senior civil servant, while her husband was away reporting on the war. Her victim had to be a man vain enough and naive enough to think she wanted him simply for himself and not for his secrets.

In France, no one would suspect that the suitcase carried by a girl, dressed in a school uniform, contained wireless equipment, or that the girl in question had the intelligence and courage to transmit messages to her spy masters in Britain from enemy-occupied territory.

And who would suspect a travelling hairdresser, clipping along in high heels and a tight skirt, of being a messenger for the Resistance?

Writing this from my comfortable armchair, I can only imagine the courage of the women who carried out similar tasks, and remain forever in awe of them. Their bravery is even more inspiring when you consider this kind of covert work was still in its early days. This was a completely new kind of warfare, where lessons were learned on the job, because nobody really knew how to prepare agents for the field. Women and men were sent into enemy-occupied territory not knowing what they might encounter, relying on their wits to survive, and the training that might or might not prove useful.

It was this that led me to consider how a woman, wholly unprepared to work as an assassin, would set about fulfilling her mission without laying herself open to suspicion.

It's commonly said that poison is the murder weapon of choice for women. It doesn't involve brute force or a physical confrontation with the victim, and many poisonous substances can be found in the domestic environment, in cleaning products and medicines, and as I've chosen to demonstrate, in everyday plants.

Poisoning seemed the perfect solution for Iris's situation, until you look at the risks, the lying and the subterfuge that are a consequence of any murder, and the toll it takes on the perpetrator, which brings us back to the personal sacrifices that were made by so many people to win the war.

The French Affair is a work of fiction. I've taken the history of the war and the locations, and used them as a jumping-off point for my imagination. I've also used a lot of creative licence when it comes to describing the effects of poisoning, so please don't take anything I've written as an instruction manual for murder!

Having said all this, I've tried to remain true to the spirit of the times and the places in which the story takes place, and *The French Affair* is my tribute to all those who sacrificed their lives and lost loved ones during the battle to win the freedoms we all enjoy today.

Thank you for choosing to read *The French Affair*. If would like to be the first to know about my new releases, you can follow me on Twitter or visit my website for updates.

If you enjoyed *The French Affair*, please consider leaving a review. I love to hear what readers thought, and it helps new readers to discover my books.

You might also be interested in my first novel, *The Secrets We Keep*, a story of love and Resistance, set in the South of France during the German Occupation of the Second World War.

Until next time,

Theresa Howes

Twitter @Howes_Theresa
www.theresahowes.co.uk

The Secrets We Keep

1944, the Cote d'Azur.

Artist Marguerite Segal is recruited by British Intelligence into befriending Etienne Valade, a local priest. Her mission is to persuade him to pass on information from the high-ranking German officers who attend his church: evidence of their war crimes.

Connected by a passion for art, Marguerite and Etienne soon fall in love, but their association increasingly puts her at danger of violent reprisals. With his church frequented by Nazis, Etienne is a suspected collaborator, and distrust is high.

And Marguerite is keeping her own secret too. Like the Jews whose identity cards she forges to hide them from the Third Reich, she is hiding behind a false name, her true identity and past known only to her closest friend.

Marguerite must get hold of the documents that will condemn the German officers but, in a world where everything is at stake, can she truly trust anyone – even the man she loves?

Acknowledgements

I'm so grateful to everyone who has worked tirelessly behind the scenes to help me create *The French Affair*. My most special thanks go to my fabulous agent, Juliet Mushens, who loved the idea of the story from the start and encouraged me with her insightful notes and suggestions along the way. I wouldn't be here without you, Juliet x

Behind every great agent, is an equally great team! Thank you to everyone at Mushens Entertainment for everything you do – Liza deBlock, Rachel Neely, Kiya Evans and Catriona Fida. It's an honour and a joy to work with you all.

My thanks also go to everyone at HQ Digital, especially my lovely editor Abigail Fenton, who always finds ways to help me make my stories sharper, clearer, better. Also thanks to the rest of the editorial team, Sophia Allistone, Eldes Tran and Michelle Bullock. Thank you to Flo Shepherd in the contracts team, and Sarah Goodey and Tom Han in Publishing Operations. Thank you to Anna Sikorska and Kate Oakley who have done such a wonderful job with the design of the book. In Production, thank you to Emily Chan, Halema Begum and Angie Dobbs, and in Sales, thank you to Hannah Lismore, Petra Moll, Georgina Green, Brogan Furey, Angela Thomson, Sara Eusebi and Lauren

Trabucchi. In Finance, thank you to Kelly Spells, Jennifer Harbord and Akifah Mendheria. Finally, thank you to Isabel Williams and Lucy Richardson for all your hard work in Publicity, and to Emma Pickard and Emily Gerbner in Marketing.

Special thanks to Emma Spurgin Hussey for your lovely narration of the audio book. You do the most wonderful job of bringing my words to life.

I owe so much to all the readers, reviewers, book bloggers and fellow writers who supported my first novel, *The Secrets We Keep*. This one's for all of you. I hope you like it. Also, thank you to all the librarians up and down the country. As a life-long library user, it means so much to know my books are on your shelves, or available to borrow as ebooks.

So many friends have helped me along the way. Thank you, Sarah Sykes, for all your sage advice. Annabelle Thorpe, it's been such fun comparing notes on our novels-in-progress. Lisa Berry, I'm indebted to you for your kind words about my work – you made me cry (in a good way). Richard and Suzanna Freeman, thank you for your enthusiasm, your wine and your jigsaws. Rif Aslam and Ray Wood, thank you for gifting so many copies of *The Secrets We Keep* to your friends.

Thank you to Mum and Dad, Brian and Janet Wood, for being my greatest cheerleaders, and for not letting visitors leave the house until they've agreed to buy one of my books.

Final thanks go to my husband, Bill. What would I do without your map-reading skills, your stone-cold logic, and your ability to remove the biscuit crumbs that lodge themselves under the keys on my laptop? I couldn't have written this book without you x

Dear Reader,
We hope you enjoyed reading this book. If you did, we'd be so appreciative if you left a review. It really helps us and the author to bring more books like this to you.

Here at HQ Digital we are dedicated to publishing fiction that will keep you turning the pages into the early hours. Don't want to miss a thing? To find out more about our books, promotions, discover exclusive content and enter competitions you can keep in touch in the following ways:

JOIN OUR COMMUNITY:

Sign up to our new email newsletter: http://smarturl.it/SignUpHQ

Read our new blog www.hqstories.co.uk

https://twitter.com/HQStories

www.facebook.com/HQStories

BUDDING WRITER?

We're also looking for authors to join the HQ Digital family! Find out more here:

https://www.hqstories.co.uk/want-to-write-for-us/

Thanks for reading, from the HQ Digital team